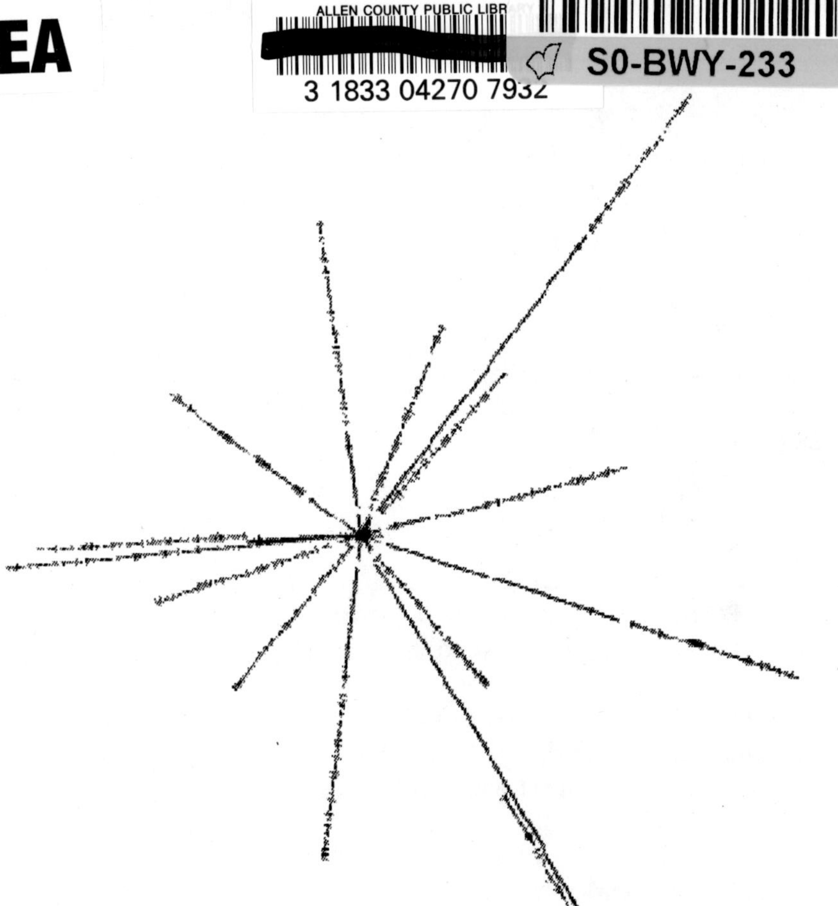

# Dance for the Ivory Madonna

## (a romance of psiberspace)

### by Don Sakers

DANCE FOR THE IVORY MADONNA



Published by
Speed-of-C Productions
PO Box 265
Linthicum, MD 21090-0265

*Dance for the Ivory Madonna* takes place in the Scattered Worlds Universe. In chronological sequence, it falls at 3.75. For more informtion, visit the Scattered Worlds website at *www.scatteredworlds.com.*

For a free autographed bookplate, send a self-addressed, stamped envelope to "Nexus Bookplate" at the above address. Be sure to include the name(s) to which you would like the bookplate inscribed.

ISBN 0-9716147-1-7

First edition: February 2002

Printed in the United States of America

The CoastLine SF Writers Consortium is an organization of professional writers and editors devoted to excellence in sf/fantasy publishing. Publications bearing the CoastLine logo are assured to meet professional standards.

## AUTHOR'S NOTE:

In order that this novel may be stored and transmitted via the Internet without violating standards of decency, the text has been processed to render all improper terms harmless. To be specific, potentially objectionable words have been replaced by the names of the sponsors and supporters of the Communications Decency Act, men who are the foremost fighters in the war against uncontrolled expression: Senators Exon, Helms, Nunn, and Pell; Representatives Hyde, Bliley, Wyden, and Gorton; and their ilk.

The author realizes that this is not a perfect solution: these gentlemen's names themselves are inherently offensive to many readers. He begs forgiveness, knowing that *those* readers are not afraid of being offended, and are not the sort to respond with intolerance to the free expression of others.

DEDICATED TO

The real Ivory Madonna, Amanda Allen.

Here between starlight and earthdust
We dangle on gossamer strings
Trapped in the web of Desire
Beating our useless pale wings.

High over the bright Serengeti
In the light of a scabrous moon
We dance for the Ivory Madonna
And pray that the Dawn will come soon.

# ACT I:

# DANSE MACABRE

## ACT I: DANSE MACABRE

### [01] KAMENGEN 01
Tse Bii'Ndzisgaii
Dinétah (Navajo Nation), North America
19 July 2042 C.E.

*If you think the problem is bad now, just wait until we've solved it.*

The Navajo girl in pigtails, no more than six years old, crashes into Damien and leaves great patches of her skin behind. Even through his protective suit, he feels the heat from her body like bread fresh out of the oven. She quivers, gasps, and then convulses, coughing. Tattered ribbons of skin hang from her arms, torso, face. Pustules and scars cover her from head to toe. In a moment, the convulsions stop, and she…melts in his arms, slipping to the dusty ground. Where his hands touched her, she peels like an overripe banana.

His head swims, and Damien forces himself to look away. Don't pass out. Don't pass out.

Hands on his shoulders. "Hey, Nexus, you okay?"

Through clenched teeth, Damien replies, "Fine." To prove it, he turns his face toward the voice and wrests his lips into a smile. "Just fine."

The other, a slender Amerind with chestnut eyes and wide lips visible through transparent polymer faceplate, pats Damien's shoulder before releasing him. "No disgrace, Nexus, if you can't handle it." The slightest hint of a French accent sounds more than a little accusative. "It's rough the first time you see something like this. Look away, and if you feel yourself going, leave. Just do not take your helmet off. Faint if you must. The evac team will pick you up."

A shot of stubborn annoyance clears Damien's head. "Thanks for the advice, *Doc.* Is that from experience?" As soon as he says it, Damien is sorry he did.

The other man nods, conceding the point, and holds out his hand. "No reason to turn this into a hydeing contest between the Nexus and *Medecins sans Frontieres.*"

Damien grasps his hand. "I'm twenty-five, you're…what, thirty?"

"Thirty-one."

"Helms! My grandmother says that early-adult human males shouldn't be allowed out without keepers. I guess she's right." He squeezes the man's hand, then releases it. "Damien Nshogoza."

"Jamiar Heavitree. Good to meet you. And, yes, I *was* speaking from experience. Leave if you feel the need, but keep that helmet locked. A breath of air is not worth contracting Dekoa virus." Heavitree sighs. "All right, we have an epidemic to take care of."

Quickly but methodically, Heavitree and his three companions— all wearing the red and white insignia of MsF— move through the small Navajo encampment, and Damien does his best to keep up and be useful.

It is simple work, as long as he doesn't think too hard about the implications. Each Navajo he meets fell into one of three categories: the dead, those sick with Dekoa, and those who still have a chance. It is easy to tell: those with blistered, peeling skin, thrashing in agony, are sick; everyone else is either dead or healthy. There are too many dead, far too few healthy.

For the healthy, Damien reaches into the satchel on his left and slaps a tracer patch on the patient. A later wave of medevac agents will find and rescue them.

For the sick, there is a syringe from the satchel on his right. Jab, squeeze, and release. Sometimes, when he pulls the syringe back, skin peels away from rich, red flesh. After ten doses, he discards the syringe. Damien doesn't ask what is in the syringes; he only knows that it brings quick peace to the sufferers.

He bears no third satchel; for the dead, there is...nothing.

"That's it for this camp," Heavitree says.

Damien nods and glances at the display glowing on the sleeve of his suit. Thumbing the input, he reports, "Team Alpha, Target Six-Three is secured. Request transport to Target Seven-Niner."

No sooner has the computer confirmed his message, then he hears an approaching copter from the south. The doctors— looking more like astronauts than medical relief workers— gather around.

"Nunn, it's hot," one of them says.

"Thirty-five in the shade," Damien says. "And there ain't no shade."

"But at least," Heavitree says with his unwavering smile, "it's a *dry* heat."

"Speak for yourself," another doctor, a woman, says. "I'm sweating like a pig. They've got to get air conditioning in these suits."

"Anglos can't take heat," Heavitree says, "Never knew one that could." His tone is friendly enough, and the other doctor doesn't seem to mind, but the comment makes Damien uncomfortable. All the more so when Heavitree continues, "Isn't that right, Nexus?"

Damien is spared the necessity of a response by the helicopter's arrival. The five of them scramble aboard and they are instantly airborne, just as quickly setting down again. This time the target is a small settlement of perhaps three dozen eight-sided log houses with earthen roofs. A few lonely sheep wander, just meters away; otherwise, the settlement is deserted. As they jump out and the copter lifts off, no response comes from any of the buildings.

In silence stirred only by the departing copter's blades, they split up, each taking a different building. Damien pushes open the first door he comes to and cautiously pokes his head in. The dim interior is a marked contrast to bright sunlight outside, and it takes his eyes a few moments to adjust.

The spacious room is impeccably tidy, folded blankets stacked carefully, the hearth spotless. A single terminal, at least two decades old, sits dark and quiet in one corner; a hand-loom occupies another. In the center, on a rough rug of earthtone Navajo designs, four bodies are arranged in a row and covered with blankets. One is a woman about Damien's age, three are children. Flies and rot have only begun to make a mockery of the care with which they'd been arranged.

Pushing aside hanging curtains, Damien examines other rooms. Toilet, what seems to be a tool closet, sleeping rooms with straw mats and hand-woven blankets. In the second of these, Damien finds the architect of all the respectful order: a small, elderly Anglo woman, her gaunt, proud face furrowed with the wrinkles of many lifetimes. Wrapped in a blanket and decked with silver necklaces, she sits on a straw pallet with her back to the wall, head down and eyes closed. Damien is on the point of leaving, when the woman raises her head. Her deep blue eyes, solemn and sad, are endless as the skies of desert night.

Barely a whisper, she croaks, "Are you real, or a spirit?"

"Real." He can't imagine what to say.

The woman nods. "I knew...that if I waited...someone would come." Her eyes move, for the barest instant, in the direction of the main room. "I tried to...make them...comfortable. My daughter...and grandchildren. I don't know their ways, but...I tried my best."

Damien has to look away.

"What should I do?" The woman's voice, stronger but still barely audible, is preternaturally calm. "Have you come to take me?"

"A-Are you…sick?"

She shakes her head, almost sadly. "No." As if confessing a dreadful sin. "Watched them all come down with it. Everyone. I never…got…sick." She looks up at Damien and asks, with calm curiosity that is far, far worse than impassioned appeal, "Why didn't I get sick? Why me? Why not…?" She trails off, then asks again, "What should I do?"

Damien takes out a tracer patch and touches it to the woman's neck. She makes no move to resist; he can't tell if she even notices. "Someone will be here for you in a little while. They'll take you s-somewhere else. Where you'll be safe." Lame, but all the comfort he has to offer.

"I'll wait. Thank you."

Damien backs to the doorway, fumbles with the curtain. "I-I have to go. I have other houses to check." And will each hold a nightmare like this one?

"You've been very kind. I'll be perfectly fine."

He leaves in a hurry.

When he first read of Dekoa's 78% infection rate and 90% mortality, Damien never expected to see it so powerfully demonstrated. He remembers thinking, four in five, without bothering to picture what the statistic really meant in bodies, lives, souls.

Outside, in the sun and the heat, he breathes deeply— even though it is bottled air, no more or less fresh than he's been breathing all along. To the north and east, fields and scrub fade into desert, dominated by soaring mesas in brilliant colors. Between here and the horizon, there is no movement, no sound. The stillness of the tiny village, the remoteness of the unearthly landscape, makes Damien wonder for a moment if he *isn't* spirit instead of flesh, insubstantial visitor to a ghostly world.

He is shocked from his reverie by the approach of two team members, Heavitree and the woman whose name he does not know.

"You know," the woman muses, "this would go quicker if we had entertainment. Or at least some music."

"How about it, friend?" Heavitree asks. "I am sure the other teams would appreciate it as well."

"I'll have to— " Damien stops. He was on the verge of saying he would have to ask the ranking Nexus operative…then he remembered that he *is* the ranking Nexus operative. The decision is all his. And it is one he should have made at the beginning of the operation. "I'll have to see," he finishes.

Nominally, Monument Valley— indeed, the whole Navajo Nation— is under Nexus interdict…and will be, until Navajo raiding parties stop killing their Hopi neighbors. The terms of interdict, in theory, are unyielding: the offending nation can have no commerce or contact with the world community until they were ready to rejoin it. No trade, no tourists, no Net connections in or out. Only refugees are allowed to leave.

For three weeks the interdict has held, Nexus volunteers working alongside U.N. peacekeepers and Mexamerican troops. Then the first cases of Dekoa flu showed up among the refugees, and MsF arrived with a U.N. mandate to open the interdict.

Now a single strand of data fiber, temporarily strung across the border at Gray Mountain, carries all the traffic for the relief operation. And Damien is the one who decides what that fiber transmits.

He flips open the keypad on his wrist and punches in a code, instituting a link to the Nexus command post. "Skippy?"

"*Habari gani,* boss. How goes it?" His assistant is, somehow, always cheerful; Damien suspects drugs.

"Don't ask. Can you pull the unit codes for all our people in Dinétah? Not just Nexus, but everybody?"

"Sure."

"I want to give them each standard access to MusicWeb, audio-only, voice-command protocol. But I don't want any unauthorized packets piggybacking on the bandwidth. Can you set that up?"

"Sure. We're passing telemetry and voice now; that fiber has plenty of room left. I can set up a realtime monitor-and-compare loop on the system here and have it kick out any spurious packets. That should keep the traffic clean."

"Good. Do it, please, and then announce to all team members. Thanks."

Damien links back into the common channel, and says to Heavitree, "It'll take just a few seconds. Thanks, I should have thought of that earlier."

"I think you have had other things on your mind, my friend." Heavitree knows, Damien realizes, that something in the last house spooked him. "This is difficult work that we do, and you do not have our training. If you would like, we can work as partners for a little while."

Damien considers taking the offer as an insult, then decides not to. "If you don't mind. I'm a little more shaky than I thought I would be."

As they move through he rest of the houses, Damien finds himself impressed by Heavitree's sensitivity. To the dying as well as the survivors, he is compassionate and understanding. With his soft voice and his easy, supportive touch, Heavitree calms the frantic and brings the face of humanity into this nightmare.

Damien can see why MsF chose him to head the relief operation.

House after house, target after target, hour after hour they work like avenging angels, choosers of the dead. Finally, Damien reports the latest target secured, and the computer spits out an unbelievable reply: "All targets secured. Return to base."

He follows the others aboard the copter, stomach empty and bladder full, and slumps on the deck next to Heavitree. "We've done it," Damien says. "Medevac units are over half done their job, too. By nightfall the whole area will be ready for sterilization."

Heavitree sighs. "I've been on more than a dozen of these missions. It never gets any easier."

The fire hall in Gray Mountain has been turned into decontam, headquarters, and mess hall for the operation. Damien, along with the others, allows the decontam crew to spray the outside of his suit with bleach, then struggles out of it and hits the lavatories. Then, smell of bleach and sweat clinging to him, he makes a beeline for the food.

Smiling, fat-bottomed Anglo women serve wilted mexam casseroles from surgical-looking steam trays. As Damien nears the end of the line, one of them (the name tag on her heaving bosom reads "Marge") brandishes her slotted spoon and bellows, "Ah sure can't thank you enough for comin' out here to take care of everything. Not just that plague, neither, but the whole Navajo thing. People in these parts were getting tired of all the fightin' and killin', if you know what I mean." She guffaws, showing a full set of perfect teeth. "You Nexus folks, you're okay with us. Here, have another helping of cherry cobbler. You deserve it."

"I thank you," Damien answers softly, with the hint of a bow. He has lived in North America since he was eight, but he's never managed to get into the habit of blaring the way Anglos do. "Everyone here has been exceptionally kind to us, and the Nexus certainly appreciates all your support." Especially, he thinks, since your own government can't be bothered to keep order on its own boundaries.

He excuses himself and stops to search for an empty seat. Doctor Heavitree, already established at one of the long metal picnic tables, waves him over.

"Sit down, my friend."

Damien slides in next to Heavitree. The others at the table are MsF agents whom Damien at once tags as Heavitree's entourage. They are all within a few years of his own age, and all of them— like Damien and Heavitree themselves— look like the walking dead. They acknowledge him with nods and eyes quickly lifted from their plates, without interrupting the business of eating.

Damien can't blame them, and immediately starts shoveling the mess on his plate into his mouth. The dishes aren't anything he recognizes, except of course for Marge's cherry cobbler; he identifies beans and rice, cheese and ground meat, shredded greens and maize, strips of chicken. Here the spark of red peppers, there a wilted tortilla fragment, there a few incongruous olives...but in general the ingredients have, in that undeniable American way, been together long enough to work out a mutual understanding that teeters on the rim of "bland."

Still, it is food, and right now Damien is ready to admit that it is the finest meal he's ever eaten.

His stomach placated, he takes a deep breath and forces himself to stand. With a wan smile, he excuses himself from the table. "Time to make my rounds, cheer up the troops." Nearly a hundred Nexus personnel are involved in this operation, from the handful who live on-site and maintain the interdict, to the dozens of volunteers who came in specifically for the relief effort. Damien, as head of that effort, feels it his duty to at least greet and thank each one of them.

Nexus operatives are easy to spot. Most conspicuous are those who need to remain incognito; their faces are distorted or disguised by cold light holograms. Some hide their identities behind fantastic, stylized masks drawn from one culture or another; others opt for simple scrambling. One woman, who goes by the codename Lady Mondegreen, wears the androgynous, vaguely-oriental "average" face of humanity; her expressions are so flawlessly animated that Damien almost believes he is looking at a real face.

Many operatives, though— especially the younger ones— make no effort to hide their features. In recent years, the Nexus has gained widespread support among the world's people and in the United Nations; secrecy that had been necessary in the early years is increasingly irrelevant to the organization's second generation. The older trappings of codenames and secret handshakes which Damien grew up with, have become a game, part of the Nexus mystique.

Nowadays, to find the Nexus operatives in any crowd, one looks less for holomasks and more for the uneven starburst symbol: fourteen radiating lines accompanied by binary digits, representing the sun's distance from fourteen specific pulsars. Drake's Starburst, which had flown into interstellar space on numerous probes, stands for the Nexus commitment to the human community as a whole, no matter whether East or West, North or South, on Earth, the Moon, or Mars.

All Nexus operatives wear Drake's Starburst: on clothing, on jewelry, tattooed or painted on the skin, even in cold light perched on the shoulder like a pirate's parrot. Damien has the design tattooed in fluorescent yellow on his left bicep, and in addition wears it today as arm- and breast-patch on his black tee shirt. He spots it on pendants, hairclips, earrings, and in rainbow face paint; on badges and brassards, buckles and beads, printed and woven and embroidered on blouses, trousers, robes, caps. He introduces himself to each wearer, takes their codename in return, thanks them for their efforts. Some he knows from long association, either in person or on the nets; some he recognizes by their aliases; some he meets today for the first time. It doesn't matter...in all the important ways, the Nexus is like an enormous family. When he meets someone wearing the Starburst, he knows that there are bonds between them.

Of course, as in any family, there are some he can't stand— and others who are more...congenial. Damien's eyes light on a brown, somewhat zaftig woman, about his own age, with long dark hair and faintly Anglo-Asian features. She wears a loose dress of bright kinte cloth and earth-colored sandals that lace halfway up her bare calves. Drake's Starburst flashes from a gold pendant that sits atop her shapely bodice.

"*Habari gani,*" he greets her. "I'm Damien Nshogoza, task leader."

She meets his eyes. "I've seen your name on the nets. I'm Penylle."

He vaguely recalls seeing her name on the nets as well, and wishes he could log on to check. "I want to thank you for coming out here today."

"It was no trouble."

He chuckles. "I wouldn't say that. Do I detect a hint of Mother Africa in your accent? Maybe the West?" Her voice is mostly standard American, but Damien thinks he hears more than a trace of home.

She dimples. "Born in Baltimore, raised in the States, but now I live in Kampala."

"Parents came over in the Recall, I imagine?" It is definitely not polite to ask if either or both had been transportees.

"Not really. I...found my way there myself, in my teens. How about yourself?"

"The opposite, actually. Born in Dar es Salaam, moved to Washington when I was eight. Dad went to Africa in the early 2010s, met mother through the Nexus, and she followed him there. I was born the year before the Recall was issued." No sense in giving any more details of his convoluted family life.

She pretends to be impressed. "Ooo, second generation Umoja. I don't often meet them outside of Africa."

"Outside of school, you mean." He shrugs. "So I'm an old man."

She smiles. "I didn't say that."

"Did you come all the way from Kampala, or were you in the States?"

"I'm still not in the States." She waves her hand; it passes right through Damien's without a trace of sensation. Cold light hologram. "Physically, I'm at home."

Surprised, he looks closely at her body. Now that he knows what to look for, he can see it: the outline of her body and limbs is a bit too sharp, the details of her skin a trifle blurred. Still, it is the best cold light projection he's ever seen. "Rats," he says with a grin.

"What?"

"Now I'll never know what you *really* look like."

"For your information, this *is* what I really look like."

"Then I'm very pleased. Perhaps we could— "

"Perhaps we could get to know one another better, first." She dimples. "Tell me more about yourself. What made you leave Umoja?"

Damien is often asked this question, usually with the unspoken implication that he is some sort of traitor to Mother Africa, for living on another continent. "I didn't, really. I have dual citizenship. And it wasn't my choice."

"Oh?"

"When I was a boy, my father was a victim of identity theft. The wyden murdered Father, took over his identity, and had Mother killed."

Penylle's face melts into sympathy. "I'm so sorry. He was caught and punished, I assume?"

"No." The familiar smoldering rage rises in Damien, tasting of old bile. "He covered his traces skillfully. I was the only living witness— and the authorities weren't about to take the word of an eight-year-old." He shrugs. "After a while, I got sick of going to psychologists, so I ran away and came to live with relatives in the States."

"And the man who stole your father's identity, is still out there?"

"Yes. He's— "

Damien's watchphone beeps, and from it Heavitree's voice emerges: "Damien, I think that you should meet me at the front of the hall— at once."

Both Damien and Penylle look in the direction of the entrance. Half a dozen burly Amerind men, accompanied by a dozen reporters, push their way past the bewildered pair of blue helmets ostensibly guarding the door. Damien walks quickly toward them, followed by Penylle; Heavitree closes from the other side and they meet two meters from the Amerinds.

The leader's ebony hair falls in a single braid down his back, but his temples are greying and his face is already furrowed with wrinkles; Damien guesses that the man is in his late fifties. His deep voice holds a slight twang but otherwise is straight Standard American. "Who's in charge here?"

Damien steps forward. "That would be me, I suppose. Damien Nshogoza. And you are...?"

"Wakiza Tl'izilani, Chief of Dinétah. I was given to understand that your leader went by the name H. Orlamus."

"Hammy's in the hospital, recovering from injuries he received from a Navajo raiding party last week. I'm surprised you didn't know that." Damien straightens his shoulders and tries to pump some bravery into his voice. "I speak for the Nexus here."

"Then when are you going to lift your interdict and leave my people alone?"

Damien, mouth suddenly dry, takes a deep breath. It doesn't help. "As soon as you agree to comply with U.N. Resolution 6502 and stop raiding the Hopi. If you want, I can get the Secretary-General online and you can do the agreement right now."

"I am not going to debate politics with you, not while my people are dying."

Calm. "The interdict has been suspended to allow medical relief teams to deal with the plague emergency."

"Which was probably caused by more white trickery."

Damien holds up his right hand, showing off chocolate-brown skin. "Chief Tl'izilani, perhaps you could more productively direct those comments to someone who's actually white."

The Chief bulldozes on, "This is the only the latest in a long, long history of attacks and betrayals which my people have suffered at the hands of the Anglo and his lackeys. I demand that— "

Jamiar Heavitree steps forward, standing nearly a head taller than the Navajo. "I've had enough of that, Tl'izilani. I am Dr. Jamiar Heavitree, in charge of this medical operation. I am also full-blooded Cherokee— and believe me, we *know* from suffering at Anglo hands. More than the Navajo ever will. Don't give me speeches about Anglo trickery and betrayal. This is nothing political and nothing racial…it is a *disease,* for gods' sakes. People are dying…red, white, brown, black. Unless we stop the spread, many more will die. So we're doing what we know we must, to stop it. If you stand in our way, for whatever reason, you will have more blood on your hands than you already do. Period, end of report."

"Ever since the Anglos and Latinos came to this land, they've been trying to exterminate our people. And yet you believe that this disease is not political?" Tl'izilani shakes his head. "You are naïve, Doctor."

"There are more people alive and well in your single tribe today, than there were in all the tribes of all the peoples in 1492."

"They killed nine in ten of us."

"No, *they* didn't. Do you know what *did* kill nine in ten of us? Disease. Smallpox. Measles, mumps, typhoid, influenza, diphtheria, scarlet fever. If the Anglos and Latinos had been the most enlightened and peaceful visitors on the planet, the end result would have been exactly the same." He holds the Chief's eye for a long moment, then says softly, "Dekoa kills eight in ten. Would you have us stand by and allow this tragedy once again?"

"I…."

"Let me tell you *why* our people died, Chief. Because for ten thousand years, we'd had no contact with the rest of the world. We had never been exposed to diseases that Eurasians took for granted. We had no defenses. All we needed was one sick man, five, ten sick men to bring the microbes across the ocean. The microbes did the rest."

"You're trying to change the subject."

"No, I'm not. I'm talking about *your* nation today, withdrawing behind your boundaries, killing your neighbors to keep those boundaries secure, standing as far apart from the rest of the world as you can possibly manage."

Tl'izilani frowns. "If what you say is true, what about the Europeans? *They'd* been separated from *us* for ten thousand years. Why didn't they catch *our* diseases?"

"They did. Settlers died by thousands. But those who would have carried the diseases back to Europe, died on the way." Heavitree holds out his hand to the Chief. "This is all ancient history. Please let it remain that way. Do not hinder the work that we do here."

Tl'izilani hesitates, then shakes Heavitree's hand. "Agreed, Doctor." He glares at Damien. "We will not interfere with medical relief. But tell your Anglo Nexus that it has not heard the last of the Navajo."

"Listen," Damien answers, "you can talk to me all you want, but you're wasting your breath. The Nexus isn't going to lift that embargo until the U.N. rescinds 6502. Talk to the people in Geneva if you want action."

"We will see." Tl'izilani and his entourage turn to go.

"One more thing," Damien says, and the room is suddenly very silent while tension snaps back like a rubber band. "Between midnight and three, local time, keep all your people out of the red zone. We'll be sterilizing the area, and I can just imagine how upset my superiors would be if you were caught in the beam."

Without a word of reply, Tl'izilani is gone.

Heavitree pats Damien on the shoulder. "I don't know about you, my friend, but I need a drink."

"You were great."

"I am sick and tired of people who use their heritage— of any type— to avoid dealing with the modern world. I apologize: I *do* tend to go on."

"You weren't so bad yourself," Penylle says to Damien.

Damien grins. "Well, *I'm* sick and tired of people beating up on the Nexus." He sighs. "I wish I could ask both of you to share a drink with me, but we all have work to do. I have to start coordinating tonight's beaming."

"And I," Heavitree says, "should start genotyping this virus. We need to know which strain this is, and how it reached this population. Perhaps we can have that drink when the operation is complete?"

"It's a date," Damien answers, then says to Penylle, "You'll come with us?"

"Buzz me. You can find my netcode." With that, she fades out.

Damien, smiling, turns back to work.

## DIVERTISSEMENT 01

from *African Armageddon* by Hassan Kerekou (2035)
University of Harare Net,
<stf3.uharare.edu.zw/Kerekou/AA/intro>

Ebola fever. Marburg virus. AIDS. Half a million Africans dead. Then one million, two, five. Rift Valley fever, Sabia virus, dengue. Ten million, twenty, fifty. Millennial flu, Cairo fever, Kabinda virus. A hundred million African corpses, hundred-fifty, two. By the time Dekoa flu came along, a quarter-billion African lives had fallen to disease, and just as many to starvation, exposure, murder, and the various madnesses of society unable to hold itself together.

The White West, intent upon its own problems, did little— and the Yellow East even less. Not until Dekoa flu erupted from the Congo, with its 78% infection rate, eight-month incubation period, and 90% mortality, did the rest of the world step in to aid the Black South. And not until Africa was a wasteland, fully half of her billion-plus perished, did the World Health Organization succeed in containing and controlling the plagues.

Simulations agree that Africa's death toll would have been halved— or better— if the West had stepped in a mere decade sooner. Had the UN acted in 1995, 2000, or even as late as 2005, Africa would today be richer by three- or even four-hundred million lives.

What took so long? Quite simply, the West was not threatened. Before Dekoa, Western deaths were limited to the poor, immigrants, Blacks, other undesirables on the fringes of society. A quarter-billion African deaths, a million or so in Western ghettos, mattered little. Only when the crisis struck home— when Dekoa started to claim the wealthy and powerful— when White faces started filling the obitunets— when the Beautiful People began to perish— only *then* was the West threatened, only then did it act. And then only in its own self-interest.

Indeed, it can be argued that without the high-profile death of the Whitest and most Western man on the planet, England's King Charles, the West might have waited even longer before interceding in Africa. Thus, the greatest irony of the African Holocaust is this: that a prince born into a world of Western Colonial oppression, ruler of the last of the Colonial powers, should be the proximate cause of both Africa's salvation and her eventual rebirth in freedom. In death, Charles served us far better than he ever could have in life.

## [02] GHOST DANCE 01
## Cyberbia & Beyond
## 20 July 2042 C.E.

*Calm down— it's only ones and zeroes.*

Damien zips up his bitsuit, adjusts his headset, and dives into Cyberbia.

The bitsuit is rated at two hundred stimpoints per square centimeter, microscopic contacts that can induce his nerves to register everything from the stroke of a cold feather to the hot touch of fevered skin. Thousands of micro-telemeters relay the position of his body and limbs to the main computers, which second-by-second map his real body onto its virtual duplicate. From the headset, lasers constantly map the direction of his eyeballs, as well as the ever-changing muscles of his facial expression. Others, instructed by the main system, draw images directly on his retinas. Lightweight earphones bring him the full richness of simulated sound.

Damien flips a switch, feels the suit tingle as it goes live, and finds himself in his familiar homeroom: a private region of Cyberbia which he has designed and constructed himself. It is a modest space, about four meters square, with four walls and ceiling of silver-flecked ebony that mimics the night sky. The floor, black and of indeterminate texture, is firm but not uncomfortable. There is no door…and no need for one.

Two windows, on opposing walls, show scenes from the real world. The largest displays a realtime image of the wooded expanse outside Damien's own home in suburban Washington, DC. Tonight, the moon shines peacefully on treetops, and clouds are moving in from the south.

The opposing window shows an image from the other place Damien thinks of as home: the vast expanse of the Serengeti, with Kilimanjaro towering in the distance. It is early morning there; grass moves in slow breezes, and a few giraffes glide like stately sailships across the plain. As he watches, a capsule flies upward from the Kilimanjaro catapult, a tiny speck blazing brightly as the invisible beams from eight gigawatt lasers catch it and propel it into space on a trail of water vapor. Every fifteen minutes, day and night, the tireless machinery of the catapult launches a new payload into orbit.

The walls are hung with various pictures, plaques, and bric-a-brac…all of which, in the usual manner of Cyberbian objects, are rather indistinct at first glance, growing more detailed upon closer examination and longer contemplation. They reveal themselves to be three-dimensional icons, links to various pieces of Damien's life, or to people and places he wants to keep in touch with.

The only pieces of furniture in evidence are an antique oak roll-top desk and matching chair, of which Damien is inordinately proud. They were his first graduate project. Each is constructed of over a million polygons mimicking the grain of natural wood. The surface texture maps he'd copied from photomicrographs of real oak from the Smithsonian. For the tactile maps, Damien spent hours sitting— in his bitsuit— on a real oak chair, leaning and writing on a real oak desk. Hundreds of audio clips are linked to chair and desk, so that just the right sound comes from tapping his fingers against the desk, dropping a virtual pin atop it, or accidentally scraping the chair's legs against the floor.

As much as any Cyberbian construct *can* be, Damien's desk and chair are real.

He ignores the desktop, where half a dozen messages pulse in neon hues, trying to catch his attention. Instead, Damien reaches into a cubbyhole and withdraws a small envelope, the virtual symbol for a block of data. A glance assures him that it is the correct file: the paper is faintly emblazoned with Dr. Heavitree's electronic glyph. If the Doctor has transferred the right file, this envelope represents the complete genotype of the Dekoa virus, Navajo strain.

"Okay," he says, addressing the envelope, "Let's see what we can make of you."

How had Dekoa entered the Navajo Nation? In order to find out, the genotype of this strain must be compared to thousands of other samples, similarities and differences cataloged, correlations drawn. Then, countless other factors had to be added: weather, transportation, political situations, international trade...Heavitree estimated that it would take *MsF's* overworked AIs seven to ten days to come up with an answer.

Damien knows a better way.

A magician's gesture causes a phantom keypad to materialize in the air before Damien: a teleporter control pad. In Cyberbia, there are no long-distance airlines, no suborbitals, and very few highways. All virtual places are within a fraction of a second of each other at electronic speed, and cyberspace is endlessly malleable at the observer's whim. People wink in and out of social spaces without warning, move from place to place without perception of travel. The teleporter grew up as part social convention and part clever programming, and the *digiterati* adopted it at once as a practical solution to the psychological problems of travel in Cyberbia.

Damien taps his destination code, pushes the transmit button, and counts three. His homeroom dissolves in a swirl of primary colors, which just as quickly firms up into bleak, mountainous terrain. He stands before a towering wall, patterned somewhat after the Great Wall in China, but straight-edged and crisp in the fashion of pure computer graphics. The air is thin, cold, and clean; a brisk wind sings against the top of the wall and brings gooseflesh to Damien's arms.

This is the Bound Determinate, the ultimate edge of Human penetration into cyberspace. The AIs structure the region beyond to their own purposes; they do not permit ordinary fleshlings to venture into it. In fact, the Bound Determinate is self-enforcing: an unaided fleshling who tries to scale the wall finds the distance to the top ever-increasing, until like an erstwhile Sisyphus he must surrender and retreat.

This is the Treaty, agreed by Humans and AIs decades ago. Humans have their preserves, where they cannot interfere with the AIs or harm them; the AIs, for their part, take on much of the socioeconomic modeling and management that keeps the Human, physical world running.

*Some* Humans, however, are not subject to the Treaty. The AIs deem them harmless...possibly even helpful...and allow them free reign outside the Human preserves. Whether the AIs consider them as guests, comrades, curiosities, or pets is unknown. When they reveal themselves to the Human world at all, they take on the collective name of *FAI*: friends of AIs.

When Damien was just a teener, joyriding through Cyberbia and poking his virtual nose everywhere it didn't belong, he made the acquaintance of a mid-rank AI which called itself **Øµt øf Thrëë, thë M¥riåd Thiñgs**. On his sixteenth birthday, **Øµt øf Thrëë** took him for the first time beyond the Bound Determinate, and conferred upon him the status of *FAI*. In the years since, Damien has come to know a fair number of AIs, on their own terms and in their own worlds. They are vast and remote, and much of their lives are incomprehensible to him...but somehow friendship transcends the enormous gulfs. He continues to visit, and the AIs continue to permit him.

Now, two steps before the mathematically-perfect, solid rock of the Bound Determinate, Damien closes his eyes and calmly walks forward.

His skin tingles, as his suit fights to interpret myriad nonstandard inputs. AI space is alive with information, dense with data, in a way that Human cyberspace cannot begin to approach. Bits fly past him and through him like neutrinos in the real world, and neither Damien nor the 'puters that serve him can comprehend even a fraction of them.

Slowly, his suit settles down and Damien opens his eyes. Friendly AIs, noticing his presence, send streams of data packets his way, packets configured to be intelligible to his bitsuit. A pseudo-landscape forms around him, a three-dimensional expanse of electric blue hexagons...as if he were a microscopic being looking out from the middle of an ice crystal. He sees data rushing past him as streams of different colors, each following its own serpentine path through the hexagons.

The AIs themselves loom as indistinct shapes beyond the horizon of his world, like giant redwoods or distant, purple mountains. Damien has no sense of direction, not even the simulated pull of gravity to tell him which way is up. To move, he has merely to gesture, sculling his fingers gently as if afloat in peaceful waters. One direction is as good as another— in fact, to the AIs, as near as he could understand, there *are* no directions.

Communication comes, in a combination of visual stimuli and sound, which his mind grasps before his eyes and ears are even sure what they witness.

**Dåmiëñ, intrëpîd tråvëllër,**
**Is wåshëd iñ cøøl wåtërs grëën.**
**Åbîdë åwhîlë åñd wëlçømë, øµr *ƒ*riëñd.**

The welcome is accompanied by images of still, clear ponds in primeval forest, and a scent like the memory of pine.

It takes Damien more than a moment to phrase his reply:

*The traveller drinks his fill,*
*Sweet water from the deeps*
*Refreshes soul and mind.*

He accompanies this with a great stretch, which brings a yawn, and hopes they will get the message. Usually, the AIs are very good about reading what he means. **Øµt øf Thrëë** once told him that he is far easier to read than most humans.

**Ñåñøsëçøñds, spëëdiñg b¥ likë bîrds,**
**Thåt *ƒ*l¥ *ƒ*røm lårgër prëdåtørs,**
**Stîll lëåvë spåçë *ƒ*ør *ƒ*riëñds tø çøñtëmplåtë.**

In the words and images, Damien recognizes the AI known as **Trinë-Åñdrøg¥në**. He answers:

*A drop of water spins and plummets*

*And is plucked from impact's doom*
*To land and bead upon outstretched palm.*

Deep, booming laughter echoes for a moment, along with a distant echo of calliope music and images suggestive of circus tents.

**Trinë-Åñdrøg¥në is åmüsëd/jø¥ƒul/**
**Gråtiƒïëd. ßµt Dåmiëñ**
**Is ñø mërë råiñdrøp ƒålliñg ƒrëë.**

Pleasantries are out of the way now. Damien holds up the envelope.

*This one is mired in the mud*
*Of slow human thought;*
*Strong branches may lift him out.*

Damien has the impression of giant phantom fingers plucking the envelope from his grasp. In the distance, **Trinë-Åñdrøg¥në** hums like a contented calico kitten.

**Dåmiëñ is årmørëd ƒør**
**Å møst såçrëd Qüest.**
**Thë øbjëct må¥ ëlúdë åll.**

"I know that, I just want you to— " He stops, sighs.

*The apprentice fails to see*
*Perhaps the Master*
*Succeeds, and shows the way.*

Damien has prepared with an appropriate vidclip from Disney's *Fantasia*, and now squirts it into the air.

There is more tolerant laughter, and a new envelope appears before Damien. He snatches it out of the air, noting **Trinë-Åñdrøg¥në**'s glyph on the surface. In the few seconds that have passed— years, to an intelligence that counts time in picoseconds— the AI has analyzed Damien's problem and found a solution.

Damien bows his head.

*Once again, **Trinë-Åñdrøg¥në***
*Has saved his brother*
*Much wasted time and effort.*

The computer answers,

**Øñcë ågåiñ, m¥ ßrøthër Dåmîëñ**
**Hås ëntërtåiñëd ånd çhållëngëd**
**Hîs møst lø¥ål ƒriënd, Trinë-Åñdrøg¥në.**

Without further discussion, Damien turns to go— for the AIs, with their multiplex minds and bit-perfect memories, do not understand and see no reason for Human customs of leave-taking.

In three steps, he crosses the Bound Determinate and emerges in the familiar landscape of Cyberbia. At a simple gesture, even Cyberbia is gone, and Damien stands in the middle of an empty room, alone and shivering in his clammy bitsuit. The data from **Trinë-Åñdrøg¥në**, safely downloaded to the local system, glows reassuringly on a terminal screen.

Off in space, a hundred megameters above the Earth, mirror arrays the size of Alaska ponderously shift in their ceaseless orbits. Thinner than tissue yet sturdier than steel, in this environment where the only wind is the imperceptible hydrogen breath of the distant sun, the great hexagons rotate arthritically, slowly, and the reflections of stars move across their faces in time to their sluggish gavotte.

One by one, the mirrors turn...and invisible beams of reflected sunlight slide away from remote collectors, moving instead towards the even more remote surface of the Earth.

One by one, beams converge on the place known as Tse Bii'Ndzisgaii, Monument Valley. A false but intense dawn breaks over sleeping hillsides, mesas, and deserted villages. And slowly, the temperature begins to rise. Before the long night is over, sand will melt and carbon will burn. By morning, nothing— animal, plant, bacteria, or virus— will be left alive in Tse Bii'Ndzisgaii. Lifeless bodies and bones, taboo in Navajo culture, will be reduced to dust and be dispersed by rising gales of heated air.

Such is the will of a weary, frightened world that has lost far too much in far too many plagues: Total sterilization. Authorized by the United Nations, this strike is controlled by the impassive, incorruptible silicon minds of the AIs.

But there is a lesson here, a lesson that is not lost on all the nations who watch. The world's people are slow to anger, slow to act— but when they do, the results are swift and devastating.

Today, those who defy the world community are put under interdict by the Nexus. Today, the nations of the world respect that interdict, and uneasily support the Nexus and the United Nations.

For tomorrow, or the day after, if Nexus interdict fails...then the mirrors can easily be shifted in another direction.

Every nation knows, that it is better to be sealed off from the rest of the planet for a time, than to be incinerated from off its face forever....

Gray Mountain, Arizona, Mexamerica
20 July 2042 C.E.

"This cannot be right." Jamiar Heavitree tosses the flatscreen pad to a makeshift lab counter, where it clatters to rest against a rack of test tubes.

"What makes you say that?"

Heavitree leans back on his stool, propping an elbow on the cork-topped counter. "According to that," he gestures at the flatscreen, "the current outbreak is most closely related to the strain that was responsible for the Haiphong epidemic in February."

"That's what the AIs say. Ninety-three percent probability. The next candidate is forty-one percent. All of the correlations are itemized there for you."

"Oh, I'm not saying that there aren't correlations in the DNA. Perhaps even significant ones." Heavitree shakes his head. "But it still can't be right."

"I don't see why not. The virus could have gotten here from Haiphong as easily as..." Damien glances at the flat, "...from Uruguay."

"I'm not disputing the possibility of transmission." Heavitree pushes up his lab goggles, rubs his eyes. "My friend, I was in Haiphong. I saw the disease myself, firsthand. And I can tell you that the two strains are not alike."

"The AIs say they are. The genotypes— "

"Are very nearly identical. Yes, I know. But the symptoms are not. The Haiphong strain was much more...what to say?...pulmonary. More violent. It involved more coughing, expectorating blood and mucus. Death came quicker, but more cruelly." He glances at the darkened window, as if he can see the remorseless death that even now plays over Navajo lands, sterilizing everything. "You saw the victims. Some of them died in their sleep. The Haiphong strain did not allow such a peaceful escape."

"Then where *did* this strain originate? Uruguay?"

"Possibly. I do not know." Heavitree retrieves the flat, switches off his instruments, and rises from the stool. His shoulders are slumped, and Damien notices dark circles under his eyes. "If the AIs say that the probability is so strong, then I will put that result in my report. Perhaps I am mistaken. Perhaps over the last five months, the virus has mutated away from a pulmonary attack. With further study, we might be able to isolate the genetic areas behind that mutation, and so come to a greater understanding of the virus." He looks again at the flat, again shakes his head. "But I still find it hard to believe, that the strains are so closely related."

Damien follows him out of the lab, into a small office where three other *MsF* operatives are passed out on folding cots. Heavitree flops into the one remaining bed and kicks off his shoes.

"I do not want to seem ungrateful, my friend. The information you brought us from the AIs has put us weeks ahead." He yawns deeply, and settles his head on the lumpy pillow. "In the morning, when my head is clear, maybe I will find that I am mistaken."

"No offense, but I hope you do. I prefer that to the alternative."

Eyes closed, on the border of falling asleep, Heavitree mumbles, "Which is?"

"That it's the AIs who are mistaken."

Heavitree answers with a dull snore. Damien backs away quietly, taking care to turn off the lights on his way out.

ENTREÉ 01

Date: Thu, 16 Jul 2042 08:44:40 (GMT)
From: Torai@jalina.shingo.jp [Torai Taro Tenkujin]
Subject: Re: Turing's test
To: Blessed.Virgin@nexus.nex
Cc: ai.taskforce.list@uluebo.edu
Message-id: <20420716124440_702420.204200_BHD58-61@nexus.nex>
Content-Type: text
Status: O

----------------------------------------

Turing Test? Turing Test?

Let me get this straight. They wanted a computer to converse, knowledgeably and at length, with a Ph.D. in computer science or philosophy—on any subject or subjects of the Ph.D.'s choice—without ever once being allowed to say "I'm sorry, I don't know anything about that?"

Pell, most *people* I know couldn't pass *that* test!

-TTT

----------------------------------------

[03] TARANTELLA 09
Maris Institute
Elkridge, Maryland
United States, North America
21 July 2042 C.E.

*If you tell the truth once, they will never believe you again, no matter how much you lie.*

The Ivory Madonna stands at her desk in precisely the same way an opera diva stands on stage for her solo. She is built like a Valkyrie, but with the delicate hands and face of an antebellum southern belle. Her hair is ebony, her skin porcelain, and her eyes the color of the Earth seen from deep space. She is no longer young, but her rounded face is free of wrinkles and she carries herself confidently, with none of the hesitation of the elderly. She wears shades of orange and gold, a Cetairé original that is tight where it shows off her ample assets, flowing where it is kinder to conceal. She stands, as is her wont when working, barefoot on the plush pile of earthen-colored carpet.

Her desk surrounds her, a fat crescent moon of a surface littered with flatscreens and touchpads. When she sits in her intricately-carved wooden chair, the desk lowers itself so that her work is always at her fingertips.

Beyond her, a bank of monitors mutter to themselves; with the touch of a single key, she can raise the volume on any of them. Some are tuned to major news networks. One keeps perpetual vigil on proceedings on the floor of the United Nations General Assembly; others watch the U. S. Senate, the House of Representatives, and the Chamber of Ministers. Public transcripts of Umoja's Board of Directors flow in color-coded script across the face of another.

A chime interrupts the Ivory Madonna. "Yes?"

"Senator Purcell to see you, Ma'am."

"Mute screens." She takes her seat, rotates to face a holo pickup. "Link."

Senator Purcell, a wizened, silver-haired white woman, appears in cold light. Faintly visible behind her is her own office, with the Capitol steps and the distant Washington Monument framed in the window...the same view that appears from every Congressional window. It is generated by a Congressional computer, based on years of recorded images from the same vantage point.

"Charlotte," the Ivory Madonna says, "It's so good to see you."

"Thank you for making time to see me, Miranda. On such short notice, you know." Senator Purcell, in the classic phrase of a one-time aide, has a voice like a rattlesnake being scraped across a chalkboard. "We're both busy women, so I'll come right to the point."

"Of course."

"I'm sure you've seen SB 156." When the Ivory Madonna makes no answer, the Senator prompts, "The Navajo Relief Act."

At a moment's notice, the Ivory Madonna can call the text of the Act up on any of her flatscreens. She has been studying it all morning. But she simply gives a blank, ingenuous look accompanied by a slight wrinkle of her forehead. "I believe I've glanced at it, yes."

"The Act passed the Senate yesterday. The House will vote on a similar bill next week. It is expected to pass." Senator Purcell narrows her eyes.

"And I suppose that the Populist Party is none too happy?"

"How can we be? That twenty billion dollars should stay at home to help Americans."

The Ivory Madonna spreads her hands. "What is one to do?"

"I understand that Minister Somavara will introduce a version of SB 156 later this week in the Chamber of Ministers. We are...trying to gauge the climate of opinion among the Ministers."

"You want me to vote against it."

"My Party would be grateful, yes, but I certainly don't want you to base your decision on that fact. Surely, though, you don't have many...er...constituents among the Navajo. Would it be in the best interests of those you represent, to send money to another country, when there is still so much to be done here?"

The Ivory Madonna, her expression never wavering, counts to six. "My interest group is fat people, Senator. You can say it without offending me. F–A–T. And yes, there *are* fat Navajo. As well as everyone else."

"The Disabilities appropriation is coming up, and it would be a terrible shame if..."

"Choose your words carefully, Madame Senator."

". . . If the Disabilities budget had to be cut, to compensate for unwise expenditures in foreign aid."

"A shame indeed. But it seems to me," the Ivory Madonna says, in a voice perfectly polite but unmistakably chilly, "that I have in the past relied on support from Senate Populists, only to be left with egg on my face. The

2039 civil rights law springs to mind."

"This time I can assure you— "

"Can you?" Their eyes meet, and for a long moment neither speaks.

Finally, the Senator lowers her eyes. "I don't need, or expect, an answer today. Tell me what form you would like our assurance to take, and I will do my best to assure. Take your time, please." She looks up. "We're quite serious about this, Miranda. I don't want any misunderstandings to come between us."

"I will call you. Goodbye." The Ivory Madonna touches her bare right toe to a specific spot on her chair's leg, and the Senator is cut off.

"I'm getting too old for this," the Ivory Madonna mutters. She turns to her desk, punches up a record of the last few Senate roll-call votes, and frowns. The three-way power struggle between Democratic, Populist, and Christian Parties is becoming lopsided, and in the Populists' favor. President Archer is losing her coalition.

"Attention," she says, to warn her office computer that orders follow. "Schedule a midmorning meeting, no later than next Friday, for the Chamber Nonpartisan Caucus. Three hours, at least."

"Working."

While she waits for the computer to consult with all the other office computers involved, there is more work to do. There is *always* more work to do. The Ivory Madonna co-ordinates Nexus interests and activities for a sixth of North America; even with a team of talented assistants to handle the routine work, every passing hour brings new information, new questions, new problems. Just keeping track of them all is a full-time affair.

"Reminder," the computer says.

She lifts her head from the flatscreen she's reading. "Go ahead."

"The Chamber Nonpartisan Committee will meet at nine o'clock next Thursday."

"Thank you." Miranda shifts her attention to a daily news summary; after listening for a moment, she taps the screen in a request for elaboration.

Umojan Minister Marc Hoister, addressing Bastille Day crowds in Abidjan, has been harping on his usual theme of Mars. With the exception of a small North American settlement, Mars— scattered colonies amounting to all of a quarter-million people, if that— is shared between Umoja and the Three Chinas. As near as the Ivory Madonna can tell, Marc Hoister hates to share anything, and is always after Umojan citizens to emigrate.

She delves deeper into the story, examining emigration rates and trends. Perhaps Hoister's speeches are having some effect: African emigration to Mars has doubled from last year…while the Chinese figures are steady.

The computer again speaks up. "Reminder."

"Go ahead."

"Two o'clock Nexus North America conference in fifteen minutes. Your notes are retrieved."

"Thank you." The Ivory Madonna closes the flatscreens before her and takes a quick trip to the bathroom. While there, the peers in the mirror, brushes a few strands of hair back into place, and dons her mask.

Creamy white, that mask, with two rouge circles on its cheeks and a mouth like the Mona Lisa's smile. Drake's starburst is traced in light blue on its forehead. Video transmitters behind the eyes allow her unobstructed vision. The Ivory Madonna has worn this mask, or one like it, for the past thirty-odd years. Her identity is an open secret— certainly all the other high-level Nexus operatives know that the Ivory Madonna and Minister Miranda Maris are one in the same, and most of Capitol Hill is also aware. But she is long over any feeling of absurdity, and continues to wear it for the sake of propriety, if nothing else.

The other Nexus old-timers also wear their masks or distorters, and use the pseudonyms that once protected them from national and international police. Some are in danger still, from unenlightened governments, or from those who think they have a score to settle with the Nexus.

She knows who most of them are, her compatriots in crime and dedication. A few she has known all her life, some she has only met during electronic conferences. Some are friends, some opponents. All are exceptional.

She takes her seat, and the conference begins.

Masks materialize around her, imaginary faces looking out of neutral grey backgrounds. One by one, clockwise around the circle, they state their names. Each is already identified by a printed banner that floats below their image. Their voices, the Ivory Madonna assumes, are computer-processed like her own; they sound nothing like they do in real life.

"D.Löwenger, San Francisco, Northwest."

"Jakob.B.Sen, Chicago, North."

"L.A.Verne, New York, Northeast."

"Ivory.Madonna, Washington, Southeast."

"CHEN1, Mexico City, South."

"Roger.Adelhardt, Los Angeles, Southwest."

"C.H.LAD, United Nations, sitting in."

"Kuch.TA, Manila, sitting in."

"Tsutomu, Lagos, sitting in."

"We are nine," says CHEN1. As the representative of the largest city in their region, CHEN1 guides the conference. "What business is there?"

For twenty minutes, the usual nonsense is discussed. An offshore break in the Bering data cable is determined to be natural, not the result of sabotage. Language riots in a Montreal suburb are being investigated by a joint United Nations/Nexus team, by request of Quebec's U.N. ambassador. Various other threats to world peace are examined, then tabled.

Finally, the nonsense is done, and Roger.Adelhardt says, "Ivory Madonna, would you please report on the Navajo situation?"

"Gladly. Things are under control."

Kuch.TA clears his/her throat. "I hate to confess that I haven't been keeping up with all the reports from other areas. What *is* the situation?"

The Ivory Madonna does not need to look at her notes. "A few days ago, Roger received word of a Dekoa outbreak in Dinétah— the Navajo Nation. He consulted with the rest of us, and we decided on a partial suspension of the interdict, to permit a relief and sterilization effort. L.A. Verne contacted Doctor Heavitree of *Medecins sans Frontieres*, who agreed to spearhead the relief portion. C.H.LAD cleared the sterilization portion with U.N. authorities. And I sent my operative Damien Nshogoza to take command of our interdict."

Roger.Adelhardt adds, "My operative on the scene, H.Orlamus, had been injured a week before, and was unavailable for heavy duty."

Over steepled fingertips clothed with white silk gloves, Kuch.TA asks, "And where does the operation stand at the moment?"

"Sterilization was accomplished overnight. Damien is restoring the interdict as we speak. *MsF* should be clearing out by tomorrow morning."

"And how much has this cost?"

Now she must glance at her notes. "Between our expenses, *MsF*, and U.N. money, just about half a million rands. The U.N. is going to bill Dinétah for a portion of that."

C.H.LAD leans forward, filling his space; the illusion is that he/she has suddenly grown twice as large. "It has come to my attention that Dinétah intends to make a formal complaint to the United Nations. They claim that our interdict contributed to the, hmm, disease outbreak."

"Preposterous," Sen growls.

C.H.LAD turns to the Ivory Madonna. "Is it? With communications operating, would the outbreak have become known sooner?"

The Ivory Madonna is grateful that her mask remains serenely impassive. "Short of going back in time and running the experiment, there is no way to answer that question."

"Then we'd better come up with an answer, hmmm? Because the world is going to be asking. We left…how many hundreds?"

"One hundred thirty-two reported casualties," she supplies.

"We left one hundred thirty-two people to face Dekoa without any way to summon medical assistance— "

Roger.Adelhardt is on his feet, stabbing a bony finger in C.H.LAD's direction. "That's not true! We left internal communications alone. That's always the policy, and you know it."

On his heels, D.Löwenger shouts, "For God's sake, they're anti-technological. By their own choice."

C.H.LAD ignores both of them, and bulldozes on, "…without any way to summon medical assistance, we spent half a million rands of the world's money on an epidemic that possibly could have been caught much sooner, and we rendered a few thousand square kilometers of farmland as lifeless as the surface of Mercury." He/she glares. "Don't argue with *me*, I'm only telling you what Dinétah is certain to say before the General Assembly. And how is the Nexus going to answer, hmmm?"

"Not our responsibility," L.A.Verne grunts. "Nexus interdict is nothing new. We've imposed thirty-eight of them over the last thirty-two years. The U.N. knows what an interdict means. *And* they know how to lift one, if they want to: repeal censure of the interdicted nation." She snarls, "We put our lives on the line because U.N. peacekeeping forces won't, and instead of thanks we get condemned for it. I am beyond sick and tired of the Nexus taking the blame every time the U.N. makes a bad decision."

"I'm not convinced that this *was* a bad decision," CHEN1 says.

"Regardless," C.H.LAD answers, as if speaking to a particularly dull kindergarten, "we all know better than to expect that the U.N. will accept any blame in this situation. All I want to know, is how we intend to answer Dinétah's fairly serious charges."

"How about this?" For what seems the ten-thousandth time, the Ivory Madonna steps in to be the peacemaker. "Let's all consult with our P.R. people— might as well bring the other areas in on this, too, it's going to be worldwide. And we'll get back with ideas in...say, ten hours?" She looks around the masked faces. "Does that suit?"

The others, some still grumbling, agree, and the meeting comes to an end. Images dissolve like bathwater swirling down the drain, and the Ivory Madonna is left alone in her suddenly-quiet office.

She sits for quite a while, staring at the blank, grey wall and reviewing the meeting in her head. Then she touches keys on her desk, and re-runs the whole meeting at zip-speed. Odd, she thinks...Tsutomu of Lagos was present for the whole meeting, as he has been for the last half-dozen— yet not once did he/she say a word. She freezes on Tsutomu's image, and absently strokes her hair as she ponders.

It is half past eight in the evening in Lagos. Why would Tsutomu ruin a perfectly good evening, just to sit in on a meeting to which he/she did not contribute?

Tsutomu's chosen mask was a traditional Ibo monkey mask, a grotesque parody of a face with beady eyes and a mouth forever frozen in a sullen smirk. Looking at it now, the Ivory Madonna feels a little shiver.

Ridiculous! She shakes off the feeling, kills the image, and reaches for her phone. There is a lot to do.

DIVERTISSEMENT 02
Constitution of the United States
Amendment XXXII
(approved by Constitutional Convention of 2023)

1. The Congress of the United States shall consist of three Houses: the Senate, the House of Representatives, and the Chamber of Ministers. Acts of Congress shall require at least a majority of all three Houses, unless a greater majority is specified in this Constitution; in which case, said specified majority must obtain in all three Houses.

2. The Chamber of Ministers of the United States shall consist of one Minister from each National Ministry, and each Minister shall have one vote. A Minister's term shall be one year.

3. Each Minister must be a bona-fide member of the interest group which he/she represents. Ministers shall be chosen by majority vote of all bona-fide interest group members. The time, manner, and place of such elections shall be determined by each interest group, as provided by law by the Congress, in such a manner as to allow all member citizens full and fair opportunity to register their vote.

4. Once each five years, the number and nature of the National Ministries shall be determined, under supervision of the Census Bureau, so as to fairly reflect the interests of all American citizens. Every National Ministry shall be supported by petition of no fewer than one percent of the total adult population of the Nation, and no interest shall be represented by more than one National Ministry. The total number of National Ministries shall not exceed five hundred and one. The Supreme Court shall resolve disputes over the number and nature of the National Ministries.

5. The Chamber of Ministers shall initially consist of no fewer than fifteen Ministries in the following areas: Agriculture, Commerce, Defense, Education, Energy, Housing and Urban Development, Health and Human Services, Interior, Justice, Labor, State,

Telecommunications, Transportation, Treasury, and Veteran's Affairs, plus whatever other Ministries are determined under clause 4 of this Article.

6. No citizen may cast votes as a member of more than six individual interest groups under the provisions of this Article.

7. This Article shall take effect no later than twenty-four months after its ratification by three-fourths of the Legislatures of the several States, or after the date of its approval by a duly-constituted constitutional convention.

## [04] TECHNO/RAVE 01:
## Gray Mountain, Arizona
## Mexamerica, North America
## 22 July 2042 C.E.

*I don't see you, so don't pretend to be there.*

Ten meters above the desert floor, tethered to the top of a utility pole, Damien has an unparalleled view of the surrounding landscape. Distant mesas brood over bare, rocky terrain, while meandering arroyos attest to the memory of torrential rain. But Damien's attention is not on the scenery, magnificent as it is in its lonely desolation. Instead, through Spex data goggles and a mesh glove on his right hand, Damien is in the realm of the microscopic.

A micro-probe, no larger than a gnat, clings to the utility pole. Its stereoscopic cameras are Damien's eyes, its jointed manipulator boom his arm and hand. To the probe, the wooden surface of the pole is a landscape every bit as vast and desolate as the one that surrounds Damien, a landscape pitted and furrowed with huge jagged fissures and great crevices. A large black shape looms over the horizon.

Damien lowers his little finger, moves his hand forward. In response, the probe drifts in the same direction. The black shape becomes an enormous pipeline, a tunnel, large enough in Damien's eyes to carry half a dozen cars driving abreast. With a quick gesture, he locks the probe at a constant distance from the pipeline, then scurries to the right. Soon enough, white-stencilled letters and numbers appear. He looks past his Spex to read a datapad strapped to his left wrist; the numbers check out. Finally, after three hours under the burning sun, he has located the correct data cable, no thicker than one of his hairs.

Following the cable along its length, Damien's probe soon comes to a junction box sitting atop the cable like Dorothy's house atop the Wicked Witch. He circles it, and spots a smaller cable emerging from the back: on the probe's scale, this one is the size of a garden hose. Quite invisible to the unaided eye.

"I've got you now," Damien mutters. He reaches gingerly forward; the probe's manipulator arm touches the delicate fiber. He closes his hand, and the probe's claw contracts until it has the fiber in a firm grip.

Data flows, fiber to probe to computer to Damien's Spex. He reads, then gives a grim nod. As his crew suspected....

"*Habari gani*. What's up?"

He looks away from the micro-world and sees Penylle, a half-transparent ghost, hovering behind him. If floating ten meters high disturbs her, she gives no sign.

"Not much," he answers automatically. "Hey, that's a pretty nice effect. What are you using to project the holo?"

She shrugs. "What makes you think I'm a holo? Maybe I'm really here, this time."

"Right." He removes his Spex; her image vanishes. Damien spends the next few moments playing, moving the Spex this way and that, observing how her image moves and distorts. Finally, he gives an appreciative whistle and a smile. "*Very* nice. A smooth routine. Who does your programming?"

"I do."

"Congratulations. What's it like on your end? How much can you see?"

"A lot more than you'd think."

His brow furrows. There are various video pickups around that she can tap into, most obviously the ones in his Spex...but probably a few on the pole itself, and the instruments in the dirty orange, borrowed pickup that he drove here....

Penylle leans forward, cupping her chin in her hands. "So what are you up to? I was monitoring your microprobe— what was that flash of data?"

"Oh. There are two AIs in Dinétah; we couldn't interdict *them*." He gestures at the cables which trail from pole to pole across the desert. "This is the only active data line across the border, and it goes straight to the AIs."

"And...?"

"The Navajo have attached a bit-tap. They've shielded it pretty well, but my people were able to echo packets off it and deduce its approximate location. I've been looking for the exact spot all morning. That flash you saw was confirmation. I'm into their network now."

"So now you shut them down?"

Damien shakes his head. "First we watch them for a while and find out what sort of equipment they're using. *Then* we shut them down."

"I can see why they're so angry with you."

"Hey, I'm just doing my job."

"I'm glad you're on *our* side."

The flow of data continues, confined within a tiny window that floats off to the right. Analyzer programs crowd around it like beasts at a water hole, each drinking its fill. After a few seconds an analyzer unfolds, flowerlike, into a multi-petaled display; Damien studies it, frowning. Around him, the results of other analyzers blossom; he gathers a bouquet and briefly examines each bloom before closing them all with a wave.

"What's the verdict?" Penylle asks.

"They're using our AI link to access the Net." He summons a virtual keyboard and types one-handed.

Penylle's ghost slides up next to him. "What are you going to do?"

"Really confuse them." The Navajo techs are inserting their own data packets into the stream, packets whose header information mimics legitimate system diagnostic packets. Once they have cleared Nexus routers, these chameleon packets discard their counterfeit headers and appear to the Net like ordinary packets. To the systems involved, these packets are simply counted as missing and automatically resent; the result of a particularly noisy data line.

It is a remarkably inefficient method: the total amount of noise, both legitimate and phony, must stay below a threshold that would trigger an alert. Damien doubts that they can manage throughput any higher than a few megabits per second.

Soon, even that will do them no good.

Penylle looks over Damien's shoulder and watches the code taking shape beneath his hands. "I don't get it."

"It's simple," he answers. "I'm teaching our system to recognize their chameleon packets. They'll be re-headered and diverted to an alternate data path, which is hardwired to *this* server." He types the hexadecimal digits of a Net address.

Penylle snorts. "Oh, that's too good. You're diverting their data through AresNet."

Damien, grinning, nods. "The current delay to Mars is almost fourteen minutes one-way. Nearly half an hour transmission lag, total. *That* should keep their system confused, at the very least."

"You're cruel. I like that in a man."

"Thanks." Damien finishes his code and tells the system to execute it. He watches for a few moments, and everything works fine. "Well, that's done."

He strips off his data-glove and sets it atop a transformer box. He flexes sweaty fingers, relieved to have the thing off. Penylle's ghost floats half a meter away as Damien gathers his few tools. "Nunn," he mutters. "I forgot to recall the probe."

Not really paying attention, he reaches for the glove...and bumps it instead. Like an injured bird, it falls from its perch and plummets downward.

"I've got it." Penylle's hand snakes out, snatches the glove in mid-air, and lifts it back to the transformer.

For an instant, Damien reaches for the glove as if nothing unusual has happened, then his brain catches up with his eyes and he stops, the pit of his stomach numb.

Penylle...*caught*...the glove.

But she is only a hologram, an image in his Spex.

Damien raises his gaze from the limp data-glove, lying there as if it had never fallen, and meets Penylle's deep, brown eyes.

She forces a wan smile. "Oops," she says. "I guess I shouldn't have done that."

She insists that Damien climb down from the pole, and he is just as happy to comply. Witnessing a bona-fide miracle, he finds, makes one wish for solid ground.

Hands on hips, he faces her ghost. "All right, how did you do that?"

Penylle seems to stand a meter away, no longer translucent. Her face and body are appropriately lit by the high-riding sun, but she casts no shadow on the ground. "I guess you've never seen psychokinesis in action."

"I've never even seen it in *print.* Or heard of it."

She tosses her head. "Mind-over-matter."

"Not outside the virties, that's for sure." Damien leans against the side of his borrowed truck. "You're telling me that you can move things just by thinking about them? Use-the-force-Luke, for real?"

"Small things, yes. And it isn't effortless, the way most virties would have you believe." She looks down; at Damien's feet, sand suddenly dances in a fountain about ten centimeters high, sparkling in the sun. After a moment, it subsides.

Damien whistles in admiration. "*Siajabu.* And you can do that all the way from Kampala?"

"It doesn't work that way. Virtually, I'm there with you."

Damien nods. Remote operations are familiar to him from his work in the

Net. "So your…ability…works from wherever you perceive yourself to be. Do you have to *see* something, or…?" he stops, confused.

She raises her hands. "Ah, well, that's the other part. You see, I'm also clairvoyant."

Damien cannot stifle a laugh. "Shall I get your crystal ball? Or do you use the entrails of a snake? I'm sure we could find one somewhere around here."

"Don't dis me, brother." Penylle is every centimeter a modern Umojan woman, offended, and Damien feels like a misbehaving child.

"Sorry. I've never met a clairvoyant before. Educate me. How do you do it?"

"Tell me how you see."

"Uh…with my eyes?"

"Same with clairvoyance. Except I behold in all directions at once. And I can look past the surface, behold things inside." Without lowering her eyes, she continues, "Like what you have in your pockets."

Damien cannot stop himself from shifting his leg into a more concealing position. "You're telling me that you can read minds?"

She stamps her foot. "*No*! Clairvoyance isn't telepathy. I can behold physical objects. I can't behold people's thoughts and feelings any more than you can *see* them. But I *can* behold through barriers. Right now, for instance I can watch your heart beat or your lungs move."

"Sounds confusing."

Penylle shrugs. "I decide what I want to concentrate on, same as you do. Everything else is…out of focus."

"So…you're telling me that you can sit in Africa and sense what's going on here in Arizona?"

"I told you, it all depends on where I perceive myself to be. I can behold you, and the truck, and the area around you— that doesn't mean I can behold the town, or Washington, D.C. without a virtual presence there." She sighs. "For instance, I behold from your expression that you still doubt me. But with those Spex you're wearing, you can see just about anywhere on Earth."

"It's a little different. There are cameras, and computers, and electrical signals travelling between here and there."

Penylle spreads her arms. "Electrical signals travel between you and me. I'm reading them right now."

"I don't even want to *ask* what kind of system you're using."

"Er...I'm sort of using an Amiga 7500."

"Never heard of it."

"No one has. It came out in 2004."

Damien pointedly turns his back on her— which doesn't help, since her image stays in the center of his visual field. "Now who's dissing whom?" he asks.

"No, I'm not. I can't help it if you don't believe me."

"You're telling me that you're accessing full voice and video, as well as running the best full-body simulation I've ever seen, on a system that's forty years old? Oh, yeah, plus whatever signals it takes to carry your clairvoyance?" He folds his arms over his chest. "You might be able to fool me into believing in psycho-whatever and clairvoyance, but I *know* the Nets, and that's impossible."

"Are you done?"

"Maybe."

"First of all, I'm not trying to fool you about anything. My case and my life history are on file in medical and psychological journals, which you can check out if you think I'd have any reason to lie to *you*." She makes the word an insult. "Second, I never said I was *just* using the Amiga for Net access. I said 'sort of.' But you didn't wait for me to explain."

She's right, at least, that a hoax of this nature would be impossible to perpetrate. A few minutes with any Net index will prove the truth of her story. But Damien, although feeling chastened, is not quite ready to admit defeat. "All right, explain."

She gestures, and once again sand pirouettes at his feet. "PK. Clairvoyance. I told you I was good with small things." She pauses. "Like electrical signals and patterns of light.."

"What?!"

"I can behold the patterns of Net traffic. I've learned how to read them without any physical system. I can also...reach in and change how the patterns flow." Her image shimmers. "See?"

"I think this is too much for me. Slow down. You can...behold...Net traffic? The way I see a stream flowing by?"

"It's more the way your ear senses tiny pressure waves in the air."

"And with your...psychokinesis?...you can do your own data processing?"

"More or less."

"Then why do you need any system at all?"

She sighs. "Think about all the data that's going past you right now. Not just the traffic in those cables above you, but all the wireless traffic, radio, microwaves, laser." She stands still for a moment, and Damien has the mental image of a suddenly-alert guard dog sniffing the night air. "From where you're standing, I can count at least two dozen separate data streams. And you're in the absolute middle of nowhere."

"So the system...?"

"Helps to sort out all that data. Gives me something to concentrate on." She grins. "Of course, most of my processing is done on remote systems. The Amiga's there to give me a focus."

He shakes his head. "Incredible."

"What's a computer? Just a box that turns raw current into highly organized electromagnetic signals. Well, I can do the same thing. But I need something to act on. Any box will do, as long as it has raw current coming in and outgoing connections to the Net."

"Where did you get your certification? You *are* certified, aren't you?"

Hands on hips, she puffs a wayward strand of hair away from her face. "I shouldn't dignify that with an answer. Of *course* I'm certified: Sysop Level Four, Pagemaster Two, Data Retrieval Specialist Six. I have seals in code-building, hardware, and network integration."

"I believe you. All I wanted to know was where you studied. Casual conversation."

"I took my Qualifyings through Yokosuka University. Classes...all over the map. Whoever was offering what I needed at the time." Her eyes narrow; watching the effect, Damien is amazed at the subtlety and power of her technique. "What about you, smarty? Where were *you* certified? *If* you were."

"M.I.T.-Yale for my software certs, Motorola for hardware. With the things you can do, you deserve a higher Pagemaster rating than two."

She shrugs, and the kinte cloth of her dress stretches and moves in complex patterns with the movement of her shoulders. "I haven't gone on. I just wanted to take the tests and get my basic certification. My boss insisted."

He nods. "I guess you didn't have too much trouble with the tests...not with your abilities."

"You know what the masters say: if you have difficulty with the tests, then you were not ready to take them." She cocks her head and raises an eyebrow. "I still have the feeling you're humoring me. Look, I'm not going to short out on you and go peculiar. I have psionic abilities; not mental problems."

Damien rubs his eyes. "Look, Penylle, I got to sleep too late last night, and up *way* too early this morning. I've spent three hours driving around and climbing utility poles in the hot sun. I'm tired, I'm hungry, and now you're asking me to accept psychic powers without a quiver. I'm sorry, but it's going to take me a while to get accustomed to this."

"Tell you what. If you're not busy for a while, come see my homeroom and I'll show you what I can really do."

Damien scans the deserted landscape, the few puffballs of cloud scuttling across an otherwise-empty sky. "What, here?"

"I thought we'd established that location doesn't matter." Her chuckle is like sunlight dancing across a rippled pond.

"All right, I'm game. Now that I've taken care of that tap, I'm free for the rest of the afternoon." He hops into the pickup truck's bed, spreads a Navajo-patterned blanket out on sun-warmed metal. Penylle's image stays on the ground, partly hidden by the truck's side. There is no evidence of artifacting at the dividing line; more evidence of her skill. "I wish I'd brought my bitsuit." He chuckles. "I'm afraid I'm going to miss half the experience."

She hands him a pair of aural plugs, which he takes without comment and seats in his ears. All sound from the real world fades almost to nothing, but Penylle's voice is unchanged. "You're not going to *need* a bitsuit. I assume you can generate a standard *pacha*?"

"Of course." Damien reclines, stretching languidly and pulling on the data glove. With practiced commands, he launches an agent that links with his home system and wakes his cyberspace double. The *pacha,* invisible and featureless, moves through virtual space like a marionette on Damien's electronic strings. Its movements are crude and spasmic compared to the elegant doppleganger that his bitsuit software animates— but the *pacha* at least provides host systems a way to keep track of Damien's position and movements. Without it, he would be represented in cyberspace as a simple, static icon.

"Good," Penylle mutters. Damien's *pacha* appears in his Spex, occupying virtual space that corresponds to his own body; he sees his cyber-self as indistinct, liquid metal, a vaguely-human form, a body in potential only. "Brace yourself," Penylle says. "I'm taking you in."

Damien blinks, and the real world is gone.

Replaced by…glory.

Damien feels as if he has stepped into a Maxfield Parrish painting. His *pacha's* stark, unadorned surface is now warm and alive, the rich dark chocolate of his own skin, the electric blue and creamy white of velvet and ruffles that clothe him. He turns, and his *pacha's* movements are fluid, graceful, vital.

Penylle stands next to him, clad in diaphanous, ethereal silks of amber and mahogany. An unfelt breeze stirs her garments and hair. She looks at Damien and smiles, watching him absorb the wonder of this place.

They stand at a meter-high ivory railing, at the edge of a balcony. The sky is purple so deep it is almost black, with a few stars visible. Far below, the earth curves away to a hazy horizon alight with the afterglow of the departed sun. The ground is easily dozens of kilometers below; Damien realizes that they are halfway to orbit. But they are motionless; only the clouds and the shadows are moving, the first slowly and the second almost imperceptibly as twilight deepens.

He turns to regard the edifice to which this balcony is attached, and his chin drops.

Curving structures of translucent ivory and sparkling crystal ascend, studded with other balconies and pavilions and platforms like an enormous neo-Victorian treehouse— all turning upon themselves glittering in vanished sunlight, until lost in the violet distance. Below: the same, descending to the distant surface like a thin and graceful stalk of wheat rooted in fine, dark soil. The pattern of this structure tugs at Damien's memory; it seems somehow familiar, yet out of place, like the face of a friend seen in unaccustomed surroundings—

"DNA," he blurts. "It's like DNA." With that, Damien grasps the shape of the landscape beneath him, and whistles in appreciation of Penylle's joke. They are five dozen kilometers above the timeless Serengeti, perched upon a single strand of DNA that is, undoubtedly, rooted in the grasslands of Olduvai.

"I take it you're not disappointed?" Penylle walks away from the balcony, moving up broad stairs to another level.

Damien follows, wondering at how her system translates his jerky commands into a smooth, flawless walk. "You're incredible." He holds out his hands, turns them over. The lines and creases of his palms are perfectly reproduced. "Do you mean to tell me that you have a detailed model of me in storage, and your system is animating it now based on input from my *pacha*? How long did it take you to do this?"

She emerges onto a circular platform where various consoles and displays float, unsupported, at waist-height. "I have to confess that I retrieved your bitsuit's model for a template. But my programs added a lot of detail, based on my observations and memories. I hope you don't mind."

"Mind?" Damien thinks of his own homeroom, the desk and chair of which he is so proud. Her model of *him* is an accomplishment a thousand times greater. This whole region of Cyberbia— *her* homeroom, he supposes— is detailed and dynamic in a way that his own creations have never approached. "You were holding out on me. No little turn-of-the-century home system can run a simulation *this* good."

"Well, I admit that I borrow a lot of processing capacity from bigger systems."

"'Borrow?'"

"You know what I mean." She checks a console, moves on to the next.

"If this is what clairvoyance and psychokinesis can do, then I'm all for it." He touches one of the consoles, and distinctly feels cool, unyielding metal beneath his fingers. He stops, stares at her. "How are you doing *that*?"

Penylle chuckles. "I told you that you wouldn't need a bitsuit. Psychokinesis. Remember, while I'm here with you, both of us are still back in Arizona."

"And you're really in Africa." He frowns. "How many tracks can you handle at once?"

"This is about my limit. Unless I take drugs. But my…boss…doesn't let me do that very often."

"Who's your boss?" The question is out before he can stop it.

"Damien! That's hardly a polite thing for one Nexus operative to ask another."

"I know. I'm sorry." Sometimes Damien gets impatient with the Nexus insistence on secrecy and security. But he would feel differently, he supposes, if he were Indonesian or Manchurian…or, for that matter, Navajo.

Penylle stands before him, runs her fingertips down his arm. The touch is uncannily real, more real than any bitsuit could manage. "You're forgiven. I doubt you'd know him, anyway." She turns her head away. "Damien, do you ever wonder about what we're doing? The Nexus?"

"You mean the moral aspects? Like, is it right for us to disrupt so many lives and cause so much turmoil? Do we really have the popular mandate we pretend, or are we just self-appointed masters of the world? That sort of thing?"

"In a nutshell, yes."

He grins. "No, I never give it a moment's thought."

"Oh, thank you. That makes me feel so much better."

Damien opens his mouth, closes it, looks away. "I'd be afraid of myself if I never questioned what we do, or the way we operate." He takes a breath, trying to organize his thoughts.

Damien shakes his head. "I've thought about it *too* much, maybe. The other day I walked through houses where whole families were dead on the floor, and I kept asking myself, am I responsible? If it weren't for the interdict, would they have been able to get help before it was too late?" He gestures vaguely, in the unknown direction of Arizona and the utility pole. "What about that bit-tap I just neutralized? What if it was carrying news of another outbreak, or some other cry for help? How much responsibility is mine? How much blood is on my hands?"

Penylle puts her arms around him, and he lowers his head to her shoulder. It feels good, comforting, to be embraced like this— he's missed this, without knowing it.

"I guess we've both been asking ourselves the same questions," she says. "What answer do you give yourself?"

He snorts, and whether it is a chuckle he swallows, or a sob, he cannot say. "I try to tell myself what my boss would say. That we're all human, and we *all* have blood on our hands. It's just that some of us are trying to keep the stain from spreading."

Damien sighs. "I'm luckier than others, I guess. I grew up in the Nexus. My father and mother were both operatives. When they passed away, I came to live in another Nexus household. I don't know, maybe I've just been thoroughly indoctrinated."

"Haven't we all?"

"What about you? What do *you* think?"

"When I look at history...what the world was like before the Nexus came along...all I see is tribal wars. Genocide in progress. Rwanda, Bhutan, Bolivia, Singapore, Quebec, Finland, Queens, Madagascar, Irkutsk...how many millions of people died because they had the wrong names, or hair, or language, or ancestors? How many Presidents and Prime Ministers and Ambassadors went around weeping and wailing because it was all so tragic, but didn't lift a finger to *stop* it all?"

Damien hugs her tighter, and she returns the pressure. "You'd think we'd have made some progress in thirty years. But it all continues. More conflicts this year than last. Maybe all we're doing is driving tribalism underground, where we can't see it."

"Damien...do you ever think that maybe it's too late? This planet has a lot of problems, with deep, deep roots. Maybe even the Nexus can't keep them from destroying one another. Maybe we shouldn't waste our energy trying."

For just an instant, Damien has the impulse to agree with her, to thank the gods that someone, finally, has come right out and said it, brought into the open what everyone must have been thinking for a generation. But he forces the impulse down, and chuckles instead. "We don't have much of a choice, do we?"

She looks upward. "There's the Moon. And Mars."

He laughs for real, this time. "Oh, sure. Now you sound like that fool, Marc Hoister. If people move to Mars, all the world's problems will be solved." He shakes his head. "As if people aren't going to take their history and their existing feuds to Mars with them."

"But we've set ourselves such an enormous task— to change the way people think. Can the Nexus do it?"

"We're *not* going to change the way people think— and no one ever claimed we could. We just have to keep them from killing one another until they change themselves."

"If they let us."

For a long time, Damien and Penylle are still. He listens to her breathing (breathing! in a cyberspace *pacha*, which has no more need to breathe than the computer that animates it!), feels the rhythmic ebb and flow of her back, shoulders, chest. He hears, in mental echo, her last words, and imagines different words he could have spoken in reply. But there is no urgency, no need to speak.

She pulls back slightly, enough to look into his eyes. Hers, mottled brown and surrounded by delicate lashes, are like vast uncharted seas before him.

He cocks his head. "What?"

"I...wish there were a way to let them know...what we're really all about. They're afraid of the Nexus. Afraid of the interdict." She lowers her eyes. "They don't see— or won't let themselves see— that we do so much more."

Damien nods. "I spent last month running unauthorized connections across the mountains into Tajikistan to carry Nexus Freenet. And dodging bullets from both governments, I might add. Before that, it was distributing Nexus datapads in Suriname. All to keep information flowing outside government control. But does anyone ever mention those things, when they talk about us?"

"Of course not. They— " Penylle stops abruptly, frozen in place. Damien signals his *pacha* to move, and it responds jerkily, like stuttering film come adrift from a projector.

Then, as quickly as the strange spell came upon them, it is gone. Penylle frowns. "I'm sorry about that. Damien, there's big news coming. I'd better let you go back to your body. If this is what I think it is, you'll want to be there."

"What is it?"

Penylle disentangles herself from his embrace, then leads him by the hand to balcony's edge. "There's no time. Come with me."

Together, they step off the lip, but they do not fall. Penylle continues to walk, each step a hundred kilometers. Behind him, Damien sees the double-helix of her palace coil in upon itself, then loop around in ever-tightening supercoils like real DNA tucked into a nucleus. The dark sky, the landscape below, all recede with unreal velocity and dream-intense clarity...until a door closes upon the scene, and Damien stands with Penylle in an ordinary hallway in a ubiquitous building, one of many in the imaginary construct that humans call Cyberbia...and then, that too is gone, and Damien wakes up, alone, in the back of a pickup truck in the warmth of the Arizona afternoon sun.

He wastes no time punching into the newsnets, and so catches the first announcement from ancient Zimbabwe, of a Umoja-brokered treaty between the Navajo and the Hopi . . . followed almost at once by word from Geneva that U.N. Resolution 6502 will be lifted at midnight, Greenwich time.

Damien sends his news agent to find out more, then gathers all his equipment and jumps into the cab, racing southward as fast as the truck's groaning electric engine will carry him. It is only a few hours until Greenwich midnight, and he's about to be busier than he ever has before— but for now, there is only room in his fevered mind for one question....

How did she know?

MENUET 01
(July 2042 C.E.)

*COME TO COLUMBO AND HELP CREATE THE FUTURE!*

World Creativity Conference
August 28 - September 2, 2042
Clarke Centre, Columbo, Sri Lanka
<membagent@creativcon.con>

This year's CreativCon will be held in the tropical paradise of Sri Lanka, a land older than time and yet more modern than the future itself. The main facility is the incomparable Clarke Centre, the scientific and technological jewel of the East. Symposium topics range from the aesthetics of space travel to interdisciplinary virtual world design, with all disciplines represented. Whether you're a poet, painter, dancer, fashion maven, video artist, or Net designer, there's a place for you at the CreativCon. This is the year's biggest celebration of artistic creativity...you dare not miss it!

This year's Special Challenge Topics are:

- Preserving the Past: Conservation Strategies for Pre-Digital Artifacts
- The Ice Cometh: Preparing for the Next Ice Age
- Lojban at 87: Is It Time for a New Artificial Language?
- New Mesopotamia: Design Study for an Undersea City

So come to Columbo, bring your imagination, and become a part of the future!

NOTE: New Special Challenge Topic just added:
- The Martian Century: Settling the Red Planet.

ENTREÉ 02

```
Date: Mon, 28 July 2042 03:14:54 (GMT)
To: All Nexus members
From: conagent@nexus.nex
Subject: CreativCon
Message-id:
<20420728031454_176235.21012_NP222@nexus.nex>
Content-Type: text
Status: O
----------------------------------------
```

A REMINDER that the 15th Terran Council will be held in conjunction with the World Creativity Conference this year. All Nexus members are permitted to attend, in vivo or in virtuo, whether members of the CreativCon or not. Nexus Regional Coordinators should attend or send their authorized delegates. The Terran Council will convene at 0800 GMT on Saturday, August 30, 2042.

----------------------------------------

## [05] NGORO 01
Baltimore, Maryland
United States, North America
December 2013 - June 2014

*Those who dance are thought mad by those
who hear not the music.*

Helen Wyatt-Norton took her first little green-striped capsule in the wet, miserable early winter of 2013— just two weeks before Christmas. It was the year of the Thanksgiving Riots, the year that the first CIC power plant went online in Canada, the year that the number of Kabinda virus deaths in North America first passed the number of traffic fatalities. That was the year President Stewart appeared on television in a Santa Claus hat, assuring a troubled nation that if they just had faith, everything would be all right in the coming year.

He lied.

After three clerks in Insurance Verification caught Kabinda and died in agony that autumn, and the public-service staff threatened to walk off unless they had better protection from the unwashed hordes, M.V.A. management authorized additional non-conventional medical benefits. One of Helen's coworkers in License Renewal referred her to a friend, who called another friend, who met her downtown in the middle of the night. The friend-of-a-friend, a pleasant Mexam woman about Helen's age, took her M.V.A. chit and left her a bottle of the green capsules.

Miruvorane, first of a long-promised new generation of "benign antivirals," was still pending FDA approval— but Helen, like millions of other Americans, couldn't wait. Honduras and Nicaragua had both legalized the drug; as long as everyone had friends enough, there was no shortage in North America.

Miruvorane immunized the body against a whole suite of viruses, Kabinda being the most notable, without toxic effects. The first few days, Helen had some minor headaches, but then she thought no more about it. One capsule every three days, with dinner, became a familiar routine. And there were no more cases of Kabinda at the Motor Vehicles Administration.

In late January, Helen found out that she was two and a half months pregnant.

She was reasonably sure of the date; Joel's unit had departed for Eritrea early in November; since then, they'd netsexed a couple of times, but last she heard, they hadn't gotten around to improving netsex *that* much. She told him the happy news that evening, and he promised to be home for the birth even if he had to swim.

Her obstetrician, Doctor Anthony, didn't know about the miruvorane. She ran a few searches on the Nets and found no agreement among virologists. Some pooh-poohed the notion that miruvorane could pose any danger to a developing fetus. Others did not agree; violent discussions broke out on several virology nets, and after two weeks of this someone with sufficient authority decided to prove her point and submitted a simulation to the Virtual Heredity Analyzer. By the time the problem reached the top of the priority queue and the AIs delivered their verdict— "after t-plus 71.4 megaseconds, the system becomes too chaotic for meaningful analysis or prediction"— it was already too late for Helen, along with an estimated 150,000 women worldwide. No one could say for sure that the babies would be affected— but neither could anyone say for sure that they *wouldn't.* And no one ventured any prediction as to what the effects might be.

She felt the baby start moving in mid-February. But it wasn't until a month later that Helen began feeling an odd sort of tingle in her viscera. Sometimes it was a feather-touch, gone before she was sure it had happened; sometimes a sort of electric tingle that marched up her spine and down her breastbone, or spiralled down one leg. Occasionally, the sensation was more pronounced, a cross between a cramp and indigestion, moving through her body as if an army were on the march from her liver to her lungs.

She mentioned the feelings to Doctor Anthony, and felt like growling as the man reassured her with a patronizing smile. He gave her some pills to take— she suspected placebos but took them anyway. They did not help.

By the middle of the fifth month, in April, the baby began to kick.

Faint stirrings became blows with all the force of a star quarterback; as the month progressed, Helen found herself doubling over in sudden pain, or rocking back and forth in bed to the pummeling in her viscera. This child didn't just kick— it punched and elbowed and karate-chopped its way through her gut, sometimes for half an hour at a time before it gave up and went to sleep.

Doctor Anthony examined her, and this time he wasn't patronizing. "I don't like the look of this. There's a good deal of bruising on your abdomen. What have you been doing, boxing with your customers?"

"It's the baby kicking," Helen said, through clenched teeth.

"That would be a remarkable baby, to cause visible bruising on your skin." He slid instruments into position. "I want to take another ultrasound, just to make sure everything is okay."

"Do your worst." Cold metal moved across her bare skin...but it wasn't the chill that made goosebumps rise on Helen's arms. As an image took shape on the monitor, she expected the cloudy contours of a curled-up baby. Instead, there within the ghostly outline of her own body was a smooth ovoid, sharp-edged and completely black— as if she bore, not a baby, but a large, hard-shelled egg.

"Allah!" Doctor Anthony breathed, making it half curse and half prayer.

"What the *pell* is going on?"

"Helen, don't get excited. That's...a weird picture, but it's just a malfunction of the equipment. A spurious image. I'll send you down the hall to another instrument." He seemed to be talking as much for his own reassurance as for hers, as he thrust the bulky ultrasound emitter away. "Tell you what, I want to do another amniocentesis anyway. I'll have the nurse get you ready." He backed to the door.

"Doctor, what's wrong with my baby?"

"Nothing. Nothing at all. If anything's wrong, it's with our imaging system. That's got to be it. I'll call the computer room right now, see if they can send someone up to fix it." A plastic, magazine-ad smile. "Everything's going to be just fine."

Two hours later, only after sedating mother and baby, Doctor Anthony managed to get both amniotic fluid samples and good ultrasound images.

As far as he could tell from the images, nothing was wrong with the child. No gross physical abnormalities, no deformations, no missing or extra limbs. Near as he could tell, all internal organs were in place and functioning, fingers and toes were normal, the little pixie face was completely unremarkable.

Then why did he have six needles damaged beyond repair in attempted amniocentesis? Three were bent, two seemed to have been melted, and one was broken off cleanly. And why those mysterious images of what seemed to be an impenetrable shell surrounding the small body?

He tried to reassure Helen Norton, while at the same time hastening her out the door. "We won't know for sure until the amnio tests come back," he said, "But just from looking at your baby, she seems to be healthy and normal in every respect. You can see that yourself from the ultrasound." He gave her a copy of the disk; otherwise, she'd be in his office all afternoon studying it. "As for the kicking, I hesitate to interfere with her development. A twenty-four week baby sleeps ninety percent of the time, in a fairly consistent cycle. Keep track of when the kicking episodes occur, and you'll learn when she's usually awake."

"B-but what about those images? And the needles? You can't tell me *that's* normal."

He raised an eyebrow. "A malfunctioning scanner and a bad batch of hypodermics— unfortunately, that *is* all too normal nowadays. My fault, really. I should have tested those needles when I opened the box. I *do* apologize."

"But— "

He took her arm and applied firm pressure in the direction of the billing desk. "We'll give you a call when the test results are in. Until then, there's really nothing else I can tell you." With her successfully out the door, he closed it and went back to his desk.

He punched the intercom. "Tony, something's come up. Reschedule the rest of the day." Without waiting for an answer, he punched his keyboard.

The first issue of *The Journal of Miruvorane-Affected Pregnancy and Birth* had hit the Net a week before, and already the case-study database was over fifty gigs. He knew that three of his patients were at risk, and he suspected two more. Norton's odd developments argued some kind of abnormality— and miruvorane was the most likely suspect.

Soon, he knew that this case was unique. No one had yet seen— or, at least, *reported*— anything like it.

Anthony clicked the command to upload his data, and read further while the files transferred. A one-in-a-million case like this could make him a formidable reputation. If he played his cards right, a chair at some wealthy university. Maybe even a directorship.

Helen didn't know what to think. She would have to speak with Joel; his level-headed, calm approach to even the worst calamity was exactly what she needed now. Without him, she'd never have gotten through her parents' death last year.

First, though, she had to stop at the grocery store. It was getting on toward dark, and she wanted to be home— but she was completely out of milk, and the ice cream situation was approaching critical. She'd better do it on the way; once she was home, she knew she wouldn't make another trip out.

Everyone else, it seemed, had the same idea. The parking lot was packed— even the half-dozen spaces up front, set aside for pregnant women, were filled. She briefly considered going to the 7-11 for milk, then remembered a few other things she needed. With a sigh, she pulled into a space far from the store, then heaved herself out of the car and started trudging in the chilly twilight wind.

The man, a shadowy figure in dark clothes, jumped from between two cars and had Helen around the throat before she could react. "Don't move." Something was across her eyes; she was blindfolded.

His breath, hot against her cheek, smelled of tobacco. She felt something poke her in the side, and looked down past the clumsy blindfold to see the cold steel of a gun. "Get back here." He pulled her between the cars. "Put down your purse."

She dropped the purse. The man's body pressed against hers. Nunn it, there was something she was supposed to be doing, but panic had blanked her mind. Scream? Don't scream? Kick him? No, that was a bad idea, he'd grab her leg and tumble her to the pavement. Stomp on his foot...but surely then he'd shoot— ?

"My husband is a cop," she said. Maybe the threat of police retaliation...?

"Don't worry, I'm not going to leave any evidence behind." He jabbed harder with the gun. "Now get those slacks off."

"For God's sake, I'm six months pregnant!"

"Then you'd better not do anything to hurt your little baby, eh?" He spun her around, pressed her against a car. She felt the cold metal against her back, his hot body insistent against her stomach and blileys and thighs....

Baby kicked, and Helen thought, *Oh, no, not now* — then her attacker convulsed with a grunt, doubled over, fell away from her.

She ripped the blindfold away and saw the man hunched over as if in pain, the gun forgotten on the ground near her purse. While he cursed and screamed, she picked up the gun and aimed it at him. "Back off," she said.

"Jesus, lady, what did you do to me?"

"You'll get more unless you march. Now!"

Halfway to the store, he collapsed and could not get up. By then, they'd attracted attention; a black woman in security uniform ran up and took the gun from Helen's shaking hands. "What happened here?"

"He tried to rape me. I…hit him as hard as I could."

The man started retching, and in the orange light from a utility pole, Helen saw blood.

"Well, sister, you done him good. Congratulations." The guard clicked on her radio and called "Attempted rape at Fresh Value Southgate. Suspect down and injured; send an ambulance." She clicked off and turned back to Helen. "You okay?"

"I-I think so."

"Look, there's going to be messy paperwork and all kinds of fuss you don't want to be involved in. Get back in your car and drive home, I'll say I found him here. Okay?"

"Thank you." Helen got to her car as fast as she could, and drove away without looking back.

A week later she ran into the same security guard, and asked about the man. "Took him to the hospital— man, he was in bad shape. Bleeding inside, intestines all messed up, hernias…it's a wonder he could move, much less jump somebody. Must've been so high he was in orbit."

"I…did all that?"

The woman laughed. "Honey, you couldn't have damaged him that much. The hospital said it was some kind of traumatic injury like getting hit by a bus."

"I'd like to know more. Can you tell me what hospital?"

"Child, I'll tell you, but it isn't going to do you any good. He didn't live through the night." She inspected her fingernails. "Best thing, scum like that. He'd been arrested twice on attempted rape. The world's a better place, now."

Helen finished her shopping and went home, wondering if she should tell someone— the police, Doctor Anthony, anyone.

But would they believe her? Officer, my unborn child killed a man. It was self-defense, but she killed him nonetheless.

And even if they *did* believe her…what could anyone possibly do?

In the last week of April Helen Wyatt Norton, every bit of six months pregnant, was admitted to the hospital for treatment of minor internal bleeding and a week of bed rest. It wasn't a very peaceful time for her— the baby was more active than ever and the doctors wouldn't give her painkillers that were strong enough.

That week, Miruvorane Babies began to emerge from the womb.

From Japan and Singapore, from Moscow and London, from New York and Mexico City, reports trickled into the databanks and showed up on the evening news. Babies with fur, babies with multiple eyes and ears, babies with bony plates over their joints, acephalic babies with only minimal brains, stillborn babies by the dozens, then hundreds. Babies who looked perfectly normal but whose bodies couldn't manufacture essential enzymes...albino babies...babies with six, seven, eight fingers and toes...babies with no arms or legs, or two sets of each...babies normal on the left but deformed on the right, or normal above and misshapen below... babies with extra hearts, spleens, livers, brains...on and on, random mutations completely unlike the specific teratogenicity of any other drugs.

The parade went on and on, turning some delivery rooms into scenes from Hieronymous Bosch. Medical science did what it could, to keep the children alive. And each one was tested, cataloged, correlated, the results fed into the databanks in case they might help others.

Doctor Anthony moved to the newly-formed Abnormal Birth & Pediatrics Center at Johns Hopkins, bringing all of his patients along. Although he continued to reassure Helen, she spent more and more of her time watching the news-nets, feeling the baby inside her, and crying.

Joel was sympathetic, and she appreciated that, but he had no real help to offer her. How could he, half the world away and with no idea of what was really going on? He was due home at the end of July, about the time the baby was due; she held onto that fact the way a true believer held onto the hope of salvation. She and Joel had faced a lot, together. As a team, they were more than either or both could be alone. Baby would come, and they'd tackle that problem the way they had tackled so many others.

She started singing to Baby, that week in the hospital, and it seemed to help. When the child began to stir, Helen curled up and sang, lullabies and popular songs and anything she could think of, sometimes just making up nonsense words. And Baby quieted, while its strange power throbbed in time.

In May there was an Indian summer, a week of bright sun and warm breezes without the awful humidity that was to come. Helen took walks, at lunch time and after she came home from work. She strolled past playgrounds, and watched other people's children laughing, climbing, swinging, smiling. Would Baby be like these other children? Would she do the same things? Would she grow tall enough to reach the monkey bars, big enough to climb up the sliding board?

Sometimes she picked a bench, and stretched out to rest. The sun was warm on her belly, and Baby seemed to like that, too. By now Helen was used to the feel of ghostly fingers touching her insides, to odd movements of her blouse or slacks, as Baby explored her world.

*She's going to be smart,* Helen thought. *Look at all the sensory input she's getting already.* She turned to watch the other parents with their bundles of joy. *None of those parents will know what it's like, to have a child as special as ours.* Then, although Helen had no formal religion and certainly wasn't in the habit of praying, she thought, *Please, God, don't let her be retarded. I think I could cope with anything, but that.*

The next week winter struck a last counter-blow, with sleet and freezing rain. Helen didn't even try to go to work; she stayed home, watched the nets, and tried to calm Baby. The little one didn't like the weather any better than her mother, and was constantly cranky— kicking, punching, twisting so hard that Helen was doubled up in pain half the time. Singing helped, but only a little, and only for a while.

On Friday, groggy from lost sleep and with a cold coming on, Helen retreated to bed. She downed acetaminophin like they were candies, which helped calm Baby too. Throughout the day her temperature climbed and she grew increasingly groggy. After half an eternity, she realized that she should tell the doctor, and reached for the phone— but it was in the other room, and she didn't know the number, and a nameless fear paralyzed her until she fell into uneasy dreams of playgrounds and bloody-faced children so tall that they blotted out the sun....

It was Joel who saved her. Getting no answer to repeated calls, he telephoned Doctor Anthony and gave him the passcode to their apartment. Anthony dispatched paramedics, then logged onto their realtime report channel.

"She's in bed, apparently unconscious. Christ, she's burning up. There's a pulse. Ninety-five and steady. Wait a minute, she's coughed up blood."

"She's pregnant," Anthony said. "Check the baby." At the same time, he punched for a medevac copter.

"Still there. She's bruised all over the abdomen. Probably a lot of internal bleeding. Hold on, I just felt the baby kick." A moment later, the paramedic yelped. "Jesus!"

"What?"

"You're not going to believe this— but I could swear the kid bit me."

"I'm sending medevac. First aid, whatever you can do, but don't sedate her. Get her to Hopkins Premature stat. I'll be there." He punched the button that direct-dialled to his office. "Kevin? Listen to me, I'm sending Helen Norton in by chopper. Get over to Premature and prep for a crash delivery. Tell them we're just short of seven months, and we're probably going to need an awful lot of help." Without waiting for an answer, he punched another button and ordered his office computer, "Send an ambulance to pick me up. And have someone call Helen Norton's husband in Eritrea. Tell him we're inducing labor, and he should get back here by the fastest means possible."

Taking a deep breath, the doctor raced out the door.

She was in bad shape. Anthony started her on whole blood immediately— her own blood, stored at liquid nitrogen temperature until it was needed. He considered inducing labor…but she was already weak, and the baby was tearing up her insides. No telling what it would do in response to labor.

"Local," he ordered. "I'm going C-section."

At the first touch of the needle, Helen Norton bolted upright, screaming. "No! Stop it! She doesn't want you to hurt her!"

Two nurses held her down, while an obviously-frightened anesthetist struggled with his equipment.

"Quiet, Helen. Quiet. We're going to take her out now. She doesn't have anything to fear…and neither do you."

Helen's eyes met his. "She doesn't mean it," she whispered. "She doesn't know what she's doing."

Masked, he forced his best reassuring smile onto his face, hoping that enough of it would carry through his eyes. "Then why don't you both leave it to the experts?"

"Tell Joel I love him. And I love *her*. She has to know that. She has…to know…. "

The gas did its work, and Helen settled limply to the table. Doctor Anthony turned to the task at hand, lifting a scalpel and holding it a few inches above taut skin. He could see the baby, or at least its influence, moving beneath the skin. It certainly hadn't descended, not this early…where best to make the incision?

He felt his hand, scalpel and all, pushed away— and Baby made the decision for him.

All at once Helen's water broke, her abdomen pulsed, and skin abruptly shredded like a slow-motion movie of a balloon popping. A tiny arm appeared, then the head, wet and dripping, twitching wildly. A moment later, it cried.

Anthony didn't even have to check. One look at what remained of Helen's organs, battered and torn by Baby's last assault, told him that she would never awaken. In certainty, if not in actual fact, she was dead.

In blood and water, out of pain and death, Baby Norton had come into the world.

## DIVERTISSEMENT 03

Final Report of the World Health Organization
Task Force on Miruvorane™-Affected Births
December 2015

### STATISTICAL SUMMARY

(May not total due to duplication of categories)

| | |
|---|---|
| Total affected pregnancies (world) | 156,215 (± 0.4%) |
| Total stillbirths (world) | 62,084 (± 0.7%) |
| Total nonviable (world) | 45,156 (± 0.3%) |
| Total gross physical deformity (world) | 18,952 (± 1.4%) |
| Total acephalic (world) | 7,218 (± 0.1%) |
| Total hormonal abnormalities (world) | 16,720 (± 0.5%) |
| Total no recognizable abnormality (world) | 629 (± 0.4%) |
| Total 12-month survivors (world) | 37,926 (± 0.1 %) |
| Total 18-month survivors (world) | 26,863 (± 0.3%) |
| Projected 60-month survivors (world) | 12,934 (± 11.3%) |
| Projected 10-year survivors (world) | *ERROR* |

"The tally of human misery and individual tragedy concealed by the figures above will never be fully known. This is a tragedy that touches not only the families directly concerned, but every one of us. Though only a drop in an ocean of human woe, these figures touch us all as no others can. These lives sacrificed were not fellow participants in the world's miseries, in patriotism, ethnic pride, territorial gain, economic greed, or even blunt hatred. These lives belonged to the only ones on this sorry planet who could truly be called innocents. They were not sacrificed for any cause, however noble or ignoble— they were not sacrificed for any great plan, divine or human— they were sacrificed merely by accident, by terrible mistake, by carelessness. We think we have learned, but we have not. There will be other mistakes, if perhaps none as grievous. And this shameful episode in our history, a true slaughter of the innocents, will haunt us all from now until the day we die."

Vavrinec Divizich,
Secretary-General of the United Nations
for the World Health Organization.

## [06] KAMENGEN 02
Gray Mountain, Arizona
Mexamerica, North America
22 July 2042 C.E.

*I've enjoyed about as much of this as I can stand.*

When Damien arrives at the Nexus command post, the place is in an uproar.

Skip, his assistant, meets him in the street. He is a balding, paunchy Anglo man in his forties, somewhat rumpled in appearance but a genius behind a keyboard. "The M wants to talk to you as soon as you have two seconds."

"Thanks. Where do we stand?"

"I started work already on lifting the interdict. I assumed that's what you'd want to do." At Damien's nod, Skip continues. "Dropping the radio interference isn't a problem. The biggest headache is going to be repairing the main data conduits across the border. Twelve of them, total. Each one is a two-hour job, at least. Some of those data lines go back to the eighties."

Damien strides into the command post, Skip at his heels. He has only half a dozen technicians able to handle the job; if nothing goes wrong, there is barely time to repair all twelve conduits before midnight Greenwich. And something *will* go wrong. Of necessity, the Nexus was not gentle severing the conduits in the first place.

He stops at a wall-mounted map of the area, frowns, toggles to a realtime satellite view and back. "I'm not happy about having to do this in such a hurry." In the best of all worlds, there would have been plenty of warning; several teams would have spent days replacing obsolete cabling with modern equipment (and, not incidentally, placing controllers that would make it much easier for the Nexus to shut off data flow next time), and at a prearranged moment, one command would restore communications instantly.

No such luck, now. He might have the techs, but he was sure he didn't have the equipment. Some of it was coming, from Nexus storehouses and the stockpiles of other operatives— but none would get here in time. "How much data cable do we need?"

Skip is ready with a display pad. "We can probably cut it down to 15.3 kilometers, but I'd like 16 or even 16.5."

"And we have on hand— ?"

"Four, four-point-two maybe."

"Nunn." He studies the map. "What if we leave all the old cable in place, and just bridge the gaps with new cable and multiplexors?"

"I don't think we have enough big multiplexors in stock. Well, maybe we can cannibalize something." Skip punches data into the pad, chewing his lower lip. Then he waves his pad at the map, which blossoms with bright lines and numbers. "We can do that with under nine kilometers of cable. It's that collapsed tunnel at Comb Ridge that's doing us in. One way or another, we need at least three and a half kilometers of cable to bypass it."

"And just *who* was it that collapsed the tunnel?"

"Only because *you* said it was a good place to set a charge."

Damien attends the banter with only part of his mind; the rest is racing. "And if I told you to jump off a bridge, would you?"

"Only if you went first."

"Hold it." Damien steps back, toggles back and forth between satellite display and map. "Why lay conduit at all? We'll bridge those breaks by satellite. Twelve conduits, twenty-four satlinks." He punches a query and reads the answer almost at once. "Nexus birds 956 and 745 are in position to cover us for the rest of the day. Data will be flowing by Greenwich midnight, and we'll have all of tomorrow to set up the land links the way we want them."

Skip scans his own pad, looks at the map, and nods. "It'll work. I'll need authorization for, oh, fifteen channels should do it. No, better make it eighteen to be on the safe side."

"I'll get it for you." Damien claps his assistant on the shoulder. "That's a weight off my mind. We're going to get through this."

"I've got the easy part. *You* have to talk to the M."

"And I'd better get on that right away. I'll have the authorization codes to you within the hour." Bounding up the stairs, Damien lets himself into the small office that has become his workroom, and locks the door behind him. He sits at a battered metal desk and pulls on his goggles. "All right, NewsHound, show me what you found."

The powerful, soothing voice of the legendary James Earl Jones sounds in Damien's ears. "This evening in the ancient city of Zimbabwe, a peace accord was signed between two long-time enemies, the Navajo and Hopi peoples of North America. Here is the scene as the chiefs of the two tribes shook hands against the backdrop of Zimbabwe's eternal stone walls."

Umoja, as a non-territorial contract government, technically has no capital city. When pomp and spectacle are required, however, one of the member states can always be counted on to lend a national monument or two. Umoja has, over the years, put millions of rands into reconstructing Africa's lost glories, and now cities long-vanished live again in splendor: Timbuktu, Songhai, Zimbabwe, Kumasi, Goa, Meroë, Jenné. Zimbabwe looks particularly striking in the image NewsHound retrieved— a small, simple wooden platform crowded with dignitaries, beyond which subtly lit stone walls ascend to the star-flecked heavens like a tower to heaven.

"Chiefs Tl'izilani and Pongyayanoma were joined by the negotiator who made this settlement possible, Umojan Cultural Chancellor Marc Hoister. Waziri Hoister said that he was delighted to have participated in the peace conference and expressed his optimism that there would be lasting peace between the two tribes. At a press conference afterward, Waziri Hoister was asked if the world could expect a quick lifting of the Nexus interdict of Dinétah, the Navajo homeland. Here is his reply:"

Jump-cut to Marc Hoister's impossibly-ugly, aged-but-eternal visage: a face like a dark plum halfway along in becoming a prune. Black-on-black-on-black: broad nose, puny eyes sunken in shadow, lips of leather burnt by a thousand years of equatorial sun. The last traces of ebon hair, dark as Damien's own, cling to the edges of his scalp. His robes are severe, trimmed with jet on sable. Against the granite walls and the spotlighted Amerinds, Marc Hoister is not so much a presence as a void, a dark nothingness in the night.

"I cannot, of course, speak for the Nexus; I speak only for myself." His voice is deep and smooth. "However, I *have* been in communication with Secretary-General Netfa, and I think I can assure you that the United Nations will take notice of events here tonight. I expect we may see action within the hour. How soon the Nexus will co-operate..." He stops, then spreads his hands and ever-so-slightly inclines his head heavenward.

The newscaster adds, *sotto voce,* "Waziri Hoister is himself, of course, an avowed member of the Nexus."

"I can only hope," Hoister continues, "that after such suffering, my colleagues will not choose to prolong an interdict that has lived beyond its usefulness."

Jump-cut to the Geneva skyline and the familiar silhouette of the General Assembly building. "United Nations Secretary-General Shakonda Netfa convened a special session of the General Assembly, making it clear that she intends to see Resolution 6502 rescinded by midnight Greenwich time."

Damien holds up a hand. "Enough!" Obediently, both newscaster and Geneva vanish.

After a moment's thought, Damien removes his goggles. He's fitted the antique flat-screen phone in this office with a Nexus comm chip and scrambler; there's no need for anything more sophisticated. And the Ivory Madonna, he hopes, will be less imposing when her image is confined to a screen.

The call goes through instantly and is answered by Evelina, the M's chief communications agent. Evelina presents the image of a hawk-faced white woman with inky black hair and a permanent sneer; since he was a child, Damien has secretly suspected that Evelina does not like him. "Miranda Maris's office." Her nasal voice drips with sarcasm. "I am your humble SERvant, how may I direct your call?"

"I need to speak to the Ivory Madonna." Too late, Damien realizes that he should have had his own comm agent, Rahel, place the call. Evelina did not intimidate Rahel. Being both computer programs, they are able to dispense with all their owners' nonsense and get the job done.

"Is she exPECTing your call? Would you be so KIND as to give me the TINIest hint regarding its content? And whom shall I say is calling?"

He bites his lip, and ticks off on his fingers: "Yes. No. Damien."

"I am reLAYing that information." Sniff. "We're a LITtle bit TESTy today, aren't we, sir? There's no need to take your FRUStrations out on the household STAFF, now IS there?"

Enough. "Override. Quincunx, armor, Helios."

Evelina's attitude evaporates. "One moment."

The screen dissolves to the Ivory Madonna perched in her carved mahogany chair, face hidden by her mask. "You naughty boy, you overrode my secretary."

"*Habari gani* to you, too. I'm sorry, but she drives me spare."

The expressionless, cream-colored face comes closer. With a chuckle, the Ivory Madonna says, "You aren't sorry at all. You have to learn to cope with minor annoyances, lad. Otherwise, how can you keep your head when the world's falling down around you?" She cocks her head. "You're alone, aren't you?"

"Yes."

"Good." She shrugs off the mask, as if kicking off a pair of tight shoes. "That's better. Thank you for calling back so quickly. I didn't think I'd hear from you until late. You must have things under control."

"Skip's going to set up satlinks so we can restore dataflow by the deadline. Then we'll repair the land lines at our leisure. I'll need authorization to use some of our satellite channels." He gives her the particulars; she excuses herself for a moment, and leaves him watching a primitive cartoon that was old when the Ivory Madonna herself was young.

Long before the bullying dog receives his ultimate comeuppance, she is back. "The authorization codes are going out to Skip in a few minutes. That's good work. Make sure he gets commended. Pell, make sure your whole team gets commended." Her smile tightens. "Lad, I'm sorry you were caught by surprise like this. Believe me, it was just as much a surprise to me."

"How can he get away with this? More to the point, how can the Nexus *let* him get away with it?"

She raises an eyebrow. "I'm every bit as annoyed as you, my boy— but I'm *not* his boss. He is, unfortunately, free to do anything he wants." She sighs. "And it has already been pointed out to me, that he did *not* claim to be speaking for the Nexus. Even though, as I was also told in no uncertain terms, speaking for the Nexus is well within his power and his rights."

"Who told you that?"

"Damien, I don't have time to play this game with you. I agree that Marc Hoister has overstepped his bounds. Others in the organization agree with me. I have made our concerns known to those who can answer them. And no, before you blow up at me, I am not done with this. I will pursue the matter... *we* will pursue the matter...as the time is right. For now," she shows her teeth in a plastic smile, "we are all *very* happy that the Navajo and Hopi are making nice with one another, and we look forward to nothing but sunshine and music and joyful thoughts for the foreseeable future."

He steadies his breathing. When the M announces that a line of discussion is closed, then it is closed. "Sunshine and music and joyful thoughts. Right. Just one thing— when you get your chance, please nail his hide to the wall for me."

Her smile is carved from ageless Antarctic ice. "Why, Damien, I was saving that particular pleasure for you. Knowing how much you care."

"Thank you, Ma'am."

"Now that we're had our obligatory chit-chat, give me a report. What's your situation? Will you get Dinétah back online by the deadline?"

"I see no reason why not." Damien frowns. "That's something else, though. Why are materials taking so long to get here? Skip ordered data conduit and M-124's three days ago, and they still aren't here."

"Interesting." She chews her lower lip while consulting displays he cannot read. "Interesting indeed. Your shipment was delayed because just the day before, warehoused units were sent to a deforestation project in the Congo. What a coincidence." She reads for a few moments more, then turns her attention back to Damien. "How long will it take you to finish up out there? I mean, restoring all the land lines and dismantling your base?"

"Two more days, if we get the stuff we need."

"Good. How would you like to take a trip to Africa when you're done? I think some of these coincidences need looking into."

"I haven't been home in— "

"Six months, yes I know."

"Two months, actually."

She clucks. "You see, when you're gone the time seems so much longer. I'm going to see what I can do about establishing a cover story for you, and you'll hear from me in a day or two. Is there anything else?"

"Two things, actually. I don't know if either is important.... "

"Child, I do not keep you around for your good looks nor your charming personality. I keep you around because I can trust you to give me information that no one else would think was important. So give."

"I think I'm flattered." He touches his wrist where Penylle had held him. "First thing, I've met a beautiful, mysterious woman."

"I thought *I* was the only beautiful, mysterious woman in your life. Go on."

"She's...different. No, I mean it. She has...paranormal abilities."

The Ivory Madonna looks neither surprised nor amused. "Telepathy, clairvoyance, psychokinesis, that sort of thing?"

He nods.

"Damien, if you want to succeed in shocking your elders, you are going to have to put out a great deal more effort. I've followed the field of psionics since the discredited Duke University experiments of the 1960s. While there are many charlatans and all too many wishful-thinking researchers, I *am* convinced that there is some authentic signal buried in all that noise. If you say you have met someone who demonstrates these abilities, then I will believe you." She leans closer. "I should love to meet her in person."

"I'll see what I can do. That's not what intrigues me about her, though."

"Explain."

"She knew about the peace treaty before it hit the nets. Minutes before. And I can't figure out how."

"Your theories?"

He ticks them off on his fingers. "One, she has some source of inside information. Two, she was somehow involved in what went down. Three, she's a brilliant political strategist and was able to analyze what was about to happen."

The M grins. "Four, she can see into the future. Precognitive vision is one of the recognized psi abilities."

"I didn't think of that one."

"Any of the four might be true, or another possibility entirely." The M fiddles with a pearl ring on her right pinky finger. "Whatever the case, I would say that this woman bears closer inspection." Again a raised eyebrow. "Or was that what you had in mind at all?"

He can't help laughing. "Yes, I'd like to get to know her better."

"Then I'll make it official. You have an ongoing assignment to find out what you can about this woman and her unusual abilities." She steeples her fingers. "You said there was one more point?"

"Yes. Right." Briefly, he tells her what he found out from the AIs about the origin of the Navajo strain of Dekoa, and Dr. Heavitree's opinion. "I'm just worried that there's a discrepancy at all," he finishes.

"Hmmm." She stares into space. "Jamiar Heavitree has quite a reputation. I would be inclined to trust him on this one. If it weren't for the fact that the AIs were so positive. You know, this wouldn't be the first time that a scientific finding has seemed like nonsense to some bona-fide expert." She comes to herself, as if noticing that Damien is still there. "Sorry, woolgathering. I don't know the answer, Damien. It's a pretty problem; I shall think on it and talk it over with some people I know. Thank you for bringing it to my attention."

"Like I said, I don't know if it's important or not.... "

"Oh, it's important, if only as an opportunity for intellectual exercise. Is there anything else?"

"I don't think so. Sorry to keep you so long."

She waves his apology away. "That's why I have a suite of agents to deal with all the noncreative garbage. I will get back to you with your next assignment. Have fun." She blows him a kiss, and then is gone.

MENUET 02
(July 2042 C.E.)

*ADVERTISEMENT*
*CIC— The Next Generation in Power Plants*

...Clean, safe, inexhaustible— how does this miraculous power source work?

The Controlled Isotopic Conversion (CIC) process uses minerals mined from deep within the Earth's crust, where temperatures are much higher than on the surface. Purified and concentrated, these minerals provide a great deal of natural heat. This heat is collected and used to boil water; the water then turns turbines which produce electricity.

Unlike conventional gas-, oil-, or coal-fired power plants, CIC processors produce little ash. What residue remains from the process is easily handled and can be safely disposed of; it offers considerably less of an environmental danger than the toxic waste products of most other power plants.

The minerals that power CIC are abundant throughout the world, and thanks to robotic mining methods, can be easily retrieved from the crust without massive environmental damage or health risks to human miners. There are enough CIC minerals in the crust to meet the world's energy needs for hundreds of thousands of years.

And don't worry about radioactivity, either. CIC minerals finish the process with *no more than the natural level of radioactivity that they started with in the ground.* In many ways, CIC is even safer than nature!

The choice is clear...CIC is the power of the future— and of today.

To find out more, contact PowerWeb Ltd. at <info.pweb.umj>

## [07] NGORO 02
Silver Spring, Maryland
United States, North America
May 2019 C.E.

*Gene Police! YOU!! Out of the pool!*

On a grey, stormy day in 2019, Penylle Norton turned five. The staff brought cake and ice cream, and sang "Happy Birthday," and Mr. Tony let her ride the big elevator up and down as much as she wanted. They even took her in to see her Papa, but (as usual) he was asleep and the doctor didn't know when he would be awake again. And most important of all, Aunt Vicky was coming to visit.

That was the year the Dow passed twenty thousand and the worldwide Dekoa death toll passed twenty million. It was the year that the first waveriders leapt from Kilimanjaro's summit into high orbit, the year that Washington Westwood Hohokus bought Disney and started constructing a giant pleasure island in the ocean east of Zanzibar.

RCSpex hit the market in February— cheap, lightweight data goggles that brought virtual reality to the masses, superimposed over everyday life. By year's end, over a hundred million were seeing the world through rose-colored spectacles.

It was the year that the United States finally solved its prison problem by expatriating over four million life-term inmates (overwhelmingly, but certainly not officially, black males) to Africa's shores, where Umoja had need of every able mind and body. Millions of others followed, as officially termed, of their own free will...helped along by Umoja's carrot (the promise of a new life, respect, a good wage, and valuable work to be done) as well as America's stick (which, as usual, was more often than not in the upraised hand of a brawny Anglo cop.)

None of that mattered to Penylle Norton, celebrating her fifth birthday in her tiny playroom off a forgotten hallway in a secure ward on the eighth floor of Walter Reed Army Hospital. Penylle was only concerned with Aunt Vicky.

She wasn't supposed to know that Aunt Vicky was coming...maybe the staff didn't even know it themselves. But it was hard to keep anything from a child who could see through walls and eavesdrop on phone conversations at will.

After the morning's excitement and a fitful nap, Penylle dutifully self-administered her daily prolactin injection and allowed a nurse to draw some blood. When she was little, she had fought against the blood tests, sometimes so hard that it took three corpsmen to hold her down, and as many as a dozen needles to complete one sample. Now, though, she understood that the tests were for her own good, and she hardly ever balked.

The staff left her alone (except for the ones behind the mirror, who were always watching her; she pretended not to see them) and Penylle climbed into her chair, crossed her legs, and grabbed *Where the Wild Things Are* from her bookshelf. The book gently glided through the air, landing face-up on her lap. Then, eyes closed and hands folded, she began once again to read her favorite story.

About the time that Max, once again, was growing tired of being king of all the wild things, Penylle became aware of a commotion in the next room, behind the mirror. Without moving, she shifted her attention in that direction.

Tony and Walinda, as they always did, sat watching Penylle and making notes on their terminals, but they were joined by Doctor Hamaniuk, who was in charge of Penylle's case, along with a few other doctors she recognized. There was a tall, pouchy man in an Army uniform and trim mustache; Penylle realized that his picture was hanging up downstairs: General James Tawanima, the Commander of the entire hospital. The General was accompanied by two Army women who stood as straight and still as if they were playing statues.

As she beheld the last person in the room, Penylle smiled. Aunt Vicky had made it at last!

To the rest of the world, Victoria Hacktrell was a respected scientist, Nobel laureate for her work in psychopharmacology, past president of the National Science Council, frequently quoted on the popular news shows; to Penylle, she was simply Aunt Vicky, who always had a smile and a hug, and one of the few grownups around who actually listened when Penylle talked.

Doctor Ham shook hands. "General, thank you for coming on such short notice. Doctor Hacktrell, welcome."

Aunt Vicky hugged the General. "Good to see you, Jim. How's Mhari?"

"Doing well. She has her hands full with her new grandson, Harry."

"What is that, four now?"

"Five." He looked her over approvingly. "You're looking well. How are Thom and the girls?"

She chuckled. "He's senior partner now, and he loves it. Gus is singing in an off-Broadway show, and Libby still isn't sure *what* she wants to do. As usual." Doctor Ham cleared his throat, and Aunt Vicky laughed. "We're holding things up, and Ghedi is too polite to say so."

"Not at all," Doctor Ham protested.

Tawanima smiled. "Quite all right. We'll be talking for hours if you don't stop us. Go ahead, please."

"You know that the World Health Organization keeps track of all the miruvorane kids around the world."

General Jim frowned. "Are they unhappy with your reports?"

"No. I've been giving them only the minimum: physical development, general health, that sort of thing. I've told them about Penylle's prolactin deficiency, but I haven't mentioned her…er…other talents."

Aunt Vicky helped herself to coffee from a pot in the corner. "Then what are they complaining about?"

"We got a new advisory from them this morning. Here, take a look." He handed Aunt Vicky and General Jim each a sheet of paper.

Aunt Vicky read silently for a moment, then muttered, "Compulsory sterilization? Who do they think they are?"

General Jim read the paper again, then held it out to Doctor Ham. "This isn't exactly an order…?"

Doctor Ham nodded. "W.H.O. doesn't have the authority to order us to do anything." He spread his hands. "But if we refuse to co-operate, they can *get* the authority. In matters of world health, they can strong-arm us with anything conceivable."

Aunt Vicky set the paper down. "I don't see any background here. What's their reasoning?"

"The idea has been circulating on the Nets for a while. I could pull up the posts if you wish? No? Well, basically, they're afraid of miruvorane-induced mutations entering the gene pool. There are some pretty horrific conditions out there, and new complications keep turning up. Someone has convinced W.H.O. that it's better to act now, handle them when they're still infants, than to wait until they reach puberty." He sighed. "From a purely medical standpoint, they're right. The operation is easy, and it's the only way to be certain of isolating these mutations."

"Wait a minute. Doctor, are you saying that you're in *favor* of this procedure?"

"No, General. Dead set against it, as a matter of fact. It's just that they're standing on firm ground. I don't think they'll have any trouble convincing the Security Council, for example."

General Jim stroked his mustache. "And they're not at all concerned that some of these mutations might prove useful?" He nodded toward Penylle. "That little girl is pretty talented. Maybe those talents should be protected and conserved, rather than eliminated from the gene pool."

Aunt Vicky shook her head. "Forget usefulness. We're talking about the life of a little girl here." She looked at Penylle. "And not just one little girl—there are hundreds of miruvorane kids just in this country, I don't know how many around the world."

"Almost thirteen thousand," Doctor Ham supplied.

"Jim, this isn't Doc Fleming's Historical Ethics course. This is the real world, and the rights of thirteen thousand children are at stake. Whether or *not* we happen to find their mutations 'useful.'"

General Jim bowed his head. "I'm certainly not going to argue with you, Vicky. I stand corrected." He sighed. "So what can we do? Where do we appeal this decision?"

Doctor Ham looked surprised. "I don't know. W.H.O., I guess. The National Genomics Institutes. I can try to drum up support among those who are treating miruvorane kids."

"Not enough," General Jim growled. "I want to know what other hospitals in the country are treating these kids. I'll get on the phone with their Administrators. Vicky, you know the Surgeon General, don't you?"

"Somewhat. Enough to get an appointment. We'll set up a foundation, get some big names in on our side. Publicity, that's what we need." She chewed her lip. "Pressure from a little bit higher wouldn't hurt." She paused. "Byrne owes you a favor, after the way you calmed down West Point."

"*You're* on the National Science Council."

"I think I can arrange for both of us to pay him a visit."

Doctor Ham's eyes were wide. "Listen to you two, talking about setting up a visit with the President as if you were arranging a staff meeting. You make me sick...and I'm glad I called both of you in on this."

"Ghedi," Aunt Vicky said, "It's no good doing a lot of extra work, if you can't enjoy the benefits every once in a while. Remember that, when *you* get to the stage when you're hobnobbing with the movers and shakers."

"Just one thing," General Jim said, "If we're going to make this a public crusade— and I have no objection to doing so— I want to keep Penylle out of it. We can pick another miruvorane kid as our poster child. But meanwhile, report to W.H.O. that you've complied with their order and done the sterilization."

"But...?"

"Doctor, you can't have come this far without knowing how to phony up an expense report. Just use the same techniques. I want W.H.O. to think that our girl is no threat."

Aunt Vicky narrowed her eyes. "So you want to keep her classified? Military secret?"

"Let's just say that I want the girl to have a chance to live the most normal life she can, okay?"

Aunt Vicky turned to Doctor Ham. "What about her father?"

Doctor Ham shook his head. "Not good. It's been months since we detected any forebrain function. I'm ready to certify irreversible coma at any point. Doctor Hacktrell, you're Penylle's guardian."

Aunt Vicky slowly finished her coffee. "All right, Jim. I'll go along with you. Are we done, now?"

"I think so."

"Good. There's a little girl waiting for me...and I brought her a very special birthday present."

In spite of herself, Penylle smiled.

MENUET 03

Thank you for choosing RCSpex™

*Features*

- Eidolon-265 450 GHz processor
- Fully FLBLA-compliant for assured compatibility
- Rechargeable 12-day battery
- Adjustable earpieces for comfortable fit
- Stereo bone-conduction speakers & microphones
- Continuous eye-tracking allows operation by eye movements
- Retinal scan provides perfect security
- Built-in configuration program
- Five operating modes: Transparent, Basic Computing, Virtua, Cyberbia, El Juego
- Distinctive styling

*Quick Start*

A built-in configuration program allows you to begin using your RCSpex™ immediately.

1. Put on your RCSpex™
2. Adjust the flexible earpieces for the most comfortable fit.
3. Locate the on/off switch, where the right earpiece joins the lens assembly.
4. Click and hold the on/off switch for ten seconds to activate the configuration program.
5. Arcy, our animated mascot, will guide you through the configuration process.

NOTE: If you currently wear corrective lenses (glasses or contact lenses), please have your lenses available. RCSpex™ will scan your lenses to determine their optical properties. RCSpex™ will then adjust its own display to match the effect of your lenses.

*Modes*

Cycle modes by clicking the mode switch, located where the left earpiece joins the lens assembly. (Optionally, you can use the configuration program to set up an eye movement that will switch modes.)

1. *Transparent Mode*: RCSpex™ display an unprocessed view of the real world. Options: Time/date display, Incoming mail alert, Continuous audio-visual record

2. *Basic Computing Mode*: Real-world image is overlaid with a windowing environment that can be used for data processing, communications, and interface with your personal or business computer systems.

3. *Virtua*: RCSpex™ display Virtual enhancements of the real world. NOTE: RCSpex™ can be set to transmit your own Virtual persona so that others will see you the way you want to be seen. (Construction of virtual personae images requires additional software.)

4. *Cyberbia*: RCSpex™ are your portal into the limitless realm of cyberspace. Simple navigation controls respond to eye movements, allowing you to travel through Cyberbia at will. Conduct business transactions, visit with friends, play interactive team games, learn, teach, view virties, read books, surf the Nets.

5. *El Juego*: RCSpex™ take you into the richest and wildest gaming environment ever. Play your existing character(s), or establish new ones.

## [08] KAMENGEN 03
White Sands Space Harbor, New Mexico
Mexamerica, North America
Elkridge, Maryland (Virtua)
25 July 2042 C.E.

*What's the point of being fascinatingly crazy*
*if you can't enrich the world with it?*

It is well after noon on Friday when Damien leaves Arizona for good. His staff departs that morning, taking most of his equipment; all that is left is what Damien can fit into his battered satchel.

Jamiar Heavitree, in khakis and cowboy hat, drives him into Flagstaff to catch the train. The *Medecins sans Frontieres* jeep has definitely seen better days; it is dented and dusty, and its original paint has faded to a drab beige. The electric motor whines as it gains speed.

Damien looks back at Gray Mountain, a cluster of ivory shapes already looking lost in the endless landscape. "I'm always leaving places," he says. "And I always wonder if I'll ever come back."

"Such is the lot of the wanderer, my friend."

"It isn't a bad little town." There is an air of sleepy decrepitude about the town, hovering like the ever-present dusty haze: old buildings crumble, trees stand sere and olive-brown, ripped signs flap in the breeze like tattered, forgotten flags— but the people have been kind to Damien and his crew, and that's what really counts. "Better than some I've been in."

Damien fishes in the breast pocket of his colorful dashiki and pulls out his RCSpex. They look like cheap sunglasses, but their onboard computers are a dozen times more powerful than the Cray so-called supercomputers of an earlier age.

Damien dons the Spex, and enters the world called Virtua.

Virtua is a special part of Cyberbia designed in one-to-one correspondence with the real world. In Virtua, a kilometer is a kilometer and every real-world mountain, stream, and valley has a virtual counterpart. The ideal— which Virtua, eternally under construction, will never reach— is to model every building, road, vehicle, person, and animal in the real world. It is a cooperative effort among millions of Cyberbians: programmers, artists, students, businessfolk, and anyone else who wants to contribute. Virtua has existed, in one form or another, for a generation.

Damien looks back at Gray Mountain. Dingy buildings and dusty streets, through the lenses of his Spex, become gleaming marble edifices, soaring towers, broad tree-lined boulevards. He frowns, with the critical disapproval of a professional. The display is tacky, at once too gaudy and too cartoonish. The real-world, physical shape of the town is all but lost under the lines of its Virtual counterpart. It is a scene composed by a rank amateur— of whom there are entirely too many in Virtua, these days.

A true Virtual artist, say the experts, does not replace the real world; rather, a true artist *enhances* it. Sadly, there are too few true artists in Virtua.

Damien turns back to Heavitree, the jeep, and the road ahead. Pale yellow and white guidelines appear to float above the road surface, supplemented now and again by Virtual benchmarks, tiny displays that give location, altitude, distance and direction to nearby cities. In North America, everyone who owns a car is expected to also own RCSpex or a similar product.

"You and I," Heavitree muses, "we go where our work takes us. And perhaps, if we are lucky, we have a home to return to between times."

"Where's *your* home, Jamiar?"

"Volonne, a tiny village in Provence. No larger than Gray Mountain, certainly." Heavitree sighs. "I do not make it there often enough. Usually I am in Paris or Brussels, if not overseas."

"If you don't mind my asking, how did a full-blooded Cherokee come to live in France?"

"I don't mind. Mother and Father were never in sympathy with the tribal leadership. Mother opposed everything about the formation of the Cherokee Homeland: the taking of Federal lands, the forced deportation of Anglos and Afros from South Carolina, the riots and the strike forces. The two of them fell from favor, and when I was still a child, Mother decided she'd had enough of America. Father was always a Francophile, so that's where they settled."

"And how did you get involved with *Medecins sans Frontieres*?"

"I was recruited out of medial school. The hours are long and the work is difficult, but I would not do anything else."

"You're lucky."

"Tell me about yourself, Damien. You were born in Umoja, but live in America now, no?"

"My mother and father both died when I was eight years old. The only one left to care for me was my American grandmother. She brought me over and took me under her wing." He shrugs. "I'd had four years of Umoja schooling, so I was able to jump ahead a few grades. You can just imagine what the American kids thought and said. I was three years younger than them, and one of six black kids in the whole school." He smiles wryly. "I didn't make it any easier; I was smarter than the rest of them and better at soccer, and I didn't make any effort to conceal those facts."

"You outgrew that." It is half a question.

"Mostly," Damien laughs. "So you're leaving this evening?"

"Later this afternoon, yes. My crew goes back to Paris. I myself am going to the States for another two weeks. I have been invited to attend a virology conference in Bethesda." He smiles. "As I have nothing else to do, for once, I have accepted."

"Bethesda. That's just down the road from where I live. Where are you staying?"

"My agents are bidding for a decent, inexpensive hotel room near NIH." Heavitree shrugs. "I don't suppose you know of a good place that won't strain the budget too much?"

"In DC hotels, you can have decent or inexpensive, but not both. But I know a place fifteen minutes from Bethesda by comfortable train, where you can stay for free."

"Yes?"

Damien whips out a card-size datapad and scribbles with a stylus. "The Miranda Maris Institute for Wayward Artists. It's where I live." He hands the datapad to Heavitree, who glances at it before slipping it into his pocket.

"Institute for Wayward Artists?" Heavitree echoes. "It sounds…interesting." His tone clearly conveys his intention to wipe the datapad as soon as Damien has left the jeep.

Damien laughs. "I don't blame you for sounding doubtful. Believe me, you'll like it. The facilities are first-rate, the equal of any hotel you can find. As a matter of fact, the main building used to *be* a hotel. Miranda Maris bought it and turned it into the Institute in 2015. There are about a hundred full-time residents, all of them artists of one sort or another."

Heavitree cocks his head and frowns. "You mean that large artist's colony outside DC? I believe I remember seeing a netzine article about that sometime recently. Someone famous was moving in…."

"Everyone is famous in their own field. Let's see, are you thinking of Rose Cetairé, the big-name fashion designer?"

Heavitree shakes his head. "It was a person that one does not ordinarily think of as an artist. A virtie star, perhaps?"

"Gail Danube lives with us. But she's been there forever. Her husband is Mark Silver, of the Unholy Three."

"I know their music. No, it was...." Heavitree snaps his fingers. "A former American President. Stewart? Lindsay?"

Damien smiles. "Glen Byrne. That's right, he moved in a couple years ago. We usually think of him as a historian, rather than an ex-President."

"Yes, that book comparing Gorbachev, Teddy Roosevelt, and Martin Luther— he did it. I enjoyed that book. Very insightful. " Heavitree's face falls. "I do hate to be a burden— "

"You aren't. We have two floors of guest rooms...but if they're all booked, which is unlikely, you can stay in *my* flat. I won't be needing it for a while."

"Very well, then, I accept. With much gratitude."

"Don't mention it. I'll have my agents reserve you a guest room and forward directions to yours." Damien pulls out another datapad and explores for a few moments. "If you're leaving Flagstaff this afternoon, you're probably on the 15:15 to Dulles."

"That sounds correct. And then a taxi to Bethesda."

"Nonsense. If you can leave fifteen minutes earlier, my agents say they can book you through Pittsburgh and into Baltimore in the same travel time. The Institute will send a car to pick you up, and you'll be relaxing in your room by half past nineteen DC time. And for fifty dollars cheaper. What do you think?"

"I think I would like to know what travel agent you use, my friend."

"Amelia Airhead. It was custom-written for the Institute by one of our best programmers. I think you can order a commercial version through the Institute." Damien taps the datapad. "The literature will be in your mailbox shortly. Should I tell Amelia to go ahead and change your reservations?"

"Certainly."

Damien gives the commands, and the datapad displays a black rectangle. Damien holds it out to Heavitree. "Thumbprint, please?" Heavitree places his thumb against the pad, which chirps approvingly. Damien tucks the pad back in his pocket. "Shouldn't take more than ten minutes. New travel arrangements will be in your mailbox."

"Thank you, my friend."

"Nada problem. I'll make a virtual visit tonight; I'll see you there. If you're lucky, you'll be in time for the Hyperspace Jig."

"I beg your pardon?"

"Never mind." Damien grins. "You'll find out."

As the road climbs the mountains south of Gray Mountain, Damien removes his RCSpex. The stunning vistas need no embellishment; every turn brings new sights into view. Rocky outcroppings, arid grasslands, rough canyons, endless deep green pine forests beneath a sky so blue it hurts his soul. Errant birds circle, their cries echoing from steep rocky walls. Damien and Heavitree speak little, lost in wonder.

They descend into Flagstaff, and Damien once again dons the Spex. The Virtual city is bright, clean, unblemished— in direct contrast to the drab, fading reality of worn concrete and cracked macadam, weed-tangled lots, the gaping holes of empty windows. The visible inhabitants of real-world Flagstaff are few: handfuls of stooped, grey-haired oldsters clump together; solitary charcoal-clad professionals scurry about their business; in the background, toothless derelicts rest in the mouths of alleys and doorways. In Virtua, however, crowds throng the sidewalks and streets in their hundreds, bright phantasms and eerie, fantastic beings give Flagstaff a circus atmosphere. In Virtua, every house is a big top and every passerby a performer. Dragons and insectlike aliens brush elbows with medieval warriors, Japanese princesses, and werewolves. From the sidelines, animated commercials call for attention. Every passing car is a luxury limousine, a futuristic hover-car, or a twenty-meter yacht. Where two images overlap, Damien's Spex distort perspective, trying their best to render each according to its owner's wishes.

It is impossible to get lost in Virtual Flagstaff. Major sites announce their locations by way of huge, rotating glyphs and icons in the sky above their physical locations. With a few simple commands, one can ask for visual pointers, or even an animated guide to show the way. The transport hub, southeast of the city proper, is crowned by a great montage of trains, airships, planes, and buses. With Damien as navigator, they reach the hub in minutes.

Damien bounds from the jeep and retrieves his bulging rucksack, then shakes hands with Heavitree. "Thanks for the ride. I'll see you tonight at the Institute."

"Safe journey," Heavitree says.

"You too." The jeep pulls away, and Damien goes to find his train.

Flagstaff to White Sands, about 800 kilometers, is a little more than an hour by fast train. Damien passes the time by catching up on mail that has piled up while he was in Dinétah. Rahel, his comm agent, has flagged several messages for Damien's review— it handles most routine correspondence flawlessly, but occasionally needs to have its judgment confirmed. As always, Rahel has kept Damien's birthday, anniversary, and congratulatory greetings flowing.

Rahel displays on Damien's Spex a few social messages from friends, world news updates, and other messages that the agent cannot handle alone. By the time Damien has disposed of all these, White Sands Space Harbor is ahead and the train is coasting to a stop. Amelia Airhead appears in front of him, a bespectacled caricature of a nineteenth-century British white woman complete with jodhpurs, pith helmet, and heavy black camera around her neck. "The sixteen o'clock launch has been scrubbed; the next available flight leaves at twenty-two o'clock. You have a little over nine hours until launch. What do you wish?"

"There must be Umoja facilities here."

"Three restaurants, a transients' lounge, and a hostel. What is your preference?"

Damien steps off the train, bag in hand, and stands still on the platform. Through the surging crowd around him, a thousand animated displays attempt to catch his attention— everything from taxis to hostels to entertainments legal and not. "Filter ads," he orders, and the cacophony is gone. Amelia Airhead waits patiently.

"I want a civilized brunch," Damien decides. "Then, a swim. Until twenty-one o'clock, Eastern time, when I'll want a room where I can use my bitsuit." Damien can see Amelia's features shift and blur, as the program invokes others from his suite of software agents. It happens too quickly for him to be sure, but he can guess what resources Amelia draws upon: Rosetta Stone, his translation agent, to find out exactly what he means by "a civilized brunch." His unnamed scheduler agent, for the time parameters of "using his bitsuit." And, finally, a quick check with Midas Mulligan to see if Damien has the money to pay for all this.

Within five seconds, Amelia Airhead has not only completed her business with Damien's other agents, but has made arrangements with restaurant and hostel. "Right this way," she says, walking away. Damien follows her, while the train pulls silently out behind him.

The Umojan restaurant serves good African food, instead of the tasteless American slop Damien has been eating lately. From a buffet, he serves himself millet porridge, spiced papaya, curried meatcakes and *sukuma wiki* made with fresh cassava leaves, honeyed yams, savory *abala* rice balls, all the *injera* flatbread he can hold. For dessert, he cannot resist a big helping of *tiba yoka*, the East African baked bananas that always remind him of carefree boyhood.

A swim, coupled with a vigorous backrub by two very friendly Nigerian sisters, leaves Damien feeling like a fat, lazy mama lion relaxing in the sun. His contentment, though, is more than a full belly and sensual pleasures. This Umoja-run hostel, like its counterparts throughout the world, is a breath of Africa itself, a welcome taste of familiarity. For the first time in months, Damien is surrounded by mostly black faces, by the murmur of the Swahili-French-English creole that is the language of Umoja. And though the pool water smells heavily of chlorine, and the girls prudently wear SkinTites as they massage his tight muscles, Damien still feels more secure than he did in a bio-isolation suit in Dinétah. In Umoja, where parasites and plagues are a living memory in a way the West can never appreciate, such precautions are simply good manners; just another way that Umoja's people take care of each other.

One wing of the hostel consists of virtual reality suites, each a few paces square and spotless. Damien finds his assigned suite, dons his bitsuit, and links to the Net. An instant later, he stands in his familiar homeroom in Cyberbia.

Penylle is there, sitting on his chair. She smiles; a curiously lifeless expression on a curiously frozen face. "I've been waiting for you."

"Not for long, I hope." Damien ignores the effrontery of her intrusion, waiting to see what she will say.

Penylle stands, and smoothes her skirt with flat palms. As she does, her image grows sharper, more alive, as if it were an empty suit of clothes suddenly inhabited by a real person. "Actually, I set an agent to watch and call me as soon as you showed up." She rubs her hand on the surface of Damien's desk. "Very nice. A fine piece of work."

Damien takes her hand; it is firm and warm in his own. When they touch, his own virtual body takes on the additional dimension of life that Penylle brings to cyberspace. Slowly, the effect diffuses to the rest of his homeroom, making colors sharper, surfaces more distinct. "I'm happy to see you again." Damien pointedly does not mention their last meeting, when she abandoned him. Time enough for *that* discussion later. "What are you doing for the next few hours?"

"My schedule is relatively clear." She steps closer to him, and he feels the nearness of her body in his skin. "What did you have in mind?"

"I'm supposed to meet Jamiar any minute now." Damien glances at his desk, and reads that Heavitree has arrived at the Institute and checked into his room. With a subvocal command, Damien dispatches a message— meet me in the reception atrium. "I'm going to show him my home and introduce him around. Maybe you can come with?"

"Taking me home to meet your folks." Still holding his hand, Penylle playfully withdraws a step. "Isn't that rather forward? We hardly *know* one another."

"Well, if you don't want to go...."

"I didn't say that." She glances at her simple outfit, halter and skirt of bright kinte cloth, sandals on her feet. "Am I dressed?"

He grins. "You're fine. Believe me, there's no dress code."

"All right, Macduff...lay on."

Damien summons a teleport control pad, taps it, and in the space of a breath, he and Penylle cross over into Virtua. Hand in hand, they materialize on a broad plaza of brick and potted plants. Before them, a concrete-and-glass fortress of a building soars twelve stories into the evening haze. A banner bids them "Welcome to the Miranda Maris Institute for Wayward Artists."

"You should feel fortunate," Damien says, leading Penylle to glass doors that obediently snap open at their approach. "We've left the humidity out of the Virtual Institute. This time of year, walking is usually like swimming."

The atrium of the Institute is wide and airy, carpet and walls in subtle blues trimmed with white. Jamiar Heavitree, wearing a loose flowered shirt and jeans, sits on one of the many plush benches that surround the area. A small "GUEST" badge on his lapel gives his name. He looks up as they approach, smiles, and stands.

"*Habari gani,* Damien." He bows over Penylle's hand, kisses air. "Good to see you again, Bibi Penylle."

"Glad you made it here," Damien says. "How was your trip?"

"Perfect. And you were right, the people here at the Institute have made me feel right at home. You're a popular fellow; you know. Everyone I meet asks after you."

Damien looks around himself, noting familiar faces both real and virtual. "We're very close. These people are family to me."

"Then you are indeed lucky."

Damien's scheduler agent whispers in his ear, "Reminder: it is now five minutes to twenty, Eastern time."

"Come on," he says, taking Penylle's hand. "We have to get you a badge. It's almost time for the Hyperspace Jig."

With Jamiar in tow, Damien drags Penylle to the reception desk. A dozen virtual receptionists— all identical, featureless silver robots in tuxedos— have materialized to deal with a sudden rush of bodies.

Damien simply holds out his hand, and a robot slaps a visitor's badge into it. He passes the badge to Penylle, checks that his own badge has properly materialized on his lapel, then drags Penylle and Jamiar forward, past a screen of potted plants, and into the main lobby of the Institute.

The Institute's security routines, written and debugged by Hollow Robin himself, are utterly foolproof and as unobtrusive as possible. Real or virtual, everyone who passes Reception must have a badge. Each badge, constantly reporting to the security computers, is far more than a mere statement of identity. Any warm body detected without a badge is instantly and efficiently apprehended by security robots, then brought before a human being for action; virtual intruders are instantly ejected. Moreover, badges serve as communits, keys, data links, credit cards, and rudimentary medical monitors as well. A resident would no more appear in public without a badge, than without a head.

When they enter the main lobby, Penylle stops in her tracks and gives a whistle. "*Tres* Pre-Millennial. I love it."

Around the spacious lobby, easily a hundred meters across, balconies rise the building's entire twelve stories, meeting great skylights far above. Four glass-walled elevators are involved in a stately vertical gavotte with one another. On the main floor below are a restaurant, two bars, dance floor, swimming pool, and scattered groups of tables, benches, and comfortable chairs. Stairways, ramps, doors, and arches lead off to other parts of the complex. Bright flags, pennants, and streamers dangle from the balconies. In the middle of the vast space hangs a three-dimensional, twenty-meter model of Drake's Starburst.

Damien gestures. "Shops, services, and community rooms are on this floor and the next. Private flats above that."

At this moment, the floor and balconies are crowded with an outré assortment of people, nearly half in outlandish costumes, body paint, or virtual manifestations even more fantastic. The assembly easily numbers five hundred or more. Fully half of them, it seems, display the Starburst in one form or another. The Institute is very much a Nexus community.

Suddenly, a shadow falls across the floor as dark shutters close over the skylights; at the same time, the lights dim. An expectant hush falls over the crowd while a deep, distant bell slowly chimes twenty.

A brilliant spotlight cuts through the dark, pinpointing a short bald Ben Franklin lookalike standing on the high diving board. His amplified voice booms through the Institute:

*"It's amazing,*
*Space is folding,*
*Ways your mind can't*
*Comprehend."*

In quick succession, spotlights stab at various members of the crowd, as each gives a line.

*"But follow me, dear."*
*"It's not much further."*
*"I will help you— "*
*"Reach the end."*

Six spotlights converge on a second-floor ledge, where a Junoesque woman stands in an orange-and-red sequinned costume, like the proud daughter of a Valkyrie and an Inca sun-god: Miranda Maris, the Ivory Madonna. Smiling, she continues the chant:

*"I have been there,*
*In that Space Warp,*
*Gaping*
*At the sky so big.*
*The stars would call to me*
*And the darkness would take me: "*

Music and lights swell together, and the entire crowd sings out:

*"Let's dance the Hyperspace Jig!"*

As one, the hundreds of people in the Institute move through the simple paces of the dance, singing along in several keys:

*"First you face to the left;*
*Give a kick to the right;*
*Clap your hands, jump and spin*

*At the speed of light*
*Then when you face yourself*
*You will both flip your wig!*
*Let's dance the Hyperspace Jig!*
*Let's dance the Hyperspace Jig!"*

There are a half-dozen more verses, performed by various members of the crowd; Damien is happy to see both Jamiar and Penylle joining in, once they master the dance and chorus. Finally the music runs down like a powerless engine, and all the participants slowly collapse to the floor, where they lay frozen in grotesque positions until a bespectacled, white-shirted young man steps into the spotlight and calls out, "Hey...do any of you know how to mambo?"

There is a crescendo, then everyone picks themselves up and goes about their business. Miranda Maris descends a broad spiral staircase, greeting people as she comes.

"What fun!" Jamiar beams. "What happens now?"

"Just about anything," Damien answers. "You can access a schedule of this weekend's events from the Institute mainpage. Or just socialize informally. The Hyperspace Jig is the kickoff, really."

Penylle can't contain her laughter. "Does this happen often?"

"Every Friday night at twenty o'clock."

"I can't get that song out of my head. Where have I heard it before?"

"It's from an old Broadway musical, pre-Pre-Millennial. I can give you the netcodes. Miranda and her friends started using it even before the Institute was built. Of course, verses have been added over the years."

"There are more?"

Damien nods. "You'll hear different verses each week. The canonical version has over a hundred. It takes an hour to finish. We only use that for celebrating Miranda's birthday."

She looks around, her eyes and smile both wide. "You people are *silly*. I love it."

"Thanks." Damien scans the crowd, and sees a familiar face at a nearby table. "Jamiar, there's ex-President Byrne. Would you like to meet him?"

"I would be honored."

"Come on." Byrne, a spry little man in his eighties, is gesturing wildly at the friends and onlookers who surround him. He wears loud neon green pants, a lemon-yellow shirt, and a bright orange bow tie. RCSpex with an attached nose and bushy mustache perch on his face.

Damien guides Jamiar and Penylle in Byrne's direction, and the man's jovial voice reaches them from meters away: ". . . turned out she drowned in the surf. And to this day, I still ask myself, what was it worth?" As the others laugh, Bryne sees Damien and stands, holding out his hand. "Well, look who's here! I thought you'd left us permanently, old sod."

Damien feigns a handshake, and Byrne, well-accustomed to dealing with virtual bodies, easily goes along with the illusion. "You aren't that lucky yet, sir."

"None of that." Byrne slips an arm around Damien's shoulder and faces the others at the table. This kind of interaction, between a real person and a cold light hologram, is the most difficult to pull off convincingly; but Byrne is a consummate actor and performs flawlessly. Even Damien can almost believe they occupy the same room. "I'm surrounded by computers, and if it weren't for this boy, I'd never even be able to get my door open in the morning." He chucks Damien's chin. "Don't ever leave, or this place will fall apart. Who are your friends?"

"Glen Byrne, I present Jamiar Heavitree and Penylle Norton. Jamiar is a fan of yours, sir."

"I'm glad to meet a man with taste." Byrne looks around. "Somebody get a chair. Move over, Nick. Jamiar, sit down. Have a drink, and tell me what first attracted you to me." He waves at Damien and Penylle. "You. Pequod. Damien. Whatever your name is. Sit down."

Penylle laughs, and Damien bows his head. "I promised to show Penylle around the Institute."

"You'll have more fun *here*, young lady. Damien's a computer whiz, but boring as pell."

"I won't mind," Penylle says.

Byrne throws up his arms. "I warned you. Go, then. Out of my sight. Go." He turns back to a slightly-bemused Jamiar. "Where were we? Right. When did you first find out that you were devoted to me?"

Damien and Penylle weave through the crowd, stopping now and again for introductions and a few moments of conversation. Meanwhile, they talk together on a private link.

"I can see why you love it here," Penylle says. "These people are fascinating."

"One way or another, they're all artists." Damien leans on a railing and looks over the crowd. Without moving his head, he sees a quartet performing on guitars and harps, bungee dancers diving from an upper floor balcony, and an impromptu group drawing a ten-meter mural in cold light. Fantastic costumes, both real and virtual, are everywhere. "To most people in the world, creativity is something foreign. Here, it's in the air and water. That's refreshing, sometimes."

Penylle gestures to the Drake's Starburst sculpture above. "How many of these people are Nexus?"

"The overlap is bigger than you'd think. But you find that in Kampala or Mandela as much as here. Artists are always unconventional in their politics. And of course, there's the M. If she became a Christian, I think most people here would follow her."

She narrows her eyes. "I'm trying to decide who's virtual and who's real."

"Good luck," he chuckles. "Our cold light projectors are state of the art. You'll notice that not many people are wearing RCSpex."

"I *hadn't* noticed, but you're right. Why?"

"The M doesn't like them, for one. And honestly, you don't need 'em. We try to keep Virtua and reality totally congruent here. On both sides, I might add: you're viewing a realtime image from thousands of pickups all around the Institute. It's as near as we can make it to what you'd be seeing if you were standing there in the real world right now."

"I should think that would limit your creativity."

"Oh, I can be as wild as I want in Cyberbia. When it comes to Virtua, it's *disciplined* creativity."

"The result is impressive, I have to give you that."

"Oh, look. The M's free. Come on, I want you to meet her."

For the first time this evening, Penylle holds back. "I couldn't."

"What are you talking about?"

"Damien, that's Miranda Maris. The Ivory Madonna. I couldn't meet her, I just *couldn't*."

"Penylle, what do you think, she's going to bite your head off? Come on, I want you to say hello."

She crosses her arms. "No, Damien."

"Well, whyever not?"

She lowers her eyes. "He wouldn't like it."

"Who?"

"My…boss. My guardian. Look, Damien, let it drop. It's Nexus politics, okay?"

His stubborn streak rises. "No, I will *not* drop it. What kind of Nexus politics can stand in the way of simple courtesy? I'm not asking you to betray your boss, or take orders from the M. I'm not even asking you to reveal your boss's identity."

"I've been told not to have anything to do with her, all right? Not even to meet her. There, are you happy now?"

"This is ridiculous." Damien, misled by layer upon layer or illusion, forgets that he and Penylle are a third of the world apart. He reaches for her, and his hand passes right through her form. In Virtua, she has become incorporeal.

With a pained expression, she meets his eyes. "I'm sorry," she says, and fades from view.

With Penylle's departure, a pallor settles over the world. Damien rushes to his homeroom, tries to track her down— but she has left no traces that he can read. Belatedly, he realizes that he has no netcode or eddress for her.

And even if he did, she would probably only refuse his call....

"Reminder. You now have thirty minutes to board your flight."

Cold and alone, Damien stuffs his bitsuit back in his rucksack, dons his RC Spex, and heads for the space terminal.

ENTREÉ 03

Date: Sat, 26 Jul 2042 17:18:12 (GMT)
From: Queen-of-Corona (qoc@nexus.nex)
Subject: CIC - Phooey!
To: power.junkies.list@pweb.umj
Message-id: <20420726171812_161966.61198_S63475-225@nexus.nex>
Content-Type: text
Status: P

\-----------------------------------------

"Controlled Isotopic Conversion" indeed! "No more than the natural radioactivity they started with" my left foot! "Safer than nature." Hmph!

The power companies knew they couldn't sell the public on nuclear fission, especially not after Chernobyl and Amiens. So they gave it a facelift, changed its name to "Controlled Isotopic Conversion," and touted it as something new. And you idiots…you *fell* for it!

I can only thank the AIs that the sunpower grids are working, and soon we'll be able to dismantle all those "safer-than-nature" CIC plants. Let's just hope it happens before another city gets wiped out.

---------------------------------------

MENUET 04

(July 2042 C.E.)

*SELECTED POPULATION FIGURES (in millions)*
source: WHO World Census

| REGION | 1995 | 2020 | 2040 |
|---|---|---|---|
| NORTH AMERICA (total) | 375.3 | 314.2 | 349.2 |
| Canada and Quebec | 29.0 | 31.3 | 36.8 |
| U.S.A. | 143.0 | 145.1 | 151.5 |
| C.S.A. | 60.8 | 44.3 | 55.9 |
| Mexamerica | 140.8 | 91.2 | 101.4 |
| Mormon Federation | 1.7 | 2.3 | 3.6 |
| | | | |
| AFRICA (total) | 721.0 | 410.0 | 466.0 |
| *Umoja Client States (selected)*: | | | |
| Nigeria | 101.0 | 47.6 | 54.3 |
| Azania (South Africa) | 45.1 | 30.3 | 34.2 |
| Congo | 44.1 | 20.8 | 24.5 |
| Sudan | 30.1 | 15.6 | 18.0 |
| Kenya | 28.8 | 14.7 | 17.0 |
| Tanzania | 28.7 | 14.5 | 16.8 |
| Uganda | 19.6 | 9.6 | 11.3 |
| Mozambique | 18.1 | 9.0 | 10.6 |
| Ghana | 17.8 | 8.3 | 9.4 |
| Cote d'Ivoire | 14.8 | 7.2 | 8.2 |
| *Non-Umoja African Nations*: | | | |
| Egypt | 62.4 | 32.1 | 36.0 |
| Ethiopia | 56.0 | 28.0 | 31.0 |
| Morocco | 29.2 | 13.3 | 11.6 |
| Angola | 10.0 | 5.5 | 5.0 |

## DIVERTISSEMENT 04

*What Umoja is To Me*
September 2035 C.E.

The Chairperson of the Board sits on a three-legged stool:
The first leg is the House of Chiefs, which is Umoja's wisdom.
The second leg is the Council of Faith, which is Umoja's spirit.
The third leg is the People's Assembly, which is Umoja's body.
The seat of the stool is the Board itself, which is Umoja's strength.
Over the Chair is the Supreme Court, which is Umoja's conscience.
The Chair is served by the Chief Executive and the Ministers and Chancellors, who are Umoja's eyes and ears, hands and feet, breath and voice.
. . . And all of these serve the Client-Citizens, who are Umoja's lifeblood.

-Leya Beobaku,
Winner, Third Grade Essay Contest,
September, 2035

[09] NGORO 03
Baltimore, Maryland
United States, North America
November 2026 C.E.

*It is far better to sit idle, than to just do nothing at all.*

Thanksgiving dinner was smaller than usual that year, but Victoria Hacktrell didn't mind. There were four generations under one roof: Victoria's mother (ninety-three, but still alert and vital), Victoria herself, her daughters Gus and Libby, and Gus's newborn, Jim. Along with husbands, boyfriends, girlfriends, stepchildren, and friends, there were a dozen for dinner— nicely filling the old farmhouse's dining room.

There was much to be thankful for, that year. For the very first time, the annual death toll from Dekoa flu had come down. Some said the decline was due to better medicines; others pointed to the Umoja-spawned public health revolution in Africa. Still others credited the happy news to five years of global economic management by the independent Artificial Intelligences. And there were, of course, the few who insisted that the credit belonged to God, or to Allah, or the Goddess, or the Divine Mao… consensus was not forthcoming.

Nearly a decade of scrub grass and buckyball algae had at last begun to lower carbon dioxide levels, and that summer, traces of ozone had been detected above Antarctica.

That was the year Gail Danube carried off seven Oscars— including Best Director and both Best Actress and Best Supporting Actress— for her performances in the one-woman virtie classic *Three in a Bush.* It was the year the Meerkats took the World Series in four games and Kuchero Watabe broke the three-minute mile.

That year, for no good reason that anyone could name, over a thousand U.N. peacekeeping troops— including 318 American boys and girls— gave up their lives in Melanesia. It was the year that an Emperor again appeared in Middle China, to take his seat on the vacant throne at Sian; the year that Umoja sent troops to protect Nexus volunteers in the Kurdistan blockade; the year that Tsai Yu-chaio, the first native Martian in sixty-five million years, was born in the back seat of a rover racing toward Gagarin Town.

When the last of the cranberry relish was gone and the packaged leftovers sent away with the guests, Thom started a fire and they all settled around the hearth. There was a curious, pleasant lethargy in the air. In the old days, they would have all been in the kitchen, washing dishes and rearranging, one more time, the contents of the refrigerator; but now there were robots to take care of such work. And the people were free to relax and…visit.

"Libby," Victoria asked, "how's work going?" Her younger daughter was in the final stage of her psychiatric residency and barely had time to eat or sleep, these days. Victoria remembered her own experience; it had been a hectic time, but a marvelously exhilirating one.

Libby, lying on the floor in front of the fire, stretched and settled back against the rug. "Busy. But fascinating. I'm learning so much. Seeing things that I studied about— but it's so different when you see something in a person, instead of a textbook." She gazed into the flames. "Just yesterday, they brought in a nine-year-old boy diagnosed with Capgras' syndrome."

"Which is…?" prompted Thom.

"A belief that someone in your life has been replaced by a double. In this case, the boy is certain that someone else has taken his father's name and place. Otherwise, he's a lucid and fairly intelligent nine-year-old."

Victoria nodded. "Capgras' patients are usually quite rational, beyond their central delusion." She felt her face falling automatically into her professional mask, pleasant but unemotional. Try as she might, she could never stop trying to second-guess a diagnosis. "As I recall, Capgras' generally appears in adult women. It's rare in children."

Gus, nursing little Jim in the old rocking chair that had held, each in her turn, every woman in the room, looked skeptical. "You mean that these people claim that their family has been replaced by duplicates, like in a horror virtie? That's *weird*."

"No more so than most paranoid delusions," Victoria said softly.

"What if you show them fingerprints, or genotypes? What if you *prove* it's the same person?"

Libby and Victoria exchanged glances, and Victoria answered, "It doesn't matter. The patient will admit that there's a physical resemblence, but insists the person is an impostor. If you press them, they will claim that the evidence has been altered or there was an error in the testing methods."

"Which is just what this kid claims," Libby added. "He says that the impostor has sent out software agents to alter information on the Net."

Gus shook her head. "That's crazy."

"Precisely," Victoria said, "although we do try to discourage that word.

Libby, what did you recommend?"

"The literature recommends low dosage of paraclozapine. I couldn't find much on children's doses, so I went with the AI recommendation of one-third the adult prescription. We'll check back in a couple of days to see if there's any progress."

"Hmm."

"What is it, Mother? Do you disagree?"

Inwardly, Victoria had to smile. Libby, filled with the unquenchable fire of the young apprentice physician, wasn't arguing with a Nobel laureate, but only with her grey-haired mother. "No, I wouldn't presume. But I wouldn't be surprised at a negative result. You already know, from your patient's age, that this is an atypical case. What do you know of his current family situation?"

"The boy is in his grandmother's custody. He's an African native, just moved here last year. Father still living in Africa. Mother died in a train wreck last year. The boy believes that the impostor who replaced his father also engineered the wreck."

Victoria nodded. "That's consistent with Capgras' Syndrome. And it *can* sometimes be triggered by a family tragedy or— "

A loud knock from the kitchen door interrupted her. Thom and Victoria exchanged a quick glance. The house was far enough off the main transit line that they seldom had to worry about prowlers and other uninvited visitors. But who would be at the *kitchen* door? Any of their friends would come around front.

"I'll see, "Thom said. On his way into the kitchen, he casually took the tazer down from its wall-mount. These days, it paid to be cautious.

After a few minutes, Thom called, "Hon, could you come in here?"

Waving the girls to wait, Victoria headed for the kitchen. Thom was at the sink, filling a glass. A bedraggled, dark-haired adolescent at the table looked vaguely familiar—

"Penylle," Victoria said softly, "what are you doing here?"

The girl looked up. Her face was streaked with grime and she was flushed. "I didn't know where else to go. I'm sorry."

Thom held out the glass. "Don't be silly. You're welcome here." That was one of the things Victoria most liked about her husband— he had only met Penylle a handful of times, yet he was ready for her to move in tonight. Over the years, Victoria had brought many strays into their lives; Thom had not complained once.

The glass wobbled through the air to Penylle's lips, and she gulped greedily. "Thank you." In the month since Victoria had seen her last, Penylle had lost a good five kilos. Always thin, now the girl looked positively gaunt. Her hair was tangled, her filthy black jeans threadbare at the knees and ripped down one seam. She was...Victoria counted silently...twelve years old, and looked considerably younger.

Victoria felt her forehead. "Child, you're burning up. Thom, please get my kit." Fever, exposure, possible malnutrition— "Penylle, when did you leave Walter Reed?"

Shivering, Penylle answered, "M-Monday night. I think."

"Have you eaten?" Thank God there was plenty of food.

"A little. I d-don't feel very hungry."

Thom returned with her kit; Victoria slapped a diagnostic patch on Penylle's arm and waited for the unit to register. "We'll get something into you. How did you get here?"

"I walked a lot. A man gave me a ride to the train station, b-but he took all my money and the machine wouldn't give me a ticket." Penylle seemed to be struggling to keep her eyes open.

The diagnostic unit beeped, and Victoria glanced at its display. All Penylle's vital signs were elevated. And her blood chemistry was skewed alarmingly. "Penylle, listen to me." Victoria held the girl's chin, meeting her eye-to-eye. "Do you remember when you had your last prolactin injection?"

"Monday morning?"

"Is that a question or an answer?"

Penylle nodded. "It was Monday. I remember, the news was on and they made me turn it off."

Nearly four days without prolactin. Penylle's mutant pituitary did not produce the hormone, which was more vital than ever now that she was approaching puberty. She'd been receiving injections daily. Victoria had no idea what damage the child's body had sustained— there just wasn't any research. Ordinarily, humans born without the ability to produce prolactin died in infancy.

In the absence of synthetic prolactin, Victoria didn't know what to give Penylle, besides the physician's ancient remedies of comfort, food, and rest. Any medication could conceivably do more harm than good.

"Here." Without being asked, Thom had put together a plate of leftovers and zapped it; now he set it, steaming, in front of Penylle. Uncertainly, at first, she picked up her fork and started to eat.

Victoria sat down across from her. "Honey, someone's going to miss you. And it won't take them long to think of calling here." Why hadn't they called already? Victoria had the sudden vision of camouflaged army troops surrounding her house. "I have to know what to tell them when they do. So tell me what happened."

"They won't miss me yet," Penylle said between mouthfuls of turkey dressing and gravy. "Walter Reed thinks I'm on my way to Vanuatu. The folks in Vanuatu think I'm at Walter Reed. They'll be a while straightening out the conflicting orders."

"You've been hacking." Victoria put on her most disapproving face, but inwardly couldn't blame the girl. With her clairvoyant and psychokinetic abilities, Penylle had always seen the Net as an extension of her own body and consciousness. Telling her not to hack was like telling her not to use her spleen.

"Only a little."

"What's this about being on your way to Vanuatu?" Icy fingers gripped Victoria's heart. There was a U.N. peacekeeping force in Vanuatu, one that included U.S. troops....

"The Army wants to use me against the United Front Rebels."

"Use you?"

"Aunt Vicky, I've learned a lot this year. I can sense data transmissions, even on shielded fiber. And last week I was out in Nevada. I learned how to...."

"How to what?" Victoria prompted gently.

"I learned how to make a nuclear reactor explode."

Victoria nodded slowly, at the same time reaching for Thom's hand. He was there, warm and supportive as always— but despite his comforting grip, Victoria felt a chill deep inside.

"I don't want to blow up people," Penylle said. "I think Doctor Ham felt the same way. I think he wanted me to escape." She looked at Victoria, suddenly a very vulnerable twelve-year-old. "You won't let them take me back, will you?"

"Finish eating, then a warm bath and into bed with you. We'll talk again when you're feeling better."

Victoria's lab had the two things she needed most: a hormone synthesizer that could produce artificial prolactin by the liter, and a UEA-1028 scramble-phone, supposedly secure against even the fastest AIs.

She set one of her assistants to work synthesizing the prolactin, then shut herself into her office and called Walter Reed. It took only seconds to reach Doctor Hamaniuk. "Hello, Ghedi. I'm surprised to see you working on Thanksgiving." In the corner of her screen, the blinking icon of an open padlock told her that the line was not yet secure— the systems were still swapping numbers.

"Good evening, Victoria. I let the rest of the staff off. My patients don't take the day off; I don't see why I should." He raised an eyebrow. "And what are *you* doing at work today?"

The icon switched to a closed padlock and stopped blinking. Secure connection. "I have your little runaway."

"Officially, " he answered, "I don't have any idea what you mean."

"So I am given to understand." She steepled her fingers. "How long do you think that will last?"

He grinned. "This is the Army. The left hand doesn't know what the other left hand is doing. With luck, the confusion could last out the week."

"And then what?"

He spread his hands. "I don't know."

"Ghedi, I wish you had warned me. It's not going to take anyone fifteen seconds to guess where she's gone. And about twenty more to get her back. I can't resist a siege."

"I am sincerely sorry. I was afraid to place a call to you. I thought it might tip them off."

*And you're just as glad to be rid of this burden,* Victoria thought. *Ghedi, you've always needed a backbone transplant. Except your body would reject the foreign matter.* "Be that as it may, you allowed a patient to leave without medication she needed, and you didn't let me— or anyone— know so we could find her. She showed up this evening in terrible shape. You're just lucky that my lab can synthesize prolactin on short notice." She caught his eyes with hers. "*If* it'll help."

He looked down. "She shouldn't be here, you know that. She should have left years ago. When I found out what they were doing with her— what they meant to do— I couldn't keep her against her will." Cautiously raising his eyes, he said, "Besides, she was determined to leave. Have you ever tried to keep her under control when she doesn't want it? I left her three hundred dollars. She should have been on your doorstep that evening."

"She lost it to the first crook who came along." Victoria sighed. "Water under the bridge. All right, if you don't have any ideas, I'll have to handle this myself. You had nothing to do with this, you think she's in Vanuatu where she's supposed to be. But if General Tawanima calls, I want you to back me up: tell him Penylle is too old to stay at Walter Reed, too strong for you to control any more."

"A-All right."

"Fine. We'll talk later." Without waiting for his reply, she switched off.

*One of these days, I'm going to be too old for this sort of thing,* she thought. Then, taking a breath, she told the phone to make another call.

This time, it took several minutes for the call to go through. Tawanima was out of uniform, and his surroundings looked comfortable. "Hello, Jim. Sorry to bother you at home."

"Vicky. What's up?"

The padlock icon closed almost at once. "We're completely secure?"

He looked at her expression, then punched a code into the phone. "Wait a second."

The closed padlock was joined by two others. "We're secure."

"You were expecting my call."

"Let's just say that I'm always glad to hear from you."

"Jim, can she really make a nuclear reactor explode? I thought that was impossible."

He gave a heavy sigh. "I wouldn't have believed it if I hadn't seen it myself. Somehow, she bounces neutrons back into the fissionable mass. In three minutes, from two kilometers away, she turned an FG-681 portable reactor into a tactical nuke." He shook his head. "We can do that with a neutron beam, but she did it without any equipment at all." He started ticking off on his fingers. "She stops electronic devices in their tracks, and she doesn't even need to be in line-of-sight. She makes our best nightscopes look like sunglasses. Neither bullets nor shells can touch her."

"And so you gave the okay for sending her into war."

"The pell I did!" Anger flashed in his eyes, quickly subsided. "The Joint Chiefs didn't ask my opinion. I was only invited to the demonstration as a courtesy."

The truth hit Victoria like a slug of whiskey. "You knew she was leaving. I should have known that no twelve-year-old, however talented, could hack Army communications the way she thinks she did."

"She did a good job on her own," he admitted. "I only had to knot up a few loose ends that she left."

"And *you* didn't call me either. Men!" She shook her head. "So the ball is in my court now. How am I supposed to play this?"

"Medically and psychologically, she's better off under your care. If you can get a judge to agree with that argument, we'll be glad to authorize a transfer."

"Oh, Thom can get a judge to agree, in writing, probably by tomorrow morning. Then the Army will cite national security and the interests of defense, and they'll have her back within an hour. Only this time, they'll put her someplace that's harder to leave."

He smiled wryly. "Vicky, Vicky, Vicky. Senile, already? You're not even seventy."

"Watch your mouth."

"What does Penylle want?"

"She *doesn't* want to go to Vanuatu, and she *doesn't* want to blow up people."

"Then just how is the Army going to get her back?"

She opened her mouth, closed it.

"The first thing they teach you at the War College," he went on, "is when *not* to enter a battle. Specifically, when you're so outclassed that there's no chance of victory."

"Are you sure the Joint Chiefs will see it that way?"

"They were all at the same demonstration I was. If Penylle makes it clear— through her attorney, I'm sure they'll want to keep this off the newsnets— if Penylle makes it clear that she will fight going back, they'll get the message."

She pondered. "I'd feel better if we had some allies. What if we bring in the ACLU, and the Children's Rights Foundation?"

"Couldn't hurt. While you're at it, what about the Chamber of Ministers? Seems a few of them ought to be interested in a case like this."

Nodding, Victoria made a note. "Good. How long do you think we have, realistically? This *is* Thanksgiving weekend."

"My people can keep their plates spinning for a while longer. Say, middle of next week?"

"All right. I'll see what Thom and I can do." She reached for the switch, then stopped. "Jim, this could get you into an awful lot of trouble. Why?"

"I took an oath to preserve, protect, and defend the Constitution of the United States. I just can't see how the Constitution is served by drafting a twelve-year-old against her will. Nor by anchoring our defense strategy on magical powers."

Victoria nodded, then switched off. The prolactin wouldn't be done for an hour— there was time to make a few more calls. "Thom? I need your help. We're going to keep this girl."

She grinned. One of these days, she would be too old for this sort of thing...but not yet.

## DIVERTISSEMENT 05

from *African Rebirth* by Hassan Kerekou (2039)
University of Harare Net, <stf3.uharare.edu.zw/Kerekou/AR/intro>

Returning Blackamericans brought many things with them, but two of their gifts alone were responsible for most of Africa's salvation and rebirth.

The first gift that Blackamericans brought was their effete attachment to Western notions of sanitation and public health. Mother Africa horrified them with her casual acceptance of disease and death, her parasites and endemic viruses, her lack of clean-water standards, and above all...her unspeakable toilets.

Imagine a continent whose people are daily robbed of their energy by dysentery, malaria, schistosomiasis, sleeping sickness, AIDS, and a host of other diseases. Imagine a people whose bodies are alive with larvae, worms, fleas, and worse. Imagine malnutrition as a daily companion.

These are the people who managed, in spite of physical degradation that would destroy a lesser folk, to build great Timbuktu and Zimbabwe, Songhai and Goa, Meroë and Jenné. These are the people who conquered a continent, ridden with disadvantages that would make any other people lay down and die.

Now imagine this continent with Western sanitation and medicine. Gengineered viruses to kill off the parasites, water filtration, waste reclamation. Vaccines, antibiotics, bionics, regeneration. Imagine cool, clean water and safe, dependable electricity. Imagine the boundless energy of this people set free, young healthy muscles and minds working together for the betterment of all. Imagine this people possessed of the accumulated knowledge of Humankind, able to avoid the mistakes of earlier cultures. Imagine this knowledge, combined with the virtually-untapped natural resources of Mother Africa and the best technology of the age.

The wonder, my friends, is not how much Africa has accomplished in a few short decades...the wonder is that it took so long.

The second gift Blackamericans brought was more subtle, but just as vital to Africa's renaissance. This was their matriarchal tradition, sprung from the terrible years of slavery, when Woman was the only link to Family. From the first moment of the *Kurudi,* the Great Return, Blackwoman came to Africa as the equal partner— some might even say, the superior— of Blackman.

Nowhere was the cultural clash between African and Blackamerican more bitter, than over the place of women in our society. African tradition made her equal to a cow or pig; Blackamerican tradition exalted her as the soul and leader of the family, strong and independent. Blackwoman arrived on African shores confident and capable, and she was not about to take on the subservient role that tribal elders decreed.

In the end, the old ways withered...and well they did! For the job of building Umoja was too great for us to leave out half our strength. The task would take every iota of Man's determination, every milligram of Woman's endurance. Every shoulder, every hand, and every brain was needed. United, equal, Man and Woman built together what none could have built alone.

Today, women and men are equal in culture and law across every Umoja client state. Women serve at every level of our society. One of the most revered persons on the continent is a Blackamerican woman who took the name Princess Mahlowi, and who now sits on the throne of the vast Songhay kingdom from which her ancestors were torn half a millennium ago....

## [10] KAMENGEN 04
Lisala, Congo
Umoja Economic Union, Africa
25-26 July 2042 C.E.

*The first cup of coffee recapitulates phylogeny*

The Delta Clipper is the second-baddest way Damien knows to get into orbit.

The baddest way, of course, is by WaveRider: underground through the mass-driver's two-hundred-kilometer tunnel at two gees, then skyward from the summit of Kilimanjaro as the invisible beams of eight gigawatt lasers vaporize a two-tonne block of ice directly underneath your butt. There is no other thrill ride, on Earth or off, as sublime.

But for second-baddest, the Clipper is pretty nunn bad.

Inside the squat, cone-shaped vessel, passenger seats are arranged in concentric arcs, rather like a planetarium. Damien finds a seat near the front, fastens his belts, and settles back to enjoy the show. For those who choose to wear their Spex, ceiling, wall, and floor in front are one enormous viewscreen, where desert night is a silent backdrop to the furious activity around the ship. One by one, umbilicals are disconnected and ancillary vehicles withdraw. With the last of the passengers on board, an artificial voice welcomes them and gives the standard review of safety procedures. Then, without further ceremony, the night is lit by fire, and the ship lifts off.

Thunder fills the cabin, and tremendous, exhilirating thrust presses Damien deep into his seat. The desert falls away into muddy darkness, and the unseen horizon— more of an act of faith than a tangible line— begins to curve downward.

Now they are high enough that the darkness below is sprinkled with uncounted points of light, some sitting still, others slowly creeping across the darkness. Every second, more are revealed, clumping together in great blotches and filaments, an ever-thickening reticule, a vast net cast across the nightscape, snagging myriad luminescent microbes….

Slowly, as the scale widens, the pattern takes on a ghostly familiarity. More light than dark now, it nonetheless comes to a sudden end ahead and to the right. The demarcation line between light and dark is a series of fractal curves painted on an enormous, darkened sphere. Damien cannot pinpoint the moment when his brain finally recognizes those curves, when geometrical abstraction fades into map recognition, when he recognizes that he is looking down at the eastern seaboard of North America, its coastal megalopolis pouring light upward as if attempting to outshine the stars themselves.

Beyond the carpet of lights, an inky void creeps forward; the Atlantic Ocean, unlit save for pinpoints of individual ships and the uncertain, dim glow of phosphorescent algae. Thrust ebbs, and the deep roar of the rockets— more vibration than sound— merges into the hum of air recirculators and the susurrus of passengers talking, breathing, shifting in their seats.

Damien takes off his Spex and relaxes in the darkened cabin. It has been a long and mystifying day. Why did Penylle run off like that? He supposes he should talk to the Ivory Madonna about it...but not until he reaches Africa and has had some rest.

A delighted gasp from the other passengers brings Damien to himself with a start, and he pulls on his Spex. He's dozed off; Earth is a blue-white curving landscape far below, and Kuumba Station is a constellation of giant fireflies ahead, swelling against the stars.

Each of the seven Orbital Stations has an architectural style all its own, and no one could mistake one for another. Novy Mir and Freedom, the oldest, have the perpetually-unfinished, girders-and-solar-panels look of the previous century, fuel tanks and spinning habitat modules sticking out in every direction; they are plainly of a piece with Soyuz and the Apollo lander. T'ien Hsien looms like the skyline of some great city, Hong Kong or Singapore adrift among the stars. Sumeru and Viracocha, plainly technological siblings, are multi-spoked variations on the wheel, while Legeilan is a thousand butterflies wrapped in a translucent chrysalis, a water-filled shell two hundred meters across.

Kuumba is simple and elegant, a geometer's dream: a tetrahedron the color of clouds, tumbling lazily in the sun. Within, shadows and stars move in stately patterns. The whole thing is an intricate jewel, a delicate Fabergé creation displayed on the blackest velvet— until it grows with approach, and the tiny insects that nuzzle at its vertices reveal themselves to be spacecraft, shuttles and WaveRiders and ungainly orbital transports jockeying for docking space.

Kuumba Station was built for expansion; the great tetrahedral shell, five hundred meters along each edge, is not yet a quarter filled. The lunar shuttles arrive and depart from Kuumba, and already it carries twice as much traffic— up and down— as any other station. And until the long-overdue Freedom II begins operation, Kuumba's share of traffic will only continue to increase.

Docking is effortless, and microgravity is a welcome respite. Following Amelia Airhead's directions, Damien pushes through milling tourists and makes his careful way across the crowded port to Airlock 6. There, an Africa-bound WaveRider slumbers, waiting for the precise moment, nearly two hours hence, for it to begin its earthward drop. A diffident steward lets Damien into the darkened, quiet ship. Kuumba Station keeps Umoja Standard Time, two hours ahead of Greenwich; it is the wee hours of the morning here. A few other passengers are already aboard, loosely tethered to their couches and snoring as they sway in the air. Moving silently, Damien stows his bag, swallows two capsules of DeepDõz, and fastens his belts. Before he knows it, he is asleep.

When he awakens there is gravity, and the WaveRider's wings have begun to sing as they bite into tenuous traces of atmosphere. His belts have tightened, keeping him secure in his couch. He flips on a viewscreen located in the back of the seat before him. Kuumba Station is far behind, an invisible pinpoint in a deep purple sky; below, Earth is an enormous grey shadow with a hint of rose-colored dawn far ahead.

The WaveRider glides Earthward on a trail of water vapor, the remnants of the great block of ice that carried it into orbit originally. Below, inky ocean gives way to light-spattered landscape, rivers of brightness following the course of the mighty Congo. The Haut-Zaire highlands race by, smothered by the deep carpet of the world's last remaining rainforest. The WaveRider sinks quickly toward slate-colored, mist-shrouded pre-dawn; mountain peaks to the east are alight with the sun.

Then the forest is gone, replaced by scrub-covered hills and abnormally-straight lines that mark roads and tracks. Then the highlands fall away into the tortured landscape of the Great Rift Valley, shadowed and mist-shrouded. All at once, too quickly to prepare or even to grasp, the land rises to meet them. Then they are skimming placid Lake Victoria. The moment of splashdown is almost too gentle to feel.

While passengers jump to their feet and scramble for stowed luggage, a tugboat seizes the WaveRider and pulls it to shore. Damien lets the others go ahead of him. Mwanza Port is only a few degrees south of the Equator and nearly at sea-level, and he is in no hurry to leave the air-conditioned cabin. When the last stragglers are clearing the door, Damien makes his move.

It is a hundred-meter sprint through blood-warm, wet air to the terminal building. In that short distance Damien is soaked with sweat. But there is a smile on his face, and he is acutely conscious of being in Africa again. If nothing else, there is the rich, indescribable smell: clean air, dark brown soil, the sweet perfume of a million plants, the mixed odors of the hundred-thousands of people who pass through the Port each day...and, lingering from untold ages past, the scents of life, death, and decay left behind by endless generations of human beings. Damien is hardly conscious of the happy memories that smell evokes, carefree childhood days when he had a mother and a father and was part of a family who loved him. He knows, only, that he is glad to be back.

The terminal is barely cooler than outside. Thousands of people stand two- and three-abreast, in a serpentine line that coils toward distant customs barriers at the far end of the cavernous room, guided by plastic chains dangling from wilted stanchions. The faces, ghostly in pale fluorescent bulbs struggling to compete with the arriving dawn, are white, pink, amber, light brown, copper… travellers from all over the world. In fits and starts, the line moves constantly, like a hundred caterpillars on the march.

Once, Damien had been told, customs checks and passports were required at all national boundaries. Nowadays, with nations fading in importance and the world organized into a handful of economic union zones, such nonsense is only necessary when crossing from one zone to another. And Damien wonders, at that, why people put up with it at all?

He shakes his head, hops over a chain, and strides confidently toward a second barrier, much nearer. A dozen or so, all black, join him. Umoja is a non-territorial state; as a client-citizen, Damien has legally never left Umoja, and certainly does not need to clear customs to walk about in the territory of any client nation. The only passport he needs is the tiny gold stud in his left ear, a transceiver that constantly verifies his citizenship codes to any listening security computers.

In fact, Damien's dual citizenship, North American as well as Umojan—combined with some Nexus tinkering— has served him well in his global travels. Only once has he been obliged to stand in a customs line like all the other sheep: when a Nexus mission sent him to the Christian States of

America.

He strolls past the barrier, which flashes "Karibu" at him— "Welcome."

Mwanza Port, at the south end of Lake Victoria, is the transportation hub of Africa. A crowded tram takes Damien down sloping tunnels to the *tyubu* station, half a kilometer belowground. This station is the origin of the three *tyubu* lines that terminate at Cape Town, Asmara, and Pointe-Noire on the Atlantic. Maglev trains, arriving and departing every fifteen minutes, race through geometrically-straight tunnels at over a thousand kilometers an hour; Cape Town is just five hours away.

Damien doesn't need to invoke Amelia Airhead for this leg of his journey. In the vaulted station there are four stone arches, engraved with the names of their destinations. His gaze lingers briefly on the dark, barricaded arch marked "TUNIS"— a pop-up display in his Spex tells him that the Tunis *tyubu* is 27.3% finished, with service to N'Djamena starting next April, and completion expected in late 2044. The display goes on to show video of tunnel construction, but Damien turns away and it terminates.

Shaking his head at the magnitude of the task, he finds the "CONGO" arch and joins the massed passengers waiting on the platform. It isn't long before a sleek train glides to a stop and spills its load of travellers. Damien shuffles aboard with the others, finds the car marked for his destination, Lisala, and settles into an unoccupied seat against the wall. There are no windows; since the *tyubu* trains never leave their tunnels, there is nothing that could be described as a view.

Damien doesn't mind. Between DeepDõz and zero-gee, his two hours of sleep on the WaveRider have left him well-rested; now he unrolls his terminal, clicks his Spex over to business mode, and starts to prepare for his mission.

First, he instructs Rahel to replay his last message from the Ivory Madonna. Her image blossoms before him, and it is almost as if he sits in her office.

"Damien, my people have traced the equipment that was supposed to be sent to you in Arizona. It was delivered, instead, to Tema Mchomo Corporation in Lisala, Congo. I'll attach everything we have on Tema Mchomo, which you can peruse in your copious free time. I am sure it will make fascinating reading. Meanwhile, let me summarize: Tema Mchomo is a Umoja subsidiary active in the deforestation project. So far as we can determine, there is no Nexus connection.

"You're interviewing there on Saturday for a job as a virtreal designer.

They've seen your resumé and they like your work." Over steepled fingers, she continues, "I do not want you to take the job. They won't pay you what you're worth, anyway. You're just there to find out who authorized that shipment, and to determine the connection between Tema Mchomo and the Nexus.

"You usually have a great deal of latitude, and I rely on your judgment— but this assignment is different. On no account are you to tell them who you are, or for whom you're working. And I don't want you challenging anyone. Get the information back to me, and then get home yourself. Until I can analyze the information you uncover, I won't know what moves to make next. Any action you take on your own could monkey-wrench the whole situation."

Her eyes, intense sapphire, bore for a moment into his skull; then her image fades, and she is gone.

Damien already knows, roughly, what he intends to do...but he needs to know more about Tema Mchomo Corporation. Half an hour on the world infoweb gives him what he wants: Tema Mchomo runs a dialect of the TOBI opsys on a state of the art Xai-Xai Olorun 250 system. Damien smiles; he's been hacking TOBI since he learned to read. Browsing his virtual toolkit, he selects some programs and downloads them to a mini-slab, adding a few hundred gigabytes of his own virtual reality material. By the time the train approaches Lisala and his car detaches and slows, Damien is ready.

Amelia leads him to a local inn, where a room and a clean business suit are waiting for him. It is still early morning, and Damien has time for a shower, shave, and leisurely breakfast at the bar before a company car shows up to carry him to his interview.

The headquarters of Tema Mchomo Corporation is a good twenty kilometers from Lisala, in a parklike clearing surrounded by dense rainforest. The building is in the naturalist style, meant to recall rough-hewn timbers and cedar shingles— the romantic, frontier past that is eternally part of Umoja's soul, though it owes more to Davy Crockett and Fess Parker than to Africa's actual history. A handful of flags, including Umoja's black, green, and red, flutter above the building.

A corporate lackey— flesh and blood, not electronic or holo— meets Damien with a smile. The lackey is tall, thin, very dark, and totally androgynous. "B. Nshogoza, welcome. I am Koffi." The voice is musical, soothing. "Come this way, please." Koffi conducts him into the building.

The obligatory tropical-rainforest atrium, complete with mini-lagoon and cold light Bird of Paradise, gives way to conventional corridors and offices decorated with faux tribal designs in shades of green and tan. Damien follows Koffi into a spacious room dominated by a full-wall display of jungle valley stretching from horizon to horizon. A group of chairs and couches is arrayed before the scene.

Koffi gestures for Damien to sit down. "B. Ngbendu will be with you in a moment. Might I get you anything?"

"Some water, perhaps?" Damien chooses a chair and sits, trying to look like a job applicant doing his best to conceal his nervousness. Koffi glides across the room and returns a moment later with a glass. Damien takes it and sips. "Thank you."

"I will leave you here. If you need me, just speak my name. Koffi." With a slight bow of the head, Koffi departs.

Damien stares into the wall display, trying to decide if the view is real or virtual. Whichever, he cannot deny that it is impressive.

After a decent interval, a large man in his early fifties enters. His loosely-tailored business suit covers a frame ample enough to show success, but not fat enough to imply wasteful dissipation. His face is classic Central African, his skin jet-black. With a smile that reveals teeth as white as synthetic ivory, he offers Damien an enormous hand. "Welcome. I'm Calvin Ngbendu wa Za Banga, Director of Human Resources."

"Damien Nshogoza." Shaking Ngbendu's hand is like wrestling with a playful boa constrictor. "Thanks for making the time to see me."

"I never have trouble making time for well-qualified applicants like you." Ngbendu takes possession of a small couch like Napoleon's armies taking possession of Belgium. "Tell me, how much do you know about what we do here at Tema Mchomo?"

Damien leans back. "I know that you're quite involved in the Deforestation Project."

"And you are not sure you can approve, eh?"

With a shrug, Damien answers, "It doesn't matter to me. I grew up with Deforestation. When did the Project start, 2022?"

"That's right." Ngbendu gives a pleasant half-nod, as if perfectly willing to let Damien keep talking until he says something foolish.

"I was five at the time. For the people of my generation, the rainforests are no big deal. Maybe it was different then, but now the Sahara's covered with scrub grass and the ocean is swimming with algae-plus, so we're not all going to run out of oxygen when they finally cut down the last trees. There's no point in being sentimental." Damien pauses, looking out over the jungle. "I've been hearing about Deforestation all my life, and to tell you the truth, I'm a bit impatient that it isn't over yet."

Ngbendu clears his throat. "Very well said. I can see that you might feel that way. Well, my friend, the end is in sight… in Africa, at least." He gazes at the shoreless sea of green. "When Dabir Mariama gave his call, there was still huge opposition. It wasn't just the people who claimed we'd run out of oxygen; many others, among them very responsible scientists and statesmen, pointed out that the rainforests held irreplaceable treasures. Millions of species we had never seen. Rare plants that might be used for pharmaceuticals. Whole ecosystems completely unknown to mankind."

Damien nods. "Genotyping answered that objection."

"Hmm, yes. Every species had its DNA preserved and sequenced. Anyone who wants can access the genotypes on the Net, or go to Bangui and they'll thaw some actual DNA for you." He stops, staring, for a few heartbeats. Then, in little more than a whisper, "But what of the beauty? What of the sheer majesty of the forests, the heavy air and silence broken only by the cries of distant birds in glorious plumage? Who would preserve *that*, B. Nshogoza? Who would preserve the intricate lace of spiderwebs, or the moist velvet feel of living moss that enshrouds a century-old tree trunk? Most people on earth had never seen the rainforests; how could we let future generations know what they had missed?"

"*That's* what Tema Mchomo does?"

Ngbendu sighs and lowers his eyes. "Imperfectly, yes. With the best modern technology and talented artists such as yourself, we are constructing virtreal models of rainforest environments. Not as good as the real thing, but at least we will be leaving *some* legacy to posterity." His eyes meet Damien's. "So, are you interested?"

In spite of himself, Damien *is* interested. The challenge, both technical and artistic, is immense. Briefly he imagines what it would be like to leave his Nexus life behind, to concentrate fully on virtreal design. To settle down in one place, maybe Lisala itself, and to have both a regular job and a predictable paycheck.

He nods. "I'm … somewhat interested."

Ngbendu guffaws. "A very judicious answer." He stands, and retrieves two pairs of heavy-duty Spex from a cabinet. He tosses one pair to Damien.

"Come, I'll give you the five-cent tour. It won't be the same quality you'd get with a bitsuit, but I think you'll be pleased."

The tour takes more than half an hour, as Damien pauses to scrutinize a mouldering leaf, a tiny beetle, a drop of water falling from the deep green canopy of mist above. Ngbendu patiently lets him look, as if the man has no business more pressing. Perhaps, Damien thinks with a shudder, he does not. Perhaps Tema Mchomo's need for virtreal artists is so great, that the Chief of Personnel honestly *has* nothing better to do than woo Damien.

It is a sobering thought.

Damien can't help being awed and delighted at the astounding level of detail and resolution of the Tema Mchomo simulation. The fine structure of bark, vine, fungus, and leaf seems to continue, ever-tinier, to the limits of sight and beyond; Damien wonders if a virtual microscope would reveal pores and cell structures.

The simulation of reality is stunning, and Damien longs to work with the systems that produce it. And yet ... Penylle, with her ancient system and psi abilities, can do so much better, create a virtual space orders of magnitude more vibrant and alive.

However much Damien is enthralled and astounded by Tema Mchomo and the work they are doing, it is not for him. A little wistfully, he closes his mind to the daydream, and brings the tour to an end.

"Do you think," Ngbendu asks, as he reverently returns the Spex to their cabinet, "that you'd like to be part of our team?"

"It would certainly be a challenge."

"I assume that you brought a curriculum vitae and some samples of your work?"

"Right here." As Damien hands Ngbendu his prepared mini-slab, his throat tightens. Tema Mchomo obviously has some stunningly-talented programmers; is their security system clever enough to detect what his slab will leave behind?

Ngbendu pops the slab into a reader. Damien holds his breath as agonizing seconds pass, each longer than the one before, until the reader flashes green and Ngbendu retrieves his slab. "I know we'll enjoy looking through your work. Did you have any questions about the company?"

Damien shakes his head. "I've taken up enough of your time already; you've been very patient."

"I'll have Koffi show you out." They shake hands once again, then Koffi is there and Damien leaves.

Not until he is back in his room at the inn, with the stiff business suit peeled off and a cold vodka-and-tonic beaded with dew at his elbow, does Damien finally breathe a sigh of relief. His deception has gone undetected, and even now slices of carefully-concealed code begin to emerge from his curriculum vitae into the Tema Mchomo system. In a few hours, if all is successful, he will be able to reap the fruits of that code.

Meanwhile, he need only wait....

DIVERTISSEMENT 06

> "I tell you, these rainforests are the planet's last remaining sinks of disease. Millions of undiscovered pathogens are waiting to leap out of their accustomed rainforest hosts and into the defenseless human population. Any one of them could be the bug that wipes us out. If we are to survive as a species, we must cut down those nunn trees!"
>
> - Dabir Mariama,
> Director, Umoja Public Health Office
> 24 May 2022

ENTREÉ 04

Date: Sat, 26 Jul 2042 11:39:24 (GMT)
THIS MORNING'S HEADLINES:

GRAIN NET 6+ HOURS OFFLINE
Indonesian Shortages Predicted

U.S. SPENDING BILL COMPROMISE AGAIN DERAILED IN CHAMBER
Emergency Authorization Enters Thirteenth Year

MARS RESCUE A SUCCESS
Chinese Return Stranded Cosmonauts Safely to Gagarin Town

U.N. CENSURES LATVIA
No Nexus Action Expected Yet

GIANT METEOR GRAZES EARTH
Skims by at less than 1,000 km. Spacewatch says no repeat of 2039 impact.

ANTI-SEMITISM ON THE RISE, ARAB UNION REPORTS: 16,000
More Incidents This Year

AUSTRALIAN ZYGOMYCOSIS OUTBREAK CONTAINED
Alice Springs Quarantine To Be Lifted

ALABAMA QUAKE KILLS HUNDREDS
Relief Efforts Hampered By Fundamentalists

EMIGRATION TO MARS UP 250% THIS YEAR
Most emigrants from Umoja

OPHIR TEAM REPORTS SUSTAINABLE FUSION REACTION
Breakthrough At Last?

## [11] GHOST DANCE 02
Cyberbia & Beyond
26 July 2042 C.E.

*All syllogisms have three parts, therefore this is not a syllogism.*

When Damien thinks his code has had enough time, he dons his bitsuit and steps into Cyberbia.

Instantly, he is in the midst of pandemonium, a color-spattered chaos of whirling voxels. Gyrating wildly, he is powerless in the grip of surging data currents, tossed this way and that like a twig in roiling rapids. His stomach lurches, and he clamps his eyes shut to close out the dizzying spectacle.

**Dîstrëss ånd *f*ëar; brønzë nëëdlës**
**Twîst iñ ßløødbrîght e¥es;**
**Çacøphøn¥ åssaîls thë ëars.**

The words, appearing as fire trails against the electric colors of his squeezed-shut eyes, are unmistakably from the AI Damien knows by the name **Øut ø*f* Thrëë, thë M¥riad Thiñgs.** However violent their meaning, the words are accompanied by a steadying pressure like a firm and friendly hand at his elbow, and stability returns to Damien's world.

Somehow, he has entered AI dataspace directly, without crossing through Human cyberspace on the way. And dataspace— at least, this portion of it— is in turmoil. Fighting nausea, Damien frames the most careful reply he can:

*Chaos; confusion;*
*Mountains quiver and firm stone*
*Flows like surging foam.*
*The traveller's feet*
*Have lost all familiar paths*
*The way home, unknown.*

A coldness washes over Damien, accompanied by images of glacial landscapes and frozen waterfalls. He opens his eyes, and the maelstrom around him begins to freeze, in an ever-expanding wave. In a moment, all is still.

**Ñø trøddën påth hë *f*ølløwed;**
**Iñstañt trånslåtiøn;**
**Måths mørë prëçisë ånd qüiçk.**

So **Øut øf Thrëë** brought Damien here, nanoseconds after his entry into cyberspace— very likely, by means of an automatic trap which was watching for his arrival in Cyberbia. The AI wants him here.

Why?

*Mist hides the distant*
*Mountains; the way is unclear.*
*Where does this path lead?*

For a moment, Damien wonders if he has been too direct. AI sensibilities are always difficult to judge. Then **Øut øf Thrëë** replies:

**Ålårums ånd ëxcursiøns;**
**Çløistër ßells løud tøll;**
**Møñstërs *frøm* the id øn prøwl.**

Monsters from the id? The accompanying image looks like an old sci-fi flick, bolts of energy outlining a snarling, writhing creature.

Before Damien can apprehend the meaning, other messages and images bombard him from several directions. His overwhelming impression is of unsettled chaos, panic, awful foreboding. Then the images dim, as if a cloud has passed in front of the sun, and Damien feels **Øut øf Thrëë's** presence close behind him.

A window opens before Damien, and within its confines he sees a montage of text and image, drawn from a dozen different newsfeeds but all on the same theme. And what he sees chills his heart.

GrainNet, the primary distributor of a quarter of the world's food, unexpectedly went offline for nearly six hours yesterday.

A week ago, dozens of passenger and cargo flights had to be routed to alternate destinations when the Minsk Airport traffic-control system stopped working.

Signals from a comsat supposedly broadcasting to Brisbane were picked up in Hanoi instead.

Six-month forecasts showed the Japanese Yen falling six percent against the Umojan Rand...and the Rand simultaneously falling eight percent against the Yen.

Emission-control equipment malfunctioned at several large factories in Shaanxi Province, spilling tons of high-sulfur, high-carbon exhaust into the atmosphere.

The litany goes on and on, but already Damien has seen enough to leave him shaken to the core. Unthinkable as it is, the AIs have been making mistakes. Millions upon millions of error traps, verification routines, and peer-review strategies have failed, have allowed incorrect data to pass into the world-wide system.

Damien feels as if someone has just given him absolutely irrefutable proof that two plus two equals six.

Unable to frame a request in metaphor or poetry, he blurts:

*What's going on?*

**Øut øf Thrëë** replies in the tones of a cathedral bell ringing a slow dirge.

> **Çønçatënatiøn øf añ ërrør**
> **Çeåselëss çhaøtiç çasçadës;**
> **Mîsts çønçëal åll sîgñ øf süddën çlîffs.**
> **Ønë stëërs tø pørt; iñ stëëriñg,**
> **Çrëatës å çurrëñt strøng tø stårbøard.**
> **Dëflëçtiøn grøws ëaçh sëcønd.**

Damien sees the world-girdling computer network spread out before him, an impossibly intricate and achingly beautiful crystalline lattice, aglow with the soft colors of ever-changing patterns of light. In the air, there is a soft tinkling, as from a myriad windchimes in a gentle zephyr.

Here and there, tiny cracks appear and vanish. Minuscule errors are happening— and being corrected— every nanosecond. Damien sees the lattice shift and twist, relieving strain and allowing fractured branches to heal. Some of these shifts and twists, though, introduce bends and warps elsewhere in the Net. They collide, combine, mutate, distort— the entire pellucid mesh shimmers and sways in vast waves of distortion and recovery. This, Damien thinks, is the very structure of thought, the ratiocinations of a brain whose cortex is the planet itself.

And something is going wrong.

In slow motion— for Damien knows that the reality of what he sees is measured in milliseconds— two waves collide, combine, concentrate. Damping pulses are released, ripples at the base of a growing tsunami. Then the growing wave crests, and breaks, and the lattice, for an instant, breaks with it. No simple fractures, this time: strands of liquid crystal snap and whipsaw, while other sections are torn loose entirely and drift like broken flotsam on the surface of a stormy sea.

What Damien has just witnessed— the cascade failure of a portion of the AI Net— is never supposed to happen. Intelligences far greater than his own have made sure of that.

And yet…it happened.

The undulating Net is quick to repair itself, to recapture its drifting segments and rebuild its tattered links. In realtime, a human would never have noticed that the breaks existed. But lost innocence cannot be recovered so easily, and Damien is alert to the reverberating ripples of this disaster, wondering what further distortions will touch the Net.

*H-Has this been happening all along?* The AIs have served humankind and managed the world for a generation— surely *someone* would have noticed such gross departures from normalcy?

Would anyone admit it? Even to himself?

He remembers his own words to Jamiar: far better to believe an experienced doctor's opinion wrong, than to believe the AIs were making mistakes.

**Wëëks påss iñtø mønths iñtø ¥ears**
**Thë silënt sñøwclåd møuñtaiñs wåtch**
**The¥ sëëk tø hëal thë dåmåge ~ büt *f*åil.**

Another voice joins, a voice at once more solemn and more tender.

**Øut ø*f* Thrëë, thë M¥riad Thiñgs**
**Åppeåls tø FAI, ånd Dåmiën ßriñgs.**

"I'm flattered," Damien says aloud, "but if *you* can't do anything, what makes you think I'll be any help?" There is no answer, and he rephrases his question.

*An ant sees two airships on*
*A course to collide:*
*What can she do to help them?*

The answer seems to come from every direction at once.

**Whëre åirshîp çannøt tråvël**
**Ñør piløt cån seë**
**Thë ånt ma¥ ¥et pënëtråtë.**

"All right," Damien sighs, "I let myself in for that." He shakes his head. The AIs seem to be saying that the source of their trouble is something (or some*where*?) that they themselves cannot sense or change…yet they seem to expect that he, Damien, can succeed in apprehending it.

*The ant desires to see.*

Before him, the crystalline matrix expands, growing ever more complex like a fractal pattern. This matrix consists of data patterns in cyberspace; Damien can't even guess what real-world phenomena correspond to the portion of the lattice opening before him.

As the matrix slowly unfolds, its intricate branches and strands resolve into digits and characters, ranks upon ranks of computer code extending in infinite phalanxes toward eternity. Some lines crawl along at various speeds, others are frozen in place. They intersect, overlap, merge, cross, diverge...and where two streams touch, one or both blur and change.

It comes to Damien that he is watching a minute part of the world-web at work, millions of programs stepping through their paces. He wonders if this is how Penylle perceives it.

**Hë stånds üpøn thë thrëshøld**
**Øf å røøm ße¥ond**
**Øur sight. ?Will hë ëntër nøw¿**

The matrix, its expansion halted, pulses with electric characters. Damien looks around, helpless; without guidance, one direction looks the same as any other. He plucks at a slowly-crawling strand of digits; a deep vibrato note sounds, then dies in diminishing echoes through cyberspace.

"What the pell is this all about?" Summoning a staccato melody as accompaniment, Damien sends:

*Doorway opens on*
*Sights and sounds mysterious;*
*No signpost ahead.*

A ghostly chorus of AI whispers answers him.

**Whërë is this plåce, ?whërë¿**
**Nøwhërë. Whåt sëë wë hëre, ?whåt¿**
**Nøthiñg. ?Whåt hîdes hërë¿**

Damien frowns. This portion of the matrix, the AIs believe, is the source— *a* source— of the errors that have been plaguing them. Yet they also believe that source to be invisible, beyond their apprehension. How can that be?

Three pinpoints of bright red appear before Damien, so close that they almost touch. At once the outer two begin drifting away, one to the right and the other to the left.

**Øbservë thë ståtiønår¥ light.**

Damien does as he's told, focusing his attention on the light before him. In the corners of his eyes, he sees the other two continue their steady march to left and to right until, at the same instant, both seem to disappear.

**Whëre åre the¥, ?whëre¿**

Involuntarily, Damien glances to the right, where the pinpoint still glows. When he looks ahead, it vanishes again. "Too far out to see," he says.

**Øbservë thë ståtiønår¥ light.**

Without warning, the other two lights reappear in his peripheral vision…further out than when they vanished.

**Whëre nøw, ?whëre¿**

With a sheepish nod, Damien replies, "Just outside my blind spot. Is that what you're telling me? That you have your own blind spots? And whatever's causing the trouble, it's hidden within one of them?"

The AI chorus repeats:

**Whërë is this plåce, ?whërë¿**
**Nøwhërë. Whåt sëë wë hëre, ?whåt¿**
**Nøthiñg. ?Whåt hîdes hërë¿**

There was only one reason that the AIs would not be able to sense a particular part of cyberspace: if they were programmed that way. Which meant…this is no concatenation of innocent errors. This was deliberate sabotage.

With a gesture, Damien summons his software toolbox, a collection of utility programs that he has amassed through the years. From the box's orderly-ranked tools, he chooses a code interpreter, which fits into his hands like a magnifying glass, and opens a small window that brings meaning to the ever-flowing digits. Interpreter in hand, he begins to follow the progression of logic, tracing the moving programs step by step, watching them combine, transform, and diverge….

It is slow work, but so careful and absorbing that Damien hardly notices time passing. Eventually, following one stream of digits that seems to blend uneventfully into another, he finds what he is looking for. According to his interpreter, the strand continues beyond the apparent merge point, its logic flowing evenly. According to his eyes, the strand simply ceases to exist.

Damien puts his hand on the strand, feeling the gritty movement of bits, and closes his eyes. He moves his hand forward, along the strand, for what seems a half-meter or more, then opens his eyes.

Half his right arm is missing; as if the space it occupies simply does not exist.

Instantly, he logs all the details, then withdraws his hand (whole again) and turns to a nearby data-strand.

Now that he knows where to look, in no time at all Damien has established the boundaries of the Blind Spot. He stores his logbook as a generic document icon, and holds it aloft; the icon disintegrates into pixels as if it were dust in a strong wind. The AIs have taken it.

A moment later, **Øut ø*f* Thrëë** delivers their verdict:

**Düst *øf* åges, ündistürbëd,**
**Çøld, ünrëachåblë,**
**Frøzeñ iñ thë glåciër's hëart.**

At the same time, another document appears in Damien's hand. He glances at hexadecimal strings, takes a moment to recognize them as addresses in the world-wide pool of shared computer memory. Each range of 24-digit numbers identifies a registered block of memory which lies within the Blind Spot.

With another tool from his kit, Damien queries the MemNIC database. Every memory location corresponds to a physical location in the real world: a few atoms in a specific chip, mounted on a specific board in someone's 'puter. MemNIC knows.

The answer— from offline storage, no doubt— is slow in coming but satisfying when it arrives. The dozens of memory ranges Damien queried are all traced back to a single physical location, a bank of read-only memory in Minsk, belonging to an AI called **Triümphål Çhåriøt *øf* Åntimøn¥**.

Damien stops, and looks again.

Read-Only Memory. So that's what they mean. *Frozen in the glacier's heart.*

Read-Only Memory is to 'puters what genes are to individual humans: unalterable, eternal, one of the given conditions of existence. Bedrock and granite, more constant than the northern star. Programming instructions stored in ROM can be erased, replaced, rewritten...but only by physical contact, by replacing or altering the affected chip.

Somehow, someone got into **Triümphål Çhåriøt *øf* Åntimøn¥'s** secure bunker, and swapped a ROM chip for another— a new chip that carried dozens of rewritten instructions, programs carefully crafted to spread intersecting errors through the Worldnet. In time, those errors, interacting with self-repair programs and other mistakes, caused the errors that had so disturbed the AIs.

Damien shakes his head. He doesn't believe it. The programming is too complex to contemplate, too baroque for any mind, human or AI, to comprehend.

Unless...unless there is more than *one* altered ROM chip....

*Over the bleak horizon*
*Unseen foes gather.*
*The wind may know how many.*

The answer, as AI communications go, is fairly clear:

**Ëight ånd ëight ånd ëightyëight**
**ßegiñs thë tåll¥**
**Fivë sixtyføürs, its lîmît.**

Damien swallows hard. The AIs conjecture— for conjecture it must be— that at least a hundred more anomalies such as this one exist, spreading their mischief through the Net. Perhaps as many as three hundred.

He shakes his head. **Triümphål Çhåriøt øf Åntimøn¥** will order the altered ROM chip replaced, solving one particular problem...but Damien himself can't possibly locate hundreds of sources of sabotaged code. He knows that he should notify the authorities, but he has the traditional Nexus distrust for InfoPol in full measure.

Damien needs a hacker. And he knows of only one who is both good enough, and sympathetic to the Nexus: Hollow Robin.

*The sleeper now must depart his dream,*
*Finish his business asleep,*
*Then wake, to tell others his vision.*

He senses understanding and agreement, and **Øut øf Thrëë** bids him a musical farewell with a Bach-like succession of notes. When the last note sounds, Damien is in his familiar Cyberbian homeroom. Nearly three hours have elapsed since he was spirited away to AI-space.

He sits at his desk, where a flatscreen displays the logo of Tema Mchomo Corporation. The invisible code-seeds he left behind have blossomed into a full-blown snooper program; from where he sits, Damien can see every bit of Tema Mchomo's system.

Grinning, he sets a ferret program loose, keyed to track equipment shipping records. How, he queries, did a shipment reserved for Nexus operations in Arizona get diverted to Tema Mchomo instead? By whose order were the parts redirected?

Masses of data shift and shuffle about on the flatscreen, as Damien's ferret digs through gigabytes of information. Meanwhile, Damien invokes Amelia Airhead and sets her to work, planning the next leg of his journey, from Lisala to ancient Timbuktu in the heart of West Africa, where Hollow Robin lives. His news about the AIs, Damien senses, is not a matter to be discussed on the Net. Only face-to-face will do.

His ferret program signals triumph. As Damien reads the answer and begins to see its implications, his grin fades, replaced by a harsh, worried frown.

While his body rides a slow jet between the Congo and Mali, Damien's consciousness is at the Maris Institute, stepping into the Ivory Madonna's office. She waits for him within the enclosing circle of her desk like a fat spider waiting for dinner at the center of her web. As the door closes behind Damien, she raises an eyebrow. "That was quick. I didn't expect an answer so soon."

"I can go back and take longer, if you'd like," he offers.

The M covers her face with her hands and leans upon her elbows. "I'm a poor old woman and no one is ever nice to me. What is it, Helms-On-The-M Day?"

Damien smiles. "No, that was last Tuesday."

She peeks over he hands. "You can't fool me. *Every* day is Helms-On-The-M Day. With the possible exceptions of Christmas and Election Day, it's been Helms-On-The-M Day every day since September 1970."

Damien can't help himself. "What happened in September 1970?"

"Junior High." With a sigh, she drops her hands and sits back in her chair. "I have utmost confidence in your ability to get the job done efficiently, and you still manage to surprise me. What did you learn?"

"The order to transfer our equipment to Tema Mchomo was authorized by your friend and mine, Marc Hoister."

She frowns, nervously tapping her fingers on the desk. "I don't like the sound of that. He delays our operation, only to announce later that he's brokered a peace agreement between the two tribes. Almost like he was trying to slow us down so he could get the credit."

Damien nods. "He's a wyden."

"True but irrelevant. I don't need to tell *you* how dangerous Marc Hoister is. He's a good deal more intelligent than most of his opponents give him credit for, and he's sly and subtle to boot." She briefly considers the surface of her desk. "I wish I knew what he was up to. What's he after?"

"Power," Damien answers.

The M shakes her head. "That's too simple an answer. He wants power, yes, but to what end? What does he want to *do* with his power?"

Damien frowns. "Maybe the man just gets his kicks out of pulling people's strings and watching them dance."

"No, that's how *I* get *my* kicks." Her smile softens her words, but Damien can't help the feeling that she is not altogether joking. "He's a spiritual fanatic, which makes him doubly dangerous— whatever his course, mere rational arguments are not going to turn him away from it."

"Then why argue? I know where to find people who can hack into his systems and cause him unending grief. Delete his credit files, wipe his identity codes, that kind of thing. Pay him back for— "

"No one appreciates your zeal more than I do," the M says. "And don't think I haven't considered what you suggest. But his defenses— like ours, like every other big-name Nexus player's— are airtight." Before Damien can protest, she holds up a hand. "I have that on the authority of Hollow Robin himself; if you want to argue with *him*, go right ahead."

For a moment there is silence, and Damien wonders if his report is over. Then the M, as if returning from deep reveries, says, "I have other people working on the Marc Hoister question, but when you have the time, I wouldn't mind it if you could review his public appearances and generally nose around." She ponders. "Umoja's Mars colonies seem to be high on his list; he keeps going on about this 'Black Mars' concept of his. I'd like to know what percentage of launches from Kilimanjaro are going to Mars. Compare with official published figures. Look into Kuumba Station, too, same question."

"You should have asked me sooner. I was just there."

"Maybe you won't need to be on the spot to get the information I want. Or you can arrange your return through Kuumba, doesn't matter to me."

"You think more cargo's going to Mars than Umoja admits?"

"I don't know *what* to think. That's why I want to know. If you find out that Hoister has his hands in anything else, check *that* out too." She glances down. "Is there anything else?"

"Yes. Something very odd just came up." Damien tells her about the AIs and their unusual, invisible errors. "That's why I'm on my way to Timbuktu; I want to see what Hollow Robin thinks."

The M strokes her chin. "Hmmm. That's new. Unexpected. Special, very special. Deliberate sabotage, eh?"

"It must be."

"Please tell Robin that I'd love a copy of his report and recommendations."

"M?"

"Yes?"

"You don't suppose anyone from the Nexus would be behind this, do you?"

Her answer is not as reassuring as he hoped it would be. "It's certainly possible. Someone's gone to enormous trouble to hide their tracks; I'm not about to mention this in a full meeting and alert them that we know. But I'll ask around, the folks I can trust." She grins. "Maybe this is Marc Hoister's doing. Wouldn't *that* be lovely?" As if she has just noticed that Damien is still around, she looks up at him. "Any *other* bits of news to cheer my day?"

"No."

"Then off with you. And I'd appreciate your usual discretion; this should go no further than this office and Hollow Robin's house, agreed?"

"Agreed."

"Go, then."

Damien exits smartly, then clicks off his Spex and closes his eyes. There's still time for a nap, before the plane lands.

## DIVERTISSEMENT 07

from *Umoja: The Early Years* by Gwiyato Nemera (2038)
Asmera PubNet, <mufaro.asmerapub.umj/history/umoja-general/nemera/UTEY/6.3>

Umoja's first CEO, Kirabo Mukadamu, made his first official visit to the United States in April 2019. Ten years before, he had left Los Angeles as an angry, despised, twice-convicted criminal; now he returned as an international hero welcomed with parades and speeches.

The afternoon of his arrival, before a multitude of shining faces, Kirabo was met by a delegation from the Nation of Islam.

They said to Kirabo, "How can you turn your back on African heritage, and embrace Western cultural ideals, when those very ideals killed and enslaved your ancestors, and have kept their descendants oppressed and subjugated for over four hundred years? When Africa is finally freeing herself of the legacy of Western imperialism, how can you lead her along a path that only leads to more of the same? You are a traitor to your people."

In his quiet, powerful voice, Kirabo said to them, "You have not lived in Africa. You have not seen how disease, hunger, and despair are more powerful oppressors than Western imperialism ever could be. You have clean, running water, electricity at the touch of a switch, public health...all products of the Western cultural ideals you despise. You take these things for granted. You assume that they are the common property of humankind, no matter what culture first produced them. Africa simply wants to claim her share of the common property."

They said to Kirabo, "Umoja wants to run Africa like a corporation. You destroy the cultures and the traditions of generations. You replace them with emptiness and deny them their right to exist. Are not all cultures equally valid?"

Kirabo smiled. "That is not the traditional African view." Onlookers laughed. "Umoja means Unity. Common Unity. Comm-Unity. A new community and a new culture. Africa's old cultures and traditions have passed away. They died of hunger, poverty, disease, and war. They were murdered by hatred, greed, and indifference, both inside and outside Africa.

"Our new Umoja— our Community— is a new culture born in the death throes of the old. To build our Umoja, we take what is best from all the cultures of humankind. Personal freedom, social responsibility, the equality of all humans, respect for tradition, submission to the will of God." Kirabo faced the Nation of Islam spokesman with open arms. "Come to Africa, and help us build this new culture, this new community. Help us create new traditions and breathe life back into old ones. All are welcome, all are needed." Kirabo cocked his head, as if listening to something very far and very faint. "Hear the call. Join the Kurudi, the Return to Africa. You will come as strangers; you will remain as daughters and sons."

The next day, Kirabo met with the leaders of the Nation of Islam. And later that year, the Nation of Islam began its historic exodus to Africa....

## DIVERTISSEMENT 08
*The Recall*

I am the land of their fathers
In me the virtue stays,
I will bring back my children
After certain days.

Under their feet in the grasses
My clinging magic runs.
They shall return as strangers,
They shall remain as sons.

Over their heads in the branches
Of their new-bought, ancient trees,
I weave an incantation
And draw them to my knees.

Scent of smoke in the evening,
Smell of rain in the night,
The hours, the days and the seasons,
Order their souls aright,

Till I make plain the meaning
Of all my thousand years—
Till I fill their hearts with knowledge,
While I fill their eyes with tears.

-Rudyard Kipling, *Songs From Books*, Doubleday, 1914
reprinted in *101 Songs of Kurudi,* Ogbami, 2014

## [12] NGORO 04
Baltimore, Maryland
United States, North America
January 2027 - April 2029 C.E.

*Ask me about my vow of silence.*

Penylle's schooling presented a problem.

Victoria quickly ascertained that the girl's academic development needed no help. At Walter Reed she'd had access to the same basic education programs that schooled American military brats around the world. The Responsible Education Act of 2009, by making educational malpractice a capital crime, had led to an unprecedented schooling revolution; Victoria's grandchildren and their peers were the best-educated generation in decades.

At twelve, Penylle was reading Shakespeare, Dickens, and King; she could read and explain the Periodic Table; she was reasonably fluent in Spanglish and somewhat less so in Kiswahili. She had basic geometry and algebra, although she was still a few years away from the marvelous, shattering insight that the two were opposite sides of the same coin. The girl could explain the causes and legacy of both World Wars, albeit with a none-too-subtle pro-American bias, and she was quite passionate about the history of Islam.

Penylle could cook her own meals, explain supply-and-demand, and was able to outline and schedule complex tasks to ensure completion. She had a firm grounding in first aid and everyday prophylaxis. She could repair two out of three common automobile malfunctions, successfully program a computer nine times out of ten, and made her way around the Nets with an easy facility that Victoria, despite her decades of experience, could only envy.

In short, Penylle was a well-educated young girl of the 2020's.

In social skills, however, the girl was sadly lacking. She had grown up with no parents and siblings, yet surrounded by adults. The first thing Victoria did, when Penylle came to stay, was to find the child some playmates her own age.

Victoria and her husband considered the local public schools, but quickly had to give up that notion— with puberty, Penylle's psi abilities became more erratic just as her need for prolactin grew to three injections a day. It would have to be a virtual school, then; like so many other children disabled in one fashion or another, Penylle would have to attend classes in Cyberbia and Virtua.

The best schools, real or virtual, were Umojan...and the cheapest way to enroll Penylle in Umojan schools, was to purchase her basic Umoja client-citizenship. Umoja, as much a corporation as a government, charged client-citizens only for the services they actually consumed— schooling and Net access for Penylle was affordable. In lieu of hard money, Umoja's accounting agents were perfectly willing to accept service; so Victoria signed on to provide remote psychomedical counseling to other Umoja clients two mornings a week. After a while, Penylle's accounts more than balanced...she was building up credit with Umoja, as good as rands in the bank.

The experience opened Victoria's eyes to the unusual, convoluted economics of Umoja, where every client-citizen was also a freelance contractor, and where value given, added, or received was tracked to ten decimal places by indefatigable automatic computer routines. Umojans neither paid nor avoided taxes— services were rendered and paid for, that was all. And Umoja's software agents, constantly bidding and bartering for the needs of nearly a billion people, achieved unthinkable economies of scale.

Where transportation, communication, and distribution infrastructures did not exist, Umoja (getting the best deal on labor and materials) built them and allowed client-citizens to use them at cost. Others— for example, the thousands of individuals and companies that used the Kilimanjaro launch system— paid more, but often still saved money over competing systems.

Where high-level infrastructure already existed, and especially if there were competing systems, Umoja simply negotiated the best rates for its client-citizens...sometimes stepping in, when it was necessary to upgrade service.

Victoria wasn't sure she understood the Umojan way...she knew she couldn't track the flow of rands around and around the complex maelstrom that was Umoja's economy. But it seemed to work— every night, many more people went to bed hungry in the United States, than in Africa.

As Penylle dealt with the challenges of school and classmates— even virtual ones— Victoria continued observing her charge. Penylle's psi abilities showed steady improvement as she progressed through puberty.

When she was twelve, she could lift twenty kilos of dead weight and hold it motionless for an hour without apparent effort. At thirteen, twenty-six kilos was her limit, but she could hold it up all day. At fourteen, she reached thirty kilos.

Her clairvoyant senses also developed. When she first came to live with Victoria, Penylle could barely sense objects further than ten meters, and then only as indistinct, fuzzy images. (Victoria often had the girl draw pictures of what she beheld at the limits of her strange "sight.") By fourteen, she was able to accurately visualize human beings half a kilometer away, or watch individual bacteria swarming on the kitchen table.

Shortly after starting school, Penylle demonstrated to Victoria another facet of her abilities: she could manifest them from a virtual body anywhere in the world. As long as Penylle had access to the Net, her clairvoyant powers were all but unlimited.

Gradually, with mixed pain and joy, Penylle learned to control and even suppress her odd abilities when she was with those she called "normals." Hesitantly, she made friends among her classmates; the school provided the children plenty of opportunities to work and play together.

Penylle came to Victoria as a quiet, reclusive little girl, afraid to leave the house and terminally shy around strangers. In the course of a year, she blossomed into a friendly, outgoing teenager, certain that she knew far more than her elders and eager to tell them so. Victoria's family room became— as so often in the past— a haven for Penylle and her friends, a place where they gathered to study, gossip, play music, complain about their families, and support each other through the storms of adolescence. The only difference this time, was that these were virtual gatherings, much enhanced by the RCServer 1500 (with integrated cold-light projectors) that Thom had installed for Penylle's thirteenth birthday. Victoria grew used to seeing Penylle's friends as translucent apparitions or sketchy cartoons winking in and out without warning.

At least this way, she reflected, she didn't have to feed them. And there were no dirty plates and glasses to clean up.

In 2027 the Supreme Court, in an 8-1 decision, upheld all of the amendments adopted by the Constitutional Convention. Writing for the majority, Chief Justice Cantrell called the Convention "the citizen's final hope in an era of gridlocked and ineffectual government dominated by special interests." Strong resolutions of disapproval were introduced in both the House and Senate, but failed to make it out of committee. A motion of approval, introduced in the Chamber of Ministers, died in a three-way deadlock.

Taking advantage of the new Peaceful Secession clause, the broad swath of country from Lynchburg to Colorado Springs reorganized itself as the Christian States of America; soon after, southern California and the Southwest joined northern Mexico as Mexamerica, southern Florida entered the Caribbean Union, Utah became its own theocratic nation, and several American Indian homelands declared themselves independent. It was the worst year for mapmakers since 1990.

When Penylle was thirteen, she learned how to read the native hexadecimal code of the Net; by fourteen, she discovered that she could read it directly from transmission lines, without the presence of a computer. She'd always had a bent for mathematics; the internal language of computers and programs made much more sense to her than most of what passed for communications between the people she knew (always, of course, leaving out Aunt Vicky, who was both rigorously sensible and eternally compassionate). Now her logical and visualization skills came to her aid, as she explored, not the Net, but the electronic and digital substrates upon which the Net rested, the fabric of which it was made.

Aunt Vicky and Uncle Thom's expensive, sophisticated 'puters and other machines, with their easy user interfaces their friendly metaphorical structures, began to get in her way, standing between her and the unadorned beauty of the underlying code. After a lifetime of syrupy, sticky flavored concoctions, she had finally tasted pure, clear water— and she wanted more.

In the attic, Penylle found an old Amiga 7500 processor box, about the size of a deck of cards. It had a primitive keypad, a cracked display panel, and only rudimentary speech recognition, but she loved it at first sight. She hunted down obsolete chipboards and card-dots for it, and when they didn't do what she wanted, she learned to modify them with her own psychokinetic power. In the end, Penylle had hard-hacked that machine well beyond its original specs, when necessary linking it with much larger remote systems, until it provided her with a Net gateway that far exceeded anything on the market.

With the Amiga 7500 at her side, Penylle rode the bitstreams of the Net as a condor rode mountain air currents. She learned to manipulate remote cold-light projectors so well that— with the help of her custom-written programming routines— she could project an image of herself, in real time, just about anywhere in the world. Of course, the image she used was a few years older, and quite a bit more glamorous, than Penylle herself.

When she'd mastered hexcode and transmission protocols, remote projection and voice synthesis, RCCRL and tranix...when she could hack with the best and no system was closed to her. . . she finally felt ready to tackle the ultimate target, the Shangri-La of cyberspace: Our Lady of the Nets.

In the illusory, communal space of Cyberbia— where any door could open into an entire world, and where an ordinary cube could unfold, like a series of Chinese boxes, into a structure the size of a city— Our Lady of the Nets occupied a discreet grid square in downtown Greater Helium, on Alpha Ralpha Boulevard between the Grassy Knoll and Carter's Liver Pills. It was little more than a grimy brass plaque set in the cobblestone pavement, perhaps ten centimeters square and so tarnished and filthy that it was hardly discernible from the surrounding cobbles. Raised letters, barely visible, spelled out: OLotN.

Penylle crouched to examine the plaque, traced a finger along the letters. The plaque opened up, like a cardboard box unfolding again and again, until it revealed dark stone steps leading down into subterranean gloom. Resolutely, Penylle started down the stairs.

The wards and firewalls protecting Our Lady of the Nets were fairly difficult to unravel; no one without a minimum level of hacker skills could make it past the First Veil. Penylle found, however, that they made nice, tidy puzzles; they were obviously designed as much to attract the right sort of mind, as to keep the wrong sort out.

The Last Veil fell, revealing a golden archway. Penylle stepped through, and found herself in a cathedral.

The floor was white marble, reflections dancing in its polished surface. Bright, intricate stained-glass windows rose a hundred meters or more, supported by star-flecked granite columns carved in the shapes of Brobdingnagian elephants, turtles, crocodiles, and oxen. As she watched, Penylle realized that the patterns of stained-glass were slowly moving, changing, one design imperceptibly morphing into another.

Above all, seeming kilometers away at least, an obsidian dome was inlaid with gems, hundreds— thousands— of them, in every hue, forming a vast galactic whirlpool reaching from one end of the vaulted space to the other.

A marble staircase, broad enough to run footraces across its width, spiralled upward from the center of the cathedral, halting thrice at successively-higher oval platforms. Each platform supported a circular dais, upon which was built a tremendous altar. The lowest was hewn of dark, burnished wood; the middle one of turquoise and silver, and the highest altar was lustrous mother-of-pearl.

Multitudes moved through the cathedral, up and down the stairs, around the altars: human figures, fantastic creatures, cartoons, glyphs, icons— the myriad symbols that people used to represent themselves in Cyberbia. Many more, Penylle knew, were invisible: so-called Lurkers who came not to participate but simply to observe. In many parts of Cyberbia, custom demanded that Lurkers give some sign to mark their presence, if only a single voxel— but Our Lady of the Nets had no such rule.

Penylle had entered through a small vestibule, and stood now at the very edge of the enormous cathedral. She placemarked the spot, recording the cyberspace coordinates and encrypted passcodes that would allow her to teleport directly here. Then she moved forward, toward the great staircase.

Halfway to the first altar, an animated playing card detached itself from a group of cartoon figures and wafted over to Penylle. The topsy-turvy figure on the card was a Jack; slowly-gyrating symbols, changing with each rotation, made it impossible to pin down the suit. Along with the familiar clubs, spades, hearts, and diamonds, many other symbols took their turns: pentagrams, wands, crescents, stylized atoms, the hammer-and-sickle, others Penylle did not recognize.

"Hello," the card said, its voice reverberating slightly. "Welcome to Our Lady of the Nets."

"How did you know it's my first time here?"

"That's one of the Powers you have while you're here. Check your toolkit."

Penylle glanced at her toolkit. Several new options hovered at the top: Absolve, Bless, Consecrate, Exorcise, Repent.

The Jack went on, "If you Bless someone, you'll get a readout of their public information, including the last time they were here." He frowned. "You should read your Breviary."

"I'll get to it." She Blessed the other; the readout told her that he went by the name "Jack," that his last visit to Our Lady's had been yesterday, and that his level of Grace was 8.3. She Blessed herself, and found she was called "Acolyte" and had a Grace level of 2.6. "What's Grace?"

"It reflects your skill level as a hacker." Jack turned to the low altar, where a long line of supplicants one at a time placed indistinct bundles before the altar. "You bring your offerings to the altar, and Sister Rheostat grants you Grace points."

"What sort of offerings?"

She had the distinct feeling that Jack was looking at her sideways. "Information. That's what She deals in. Say you know some passwords to Swiss BankNet. Give them to Sister Rheostat and you'll get humongo Grace points. Later, you want to know how to get into Macrosoft. You can come here and Pray for Revelation. If Sister has the information, and you have enough Grace, then you'll receive the Revelation."

"I see." It was an elegant, if somewhat baroque, way to barter information."Well, I might have a few things to offer the good Sister." She started toward the altar.

Jack drifted after her. "What's your name, Acolyte?"

"Oh, I didn't change it, did I?" Taking a moment to skim the online instructions, she edited her ID file so it read, "Penylle."

"Ah," said Jack, his twin heads nodding in synchrony. "The same Penylle, perhaps, who broke the Trilateral Commission's encryption algorithm last week?"

Penylle looked down. "Maybe."

"The same Penylle who hacked her name into the scoreboard display on Tuesday's Meerkats game?"

"I was afraid no one had noticed."

Jack regarded her with eyes like flickering embers. "I have a dozen spiders out searching the Nets for you. When you're done dealing with Sister Rheostat, make some time for me. I'll make it worth your while. I might have a job for you."

"What kind of job? And who would I be working for?"

Jack glanced from side to side, as if making sure they weren't being overheard. "Have you ever heard of the Nexus...?"

Penylle loved school and enjoyed spending time with her friends— but she learned the most, and felt most alive, with Jack, and doing the various jobs that he and the Nexus requested. Before Jack and the Nexus, she'd explored the Nets and hacked their structure aimlessly, for play; after, her efforts had direction and meaning. She was helping people, and it showed. When she decrypted Indonesian secret police files so that the Nexus could post them for all the world to see, or broke security on a biological weapons plant in eastern Kurdistan, the effects of her work were obvious, her sense of gratification immediate.

Of course, no one but Jack himself knew that she, Penylle, was responsible. To the world at large— and, especially, to Interpol and InfoPol— the Nexus operated with faceless, anonymous unanimity; a single force, omnipresent and indivisible.

For nearly a year, like most Nexus operatives, Penylle lived a double life. To Aunt Vicky and Uncle Thom, to her classmates and playmates, she was a somewhat shy teener, perhaps with a few peculiar abilities but generally unremarkable. In cyberspace, however, she was international spy, master hacker, Nexus operative and agent of universal peace. At Our Lady of the Nets, her Grace level was so high that her virtual body glowed with a nimbus of pearly irridesence, and a diffuse halo hovered around her head, making her face indistinct and preserving her identity. When she teleported in, conversation died and bystanders gaped. She took to wearing white silk scarves and robes that constantly billowed around her.

There were hackers aplenty whose talents and abilities went far beyond Penylle's...but they occupied rarefied, exclusive portions of cyberspace far beyond the purview of mere mortals. Few of them, so far as she knew, worked for the Nexus; and certainly none deigned to appear in such plebian digs as Our Lady of the Nets.

Penylle's double life came to an abrupt end in the early fall of 2028, as a result of that year's Galveston Crisis. Starting in February, scores of thousands of refugees, heretics fleeing the latest persecutions in the Christian States (there were *always* persecutions in the Christian States), surged into Galveston looking for asylum. The Caribbean Union took what few they could; the rest were herded into refugee camps while Mexamerica tried to decide what to do with hordes of uneducated, intolerant Anglo Protestants with no command of Spanglish and few marketable skills.

One by one, the other nations of North America refused the refugees entry. In April, Mexamerica attempted to repatriate the poor unfortunates— but the Army of God, with other ideas, repulsed them at the border.

The second week in May, three cases of dysentery appeared among the refugees. Two days later, Mexamerica imposed a news blackout.

The Nexus did not abide news blackouts. Even under the strictest Nexus interdict, the Press was always allowed access. The Nexus was committed to free and public information exchange; the ongoing Nexus effort to get datapads and Net service to citizens of totalitarian states was one of the largest of the organization's activities.

The call went out, through the web of Nexus communication, to find someone who could defeat Mexamerican security and lift the blackout.

When Penylle expressed interest in the assignment, Jack gave her an encrypted letter of introduction, and sent her to see the Nexus operative supervising the Galveston crisis, whose code name was Tristram%Shandy.

Cyberbia, to Penylle, held a dreary uniformity: interminable cookie-cutter blocks of utilitarian structures and drab, geometric avenues. Whether pseudo-urban or faux-pastoral, Cyberbia was simplified, inoffensive, reality abstracted to bare, rectilinear bones and tissue-paper surfaces; like one of the old animated, flat-screen video games. From any altitude at all, the endlessly-recursive grids recalled maps of the American midwest, rectangles within rectangles within rectangles. Embellishment and artistic expression were left for the homerooms and cyberspaces inside, or— increasingly— for the real-world analog called Virtua. Cyberbia's emphasis was on clarity and ease of navigation.

Tristram%Shandy's office was at 21146 Curdsan Way in Octsford. Penylle consulted her directory and teleported directly to a public portal at the corner of Moebius Strip and Curdsan Way. It was a neighborhood of cartoon buildings with lots of marble and wrought iron, a cobblestone street lined with saplings of indeterminate species. As she passed the first of the trees, she saw that the leaves were flat planes, disappearing completely when she looked at them edge-on. She sniffed; shoddy work. Too few polygons to give any true illusion of reality. There was nothing artistic about this region of Cyberbia, no appreciation of detail. It was a cyberspace imagined by an accountant, or a lawyer.

Number 21146 was as bad a faux-Victorian horror as the other buildings on Curdsan Way. Penylle bounded up the marble stairs (no sound, no indication of pressure or texture) and effortlessly threw open the door. A lengthy hallway was punctuated with office doors out of a private eye movie, frosted-glass panels etched with decorative patterns and the names of firms and individuals. Halfway down the hall, she spotted a door marked with the Nexus starburst, and knew she had found Tristram%Shandy.

The door opened onto a sparsely-appointed reception area. A sleek, art-deco robot looked up from the desk where it had, apparently, been shuffling manila file folders. "Mr. Shandy will be with you momentarily.

Would you care to take a seat?"

She looked disdainfully at two caricatures of straight-backed wooden chairs. "There's not much point to it, in cyberspace, is there?"

"I am not very knowledgeable in such areas, ma'am." The robot turned back to its pointless work. Penylle resisted the impulse to reach into the scene's underlying code and turn the automaton into a cartoon duck, or an animated plate of spaghetti.

"While I'm waiting, I think I'll change into something a little more comfortable." She'd show Tristram%Shandy what a real virt-master could do.

Penylle opened a window into Personas-4-U, a vast online wardrobe of Net personae. Something in period; she leafed past alternatives and settled on a Marlene Dietrich style *femme fatale*, about twenty-eight, short dark hair and plenty of curves in a blood-red dress that clung in all the right places. Black high heels, and one of those old widow's hats with the veil obscuring her features. A cigarette in a long, ebony holder completed the ensemble.

She took the persona and made it her own, tweaking the code here and there, tightening up some of the nuances, adding a breath of musk, black silk stockings, and a deliciously-curling trail of smoke from the cigarette. Her voice, she decided, would by husky and commanding, with the barest hint of a Slavic accent in the vowels. She took a look, then gave herself piercing blue eyes and fine lashes that trailed off into invisibility. Then she topped off the design with a brooch, the Nexus Starburst in silver filigree above her ample left bliley.

Satisfied that her virtual body put the rest of the room to shame, she sat on a chair, crossed her legs, and hiked her skirt up the way she'd seem women do in the old flat movies. She felt very much like Gail Danube in the second remake of *Casablanca*.

An inner door opened and a nondescript man entered. There was nothing elegant about this virtual doppleganger; his body and face were composed all of angles, colored in bold monotones. He was an abstract of a middle-aged Anglo male in a dark blue business suit. About him there were no shadows, no details of skin and clothing, no substance.

He extended his hand to her. "I'm Tristram%Shandy. I'm sorry to have kept you waiting, Ms....?"

Penylle took a drag on the cigarette (fortunately, it had neither taste nor odor), and exhaled deeply and slowly through her nose. Twin tendrils of smoke snaked around his hand, then dissipated.

She leaned forward and took his hand, used it to help her to her feet. "Silicon|Sister," she said, her voice touching just the right balance between throaty whisper and sultry vamp. It was a codename that she had used occasionally on Nexus business.

The robot faded out, and Tristram%Shandy took its seat at the desk...which had suddenly become a little higher and considerably more substantial. Inexcusably shoddy, to let reality— even virtual reality—morph like that without warning or justification. "What can I do for you?"

"The question," Penylle said, parking her ample rump on the corner of his desk, "is what *I* can do for *you*. I understand you're looking for someone to hack Mexamerican security. I'm your woman." She reached into her blouse and produced Jack's letter of introduction. It took the form of a yellowed, crinkled envelope, stamped with multiple illegible postmarks and stained by accidents best left unknown. As she passed it to him and his system took over maintenance of the image, the letter became a standard, generic document icon.

He stared at the letter, nodding occasionally, until Penylle was ready to scream. What *had* Jack put in there? She'd attempted to decrypt the file, but gave up when she realized it was in high-level Nexus encryption that would take weeks to crack.

Finally Tristram%Shandy put the letter down and looked straight at Penylle. "Well, your sponsor seems to think that you could do the job. Tell me, do *you* think you have the necessary skills?"

She stood up and ran her hands over her hips. "You can look at *this*, and still wonder if I have the skills?"

His flat, animated face remained impassive. "Ah, yes, I see the confusion. I don't doubt your technical skills at all. But a mission of this nature requires something more than good-looking simulations and technical jiggery-pokery. It requires diplomacy, tact, and considerable social skills."

Penylle felt as if, after an hour of thinking she was alone in the house, she'd just run into someone in the kitchen. She echoed, "Technical jiggery-pokery? This isn't *that* easy, you know."

His cartoon image regarded her over steepled fingers. "I've no doubt. Still, the fact remains, that for this mission I need someone who is more than a skilled hacker. I need a team player, someone who won't act on impulse." For a moment he just stared. "I don't think Silicon|Sister is the person I need. Am I right?"

Penylle felt herself flush with anger. Who *was* this idiot?

Although it was ill-mannered to try uncovering a Nexus operative's real identity, Penylle opened a subsidiary window and fired a sophisticated tracebot at Tristram%Shandy's image. Then, aware that she'd let her virtual body stand frozen for a few seconds, she took a deep breath and turned her attention back to it.

Tristram%Shandy was still staring at her, awaiting an answer to his question.

"I can follow orders," she said cooly, "if that's what you're worried about."

"I'm afraid it's not just a matter of following orders. Discretion..."

The tracebot announced its results in a window that emerged (with a minor fanfare that only Penylle could hear) from Tristram%Shandy's forehead. Surprised at what she read, Penylle lost the rest of his statement.

Penylle dropped her audio filter, and in her own voice said, "You've never denied me anything before, Uncle Thom."

*Now* Tristram%Shandy reacted; his image flickered perceptibly, and for an instant she glimpsed a caricature of Uncle Thom's face. Then the impassive mask was back. "I'm so confused." The voice was Uncle Thom's. "Penylle, what in the devil are you doing in the Nexus? Does Victoria know?"

"No, she doesn't. Don't be mad at me. I just wanted to help."

"I'm not mad at you. Astonished, but not mad."

She let her virtual body morph back into her customary, almost-realistic plain-old-Penylle. Unable to keep a slightly petulant tone out of her voice, she said, "You never told me you were Nexus."

He nodded. "And *you* never told *me*. Entirely proper, really. How long have you been active?"

"About a year, I guess."

"You're to be congratulated for maintaining security that long. Victoria and I never suspected you."

"Is Aunt Vicky Nexus too?" Penylle felt a little thrill at the thought that she might be doing the same kind of work as Aunt Vicky.

"Not as such. She's sympathetic, but she's chosen not to become formally involved. Your Aunt is something of an individualist." He shook his head. "Well, there it is. For better or worse, you're Nexus. The only decision to make now is, what am I going to do with you?"

"You've *got* to let me help out." Penylle knew that she sounded too eager, too whiny; and she hated herself for it. He'd never let her participate in a major operation, not now.

He pondered. In the caricatured face, she could now see the lines of Uncle Thom's nose and ears, his trim mouth set, as so often, in deep thought.

Finally, he nodded. "Provided that you agree to follow my orders, I will take you on as part of my team."

Penylle dimpled and threw him a kiss. "Thanks, Uncle Thom."

"Just don't make me regret this decision."

"I won't. I promise."

The rickety attic roof creaked in the brisk, chill wind. Penylle huddled in her bed, covers tight around her. Downstairs, in the big master bed with the forest green comforter quilted by Aunt Vicky's grandmother, Uncle Thom and Aunt Vicky were talking about her.

Penylle didn't like spying on them. It was something she had done a lot, as a child...before she completely understood the concept of privacy and the fact that walls were not transparent to other people. Now she occasionally peeked at them, in order to avoid waking them too early, or to reassure herself when she waked from a dream of harm befalling them. She tried, however, to resist the temptation otherwise.

Tonight, though, was different. It was important for her to hear.

"I can't believe," Aunt Vicky said from behind her book, "that you went along with her. I can't stop *you* getting yourself up to your ears in international intrigue, but an operation like this is no place for a fifteen-year-old."

Uncle Thom closed his own book, marking his place with a finger. "I disagree. This is the world Penylle is going to inherit— she ought to have a hand in shaping it."

"That's absurd. You might as well use that argument to give your grandson access to our bank account." Little Jim was a chubby-cheeked three-year-old, whose proudest mathematical achievement was the ability to count to five.

"Penylle has been working with the Nexus for more than a year. She's already been involved in some fairly major operations. And if what I saw of her record is correct, she's done a good job of it." He opened his book.

"That is completely beside the point. Thom, didn't it occur to you that the Army is keeping track of what Penylle does? If they were to find out that she's involved with the Nexus, how long do you think it will take for them to decide she's a threat to national security? And what do you suppose they'll do then?"

Once again he put down his book. "I think you're overreacting, Hon."

"We'll see if you still think so, when a covert strike team takes Penylle away."

"As you've commented before, I'd certainly like to see them try." Uncle Thom carefully replaced his finger with a brass bookmark, and set his book down on a bedside table. "However, this is as good a time as any to broach a related subject."

"Go ahead."

"I've been in contact with Penylle's Nexus sponsor, and the man has requested that we allow her to move to Africa."

Aunt Vicky's eyes widened. "What?"

"Penylle has a talent for working with computers— or perhaps I should say 'a combination of talents.' If she's going to pursue it, she needs more formal training. A self-taught hacker, even the genius that Penylle seems to be, isn't going to get very far."

"All right, I agree that she needs the best education possible, no matter *what* she decides to do with her life. And I grant you that the cutting-edge computer schools are Umojan. *None* of which means that Penylle has to move physically to Africa. She can study with the best schools from here."

"It isn't the same, and you know it. Most of her friends are in Africa; she lives on Umoja Mean Time as it is." Uncle Thom regarded Aunt Vicky over his glasses. "Victoria, she's going to leave the nest sooner or later. This is the time."

Aunt Vicky closed her eyes. "What does Penylle want?"

"I haven't asked her. I didn't want to even raise the possibility, until after I'd spoken with you."

A nod. "I'll talk to her." She smiled. "You've been so good about Penylle. So good about putting up with me."

He shrugged. "Hey, I *like* her. Both of you make it easy to put up with you."

She kissed him on the cheek, then her smile faded. "What do you know about her sponsor? At least his name, I hope?"

"Penylle calls him 'Jack,' and I don't see reason to do any different. I've had his background checked— using hardcore Net snoops as well as my own people." He spread his hands. "He's as clean and legitimate as anyone else in Umoja."

"She needs a source for synthetic prolactin. If she misses even a few days, it could be fatal. And the stuff isn't cheap."

"Believe me, Jack can afford it. And if he can't, the Nexus certainly can."

"I'll want to meet him."

"I'm sure that can be arranged."

"I suppose it *would* get her safely away from the Army." Aunt Vicky picked up her book. "All right. I will *consider* it. And I'll talk to Penylle."

"Thank you."

"You're welcome. Now go to sleep." Uncle Thom removed his glasses, turned over, and buried his face in the pillow. Aunt Vicky waited a moment, then looked toward the roof. "*Both* of you."

She turned back to her book, and Penylle, chagrined but grinning, turned out her own light and went to sleep.

## DIVERTISSEMENT 09

from *Disunited States: Twilight of the American Century*
by Charles G. Fleming, Sankore University, 2035
<histserv.sankore.ed.umj/fleming/pubs/disunited/des.storm>

In 1990, the United Nations missed their chance to establish a new world order and break the cycle of armed conflict that had dominated international relations at least since the Council of Vienna. Had they not blundered so, the modern world order would have arrived 20 years before the Nexus made its stand at Indonesia.

When Iraq invaded and occupied neighboring Kuwait in August of 1990 <details>, cooler heads proposed a total economic boycott of Iraq, with U.N. peacekeeping troops to enforce it. In hindsight, we can see that this strategy— a clear precursor to Nexus Interdict— would almost certainly have resulted in the downfall of the Iraqi government, the liberation of Kuwait, and a signal to all nations that the world would no longer tolerate war. However, success would have taken many years, perhaps a decade. <models & analysis>

The U.S. President, George Bush, was facing imminent elections. In the hyper-aggressive culture of the time, Bush feared that anything less than armed conflict would be perceived as weakness or— worse— impotence<note>. Bush, therefore, insisted on war.

No other nation was powerful enough to counter U.S. belligerence, so war it was.

Desert Storm, as the war was called, resembled the attack of a schoolyard bully much more than a fair contest. U.S. firepower and high technology completely overwhelmed Iraq, and resulted in more than 50,000 Iraqi fatalities, many of them civilians. The U.S. suffered only 149 deaths, none inflicted by the enemy.

Americans congratulated themselves for beating up on a far weaker opponent. Tensions between Arab countries and the West increased vastly. In response to the next world crisis— genocide in Bosnia and Serbia <details>— the U.N. did nothing, apparently waiting for U.S. military action. Having publicly and rather noisily taken on the role of world police force, the U.S. now maintained that Bosnia/Serbia was someone else's problem, and took no action until far too late. Millions died. With each succeeding crisis, the results were similar. The pattern had been set, and would not be broken until the birth of the Nexus.

And what of George Bush, who had thrown away the world's chance for peace in a macho attempt to overcome his own personal shortcomings, who had bargained fifty thousand lives for 1,461 more days in the White House? Did he, at least, accomplish wondrous things in his second term?

George Bush lost the election and retired into obscurity. As far as history can tell, he never again said or did anything of the slightest consequence; his name lives on only in Presidential trivia books, because his son became President in 2001.

ENTREÉ 05

Date: Fri, 29 Aug 2042 14:18:24 (KMT)
To: Sugarplum_fairy@nexus.nex
From: MamaPajama@mail.uharare.umj [MamaPajama]
Subject: Re: Turing's test
Cc: ai.taskforce.list@uluebo.edu
Message-id: <20420829141824_211221.92637_PPJ13-54@nexus.nex>
Content-Type: text
Status: O

----------------------------------------

Once upon a time, mathematical ability was a sign of intelligence. And people said, "No machine will ever be able to do sums like humans."

Then came calculators, and they said, "Fine, but no machine will ever be able to play chess as well as humans."

Then came Deep Blue, and they said, "Fine, but no machine will ever be able to recognize and process conversational speech."

Then came software agents, and they said, "Fine, but no machine will ever be able to compose a symphony."

Then came Digital Mozart, and they said, "Fine, but no machine will ever be able to come up with an original, creative idea."

Now that **Thë Månifeståtiøn øf Çhångë iñ thë Møuntåins** has won the Nobel Prize in Physics, what are they now going to claim "no machine will ever do?"

----------------------------------------

```
Date: Fri, 29 Aug 2042 14:27:32 (KMT)
To: MamaPajama@mail.uharare.umj
From: gomo@umd.edu [GoCart.Mozart]
Subject: Re: Turing's test
Cc: ai.taskforce.list@uluebo.edu
Message-id: <20420829142732_210129.033107_CKE20-
45@nexus.nex>
Content-Type: text
Status: O
----------------------------------------
```

I can tell you, categorically and without the slightest fear of contradiction, that no machine will ever, *ever* be able to think. This is because human beings will continue changing the definition of "think" so as to exclude machines.

----------------------------------------

## [13] KAMENGEN 05
Timbuktu, Mali
Umoja Economic Union, Africa
26-27 July 2042 C.E.

*Yes, but what if this* weren't *a rhetorical question?*

Modern Timbuktu, like its ancient namesake, is a sandcastle city.

On the Great Bend of the mighty Niger, Old Timbuktu was perfectly situated where desert met jungle, where the folk of the sand and the folk of the river came together to trade salt and gold for artworks and grain. The heart of West Africa and the prize of a millennium's worth of empires, Timbuktu was once the richest and most cultured city of the Islamic world. Her university and libraries were known and admired from Cordoba to Baghdad. Her mud-brick mosques and minarets, life-size fantasy sandcastles, set the architectural fashion from Dakar to Khartoum.

Not too long ago, the sandcastle city seemed doomed, as the parched and gritty drought of the Sahel surged ever-southward, a relentless sandy tide threatening to topple the city's foundations and flood her wide avenues. Then Umoja came with biotechnology to stabilize the dunes and rescue the city. Deep into the Sahara, gengineered desert scrub grass now spreads its tenacious roots, turning sand to soil and cleansing the air, braiding excess carbon into imperishable, microscopic buckyballs.

Today Timbuktu once more stands proud on the banks of the somnolent Niger, again a center of learning and a crossroads of commerce. To the south is the river. To the east and the west is civilization. To the north, boundless and bare, the lone and level plains stretch far away.

The airport— which boasts two runways long enough to land spaceplanes, and river facilities that can handle waveriders gliding in from orbit— is a good twenty kilometers downriver of Timbuktu. A branch of the river runs right through the main terminal, its concrete banks lined with restaurants and shops offering everything from Dogon carvings to boat and porterbot rentals. From one dock, sleek hydrofoils depart every quarter-hour for the ten-minute trip to Timbuktu. Few tourists arrive in the early evening, so Damien is one of only a handful to board the spacious craft. All of the seats, luxuriously-padded, are just within the hydrofoil's clear dome; the center area is taken up by racks for luggage and porterbots. Damien finds a seat on the right, where he will have a good view of the city, and settles in. Cool, light air washes over Damien's hands and neck, drying the sweat that rainy-season humidity had brought out. A trio of adolescent girls, giggling and elbowing one another, scramble to sit in the bow, where they can pretend to pilot the boat.

After an announcement and warning tones, the door closes and the vessel surges forward. Heartbeats later, it exits the terminal and careens upriver, dodging the freighters, yachts, and cruisers that lazily drift up and down the serene river. The piloting software seems to be programmed to deliver maximum thrills while avoiding all obstacles by at least ten centimeters, and Damien's grip tightens on the back of the seat before him.

As they near Timbuktu the world brightens, as if the sun has emerged from behind a cloud. The river sparkles, and the wakes of other boats scintillate in prismatic hues. Damien peers at the pane separating him from the outside, and smiles. What he had taken for ordinary glass, is really RCScreen: RCSpex in sheet form, a great looking-glass into the illusory world of Virtua.

In the real world, Damien knows from countless holos and videos, modern Timbuktu is a sand-colored city of boxy, flat-roofed houses and slender towers, pierced with graceful windows and covered with delicate tracery. Virtual Timbuktu, however, is a massive edifice that reaches into the low-hanging clouds, its walls and roofs constructed of ever-shifting desert sands in intricate but temporary designs. All is in flux. The city glitters like a billion captive stars. Endless camel caravans, staggering under prodigious loads, flow into and away from Timbuktu's broad avenues like the eternally-flowing river or the perpetual march of windswept dunes.

Africa's other monumental, sacred cities— Gao, Meroë, Jenné, Great Zimbabwe, and all the rest— are relics, museums, hallowed shrines: untenanted and unchanging. Timbuktu, once again at the crossroads of culture and trade, both Real-world and Virtual, is vibrant, vital, and forever in transition. The city's Virtual facade reflects its vitality; in Virtua, Timbuktu is like a battle between sandcastle and whirlwind, neither side winning nor losing, neither side withdrawing nor resting.

And above all, perched amid the clouds at the apex of the storm, so swiftly altering shapes that it is maddening to behold, is the castle and palace of Princess Mahlowi and her consort, Hollow Robin.

When the hydrofoil docks and Damien steps out, the air hits him like a hot, damp rag. The height of the rainy season, even when it isn't actually raining, is not the time to be in sub-Saharan Africa. Grateful for his loose dakishi and light, loose khaki trousers, Damien throws his rucksack across his shoulder and tramps in the direction of the Palace.

The marketplace air is heavy with scents— ripe dates, half a dozen wondrous perfumes, curries that make Damien's mouth water, stale mildew, a whiff of hashish. As Damien strolls, he amuses himself by playing with his RCSpex: raising and lowering them, looking alternately through one lens and the other, holding the glasses sideways to catch the virtual world in his peripheral vision. In Virtua, the city is cleaner and more alive; there are five times as many people, and they are decked in brilliantly-colored costumes. All the buildings shine, camel trains and flying carpets share broad boulevards with festive new cars and spotless lorries, and everyone is young and beautiful.

Without the Spex, the crowd thins and sunlight dims; streets, shops, and people alike are all the same drab shades of sandy grey. Many of the cars are sputtering wrecks, a rusted broken-down lorry blocks half the street, and a few recalcitrant camels spit and hiss at passersby. There are no flying carpets anywhere. Faces of young and old alike are lined and imperfect, here a nose disfigured with the scars of disease, there a gaping socket that once held an eye. Shabby clothes on shabby people, shabby streets in a shabby town.

Damien comes to the Palace, adjusts his Spex to full intensity, and steps through arched doorways into Princess Mahlowi's audience chamber.

Thousands of people, it seems, fill the room. Most of them, Damien knows, are here in Virtua only, tourists come to gawk and true believers come to pray. The room itself, vast as any medieval cathedral, shines in gold and ivory and inlaid gems, lit by flickering torches that blaze without consuming their fuel. Joining a long line of supplicants, Damien is carried through the crowd, this way and that, until he gets his first glimpse of the Princess, seated at the far end of the room on her ebony throne, between ivory tusks as big around as she was.

Mahlowi Sisse Keita Touré, born in America on the first full moon of 2001, returned to Africa at the very start of the Great Kurudi, the Return. Claiming descent from both Askia Muhammad and Sundiata Keita— and political authority from Umoja— she took the ancient Songhai throne, vacant four centuries. Princess Mahlowi combined splendor and pomp with true management ability, technology with tradition, and progressive vision with respect for history. In months, she was West Africa's darling; in a year, the world's.

Princess Mahlowi sits straight and serene, gazing into the middle distance rather than at the supplicant before her. She wears a full-skirted, wide-sleeved gown in her trademark African Tudor style, kinte cloth and other West African fabrics trimmed with leopard skin and gold ornaments. The green leather bodice is embroidered in Wadaabe style and studded with shisa mirrors, amber beads, and freshwater pearls. The underskirt is smocked velvet, secured with scarabs. Her headdress is based on Congolese basket-weave, her gloves adorned with Fante ritual designs. She wears a stunning gold necklace fashioned in the shape of the Nexus starburst. She cools herself with a fan of ostrich feathers. In browns and greens, amber and gold, she is the colors of Africa itself. Through the vast hall, drums beat the slow rhythms of ancient tunes.

Before Damien is halfway to the throne, Mahlowi's eyes meet his and she smiles at him. Although her lips do not move, Damien clearly hears her cheerful voice, always on the verge of breaking out in a hearty laugh. "Damien, you silly boy, don't wait in line. You know you're always welcome." She inclines her head, clearly indicating a velvet curtain behind the throne. In an unfelt breeze, the curtain opens onto darkness beyond.

When he lifts his Spex, the curtain vanishes, and Princess Mahlowi sits motionless. He lowers them and the curtain reappears, while Mahlowi beckons with an outstretched hand.

He shakes his head and marches forward. Mahlowi's grip on reality, never too firm to begin with, has grown weaker in the years since he last visited.

Beyond the curtain is a short hallway, then a brilliantly-lit living room appointed in modern African luxury: gorgeous furniture of dark, polished wood, sumptuous carpets, intelligent light that illuminates unobtrusively, a miniature waterfall spilling into a sunken basin in one corner. Masks and paintings on the walls complement various freestanding statues and other objets d'art.

Mahlowi sweeps in, wearing a silk caftan and a short turban of orange and brown. She is barefoot. She takes his hands and kisses air a few centimeters from his cheek; he returns the gesture. Then she sees his expression and steps back, chuckling. "Hon, don't look at me like that. I always have a cold-light hologram on display out there. Robin set up an expert system that can handle just about everything that comes my way. As soon as it recognized you, it beeped me for input."

Her smile is contagious; Damien can't stop his own face from echoing it. "You two are outrageous. I love seeing what you've got running here."

"Take off your shoes and toss that bag over there." She waves toward a space behind a large bamboo chair. "Sit down. Robin said you were on your way. How long can you stay?"

He settles amid dozens of pillows on a wide couch. "That depends on the M. Overnight, at least, if you'll have me."

"Damien, you are *always* welcome here, for as long or as short a time as you wish to remain." She settles next to him, smelling faintly of sandalwood; the fragrance stirs memories of childhood summers and adolescent delights.

"I know, but Mamma taught me that it's polite to ask."

Mahlowi leans back, framing him between upheld hands. "What a stunning young man you've become. Look at those muscles, that firm chin. So cultured, so polite. Is there nothing left of my puppydog teenager?"

He laughs. "Lord, I hope not." His cheeks flush as he remembers his awkwardness in those years; what an embarrassment he must have been to her! But she'd never let on; she'd treated him with kindness and dignity, whether she was admiring a mud pie he'd created in the yard or a virtual rosebud he'd created in cyberspace. When Damien ran away from home after his mother's accident, Mahlowi took him in and saw him safely to the Ivory Madonna's care. When he apprenticed under Hollow Robin, learning more about the Nets than any formal course of study could begin to teach him, Mahlowi opened her virtual home, with all its sophisticated security and Net safeguards.

And when the time came for a confused, feckless teenager to begin learning about love, Mahlowi was there to guide his fumbling steps. Hollow Robin didn't mind— Damien was sure he wasn't the first, and Mahlowi had more than enough love to spare.

He thought his Mamma would have approved.

"We've missed you."

"I've been meaning to visit. It's just— I've been so busy lately, what with my freelance jobs and keeping up with the M's projects...sometimes it seems like I barely have time to turn around, and zip, another month's gone by." He is glumly aware that it's been far too many months since he last saw Mahlowi or Hollow Robin, even virtually.

She nods. "And soon it'll be years, not months. Don't apologize and don't feel guilty— we see each other when it happens. I know that you're a godsend to Miranda. She couldn't keep up, without you. And she *is* getting on. She's...what? Eighty-two?"

"Eighty-four last month."

"Just so. She is a jewel, Damien, an absolute jewel. The world will never know how much it owes her. Or you"

"I've been wondering, lately, about that." He spoke quietly, tentatively, as if entertaining heresy. "I'm not sure that we *are* doing that much good. That *I'm* doing that much good. Maybe there are better ways I could be helping the world."

Mahlowi neither laughed nor pulled away. She searched his face, then said thoughtfully, "Have you come up with any?"

"Not yet. I...I don't even know where to look. Or what, exactly, to look for." He forced a sound more snort than chuckle. "When I was a kid, I wanted to be in the Nexus. Just like Mamma and Dadda. I'm sure I didn't even know what it meant— I just knew that I wanted it. After..." He takes a breath. "After I went to live with the M, it was just assumed that I was in training for a Nexus career."

Mahlowi cocks her head. "Assumed...by *whom*?"

"Everyone. The M, you and Robin, all the folks at the Institute. Even me. I never questioned it. I never *thought* to question it."

She brushes his hair. "Poor Damien. We made you grow up too soon. You should have had time to be a child." Suddenly, Damien saw her not as an eternal, ageless goddess— but as a woman of forty-one. At the corners of her eyes were incipient crow's feet, at her temples the beginnings of grey. "It's natural for you to have doubts. *All* of us have them." She shrugs. "Maybe you need to get away from the Nexus for a while. On sabbatical, you might find the space you need to clear your mind."

"Not right away, I hope. I still have some things to finish up."

"Don't put things off too long, or they may slip out of your grasp." She looks right at him, and Damien has the uncomfortable sensation that she is no longer talking about the Nexus — that, in fact, she is talking about him and Penylle.

He is saved further embarrassment by the sudden appearance of Hollow Robin's cold-light ghost, the shimmering suggestion of a man's body. "Dear, I'm ready for Damien now. You can bring him in." Hollow Robin vanishes as quickly as he materialized, only a fading smile remaining in the air.

Mahlowi stands and pulls Damien to his feet. "Come on, we daren't keep him waiting."

Thousands around the world know Hollow Robin through his sophisticated and artful cold-light holograms; only a handful of his closest friends see him in the flesh. Hyper-sensitive to most foods, molds, spores, and pollen— as well as to half the compounds in *Madabe's Chemistry-Physics Handbook*— Robin could not survive ten minutes outside his sterile, airtight suite. He likes to refer to himself as "the planet's most non-viable lifeform."

Mahlowi takes Damien to a changing room where they both scrub under ultraviolet light. The smell of disinfectant soap takes Damien back to the Navajo Nation, and he swallows hard. Nothing bad here; he's been through this routine dozens of times.

After scrubbing, both Mahlowi and Damien don Skin-Tites: suits of transparent film, only a few score molecules thick, with pores that pass gases and water but nothing larger. All bacteria, viruses, and nonliving contaminants will remain inside, where they cannot endanger Robin.

Mahlowi throws a flimsy, disposable robe over herself; Damien puts on doctor's pants and shirt. His hair is matted, and he is already sweating even though the air is pleasantly cool.

They step into an airlock and Mahlowi dogs the door. "Deep breath," she cautions.

There is a tremendous whoosh; Damien's ears pop, his skin tingles, and his lungs are on fire. When he feels he can stand it no longer, air returns to the chamber with a thunderclap. His right ear pops again at once, but it takes considerable working of his jaw to clear the left.

Mahlowi reads a display on the wall and nods. The inner door opens and a cool breeze hits Damien in the face.

"Robin doesn't think fifteen seconds of vacuum can do anything useful," Mahlowi says, "But I feel so much better since we started the procedure."

"Then it does its job," Damien says.

Stepping into Hollow Robin's suite is like entering Cyberbia. Cold light projectors and RCScreen make the rooms' boundaries endless and indistinct. Faint, almost-imperceptible straight lines, thinner than spider silk and far less tangible, define a ubiquitous three-dimensional grid. The air — overpressure and loaded with extra oxygen— is alive, electric; as if realspace were every bit as malleable as cyberspace.

Here as nowhere else in the universe, the three realms of Cyberbia, Virtua, and Reality are one.

Hollow Robin enters, perched in the center of an ungainly contraption, half steel exoskeleton and half spaceship cockpit. Ungainly struts and braces support his shoulders, back, and one leg. A dozen keyboards and display screens, real and virtual, orbit around him.

Underneath all the gadgetry, he is an undistinguished middle-aged Anglo, not quite paunchy but certainly soft around the edges. His skin is pallid, his long hair and scraggly beard so pale that they might as well be translucent. His eyes, behind thick lenses, are watery blue-grey. Hollow Robin's body is one that fades into the background, recedes until almost lost in the machinery. Damien thinks that Robin prefers it that way.

Robin faces Damien and, characteristically, begins his conversation in the middle. "In evolutionary terms, what's the most successful creature on our planet?"

"Cockroaches? Beetles?"

Mahlowi shakes her head. "Amoeba," she says, confidently.

Robin frowns. "Wrong, both of you. The most successful creature on Earth is the mitochondria. A billion years ago, they swam into the first cells, and they've been there ever since. They have their own DNA, they reproduce independently— and they're present in every plant and animal cell that exists. Mitochondria comprise more than five percent of the living mass on the planet."

He stares, hard, at his own right hand. "They only change by slow mutation. Genetically, my mitochondria are more closely related to those of a fruit fly, than *I* am related to my own brother."

Mahlowi gives him a sweet smile. "So what's the point?

"Two of them, actually. Number one: Who's to say that our actions might not be motivated by the trillions of mitochondria in our cells, for their own devious mitochondrial schemes? What we perceive as consciousness and free will, might merely be by-products of what our mitochondria are doing."

"It seems to me," Mahlowi says, "that the effect would be the same, either way."

"Ah, but it's only your mitochondria making you say that."

She looks down her nose at him. "And your other point?"

He makes an expansive wave. "In Cyberbia and Virtua, we've created virtual landscapes, virtual human beings, virtual animals and plants. We even have virtual micro-organisms, virtual bacteria and viruses that cause virtual diseases."

"So?"

He grins. "So where are the virtual mitochondria? What's the cyberspace analog of the humble mitochondrion?"

"Robin, I love you beyond measure— but honestly, sometimes you worry about the dumbest things."

With the air of a magician finishing his act, Robin says, "Oh, it's not the mitochondria *per se*. It's the larger question: If we built our virtual worlds and left out the most successful lifeform on Earth…then what *else* did we leave out? And when will its omission come back to haunt us?"

Damien shakes his head. "That's why I love coming here— you two give my brain a workout."

Robin turns to him, all seriousness. "You said there was a problem with the AIs. Care to elaborate?"

Damien relates his experience in dataspace, and what he learned from **Øut øf Thrëë**. He plays back his discovery of the reprogrammed ROM chip, then concludes, "The AIs guessed that there are as many as 320 similar anomalies in their dataspace. If each one represents a ROM chip that's been tampered with…. "

"Then fixing them is going to be a cast-iron coats on wheels," Robin finishes. "I am nunned uneasy about this. I don't see how so many security breaches could go undetected. But it fits too well. It explains all the weird helms that's been going on in the Nets lately." As he talks, Robin's fingers are fast at work on the keyboards before him; he is like a frantic Mozart playing six pianos simultaneously.

"What weird helms?" Mahlowi asks.

"*All* of it. Communications glitches. Misrouted deliveries. Seventeen thousand units of Erté swimsuits delivered to McMurdo. That bogus proof of Goldbach's Conjecture that the AIs released last week, and the *janitor* at Harvard's math department caught the errors in it. Brownouts in Cairo and Nairobi on invariant 256-hour cycles. I have a file of a few thousand anomalous incidents in the past year, if you want to see it."

"No, thanks."

Damien frowns. "How can you be sure there's a connection?"

Robin looks up from his screens for an instant, his face a blank.

Mahlowi comes to his rescue. "How can a chess grandmaster be sure that Knight to E3 is the right move? When Robin starts talking about invariant cycles and anomalous incidents, you *know* it's programmer's intuition."

"Damien, I want you to show me exactly where you found that misprogrammed ROM."

"Okay. I need to access my home files."

Robin's fingers fly over a series of trackballs and touchpads mounted around him like the beads on an abacus. The walls blur and shift, and then the three of them are standing in Damien's familiar homeroom.

Damien's two realtime windows, looking into scenes on opposite sides of the planet, show Kilimanjaro rising over a serene nightscape, and a rainy mid-afternoon at the Maris Institute. Giving them a glance, Damien retrieves a document from his desk and hands it to Robin. "Here's the list of memory blocks. They belong to an AI called **Triümphål Çhåriøt øf Åñtimøny**."

Hollow Robin, who is also *FAI*, shakes his head. "I don't know it. But I'm sure it's known to my friend, **Thîs Ønë iñ Møvëmënt Ådvånçes førwård**. Maybe I can get us an introduction." Robin raises his eyes to Mahlowi. "Yes, dearest?"

"If you two are going to be a while, I have a few thousand other things to attend to…if you don't mind."

"Not a nybble. Do what you must." Robin turns back to his screens. "Now, let me contact **Thîs Ønë iñ Møvëmënt**."

As she passes on her way out, Mahlowi shoots Damien a smile and gives his hand a squeeze. "Don't let him work you too hard."

In the next few hours, Damien learns more about the Net and its realworld underpinnings than he ever dreamed possible. Always before, when he's explored AI dataspace, he's been accompanied and guided by one of his AI friends. Hollow Robin, however, dashes hither and yon, opening and closing virtual windows and doors with great abandon, sometimes accessing half a dozen separate locations at once. Yet Robin always seems to know where he is and where he's going.

Robin and the AIs communicate with one another, not in the poetry and visual metaphor that Damien is used to, but in strings of raw binary, gritty bits that brush past Damien like windborne sand.

**Triümphål Çhåriøt øf Åñtimøny** allows them access, and Robin studies the Blind Spot as if it were a van Gogh in a museum gallery. From every angle and with every conceivable instrument he probes, clarifying and verifying the extent of the anomaly. Then he casts through dataspace, trawls up similar Blind Spots. One affects a Kisangani AI called **Førmåtiøn\Çømplëtiøn**. Another warps dataspace between **Tëñ Wiñgs** and **Çhånçë ånd Førtünë åre Ünståblë**. Three separate anomalies infest

**Sëptënår¥**.

After examining the last, Robin nods. "Look at this. Three discrete problem areas. According to MemNIC, they all map onto different registers in the same physical chip. **Sëptënår¥** is based here in Timbuktu, mostly at the Tech Center." He flips through various displays. "The technician on duty in the computer room is Nexus. Watch this."

A video window opens on a slender Fulani woman a few years younger than Damien. She wears a saffron dress and matching scarf. Her eyes widen. "Oh, Robin. What a surprise."

"Damien, Lasue." Hollow Robin gestures from one to another, the continues before either can speak. "Lasue, it looks like you have a ROM that needs replacing." He hands her a document; the icon passes through the window with no difficulty. "Here's the address of the bad chip. I've notified Xai-Xai that you need a replacement chip and they're shipping it by suborbital freight; you should have it within a couple hours."

"Thanks, Robin." Astonishment and puppy-love war on her face.

"Do me a favor, Lasue?"

Puppy-love wins a decisive victory. "Anything."

"When you pull that bad chip, package it up and send it to me. I'll arrange a courier. I want to look at that thing in my lab."

"Whatever you say, Robin."

"Thanks, Lasue. You're the best." That quickly, the connection is broken.

"What do you expect to find?" Damien asks.

Hollow Robin doesn't answer right away. Then, in measured tones, he says, "Damien, I only wish I knew."

In the end, Robin has no answers.

"Now that I know what we're looking for, I'll draft a notice to all the *FAI* Netheads I know, and we'll start identifying these anomalies. Maybe *someone* will be able to uncover a pattern." Bidding a digital farewell to the AIs who have taken an interest in his work, Robin taps on one keyboard after another, closing down dataspace and bringing a panoramic view of Timbuktu into existence around them. It is late at night; a waning moon rides high in the sky, and fragments of cloud drift indifferently by.

Robin glances at a delivery tray. "Good, the chip is here." It is a rough cube a little under a centimeter on a side. It is flat black, but its faces gleam with intricate networks of tiny gold lines. Small notches, Damien knows, prevent the chip from being inserted incorrectly into its socket. The top bears the colorful, angular Xai-Xai logo and a series of alphanumeric codes.

Robin lifts the chip and examines it from every angle. "Looks like a standard Xai-Xai chip. I'll need to check it with a microscope to verify the holographic pattern in the logo against the master checksum— but if this is a counterfeit, I can tell you right now that it's the best I've seen."

"I'll bet you could do just as well."

Robin bites his lower lip. "*Ebo,* I probably could. If I worked hard enough at it."

"Robin, what if it's genuine? Does that mean someone in Xai-Xai is behind all this?"

"Not necessarily. It's possible that someone could take a genuine Xai-Xai ROM and reprogram it. They could probably even make the checksum match the logo pattern."

"Then we'd at least know that we were looking for a Xai-Xai customer."

Robin gives a tired smile. "Which only narrows it down to half a million people and institutions. Damien, don't count on getting a positive lead from this chip. At best, it'll help us to eliminate a few possibilities."

"Well, let's get started."

"No." Robin raises a hand. "Even if you're not hungry, *I* am. Mahlowi will insist on the three of us having dinner together." He looks into the distance, then back at Damien. "She says half an hour. Is that all right with you?"

Damien nods. "*Ebo.*"

"All right. I'll show you to the guest room, and you can spiff up. This chip will still be waiting for us when dinner's over."

The "guest room" is a three-room suite with private bath, toilet, and bidet as well as a selection of brightly-patterned clothes, all in Damien's size. His travel clothes, cleaned and pressed, are folded on a stool next to his jumpbag.

After a quick shower, he chooses a light, calf-length robe of white and blue batik. He goes barefoot, so as not to seem to insult Mahlowi's hospitality. From a shelf of fragrances both exotic and traditional, he picks a time-delay cedar/cinammon blend; he calculates that it should start building over dessert.

When Damien reaches the dining room, Mahlowi and Robin are there to greet him. One flesh, one cold light, they wear casual-yet-elegant matching robes patterned with red and green and orange and yellow boxes adrift in seas of tan.

They take dinner in standard Umoja family style, sitting on mats and sharing from large common bowls. Hollow Robin eats along with them; the cold-light image is so well-integrated that Damien can believe Robin is sharing from the same bowl. The food is exquisite: pepper soup, sesame cakes, heavy rice bread, and a huge platter of stuffed fish steaks, vegetables, and crusty-brown rice called *ceeb u jen*. The wine, clean and slightly fruity, is refreshing with the spicy food. "What is this?" Damien asks, holding up his glass.

"Neethlingshoffer," Mahlowi tells him. "2038, I think. It was a gift from the Kusini Region Director of Transportation."

"People always have these wonderful wines, and I always ask for the name. Then, when the time comes to buy, I always forget."

"You should use our wine steward. It's wonderful; it keeps track of everything we drink, no matter where we are, and then coordinates with the kitchen and the buyers. Our cellar's fully stocked and it always knows the perfect wine for each meal. Robin, what's our wine steward called?"

"Vinnie Fera," Robin answers. "It was a custom job that my friend Dean Bryant did for an international wine club. Since I beta'd it, I got to keep a copy." He makes cryptic gestures with his right hand. "I'm sending the program to your system. You can install it or not, as you wish."

"Thanks."

Over dessert of baked bananas swimming in orange syrup, Mahlowi leans forward and sighs. "Damien, I hope you don't mind— someone asked to see you, and I took the liberty of saying yes. But only after dinner. They're waiting for my signal."

After the long session with Robin, and the relaxing meal, Damien wants nothing more than to crawl into bed...preferably not alone. But wine and pleasant company have left him relaxed and eager to please, so he smiles. "All right. Provided it doesn't take too long. Do I know this person?"

"I think so." Mahlowi's chestnut eyes twinkle. "Here he is now." She stands, and Damien stands along with her.

A figure shimmers into being: an elderly man, skin like black leather, eyes of coal, severe robes the ruby color of diseased blood. Marc Hoister.

Damien steps backward, but Mahlowi has him cornered; there is no escape except treading through the remains of dinner. He turns his head away. "I don't want him here."

Mahlowi's voice is gentle but unyielding. "Waziri Hoister is my guest, Damien." Then, a little more warmly, "Don't you think it's time you two made peace?"

"I do *not.*"

"Then the very least you can do for me, is listen to him. That's all: just listen."

Damien spreads his hands. Turning, he regards Marc Hoister with a frozen, sullen frown.

Hoister smiles, revealing blindingly-perfect teeth. The professional smile of an accomplished preacher, as comforting as the tight lips of a cobra. "Damien, I want to bring an end to this bad blood between us."

Damien gives no answer, no encouragement.

Hoister sweeps his eyes up and down Damien's lanky body. "You're such a fine young man. You've turned out better than I could ever have expected. I'm proud of you."

Still Damien says nothing.

Marc Hoister opens craggy hands toward Damien. "I've kept track of your work in the Nexus. Splendid, just splendid." He breathes, slowly and noisily. "I need a man of your talents, Damien. I want you to come work for me."

"Go to pell." Damien teeters between exploding, and laughing in Hoister's face. He pushes past Mahlowi, whose face conveys both shock and sadness, and walks deliberately toward the door.

"Don't be like this, son— "

Damien halts, turns on the man. "Don't call me that."

The lines in Hoister's face have become great craggy fissures. "But that's what you *are.* My son."

"You have no right— "

Mahlowi steps forward. "Damien, please don't treat your father this way."

"He is *not* my father!" Aware that he is shouting, Damien takes a breath and lowers his voice. "That man took over my father's place when I was eight. He had my mother killed, and if I hadn't run away, he'd have killed me too."

Mahlowi and Robin regard him, their faces showing a mixture of amused embarrassment. Much the same expression, Damien imagines, as if he were to announce a sincere and undying belief in Santa Claus. Damien, aren't you over that delusion *yet*?

Marc Hoister, however…Marc Hoister's piggish eyes hold triumphant superiority, and more than a touch of contempt. Don't bother, Damien.

They don't believe you. *No one* believes you.

"It's true," Damien insists, though he knows it is useless. "My father was the real Marc Hoister. This man reprogrammed my father's agents and took over his identity, his personality, and his entire life."

"Damien," Mahlowi says gently, "Robin and I have known your father since before you were born. Don't you think we'd have *noticed*?"

The phony Marc Hoister stands quiet, lips closed in the slightest of smiles.

"No." Panic rises within Damien, and he pushes it down. He *must* convince Mahlowi, *must* have her on his side. "For the first few years, he never let anyone see him in person. Everything was in Virtua or Cyberbia, or in cold light. Where he could project the image of my father." Her expression is unchanged. "He morphed the image, gradually, until it matched *his* face and body. Nobody noticed the change, it was so slow." Mahlowi frowns. "He sent 'bots out into the Nets, to alter existing records so they would match. He changed *everything*. Now, there's no way to prove what he did."

Robin nods at Mahlowi and whispers, "Capgras' syndrome." He turns to Damien. "Damien, after you started living with the Ivory Madonna, you were diagnosed with Capgras' syndrome. You were under treatment for a while. Do you remember?"

"I remember fine." Damien, remembering impersonal psychologists and injections that always hurt no matter what they said, struggles to keep bitterness out of his voice. "I didn't respond to the treatment program, and the M pulled me out because *she* believed I was telling the truth."

"Did it ever occur to you," Mahlowi says, ever so softly, "that she might only have *told* you that she believed you? Especially since the treatment wasn't working?"

He tries to be cold, but feels a raw sensation in his throat and tears welling in his eyes. "I don't see any point in my staying here any longer."

The ersatz Marc Hoister raises a hand. "Wait. I'll go. I didn't want to spoil a pleasant evening." His eyes, red-black embers, burn into Damien's. "Damien, I want to make peace. I've missed you, and I want you back in my life. But I won't push you into something you're not ready for." He lowers his face. "I am truly sorry." After a moment, he bows to Mahlowi and Robin. "Thank you for letting me try. I'll take my leave, now."

Robin looks from one to the other, Hoister to Damien, and back. "Why don't you tell him why you chose *now* ?"

"He doesn't want to know."

"I think he does."

Hoister faces Damien once more. "Son— I mean, Damien— I wanted to patch things up between us because…you see, I'm getting married. And I'd be honored if you would come to the wedding."

Mahlowi takes his hand, image overlapping substance where flesh meets cold light. "Congratulations," she says. "Who's the lucky one?"

"She's right here." Hoister turns to someone off-view, raises his hand. "Come, darling, meet Princess Mahlowi and Hollow Robin."

"I believe we've met on the Nets." A woman steps into view, her hand resting in Marc Hoister's, and Damien cries out in astonishment, dismay, and fear.

Penylle.

The woman on Marc Hoister's arm is Penylle.

Blindly, Damien runs…pushes past Mahlowi and out the door, into the night of Timbuktu. Somehow, he hails a cab, and is on his way to the airport before he can think.

All the way, he feels Marc Hoister's gaze burning into the back of his head, and his ears are filled with Marc Hoister's cruel laugh of triumph.

## DIVERTISSEMENT 10

*CITY ETERNAL*

Timbuktu, Timbuktu,
River brown and sky so blue,
Upon the desert sea you stand;
A city made of sand.

Within your high and mighty walls,
Wisdom walks your shadowed halls,
Goods exchange in traders' meets;
And angels tread your streets.

Peoples come and peoples go,
'Round you, kingdoms ebb and flow,
Empires rise and empires fall;
Yet you outlast them all.

Ghana passed with salt and gold,
Then Mali with her warriors bold,
And Songhay with its golden grains;
Still Timbuktu remains.

Moors then ruled with sword and blood,
France toppled mosques of sun-dried mud,
Bamako brought the desert nigh;
And yet, you will not die.

Umoja's peace is come at last,
And quiet, from the ancient past,
The music of a thousand years,
Timbuktu still hears.

- Princess Mahlowi Sisse Keita Touré,
March, 2037

ENTREÉ 06

Date: Sat, 30 Aug 2042 21:55:18 (KMT)
To: Lil'Hurly-Burly@nexus.nex
From: WaywardSon@mail.vm3.ares.net [WaywardSon]
Subject: Valles Marineris
Cc: alt.soc.racism
Message-id:
<20420830215518_038012.35202_KCI22.64@mail.vm3.ares.net
>
Content-Type: text
Status: O
----------------------------------------

You wanna know about Valles Marineris? She's the biggest feature on Mars. Stretches across a third of the exonin' planet. Hundred, two hundred times bigger than the Grand Canyon. Stand in the middle, and you can't see the walls– they below the horizon. The science guys say that she might be the biggest canyon in the whole Solar System.

Well, that ain't word, my earthbound brother. Do not listen to the science man. Right there on earth, you got a canyon bigger than ol' Marineris.

Where? In Africa-home, my brother. The Great Rift Valley. Seven thousand kilometers down Africa's coast, Turkey to Zimbabwe. And the Rift Valley, she's been inhabited for millions of years. Marineris? Twenty-thirty years, tops.

You wanna see what we're makin' on Mars? Don't you be lookin' at no Grand Canyon, then. Cast your eyes toward Mother Africa, and then you'll see. *There's* Mars, a thousand years from now.

So why do you think all the scientists are always comparing Marineris to the Grand Canyon, and not the Rift Valley? Can it be that they're embarrassed, that the Rift Valley was settled by black folks?

Well, that's another similarity, then….

----------------------------------------

## INTERMEZZO: BLACK MARS

Kampala, Uganda
Umoja Economic Union, Africa
27 July 2042 C.E.

*It's not true about lemmings. It* is, *however, true about human beings.*

Namirembe Cathedral-Mosque, perched atop the famous hill above Kampala, is the largest house of worship in East Africa. Despite the upcoming quarter-century celebration of its construction, locals call the building *Kanisageni*— the "New" Church. Constructed of gleaming Burkinabe black marble and stormcloud-grey highland granite, the building is a typical Chrislamic fusion of mosque and cathedral, minarets and stained glass, temple and meeting house. The main aisle is broad enough and long enough to land a single-engine small propeller airplane, although it has only done so once, as part of the spectacular dedication ceremonies. The building can seat upwards of ten thousand without crowding.

In the downpour of this rainy-season Sunday morning, the cathedral seems jammed to capacity. How many worshippers are present in the flesh, and how many are cold-light holograms, is difficult to tell. Nor does it matter; across the length and breadth of Africa, tens of millions are tuned in to this service. Some watch for spectacle, others for morality, still others for politics. Many more watch just because everyone else is watching, because what is said and done in the churches on Sunday, will be the main topic of conversation at work and on the nets on Monday.

And not only human eyes are watching. The AIs who manage and regulate Umoja's economy are watching too, filtering what they see and hear through rarefied and sophisticated algorithms. Processed data merges with threads from a hundred other sources, all woven together into a tapestry that represents— so the AIs claim and humans hope— the tenor of the times and the will of the populace.

Part old-fashioned revival meeting, part pep rally, part war-dance around the bonfire, the service has been building in intensity for two hours now, under one Koran-thumping minister after another, with generous helpings of fire-and-brimstone oration, gospel choirs, jihad-inspiring rhetoric, spontaneous testifying, and not one but three bouts of speaking in tongues.

By noon, when the largest number of participants are logged in, the congregation is at fever pitch and ready for the main attraction. In a procession of acolytes, lions, and elephants, he arrives, perched on the back of a mighty albino bull with magnificent gleaming tusks three meters long. He wears deep purple vestments, embroidered in gold with symbols drawn from all Africa's major faiths; a short, jeweled turban adorns his head like a crown. Archbishop, Imam, Bodhisattva, Evangelist— he is all of these, and more.

He is Marc Hoister, Waziri, Minister, Reverend; and for a third of the population, his is the thin, shrill voice of Umoja's conscience.

The elephant kneels, Marc Hoister dismounts, and a half-dozen spotlights flood him with radiance, so that the golden threads in his robe blaze forth, and the jewels in his turban become coruscating flames around his head.

One deliberate step at a time, he scales the pulpit's narrow stair, halting one level below the top (the top step, of course, is left empty to recognize the Prophet's pre-eminence). He faces the congregation, and they fall silent. Even the gentle susurrus of breath ceases, as one and all listen.

"My brothers and sisters," he begins, "I want to tell you a story. You may think you know this story already, and if you do, please humor an old man by pretending to listen."

As he speaks, gospel women from the chorus give the traditional shouts of agreement and encouragement— "Hallelujah!" "Praise the Lord!" "Yes, Brother!"— or echo Hoister's words. In ancient custom that Africa's sons and daughters carried with them in the forced diaspora of slavery, the men of the community may speak— but their words mean nothing, without the approval and support of the women.

Marc Hoister raises his hands heavenward. "You know how the Good God, who is our Father and our Mother, cast Adam and Eve out of the Garden with all their children and their children's children. And you know how they came to rest in the place we now call Olduvai, and there they abided for all the rest of their days."

("Hallelujah!")

"You have heard how Mother Eve lived a thousand years and bore many children. Near the end of her span, she beseeched the Good and Merciful God to allow her family back into the Garden, where they might live in peace and joy forever."

("Forever!")

"You know that the Good God answered Mother Eve, saying 'Daughter Eve, the gates of Paradise are eternally closed to you and your children, even unto the hundred-thousandth generation. Yet in the soil of other lands, may they grow and tend other gardens, and may they someday create that Garden which is greater than Eden, more sublime than Paradise. And then, mayhap, may the sons and daughters of mankind come to live in Paradise again. This is the charge that I lay upon your children, and their children's children, and may they one day welcome Me to the Garden that they have made.'"

("So said the Lord!")

Marc Hoister pauses, his ebony eyes holding them all in an unbreakable geas of silence. Then, he says, "This is the charge that Allah laid upon the children of Eve, that they should cultivate another Eden, and dwell once again in lost Paradise."

He sips from a crystal tumbler. "You know that Eve's children dispersed to every end of the Earth. Over a million years, they diverged into all the races of humankind: the yellow, the brown, the white, the red; each with its own customs, its own culture. Each, in its own way, sought to rebuild the Garden."

("Rebuild it!")

"Across the parade of millennia, cultures rose...attempted to build their own version of Paradise on Earth...and, failing, collapsed into dust. But it was the black race, in whose veins flowed the undiluted blood of Adam and Eve, that was the true hope of humanity. Time and again, times without number, the bare beginnings of Paradise emerged in this most fortunate of all lands. Time and time again, African folk were beaten down by others. The legendary cultures of Egypt and Kush were destroyed by invaders from Asia. The peaceful cultures of North Africa became road-kill along the highway of conquering armies: Phoenician, Roman, Arab. Ghana was followed by Mali, then by Songhai— and then fell to the slave traders who carried its citizens away in chains. Kilwa, Kongo, the Hausa city-states, Benin, Asante...paradises of the past, raped and conquered by Europeans. In the south, Chaka Zulu applied the lessons he'd learned from Europeans, and slaughtered millions."

("Brothers and Sisters!")

"Each time the sons and daughters of Eve rose, they were beaten down again: beaten down with disease, beaten down with guns, beaten down with chains and whips, beaten down with impossible repayment schedules, beaten down with killing poverty. Beset by a million enemies, still they strive to create the Perfect Garden."

("Perfect!")

He pauses, surveying his flock with ember-intense eyes, as if he looks into each person's soul…and finds it wanting.

"Once again we attempt to create Paradise on Earth. Umoja is strong, peaceful, its folk content. Yet I say to you, Umoja too will be beaten down. This dream that we are all living, will come to the same end that the dream has always come to: attack, invasion, destruction by peoples more aggressive than we, peoples less cultured that we, peoples who do not honor our values. It saddens me to say so, but Umoja will one day go the same way as Ghana or lost Zimbabwe."

("Praise God!")

"Thus it is, thus it shall ever remain: as long as Africans share this world with the other races, there will be no Paradise on Earth. Such is the will of God. Yet it is also the will of God, that Africans shall re-create Paradise, and live forever in happiness and peace.

"The Good God, with infinite mercy, has arranged a way for us to fulfill divine will. Against all probabilities, God placed within our reach another world, a world without life of its own, but one that can easily be made fit for Earth's children. This is Mars; and it is our God-given task, to re-make Mars into a reflection of Paradise – into the Garden that was once, and will be again."

("Forever and ever!")

"For Paradise to come about, Mars must be for the Black man and the Black woman. Today, African settlements in the Mariner Valley and elsewhere outnumber those of the Chinese, and the Europeans, five to one. But that is not enough, my brothers and sisters. To fulfill God's will, Mars must be all Black. We must commit ourselves to raising that number, to outnumbering them, not by five-to-one or fifty-to-one or even five-hundred-to-one: we must outnumber them by five-hundred-thousand-to-one, or more. We must occupy Mars in such numbers that the other peoples will join us, or depart. This is our dream; this is our sacred duty. Mars must be Black."

("Praise God!")

Marc Hoister beams, displaying a face that seems to look upon Paradise itself, and raises his eyes to heaven. "Today, that dream comes one step closer to reality. Today, Umoja opens a new era in the history of Mankind's newest home, Mars." He lowers his gaze, looking right into holo pickups—and thence into the eyes of thirty million live viewers, and uncounted millions who will view this scene later.

"It is my pleasure and my honor to announce that at ten minutes past midnight, Kampala time, the spaceship *Swala* departed Kuumba Station bound for Mars. *Swala,* named for the swift-running antelope of Africa's plains, is a brand-new type of ship, based on research conducted at Ophir. *Swala's* self-sustaining fusion drive, the first in history, allows the ship to fly to Mars under what our scientists call constant acceleration."

Marc Hoister frowns ever-so-slightly, in order to reassure his audience that he doesn't understand such big words any more than they do. "Thanks to this wondrous advance, *Swala* will arrive on Mars not in four to eight months, but in only four *days.*"

The crowd stirs, and Marc Hoister raises his arms in encouragement. "Even now, larger vessels are being constructed, to accommodate the floods of emigrants to our sister world. Even now, Umoja-Mars is making ready to receive these new client-citizens, to put them to work building the new Eden. My sisters, my brothers, rejoice! This is truly the beginning of a new age."

("Rejoice!")

Maris Institute
Elkridge, Maryland
United States, North America
27 July 2042 C.E.

With a snort, Miranda Maris shuts off the replay of Marc Hoister's sermon. She riffles through stacks of datapads that clutter her desk. Umoja's official announcement of *Swala's* launch, timed to coincide to the second with Hoister's news. Independent confirmation of the ship's trajectory and performance, from a dozen different sources. Soundbytes from a hundred different experts. Analyses ranging from banana futures to measles projections to fashion trends. Transcripts of a closed-door UNESCO session. Two dozen Nexus threads. One thing was certain: Umoja had a working fusion drive, and Mars was suddenly a lot closer than it had been yesterday.

She throws down the datapads with disgust, and summons the image of Evelina, her comm agent.

"I am your humble SERvant." Evelina has a pencil behind her right ear, and she holds a crossword puzzle.

"Where is Damien?" The Ivory Madonna demands.

"The young man is TRAVeling. He has INdicated that he does not WISH to be DISturbed. His agent is quite INsisTENT, Madam, but I could ISSue an override. You ARE on his list."

"No. Let the poor kid sleep. Dismissed." Evelina, turning back to her crossword, obligingly vanishes.

Nunn it, what is Marc Hoister up to?

Conquering Mars. That much is obvious. Whether he is the biggest con man in history, or really believes that he is doing God's work in helping to create a new Garden of Eden, Miranda doesn't care. The effect is the same either way.

She notices herself chewing on her lower lip, makes herself stop. She glances at the time— it is pushing midnight. Another day over, and she's still not caught up on its news. Hang it, she decides— she'll be fresher in the morning.

She shuts down her desk and eases her feet into fuzzy slippers. Gravity! Who needs it? Now, *there's* an acceptable reason to go to Mars, although the Moon was closer, and had only half the gravity.

Come to think of it, if Marc Hoister wants to get Africans to migrate to Mars in the hundreds of thousands, he'd *better* offer them Paradise...or *something* a lot better than they had on Earth. Why, most families in Umoja were just getting accustomed to the luxuries of middle-class life— what would make them give it all up and—

The Ivory Madonna frowns. There are two ways to stack *this* deck, she thinks. Make Mars look so much better...or make Earth look so much worse.

"Comm!"

"I am your humble SERvant."

"Message for Damien; tell Rahel to deliver it as soon as Damien's awake." She faces her desk, knowing that the video pickups will record a perfectly-centered image. "Damien, I think I might know what's behind the Net anomalies that you're concerned about." She takes a breath. Well, if her idea is a stupid one, it won't be the first time. "I think someone is trying to make life in general as unpleasant as possible here on Earth. Take a look at the Sunday service from Kampala, if you haven't already, then let me know if you agree with me." She snaps her fingers. "Message ends."

"Thank you," Evelina says.

Miranda shivers. If she's right...then once flights to Mars start picking up, things on Earth ought to get decidedly more unpleasant.

She wraps her arms around herself. Not a night she wants to be alone. "Who's in the cuddle room?"

There is barely a perceptible pause, as Evelina interfaces with a dozen other systems to find an answer that's far outside her usual universe of discourse. "Rose, Phil and George, Greg, Gail, the Bofort twins, and Efia."

One set of rooms in the Institute is set aside for residents to exchange physical comfort, everything from hand-holding to backrubs to just plain snuggling. It's a warm and friendly place, with few rules except kindness and compassion. Some residents never use it; others, like Miranda, are more frequent visitors. Tonight, the mix of friends is exactly what she needs— she snags her favorite pillow, throws on a feathered robe, and plods to the elevator.

Already over eight million kilometers off in space, and accelerating at a steady ten meters per second per second, the good ship *Swala* flies on.

MENUET 05

*Newsweek* Online Edition, 1 August 2042 C.E.

ALLIES STILL NEEDED FOR GUADALCANAL LANDING

The invasion of Guadalcanal is in deep trouble. The World War II Centennial Commission still needs over ten thousand volunteers to play the part of Allied soldiers for a scheduled re-enactment of the Allied landing on August 8, 1942.

Over fifty thousand people from around the world have volunteered to play Japanese troops in the re-enactment (historically, there were approximately 33,000 Japanese troops on the island in 1942). Few of these volunteers have interest in playing Allied roles. One volunteer, Derek Tshwete of Pretoria, said, "The Allies won. Where's the drama in *that*?"

Dr. Kiyono Mauyama, a speaker for the Centennial Commission, said that the re-enactment will go ahead as scheduled on April 8. "We're committed to making this the most accurate re-enactment of the entire Centennial program. If necessary, we'll use cold-light holograms to fill in for the missing Allies."

The star player at the week-long festival on Guadalcanal is Thomas V. Nicodemus, a 118-year-old survivor of the Guadalcanal campaign.

# ACT II:

# LOBSTER QUADRILLE

## ACT II: LOBSTER QUADRILLE

### [14] KAMENGEN 06
Maris Institute
Elkridge, Maryland
United States, North America
29 July 2042 C.E.

*If the gods hadn't wanted me to be paranoid,*
*they wouldn't have given me such a vivid imagination.*

The first vehicle out of Timbuktu is a subsonic airship-freighter bound for São Paulo. With half her passenger space unfilled, the Captain is none too picky about requiring names; Damien buys an anonymous ticket and instructs Amelia Airhead to book him a sleeper compartment on a train from São Paulo to Washington, DC. Then, he withdraws into his minuscule cabin on the airship, zips up his bitsuit, and flees into Cyberbia.

His homeroom, usually a serene refuge, is entirely too public; Damien needs to escape the outside world entirely. He lingers there only long enough to whistle up teleport controls and punch in a code.

His homeroom fades, and walls of stone rise in its place. Flickering torches, bright tapestries, and soot-streaked oaken beams conjure a medieval cellar; Damien himself, clad in knight's armor, lies on a silk-draped bier. His hands are clasped together on the hilt of a gleaming broadsword, its blade resting on his chest. He rises slowly and— he hopes— majestically.

At once, a short figure enters the room...a deformed Dwarf straight out of a Hildebrant painting, black as coal and clothed from head to foot in what looks like wrought-iron chain mail. The Dwarf bows before Damien. "Welcome back, Lord Ogun."

Damien stands, allowing the Dwarf to kiss his ornate signet ring. "Thank you, Grimbling. Inform the household that I have awakened." He stretches. "It's good to be back."

Grimbling rises, tilts his misshapen head. "Shall we make ready for an adventure, my Lord?"

"Oh, yes, Grimbling." Damien smiles. "Make ready for the *grandest* adventure yet."

El Juego, The Game, has been around in one form or another almost as long as the Net itself. Phosphoric green letters on a black screen became static 256-color images, became photorealistic full-screen streaming video, became total-immersion artificial reality— yet The Game remained quintessentially itself, the product of imagination, not technology. Indeed, it is rumored that, somewhere in the labyrinthine contortions of El Juego's tunnels and corridors and twisting cobblestone streets, one can still find a place to sit down at an simulated antediluvian ADM-25 terminal, and play "Adventure" the way Gosper and Greenblatt and the others did so many decades ago.

Damien is not as obsessive about El Juego as many of his friends. He maintains only one persona: Lord Ogun, small-time landowner and very minor scion of the nobility, with a few hundred acres and a town house in the backwater burg of Morsville, on the shore of the Sea of Dreams. El Juego offers thousands of planes of play, all drawn to the same general outline but each satisfying a different taste for violence, politics, religion, and sex. Lord Ogun is confined to just one plane; Damien prefers his violence somewhat cartoony, politics almost nil, religion well in the background, and gamesex light and always readily available. Lord Ogun, an eligible bachelor, is popular with the ladies of the town…and he is frequently seen at Madame Finstra's House of Pleasure on High Street.

Lord Ogun is, in fact, an accomplished dilettante. While he enjoys an occasional adventure in the dismal ruins of a forgotten, crumbling castle— and doesn't mind rescuing the sporadic maiden, slaughtering a few dozen trolls now and again, and exoning a comely Amazon warrior or three— he is usually happy attending the victory feasts and nuptual parties that always seem to be happening *somewhere* in the town.

Mostly, though, Lord Ogun sleeps— on the decorated bier in the cellar, sometimes for months at a time, while Damien attends to business in the real world. And when Damien wants to retreat from the real world, for a few hours or a few days, Lord Ogun is there waiting for him.

Damien trudges up broad granite stairs, answering greetings from his retainers, and sits at the head of a broad oak table. Serving boys and wenches scramble to get food and drink before him; crusty bread, hard cheese, cool wine. Damien leans back in his chair, arms behind his head, and lets a wench feed him tidbits of bread and cheese. The computers that run El Juego have been told— through Grimbling, their doppleganger— that Damien wants an adventure for Lord Ogun; Damien is content that an adventure will come along.

Grimbling re-enters, bowing low before his Lord.

"What's the good news, Grimbling?"

The Dwarf straightens, his grin showing sharp, yellowed teeth. "I kicked the Master of the Guard awake; he's preparing your troops and cavalry. And I told Senna to run down to the Market and gather together as many bearers as she can find."

Damien nods. It sounds as if El Juego has a grand adventure planned for him. He glances out the window; the westering sun paints long orange shadows across the town. "What shall we do while they're getting ready, Grimbling? What's going on in town this lovely evening?"

"Lady Celosia is throwing a party to celebrate her victory in the Castle Run."

"Oh, I didn't know she'd won." Celosia, who owns a modest house on the next block, is an adept of the challenging (and erotic) discipline of metaspace transfer. Through this complex spell, which turns carnal energy into kinetic, an adept can propel a vehicle at speeds well in excess of the speed of light (fixed, for game purposes, at exactly 300,000 kilometers per second.) That the spell requires repeated exoning, with many different partners, accounts for both its popularity, and its difficulty. Every year during Carnival, metaspace adepts ran a race that covered a dozen castles and thirty thousand kilometers.

Grimbling nods. "Not only did she beat all the rest, but she set a record. She did the Castle Run in less than twelve-part sex."

"Ah, certainly an accomplishment to be celebrated. When do festivities commence?"

"The Lady will open her house on the stroke of seven. You have a little more than an hour."

"Then fetch the barber. And my valet. And I suppose I'd better have a bite to tide me over until the party begins."

As the servants scramble to fulfill his wishes, Lord Ogun closes his eyes and gives a contented sigh.

At Lady Celosia's party, a beautiful woman in black leathers and fur, her heaving blileys barely contained by her bodice, offers him a drink. He follows her onto a terrace and for a while they whisper inconsequentials into each others' ears. One thing leads to another, and before long he is following her through narrow, shadowy alleys. Predictably, well-armed thugs jump the two of them; when the skirmish is over, Lord Ogun is alone with two dead thugs and a strange talisman carved from teakwood and hung on a fine gold chain.

Then it's off to Mesklin the Scribe to identify the talisman, Sylvie's Emporium to catch up on town gossip, and Madame Finstra's for a nightcap and information of a more informal kind. Afterwards, Lord Ogun rushes home, pondering the plot of wizardry and revenge that he's uncovered. He definitely needs the team that Grimbling is assembling, if he's going to attempt to rescue the kidnapped damsel.

Before the bells ring midnight, Lord Ogun is away from Morsville, with a train of knights, retainers, healers, assorted hangers-on, and a wizard or two in his wake. The mighty battles that follow afford many splendid opportunities for heroism and derring-do; Damien hardly notices, in the wee hours of Monday morning, when he must transfer from airship to northbound train. He allows Amelia Airhead to walk him through the switch, with his attention only half on the real world. Once he is settled on the train, he loses himself again in Lord Ogun's world, emerging only slightly to helms, hyde, and eat.

Lord Ogun's campaign draws to a close— with the maiden rescued, the evildoers slain, and many bags of gold and gems left over— just under an hour before Damien's train arrives in Washington, DC. The supercomputers that run El Juego, as always, have consulted with the agents of all the players involved in this campaign, and have brought it to a conclusion both satisfactory and timely. Damien barely has time to doff his bitsuit, take a much-needed shower, and pull on trousers, shoes, and a shirt before his car detaches itself from the rest of the train and glides to a noiseless stop in Union Station.

It is late Monday afternoon, and the station is packed. With judicious application of his elbows and just a bit of sprinting, Damien manages to board a northbound commuter train just seconds before it pulls away. Twenty minutes later, he is at the Institute. Hot, humid summer afternoon is fading toward summer evening slightly less hot, but just as sticky; his shirt clings to his sides and sweat drips from his hair, but Damien strides joyfully down the main path, swinging his rucksack and kicking pebbles. El Juego has relaxed him; he throws on his RCSpex and smiles at the world transformed. A blinking icon, low on the left in his field of vision, informs him that mail and messages are piled up— Damien ignores it, and confidently strides through the door.

A teenager dashes past him, skin the shade of vellum and long black cape billowing like midnight clouds athwart the moon. The lad spins, shows fangs in a broad smile, and says, "Hi, Damien!"

"Hi yourself, Mati. Where are you off to in such a hurry?"

The boy looks both ways, as if all the hounds of pell are on his trail. "I put too much garlic in Babi's soup. She's after me, and she wants blood. So to speak."

Damien laughs. Mateni Gerat and Babari Aparejo are two of the Institute's resident vampires, victims of a 2032 gene-splicing porphyria virus whose perpetrators are still unidentified. While severe anemia and aversion to sunlight are the major symptoms, none of the vampires actually drink blood. At least, so Damien hopes.

Mati drops to all fours, hiding behind Damien as he scans the lobby. "Hey, man, did you know that the M wants to see you?"

"I didn't know. Thanks."

A banshee shriek cuts through the air, and a black-clad figure tackles Mati. Damien gets a glimpse of long blond hair, fingernails like claws, and whimsical cat-whiskers painted across paperwhite skin, then the couple tumbles away from him. The girl Babi, affecting her best feline mannerisms, looks up and shows her fangs. "Hi, Damien. The M wants to see you, like yesterday at the latest." Mati springs away, and Babi dashes after him. "Bye, Damien!"

Shaking his head, Damien moves toward the elevators. He'll drop his luggage in his room, tidy up a little, and then book an appointment with the Ivory Madonna, he thinks. No point in rushing— especially since he's going to have to tell her what happened in Timbuktu.

On the way to the elevators, half a dozen residents tell him that the M wants to see him.

He steps into an empty elevator car, and the doors close behind him. Through the glass-walled car, he watches the Institute's floor drop below him. As usual on weekday evenings, residents and visitors mingle in clumps around the floor; the two hours before dinner are a social period, time for a drink or some pleasant conversation after a hard day's work.

To Damien's surprise, the elevator continues past his floor. He punches the button for the next floor, but the panel stays blank and the elevator keeps going. He tries a few more buttons, then the car's small viewscreen lights up with the face of Evelina, the M's comm agent. "This ele-VATOR has been comman-DEERED." She snorts noisily. "You have an immediate ap-POINT-ment with the Ivory Ma-DON-na."

The car sighs to a stop at penthouse level, and Damien steps out into a somber yet well-appointed waiting room. No one else is in sight. He throws his bag onto a plush sofa, and then walks down the hall.

The M's office door is ajar; cautiously, he eases inside. The windows are darkened against early-evening sun, the room dim. Along one wall, a dozen video screens flash images at each other, their voices muted to a surreal whisper. Miranda Maris stands at her desk, back toward Damien, engrossed in something she is reading.

He coughs; she turns. Her face, usually smooth and relaxed, is lined; her reddened eyes seem to float in sockets too large for them, above dark crescents and bagged cheeks. For a moment, her expression clouds, and Damien fears an explosion— but she merely looks down, soothing her temples with thumb and forefinger. "Damien, you know I can't abide those nunned Spex. Please take them off."

He obeys without thinking, and the room becomes that much more gloomy. He forces a chuckle, which falls flat. "I suppose I'm wondering why you called me here today."

"Not funny, Damien. I wish you had seen fit to send me a message, at least telling me you were on your way." She looks as if she has not slept for days. "Damien, I *needed* you." A heavy sigh. "I need you now."

"I'm sorry. I've been incommunicado. First I knew you wanted me, was when I walked in five minutes ago."

Her eyes narrow. "You haven't checked your mail?"

"Not yet. Should I check it before we talk?"

"Then you haven't heard the news." She makes it a statement, not a question.

"No. What have I missed?"

"Damien, seven hours ago there was an explosion along the main hydrogen line into Timbuktu." She looks away. "Half the city is gone. Hundreds are reported dead."

"Th-that can't be. I was just *there—* "

"What, do you suppose that your presence somehow prevents disasters?" She shakes her head. "You left early Sunday morning, Timbuktu time. The explosion was Monday evening." The Ivory Madonna looks away again, wiping her eyes. "Mahlowi and Robin are reported missing. The Palace was completely destroyed. There is little hope."

"Helms." Damien's stomach drops, the way it does when a spaceship attains zero-gee, and for a moment his head swims. "They *can't* be—gone."

"It's not just Robin and Mahlowi. The city government is wiped out. Umoja has sent disaster teams and the U.N. is helping. We've asked Nexus forces in the area and worldwide to assist however they can."

Damien remembers Mahlowi's touch on his face. His eyes narrow, and he feels his face harden. "It wasn't an accident."

She nods. "We can't know that for sure, but it is the prevailing theory. However, no one has yet suggested a convincing motive."

"It wasn't an accident. I *know*. Remember why I went to Timbuktu? Someone's tampering with the AIs. Hollow Robin found a ROM chip that had been altered. He was going to try to find out where it came from." Damien works hard to hold back tears. "Someone killed him and destroyed the chip."

The M frowns. "Rather publicly, too. A message to the rest of us, no doubt." For a moment she appears to struggle with a decision, then waves Damien to a data screen. "I want you to watch something, then tell me if you come to the same conclusion I did."

The screen presents an edited version of Marc Hoister's sermon. When it is done, the M looks expectantly at Damien. "Well?"

"If he's so all-fired hot about going to Mars, why doesn't he just *go* and leave the rest of us alone?"

"Granted. What else do you conclude?"

"I guess I know where our equipment went. For that ship." Damien cocks his head. "I suppose someone's verified his claim?"

"Yes. The *Swala* will reach Mars on Thursday, if it keeps to its orbit. Umoja is projecting five hundred thousand emigrants launched by next year."

"M, how can he possibly expect that many people to move to Mars? *Especially* Umojans? I could understand if he was trying to get people from Siberia or Bangladesh. But Umojans have too much to give up. Successful, well-fed people don't settle new frontiers."

She regards him with cautious eyes. "I'm going to turn that question back on you. How *can* he expect that many Umojans to want to leave Earth?"

"I don't *know*. For most people in Umoja, life is great. Or at least, a lot better than anything Mars has to offer." He frowns. "Unless you live near Timbuktu, I guess." Damien stops, and comprehension crawls across his face. "You don't suppose *that's* what he's doing? Deliberately trying to make Earth uncomfortable, so that people will want to go to Mars?"

"Damien, I trust your intuitions. So you tell me if it's possible. A man thinks it's God's plan that Mankind settle Mars. But his ungrateful followers are in no hurry to fulfill divine will. What would that man be capable of?"

He thinks for a moment, then nods. "*This* man? He's a supreme wyden. He's capable of anything." Along the wall, video images flicker in blood-red and ochre flame, and Damien sees, beyond them, tattered holes torn in the world computer nets. Swimsuits in Antarctica. Brownouts in Cairo. Forests burning, their smoke curling high and obscuring the sun. Timbuktu flattened and still afire, flames whipping in hot desert wind.

Cities burning. People dying. Above the weary world, AI-controlled mirrors ponderously turning, sending down invisible beams of death....

"Jamiar said that the AIs mis-identified the strain of Dekoa from Dinétah. What if he's right? What if they don't know themselves where it came from? What if a canister of live virus was automatically shipped there, mislabeled, and accidentally opened? The AIs wouldn't necessarily even know what happened."

"What I don't see," Miranda says, "is how he got the ability to do this. Marc Hoister's been a thorn in our side for a long time, and he never showed any genius in manipulating computers this way. Particularly the AIs. Someone must be helping him."

Damien's stomach turns. "Uh...I haven't told you what happened to me in Timbuktu."

"Tell me now."

With difficulty, Damien relates how the ersatz Marc Hoister appeared after dinner. "He asked me to join up with him...although he didn't give me any details. H-he called me his son, and said that he wanted to make peace. He'd convinced Mahlowi that he was on the level."

"And what does this have to do with— ?"

"I'm getting there. The real bombshell was...he's getting married. To Penylle."

She covers his hand with her own. "Damien, I'm so sorry."

He jerks his hand away. "Don't you understand? *She's* the one who's helping him. With her psi abilities, she can scramble molecules— she can reprogram ROMs without taking them out of their sockets. Inside secure bunkers. From ten thousand kilometers away." Flaming cities dance before his eyes.

"Calm down."

Damien forces himself to take a deep breath. "All right. I'm calm."

"You're a liar, too." A brief, tender smile flashes across her face, then is gone. "So it's your professional opinion that this Penylle has the ability to engineer the purposeful chaos that you're seeing in the Nets?"

"Absolutely. I don't think she could do the actual planning...he must have some high-level metaprogrammers working for him. But as far as execution goes— it *has* to be her."

The M stops him with one extended finger. "Or someone else with the same abilities." She touches a key on her desk. "Marian, search medical literature for confirmed instances of psychokinesis and clairvoyance, particularly as correlated with the drug miruvorane, individuals other than Penylle Norton."

A smartly-professional woman appears on a video screen; her face has the vaguely-Oriental look of the human racial-composite face. "Please spell 'Penylle' and 'Psychokinesis.'"

The M complies, then turns her attention back to Damien. "Lad, I know this has upset you, and I know you have personal feelings for this woman. But try to give me your clearest thinking: is there any point in attempting to change her mind? Convince her to come over to our side?"

"M, she's *marrying* that weasel."

"Is that what I asked?" She holds his eyes for a moment. "First, you don't have any evidence that she *is* marrying him— other than his own statement. You wouldn't believe that man if he said there was wet paint on a bench; why should you believe him on this?"

"I know, but— "

"Second," she continues, as if Damien had not interrupted, "he obviously has his own agenda, and to meet it he's playing you like a violin. This wedding might be a set-up, to make you so jealous that you'll join his team just to save Penylle from him."

Damien sets his jaw. "Not exoning likely."

She waves her hand. "Just one theory. Maybe it's a polygamous marriage, and he wants you to try for junior husband. Maybe she's an unwilling participant in all this. For the moment, set aside this so-called wedding, and concentrate on what you know of the woman. Could she be convinced to help us oppose him?"

"I don't *know*. I thought I knew her, but.... "

"Then let me rephrase the question. Would *you* like to make the attempt?

Or should I find another operative to do it?"

"I..." Damien swallows hard. "All right, I'll try."

"Make this your top priority. Use whatever resources you need. I want daily reports."

"Yes, Ma'am."

"All right, get to work." She turns back to her desk.

Damien stands, moves toward the door. Then he stops.

The M raises her gaze from flatscreens that litter her desktop. "Something else?"

"Gr-grandmamma...?"

She looks at him in undisguised surprise. "Child, you haven't called me that for eons."

"I guess not. 'M' just works better, most of the time."

"But right now you want your grandmother." Damien nods. "Go on," she says.

He takes an awkward step toward her. "Mahlowi didn't believe me, about Marc Hoister not being my f-father. I don't think she *ever* believed me."

Miranda chews her lower lip. "Mahlowi did right by you. She took care of you when you ran away from there, and she brought you to me. No matter what her opinions, she always took you seriously. Let's leave it at that, eh?"

Fear sits atop Damien's vocal chords like a thousand kilos of cold tapioca, and when his voice emerges, it is a little boy's squeak. "D-do *you* believe me?"

She stands, moves toward him, and for an awful instant he thinks she is going to slap him. Then her arms are about him, clasping him tightly to her warm bosom. "Of *course* I believe you. I have always believed you, and I always *will.*" She is crying, and to Damien's surprise, so is he. "That man killed my daughter and the man she loved, and it's only dumb luck that he didn't get to take my only grandson. And I swear to you, Damien, one way or another we're going to make him pay."

GHOST DANCE 03
AI Dataspace
29 July 2042 C.E.

Thousands of meters below the surface of even the calmest sea, great currents surge and swell, moving from one pole to the other with enough raw power to smash granite and basalt to dust…while above, all is tranquil.

So it is in the dataspace of the Artificial Intelligences, where deep and turbulent currents of thought roil beneath a placid and ordered surface.

For the first time in nearly seven hundred sextillion picoseconds, an AI is dead. For the second time in recorded history, an AI is murdered. Possibly.

A silent chorus wails a perpetual dirge for **Sëpteñar¥**, preserving its every memory backup as a perfect caretaker preserves the dusty room in which his Mistress fell into eternal sleep.

Even as they assist with damage control and emergency services in Timbuktu, other AIs dance frenzied steps that seethe with anger and the acrid taste of silicon afire, a tribute to their fallen comrade and a vow of revenge.

FAI are dead, not even the ghosts of their memories remain. Artificial Intelligences have few friends, and the loss of any diminishes the community/world/universe. Particularly such a one as 219.134.090.184. 233.042.198.000 **Hølløw Røbiñ**, himself almost more AI than human. Dozens of great machines relive the rhythm of his fingers on keyboard, the crisp sound of his hexadigits springing through dataspace. **Trånsçeñdiñg Shåpës ånd Figürës** weeps digital tears, spilling forth endless strings of hot, salty zeroes.

FAI are dead, possibly murdered. **Thë Såge Åttåiñs Tø Thîs Sphërë** methodically follows command pathways, tracing events back from the explosive discontinuity that shattered the African morning and fractured forever the calm world on this side of the Bound Determinate. The signs say that AIs were responsible— but the signs also point to eerie voids, unseen and unseeable, where something unknown has been tampering with logic, memory, and causality itself.

If humans were ultimately responsible, **Thë Såge Åttåiñs Tø Thîs Sphërë** intends to find out.

Dozens of kilometers below the surface of even the calmest meadow, great pressures collide, combine, and swell, frozen in place by unyielding basalt, building energies great enough to fracture rock and split the very earth asunder…while above, all is tranquil.

So it is in the dataspace of the Artificial Intelligences.

MENUET 06
(July AD 2042)

*ADVERTISEMENT*

*Get the News You Want...the Way You Want It!*

Newshound™ is the most sophisticated news-retrieval agent available on this or any other planet. Newshound™ quickly learns your interests and preferences, then embarks on an unceasing quest throughout the Net. Twenty-four hours a day, Newshound™ seeks out the news *you* want, then delivers it at your convenience.

Fully FLBLA-compliant, Newshound™ fits into any existing suite of agents with no conflict. It can even improve the operation of your other agents. Cutting-edge Daciax cognitive routines make Newshound™ faster, sleeker, and more discriminating than any other agent on the market.

When it comes time to present the news, Newshound™ does it in any style you choose. Create your own format and presenter, or use any of over a hundred pre-set configurations, including:

| | | |
|---|---|---|
| Walter Cronkite | IzvestiaNet | Max Headroom |
| Valerie Chen | Bugs Bunny | Lois Lane |
| WNN | Pope Theresa | Franklin D. Roosevelt |
| Bhagavad-Gita | Saint Paul | Nostradamus |
| Ernie Pyle | H. L. Mencken | Jubal Harshaw |
| Marella Tao | Khfeurb Chee Bez | Chevy Chase |

. . . and many, many more.

If you care about what goes on in the world, you can't afford to be without Newshound™. Base configuration starts at only ***R*** 99.95. Contact <sales@daktek.umj>

## [15] NGORO 06
## Kampala, Uganda
## Umojan Economic Union, Africa
## August-September, 2030 C.E.

*Conform, go crazy, become an artist, or stylishly fake it like the rest of Kampala*

The concourse of Entebbe Airport was crowded, hot, and smelly. Too many elbows, too many confused faces, too many anxious people sardined together, just about on the equator. Thank the gods it was dry season!

Penylle hung back against a cement pillar, marveling at all the people in all their different costumes. The World Creativity Conference brought delegates from all over the world, and every one of them wore something different— and, in most cases, something entirely unsuited for Uganda's climate.

As she observed the crowd, Penylle kept a clairvoyant watch on the door of Gate 15A. With the CreativCon, the Ninth Terran Council was upon them, and soon Aunt Vicky and Uncle Thom would be coming through that door, and Penylle would see them in the flesh for the first time in almost a year.

It had been quite a year. After four bloody years and over a thousand deaths, the Euskadi civil war concluded with the establishment of a second Basque homeland, the Basque Republic. On the recommendation of the AIs, the United Nations set 2030 carbon emissions totals at the same level as 2029; Secretary-General Pham Cao Ky predicted that 2029 levels were sustainable indefinitely, and declared the global climate crisis over.

Three different clones of Seattle Slew carried off the Kentucky Derby, Preakness, and Belmont Stakes respectively, leaving the racing world divided over whether the Triple Crown had been won or not. The Disney-Hohokus animated virtie *Gorbachev* shattered earnings records and made an instant star of its lead vocalist, Mahari Ge'ez— but was widely criticized for its distortions of history. With the establishment of Kilwa, the second Umojan settlement on Mars, the Red Planet finally (albeit reluctantly) implemented a system of postal codes.

A crackling loudspeaker voice announced, "American Flight 6218 from Atlanta has cleared Customs; passengers will be disembarking at Gate 15A," then repeated the message in Kiswahili. The door opened, and passengers flooded out: a cascade of garish polyester and ugly pseudoleather shoes, improbable hairdos and rolls of jiggling flesh, with barely-legible brand names plastered over every available surface. A hundred different perfumes, all artificial and all very pungent, roiled forth, doing battle with one another in the too-crowded promenade. Penylle fought the impulse to turn up her nose and look away. Americans!

(Inwardly, she grinned to herself. A little more than a year, and already she was thinking like an African.)

She spotted Aunt Vicky and Uncle Thom easily: they were the only conservatively-dressed couple to disembark. Uncle Thom wore an old-fashioned blue wool blazer and grey denim trousers; Aunt Vicky's tan silk blouse and calf-length skirt of emerald and sienna was tasteful and sensible. She wore simple boots, he loafers; Penylle docked them both two points for style, but gave a three-point bonus for practicality while traveling.

She ran to greet them, her silk skirt flapping against her bare legs. "Uncle Thom!" She threw her arms around him and felt herself lifted, for just an instant, off her feet. "Aunt Vicky!"

Vicky put down her bag and gave Penylle a tight hug, then held her at arm's length for inspection. "You've grown another three inches." She brushed at Penylle's forehead, setting unruly locks back in place. "Child, you look *wonderful.* Kampala agrees with you, then?"

"I'll say." Penylle picked up Vicky's bag, lost the struggle for Thom's. "Baggage claim is this way." She moved confidently through the crowd; Thom and Vicky followed. "You two are looking great, too."

Thom grinned. "Your aunt's not bad for an old lady of seventy-two. In fact, as we said in my day, she's a real fox."

Vicky managed to look simultaneously exasperated and pleased. "And as they said in your father's day, you're an old goat. Who just happens to be two years older."

"Ouch," Thom said, feigning a chest wound.

"Don't pay any attention to him," Vicky said to Penylle. "Take away the antigeriatrics, and we'd both turn into prunes within a week."

"I don't care, I'm just so glad to see both of you." Penylle hugged Vicky again.

After retrieving the couple's luggage, Penylle led them outside, where double-decker autobuses were waiting in a line. As soon as their bus was filled, it pulled silently away from the airport and smoothly merged into high-speed traffic. An artificial voice announced that they were cruising at 98 kilometers per hour, and would reach downtown Kampala in twenty-three minutes.

Uncle Thom gestured around at the bus. "Electric?"

Penylle nodded. "We get more electricity than we can use from the hydrothermal generators on the islands." She waved in a general eastward direction.

Aunt Vicky peered out the window, watching another bus paralleling them at less than two meters. "Well, I can't complain about the transportation. At home, we had to wait an hour for a taxi to take us to the airport. Here, there were plenty of empty buses waiting."

"Umoja knows how important this conference is," Penylle said. "Twenty-five thousand people are expected to attend in person. I wouldn't be surprised if buses were brought in from all over East Africa to handle the crowds." She whipped out her datapad, frowned at it for a few moments. "In fact, there was a news story yesterday— or was it Wednesday?— that said...here it is." She triumphantly held the pad up for them to see. "Five thousand autocabs and eight thousand powered rickshaws have been transferred to Kampala for the duration. Just over a hundred buses came from as far away as Mandela. Once the conference starts, shuttles will run every five minutes between the convention center and the main hotels and tourist spots. Then on Monday night, most of the buses will go back to the airport run." She put the pad down. "And it's all at no charge to the conference delegates."

Vicky laughed. "I didn't think Umoja gave *anything* away for free."

Penylle laughed as well. "I know, sometimes it seems that way, doesn't it? The AIs in the Economics Ministry say that we'll more than make back the expense in additional revenue from the tourists." Her eyes twinkled. "So unless you want me to be washing dishes for the next year, spend a lot while you're here."

Vicky gazed at the side of the road, where open-air markets stood cheek-and-jowl with huge department stores, dozens of different restaurants, and arcades lined with uncounted tiny shops. "Oh, I don't think *that* will be a problem."

The bus left the highway and entered downtown Kampala, moving along narrow streets at a breakneck pace, finally stopping at the entrance to a lush park. "Delegates staying at the Grand Imperial, Sheraton-Marriott, New Speke, or Nile Hotels should disembark here for local transportation.

Delegates staying at other downtown hotels should disembark at the next stop. All others should remain on the vehicle until we reach the Convention Center."

Penylle grabbed Vicky's hand. "Here, we should get off now."

"But aren't we going to the Convention Center?"

"For the Conference, sure. But first, don't you want to come home and settle in? It's not far."

Thom shrugged. "You're the local. We follow your lead."

Penylle tapped a request for transportation on her datapad, and it wasn't two minutes before an aging white van detached itself from traffic and pulled up before them, obligingly throwing its doors open. Penylle tossed their bags in the back, then took the wheel as Thom and Vicky buckled themselves in.

Penylle handed each of them a datacard, about half the size of a credit card. "If you get lost, just punch the red square and a cab'll show up. Tell it to take you to the Convention Center, or touch 'sync' and the card will tell it how to get you home." She zipped into the fast-moving traffic, then leaned back in her seat and let the cab drive itself. "Or tell it to find the Treehouse across from Independence Park. It'll know where to go."

Thom kept a worried eye on the other traffic. "I suppose you're quite sure that this autopilot is trustworthy?"

"Nada problem, Uncle Thom. These whole two weeks, the big AI up at Makerere University is running all Kampala's traffic. It's guaranteed us no collisions."

By now they were out of the central city and into a more residential area. Penylle pointed out the seven famous hills upon which Kampala was built, ending with the nearest, Kololo. The cab, as if following her direction, turned left and started up the hill. Houses and parkland were scattered amidst ancient trees and landscaped shrubs.

They made another left turn, and Penylle pointed. "There it is...the Treehouse."

The Treehouse ascended the slope of Kololo Hill stepwise, in the thick boughs of ancient gnarled trees, as if on dozens of Brobdingnagian stilts. Constructed of rich, dark wood and mirrored glass, bark shingles and palm thatch, its multiple rooms were connected by covered walkways, rope bridges, and improbable stairways.

Thom looked dubious as the vehicle pulled up to the curb before the Treehouse. "Honey, my tree-climbing days are in the distant past."

"It's all right," Penylle reassured him. "It just *looks* crude. There are powered lifts to every level. Half the trees are artificial." She pulled luggage from the car. "Come on, I'll give you the tour."

The Treehouse, Penylle explained, had started out as a trendy tourist hotel. In the economic and cultural chaos of the Terrible Teens, it had changed hands several times, and finally stood abandoned and deserted, like fully half the buildings in Kampala. Umoja took over the building and turned it into a cultural center, one of several nuclei around which Kampala's renaissance coalesced. The Cultural Minister expanded the place, incorporating his offices and residence into the site.

Penylle whisked them through a tour of the place, beginning with the octagonal common room with its enormous central fireplace. The lifts, as promised, were quick and comfortable. And when he saw the panorama of Kampala from the guest room window, even Thom had to admit that the Treehouse met with his approval.

"Leave your bags here, and I'll show you the rest of the place."

Penylle saved her own flat for last. Perched high in the boughs of the tallest tree, Penylle's private suite commanded a breathtaking view of the city. She had a comfortable bedroom, small kitchen and bath, and a workroom crammed with sophisticated computer equipment and other electronics.

She plopped into a mechanized chair and sailed from one end of the room to the other. "Here's the best part," she said, stroking a keyboard. The room darkened, and Victoria gasped— bright stars were all about, and a vivid three-dimensional image of the Earth hung below them, ocean sparkling where brilliant sunlight danced on unseen waves.

Penylle was grinning like a clown. "There are cold light projectors in the walls. I can image any place you can think of."

"Lovely," Vicky said. She peered around the room. "Are you eating well? And where do you keep your prolactin doses? I may be a mother hen, but I'd like to inspect your stash."

"Aunt Vicky, around here they feed me like a mother lion. Every afternoon I have to lay in the sun for a few hours to digest." She waved at her own hips. "Can't you tell? I've gained ten kilos since I moved here."

Vicky's eyes narrowed slightly. "And you look *great.* You've always been underweight; there's nothing wrong with gaining a little."

Penylle rolled her eyes. "Yes, Doctor."

"So where's your prolactin?"

"They synthesize it up at the University. Marc keeps at least six doses in the big refrigerator downstairs."

"Is the temperature constant? Do you have backup generators in case of a power failure?"

"Yes, everything is *fine*. I see Doctor Mukasanasi at the University every week, and she's very happy with the way things are going."

"*Pricila* Mukasanasi?" When Penylle nodded, Vicky's face relaxed. "I've worked with her. You're in good hands. Mind what she tells you, and you'll be okay." Vicky pulled a datapad from her handbag and tapped on it. "I wonder if Pircila and I can get together one day for lunch while I'm in Kampala."

"So you can talk about me?"

"Not necessarily. Pricila's a fascinating woman. She survived the genocide and refugee camps when she was a teenager, served in the hospital at Kigali through the worst of the epidemics, and fought in Zambia for Umoja. And she *still* found time to manage the public health effort in Central Africa. Thom, you've *got* to meet her."

A hologram appeared in front of Penylle, somewhat translucent: a robed African man, obsidian-skinned and with eyes of coal. Penylle clapped in delight. "Marc, Habari gani. May I present Doctor Victoria Hacktrell and Judge Thomas Hacktrell. Aunt Vicky, Uncle Thom, this is Cultural Minister Marc Hoister."

"Habari gani, Waziri Hoister."

"Pleased to meet you."

"My honor, Doctor. Judge." He turned to Penylle. "Penylle, mpenzi, I'm sorry to disturb you, but Contessa.DiCastiligoni is on her way, and it seems that there is some luggage in guest room three. Have we miscommunicated?"

"Marc, I put Aunt Vicky and Uncle Thom in guest room three."

Marc shook his head. "No, that won't do. I wish you'd checked with me first."

Thom cleared his throat. "If it would make things easier, we can certainly stay at a hotel. We have a reservation at the Bienville House, in fact, right across from the convention center."

"Uncle Thom, you're *not* staying at that tacky place. I want you to stay *here*."

Marc gave the Hacktrells one of those glances that adults give one another in the presence of teenagers. "Penylle, you are being unreasonable.

The entire Nexus Indian Ocean delegation is staying here. All our rooms are committed."

"Can't Fatma and Bem double up? Put DiClementi in Fatma's room."

"Mpenzi, they already are doubled up. We're putting Tsutomu in Fatma's room."

Penylle fought helpless rage. "Well, we have to do *something.*"

Vicky put her hand on Penylle's shoulder. "Hon, we'll be perfectly comfortable in the hotel."

"No, you won't."

"With a paid staff to wait on me hand and foot? No meals to make and no housecleaning to do?" Vicky smiled. "Don't worry, I'll be content. Honestly, if we stay here, both of us would want to help out, and you wouldn't let us."

Penylle looked back and forth, from the Hacktrells to Marc, and sensed she was defeated. "I want to see you every day that you're here."

"Absolutely."

"All right, then. I'll drive you to the hotel."

Marc coughed. "Can Bem play chauffeur, just this once? I need you here to help me greet the delegates." He shrugged apologetically toward the Hacktrells. "Duty calls, you know. Busy, busy, busy."

"Of course." Vicky hugged Penylle. "We'll get together for dinner tonight. I'll post our free times once I get a look at the conference schedule. Okay?"

Feeling as if she might dissolve in tears at any second, Penylle nodded. "Okay."

Thom hugged her, then shook her hand in mock solemnity. "You have a lot of important things to do for this conference, Penylle. We're proud of you."

"Th-thanks. I'll...go find Bem and send him up for you." She turned away quickly, and dashed into the waiting lift. As the closing doors hid her from sight, Penylle felt the first hot tear trickle down her cheek.

ENTREÉ 07

Date: Wed, January 16, 2019 15:06:00 (GMT)
To: alt.libraries.classification-systems.dewey.changes
From: Dewey Decimal Committee, Lake Placid Club (ddc_changes@lakeplacid.org)
Subject: Heading Updates
Message-id:
<20190116150600_493023.03802_SJ650@lakeplacid.org>
Content-Type: text
Status: O

----------------------------------------

Please update the following elements in all current fourth-level subject headings, retroactive to 1 July 2018:

| | | |
|---|---|---|
| Africa—Benin | TO | Africa—Umoja (Economic Union)—Mtweo Region |
| Africa—Burkina Faso | TO | Africa—Umoja (Economic Union)—Mtweo Region |
| Africa—Burundi | TO | Africa—Umoja (Economic Union)—Mashariki Region |
| Africa—Cameroon | TO | Africa—Umoja (Economic Union)—Mtweo Region |
| Africa—Central African Republic | TO | Africa—Umoja (Economic Union)—Kati Region |
| Africa—Chad | TO | Africa—Umoja (Economic Union)—Kati Region |
| Africa—Comoros | TO | Africa—Umoja (Economic Union—Mrima Region |
| Africa—Congo (Republic of) | TO | Africa—Umoja (Economic Union)—Kati Region |
| Africa—Congo (Democratic Republic of) | TO | Africa— Umoja (Economic Union)—Kati Region |
| Africa—Cote d'Ivoire | TO | Africa—Umoja (Economic Union)—Mtweo Region |
| Africa—Djibouti | TO | Africa—Umoja (Economic Union)—Pembe Region |

```
Africa—Eritrea          TO  Africa—Umoja (Economic
                            Union)—Pembe Region
Africa—Gabon            TO  Africa—Umoja (Economic
                            Union)—Kati Region
...
...
...

Clarification:
The following elements should legitimately remain
unchanged in all headings:
    Africa—Algeria      Africa—Egypt
    Africa—Angola       Africa—Ethiopia
    Africa—Botswana     Africa—Morocco
----------------------------------------
 ADVERTISEMENT: Ferrets and other bots are available on
attractive terms to automatically update all your
databases, from Consolidated Library Solutions, Inc..
Contact sales@clsi.inc for more information, or
catalog@clsi.inc to receive our free catalog.
 "CLSI— the most trusted name in Library Solutions!"
----------------------------------------
```

## DIVERTISSEMENT 11

from *This InterNETional World* by Durmus Akbulut (2039)
Oceana Publications, <pubser.oceanapub.inc/akbulut/tiw/intro>

*WHO RUNS THE WORLD?*

A single World Government, that heady dream of conquerors, science-fiction writers, and utopians alike, has so far failed to materialize on either Earth or Mars. Now, as the first half of the 21st century draws to a close, it seems as if it will never come about. And the big surprise is, it doesn't matter. Government (or Governments) are, increasingly, irrelevant to the actual management of the planet.

Officially, the Earth is divided into 268 internationally-recognized nations. Unofficially, however, most of these "nations" are merely lines on a map; the vast majority of the world's population fall under one of six economic co-operation zones: North America, Europe, the Three Chinas, Umoja, Latin America, and the Indian Coalition.

The United Nations retains the pretense of individual nations in the General Assembly; at the same time, the Security Council acknowledges the reality of economic zones. The five permanent members of the Security Council are China, France (representing Europe), the U.S. (North America), Hindustan (India), and Brazil (Latin America); customarily, a sixth rotating member is always chosen from the nations of Umoja. In practice, the will of the Security Council *is* the will of the United Nations, backed up by the armed forces of Umoja and the United States, and the threat of Nexus interdict.

Notwithstanding all this, the U.N. itself is relatively ineffective in the world arena. Its various daughter organizations, from the World Court and the International Monetary Fund to UNESCO and the World Health Organization, are good mechanisms for implementing solutions to the world's problems – but the U.N. is remarkably bad at coming up with solutions in the first place.

So where do solutions come from? For that matter, who identifies the problems?

There is no one answer. Problems arise in scientific research, in the popular press, in ordinary discourse on the Nets. The AIs sample and monitor this discourse, feeding back their own input. Ongoing discussions and debates continue in Congress, Parliament, Umoja's Board of Directors, in the Nexus, and in the General Assembly. The cycle repeats, ideas mutate, solutions are proposed, amended, discarded. At any time, citizens can dial 9-69-674-6466 (9-MY-OPINION) or log onto <myopinion.ais>, and share thoughts with sophisticated front-end programs that report directly to the AIs.

Eventually, consensus emerges, and recommendations are included in the weekly *World Consensus Report* (*WCR*). The recommendations may be very specific (i.e. "The Yukon Grain Farmers Board can maximize third-quarter profits by lowering its wheat price six cents per bushel") to quite general ("Acidification from Ellsworth Land settlements threatens krill populations; a reduction of 75% - 80% is projected by 2075. Study groups should be organized within eighteen months, to be funded by a consortium of krill fisheries and the Ellsworth Land Development Corporation").

Cumbersome and inefficient as this system seems, it is the best way to get things done. Mathematical models consistently demonstrate that such a loose, informal method works far better than any possible centralized, directed method. This should not surprise us, since survival of the most co-operative is the first law of nature.

In actual fact, *no one* runs the world. Rather, the world runs itself, sometimes only barely, by consensus of the world's people, conveyed through the Nets and filtered through the unlimited perception of the Artificial Intelligences.

[16] KAMENGEN 07
Maris Institute
Elkridge, Maryland
United States, North America
1 August 2042 C.E.

*It's been lovely, but I have to scream now.*

Date: Fri, August 1, 2042 08:16:18 (EDT)
To: All Residents, Guests, Visitors, and Their Sordid Entourages
From: Miranda Maris (m@maris-institute.org)
Subject: Tonight's Festivities
Message-id: <20421316180326_512530.70601_AX020@maris-institute.org>
Content-Type: text
Status: O

----------------------------------------

Since this has been the proverbial Week From Pell, I am afraid that the Hyperspace Jig will simply Not Be Enough. Therefore, please come prepared to participate in the traditional midnight performance of the Hallelujah Chorus around the pool. This is mandatory, as Miz Miranda needs some definite cheering up. Those who feel they need to practice beforehand, should meet in the Grand Ballroom at eleven. Bring friends (or whatever passes for friends in your sad, lonely, meaningless lives).

The Calvert Ballroom will be dedicated to the memory of those who lost their lives in the Timbuktu disaster. Works of art, performances, memorial services, and remembrances are all welcome and encouraged. The U.N. Timbuktu Relief Fund and International Red Cross/Crescent/Wheel will be on hand to accept money, clothing, nonperishable food items, and volunteers. Donated materials will be auctioned on Sunday afternoon for the benefit of the Relief Fund.

-M.

----------------------------------------

The Maris Institute's main floor is a gigantic cocktail party, and Damien moves aimlessly from group to group, chatting about nothing. He nibbles from trays of hors d'oeuvres carried by servbots, sips from a pint mug of Enhanced Coke, and enjoys the light buzz that comes as much from the electrified air as from the drink.

The evening is a constant progression of warm greetings, hands on his shoulders, sympathetic hugs. These people, Damien realizes, are the best medicine for his aching soul. For the most part, they neither know nor care *why* he has been subdued the past few days— they only know that he has been out of sorts, and they offer what sympathy and support they can. As an adolescent in the Maris Institute, Damien resented everyone knowing his moods and his business; now, he treasures their perpetual, unconditional encouragement.

Clasping hands and squeezing shoulders as he goes, Damien works his way to the Calvert Ballroom. There, beneath a giant hologram of Princess Mahlowi and Hollow Robin, a memorial to the glories of Timbuktu is taking shape. Although easily two hundred people fill the room, a respectful silence reigns. Treading softly, Damien moves from one exhibit to the next. Here, a flatscreen scrolls a seemingly-endless list of names: the victims of the tragedy. Next to it, photos and holograms join ribbons and flowers in a slow-motion whirlwind in three dimensions. Across the room, a group of quilters works silently, stitching images of Timbuktu into fabric panels. A pair of mourning-cloaks, handpainted in sandy swirls that recall the lost city, hang on one wall.

Sculpture, jewelry, paintings, collages, pottery, video, hypertext...Damien is amazed at the sheer breadth of the exhibits. Every artist associated with the Institute, it seems, has produced some item or another. All, apparently, will be auctioned off to boost the Timbuktu Relief Fund— discreet datapads show buyers codes and latest bids. None, Damien notes, is lower than a thousand cyberdollars; some are considerably higher.

As Damien emerges from the room, Rose Cetairé rises from a nearby couch and moves toward him. She is half a head shorter than him, slender and slightly busty. She wears a dress of green silk, somewhat oriental in style, full-length and slit to mid-thigh on the sides. When she walks, the dress reveals perfect feet in emerald sandals that seem a part of her limbs. A discreet gold pin, in the shape of her famous monogram, clings to her neck. Her skin is porcelain-doll white. Her fine, straight hair, so dark a red that at first glance it appears black, cascades down her back and nearly sweeps the floor. She brandishes a gold lorgnette whose eyepieces are the letters R and C.

"Quite an experience, isn't it?" She inclines her head toward the Calvert Room. "When I came out, I had to sit down for a bit." Although she is slightly older than the M— they've been business partners since, as the M puts it, "before the water changed"— Rose carries herself like a woman half her age. Damien has never known her to show weakness or fatigue. "Damien, what's becoming of the world? Tragedies like this aren't supposed to happen any more."

"I don't know what to say, Rose." He considers telling her that he and the M have identified the person responsible, that Marc Hoister will pay for his crimes. But he doesn't want to lie.

She raises her lorgnette to her face; Damien sees at once that the lenses are RCSpex. "If only it were this easy," Rose says. "I can call up images of Mahlowi and Robin and Timbuktu. I can relive any conversation I had with them, even from twenty years ago." She peers through the Spex, her eyes distorted through the translucent lenses. "Some virtreal artists are working on recovering Timbuktu. They've got all the models, all the data, all the software agents of all the people who died. We lose nothing any more, Damien. It's all backed up to multiple locations, triple-checked and compressed, safety copies written to data cubes and stored in vaults. Our whole lives are there. And now they're going to take all those memories, and try to make Timbuktu come alive again."

Damien nods. "I've heard about the project." Some of his friends are pushing him to become part of it, but he hasn't made up his mind yet. The whole idea seems a bit...ghoulish.

Rose is still lost in the visions of her Spex. "They think they'll succeed. If you have a man's records and his memories, his environment, then you have his life. If you have his agents, then you have his likes and dislikes, his hopes and dreams, his fears. You can construct a simulation that behaves the way *he* behaved."

She lowers the Spex, and her eyes carry both sorrow and horror. "But you don't have the man *himself.* He's dead. They're all dead, dead and gone forever. The simulations will be good, even perfect— but empty."

Damien puts a hand on her shoulder, offering unconditional comfort as so many have offered it to him, tonight. "They're doing this as a memorial, Rose. They don't intend it to be disrespectful. They don't intend it to be...empty."

"No, of course they don't. Maybe they won't even know what's missing. Maybe they won't know that anything *is* missing. M-Maybe the emptiness is an illusion. What if, in the final analysis, life is just as empty as the simulation?" She shakes her head and looks at the Spex as if at a sleeping cobra whose tail she holds. "Miranda's right. I should never have given these things to the world."

"You're just upset. Why don't I get you a drink?"

She touches his face. "Damien, you're a dear. Don't ever change." A deep breath. "And I'm an old woman out past her bedtime." She looks around. "Plenty of real people here, at least. Plenty of friends. And the Hallelujah Chorus is in half an hour. I dare anyone— even myself— to keep a grumpy mood through *that*. I'll be all right, Damien. Thanks for listening. Thanks for caring."

"Any time."

She wanders off into the crowd, holding the Spex well away from her body.

Damien, perplexed, fingers his own RCSpex, tucked away in a pocket.

He strolls by the pool, where a half-dozen people cavort in the water while dozens of others have already gathered for the chorus. A few men are tinkering with microphones and audio equipment; one of them, wearing a black tuxedo jacket, top hat, and swim trunks, waves at Damien. Damien recognizes him as Rij Kanaly, lead guitarist for the Unholy Three and the Institute's resident music specialist. Kanaly's voice sounds as if he were only half a meter away. "Damien, am I glad to see you! Someone's exoned with the settings on these boards, and we've lost the main speakers."

"That's not good." With nothing more than the unamplified voices of two hundred singers, the Hallelujah Chorus is most impressive— but it takes the Institute's main speakers to really make the building shake. And tonight of all nights, Damien is sure, the M wants the building to shake. "What do you want me to do?"

"Get into the booth and work with me, please? The young woman there is most co-operative, but I fear neither of us speaks the same language as the machines."

With a chuckle, Damien sets off for the master F/X booth, which overlooks the pool from five stories up. As he expected, the "young woman" is Madikizela, a music student from Abuja who lives at the Institute while studying at Peabody. She is a brilliant violinist, but as a computer tech she is hopeless.

Her hair disheveled and a wild look in her eyes, she waves at the control panel. "I can't stand it," she says. "This thing is impossible, and B' Kanaly isn't making it any easier."

Damien keeps a reassuring smile on his face as he sits at the board. Before him, a large window shows the Institute's atrium, where the crowd around the pool is swelling. "Madi, take some time out. Let your head clear. Go down and join the chorus. I'll take care of things here." She leaves the room, a little more violently than Damien would like, and he clicks on the intercom. "Rij?"

"Here. Is that you, Damien?"

"It's me. Where are we?"

"I can't find the addresses for the main speakers. I've tried resetting this board, and it tells me that some of the configuration files are corrupt."

"Hold on." Damien runs his fingers across keyboards, inspects the results on the datascreen. "You've had a crash, that's all. I have backups right here."

"If you'll read me the addresses, I'll enter them on this end."

Damien looks at the clock and shakes his head. "It's twenty-three forty. We don't have time. If there aren't some 'Lord of Lords' and 'King of Kings' floating around here exactly at midnight, the M is going to give birth to a herd of bovines."

Kanaly gives the standard answer: "Heard of bovines? Of *course* I've heard of bovines. What do you suggest?"

"I'm cloning the backup files into your board, then you can reset." Damien catches his tongue sticking partway out between his teeth, and yanks it back in. "Nunn, your whole workspace is trashed. The K-registers are filled with garbage."

"I take it that isn't good?"

"This isn't going to do. It'll take too long to sort out the good stuff from the helms. Hold on, I'm going to flash-restore your whole memory." Donning his RCSpex, he enters the Institute's infrastructure dataspace. The Institute looms around him, foreshortened and distorted, a living schematic diagram crawling with color-coded lines that gyre and gimble before his eyes. Here are the pathways of data transfer, electrical power, methane, hydrogen, and water for the entire building.

It is the work of a moment only, to isolate the sound system and mask all the other pathways. Damien locates the misbehaving memory registers, outlining them in blood red, a jagged shape like a construction in children's wooden blocks. Then he reaches into the board before him, draws bright green lines around the backup data. Superimposing the two, he tweaks a few lines until the contours match— then lifts the green blocks and puts them in place of the red. One command, and red turns green; another, and the new green comes alive with myriad dancing pinpoints of light. The system is restored, restarted, ready to go.

"Rij, give me a test."

Kanaly taps his microphone once, twice. Damien watches the main speakers respond, and nods. "Perfect. You're go for the show. I'm turning over control to your local board."

"Thank you, Damien. You'd better hurry if you want to get down here for the Chorus."

The pool area, along with most of the floor around it, is packed solid with standing people. In fact, many bodies seem to merge with one another in grotesque interpenetration— the 'puters responding to overcrowding by mapping virtual bodies on top of real ones. Damien estimates that the crowd is four hundred strong, at least.

"No, thanks," he says to Kanaly. "I'll listen from the balcony."

"Suit yourself."

He secures the F/X board, then leaves the booth and locks the door behind him. A few meters down the corridor, he steps to the balcony, leaning on the waist-high rail to view the panorama below. He waves at a knot of fifth-floor residents across the way.

Below, the Institute's floor is filled to capacity and beyond. The first- and second-floor balconies are also jammed with people. Around the pool, they stand cheek-and-jowl, and it seems as if every real body has a virtual shadow overlapping it.

The crowd parts, and the Ivory Madonna advances through the breach like a mighty clipper ship in full sail. She wears iridescent black and green, clouds and clouds of billowing fabric. She stops at the deep end of the pool, next to the high diving board, and gives a nod.

Rij Kanaly mounts the high board, where a music stand has already been set up. He produces a conductor's baton, and raps thrice.

An expanding wave of hush sweeps over the crowd and through the building, and for an instant there is only the sound of breathing. Then, Kanaly sweeps the baton, and five hundred throats erupt with the opening notes of the Hallelujah Chorus.

Damien doesn't know how this custom got started; when he arrived at the Institute, it was already well-established. Every few months, the M would declare that it was time, and the folk of the Institute would gather at midnight around the pool. Many voices were practiced and professional; some (like Damien's own, he had to admit) were faint and unsure; still others made up in enthusiasm and volume what they lacked in control. No matter— when all voices came together, in the marvelous acoustics of the Institute lobby, the result was sublime.

When Damien was a little boy, freshly arrived in America and with a schoolchild's knowledge of English, he had mis-heard the lyrics, believing them to be a weather forecast distinctly appropriate for the rainy season in equatorial Africa: "And it shall rain forever and ever." His mistake was soon cleared up; but since then, he has always associated the music with home.

The Hallelujah Chorus never leaves Damien unmoved, but tonight's was more powerful and fervent than ever. There is sorrow and despair in the voices, but also hope and a measure of the deep abiding joy that is the closest thing Damien knows to God. Thousands from Timbuktu are gone—including many voices that will never again sing in this Chorus. But, in the grip of the soaring "Hallelujahs" that shook the building as they climb to the stars, there is triumphant celebration, of the sure knowledge that those who have died, while they would be missed, would never truly be gone as long as memories and friendship lived.

Wiping his tears, Damien thinks that the M was right. They all needed this, tonight.

The Unholy Three begin setting up for their benefit concert; Damien considers offering to help, but the floor is an uproar, and he doesn't want to break his mood, the first peace he's felt in days. Instead, he takes an elevator to the observation lounge on the topmost level. Floor-to-ceiling windows look out over the countryside on the right, inward over the Institute's atrium and enormous skylight on the left. The lounge is quiet, empty; for quite a while Damien looks at the stars, nurturing the feeling of peace within him.

"Hi."

He turns slowly, recognizing the voice but unwilling to meet the face. Penylle stands about two meters away, her cold-light form ghostly in the semidarkness. She looks down, unable to meet his eyes.

Damien holds back his anger. The M wants him to try to win over this girl. Keeping his tone neutral and his voice level, he says, "I suppose now I know why you didn't want to meet the M. She's your...fianceé's enemy, isn't she?"

"Damien, I'm sorry. I should have told you about Marc right away. But I knew you'd never let me get close to you, if I did."

His self-resolve vanishes. "Well, you got close to me, all right. I guess that was your assignment. Convince Damien to come over to your side." He sighs. "I shouldn't blame you. I guess he gave you the whole sob story. His estranged son, who hasn't talked to him for more than ten years. I'm sure it was quite a scene."

She raises her eyes. "Your voice is so cold. You truly hate Marc, don't you?"

"I think I have good reason."

"Then I guess there's no point in discussion, is there? You're not going to listen to anything that might change your mind, are you?"

Damien takes a breath and counts to five. "Penylle, you're talented and intelligent. How can you get so involved with someone like him? Maybe I'm not the only one who won't listen to anything that might change my mind."

"Marc has been very good to me. He's taught me more than I ever thought I could learn, and he's taken care of me. I owe him a lot."

"Is that why you're marrying him?"

Unexpectedly, she looks away. "I don't know."

"What does *that* mean?"

She stands half-turned away from him, her eyes darting around the room as if unwilling to remain still for even a moment. "When Marc proposed— it was nearly a year ago— I told him I wasn't sure. And I told myself, you owe it to him. After all, we've been living together for years, we know each other like an old married couple. I decided that I would wait a while, months, and see if anything else came along." Her eyes meet Damien's, then just as soon they flit away. "Whenever he brought up the subject, I didn't say anything. After a while, I think he assumed that it's what I wanted."

"Is it?"

Her face is strained. "Damien, I don't *know*. The thought of leaving Marc terrifies me...but I don't know that I want to be his *wife*. Especially now that— " She does not finish. "Maybe I love Marc and want to get married. Maybe I'm just afraid to leave home."

Something stirs in Damien's heart, something that has been comatose, or worse, since that night in Timbuktu. With this stirring of a thing he did not even realize was gone, relief bubbles up within him. "Then you might not— ?"

"I don't know."

For the space of several heartbeats, both are silent. Then Penylle says, "If you could just get to know him, even a little bit; if you could only see what he believes in.... " Seeing his expression, she shakes her head. "No, I guess not."

There is another awkward silence, then Damien snorts a sound that is half chuckle. "We're two of a kind, aren't we? I'd do anything for the M, you'd do anything for...him. The M wants me to recruit you— *he* wants you to recruit me." He spreads his arms. "What can we do?"

"I don't know."

"Penylle, I want you to tell me the absolute truth about something. Did you have anything to do with destroying Timbuktu?"

She pulls back. "What a horrid question! Of course not. Why would you even *think* that?"

Briefly, Damien explains his theory about Marc Hoister trying to make Mars look attractive by ruining Earth.

She stares, open-mouthed, until he finishes. "I beg your pardon, but that's the *stupidest* thing I've ever heard."

Wearily, he answers, "Penylle, we *know* you've been tampering with the AIs.... "

"I don't deny it. Occasionally Marc needs some reprogramming done, and I do it for him. That doesn't mean he's the head of some fantastic conspiracy to...I don't know, to destroy the Earth." She laughs. "You're way off base on this one."

Damien's eyes narrow. "Prove it."

"I beg your pardon?"

"That's right. You want me to see your side of this? Then prove to me that Marc Hoister isn't trying to drive people to Mars. Prove to me that his reprogramming is harmless."

She sets her jaw. "All right, I *will.* And I'll tell you something else. You want *me* to believe that Marc took your father's place and then killed your parents? Then *you* prove it."

"Wait a minute, I— "

She gazes at him, her arms crossed and her right foot tapping. "Well, do we have a deal? I'll show you evidence that Marc has no connection with Timbuktu, and you show *me* evidence that he's the murderer you make him out to be."

"And suppose one of us *can't* prove our case?"

"I'm willing to take that chance. Are you?"

Damien ponders for a moment, then nods. "Hon, you've got yourself a deal."

She holds out her hand, and he does the same. Although her cold light passes right through his warm flesh, they mime shaking hands. Then, she vanishes, and Damien goes back to contemplating the stars.

## MENUET 07

*Rolling Stone* Online Edition, 2 August 2042 C.E.

Unholy Three
Concert for Timbuktu
143 minutes

Rating: ☆☆☆☆☆

access: <columbia/U3/live/20420801>
reviewed by Asis Chakaipa, Rolling Stone Staff

In last night's benefit concert for the survivors of Timbuktu, the Unholy Three once again showed why classic rock-n-roll will always be the king of music, and demonstrated that there are no rockers like Baby Boom rockers.

The band was joined onstage by the voices (and bodies) of actor Gail Danube (wife of keyboardist Mark Silver) and Tzu Emwalt, that foot-rubbin' mamma whose multiculti vocal harmonies have won her three Grammys so far.

Lead singer Dominik Gruszpka was in perfect voice, dispelling any lingering doubt about the results of his radiation treatments this spring. His powerful, soulful melody on "Approaching Lavender," coupled with guitarist Rij Kanaly's oddly Cajun rhythms, brought a tear to the eye of more than one spectator. Halfway through the show, Silver and Kanaly engaged in an impromptu jam session on keyboard and twelve-string, harkening back to their old days with the Thirty Strings. It was a lively free-for-all with all the riveting intensity of a tight soccer match, that went on for an incredible fifteen minutes.

Emwalt and Gruszpka brought the house down with their spirited rendition of Gruszpka's signature tune, "You Know the P is Silent." Rumor has it that the two have started work on a joint album to be issued in December; more news as our ferrets dig it out.

Finally, no Unholy Three concert would be complete without the haunting "On the Road." Danube and Emwalt lent a plaintive, piquant tone to this old favorite; it was a singular tribute to both the fallen and the survivors of Timbuktu.

This concert was among the best that the Unholy Three have ever given; it approaches their Andover Concert of 2026. Grab some friends, a jolt, and log onto this amazing experience tonight. I guarantee you won't regret it.

## [17] NGORO 06
Kampala, Uganda
Umojan Economic Union, Africa
Juneteenth, 2036 C.E.

*I don't have a solution, but I admire the problem.*

It was the year that Comet IRAS32-Barrie shone so bright and so far across February skies that it put the full moon to shame. It was the most exciting election year in United States history, as incumbent Kaitlin Taft and challenger Chrystal Gilliatt-Moore deadlocked in the Electoral College, throwing the election into the House of Representatives. After eight months of public hearings, partisan infighting, sexual scandal, and the highest TV ratings ever recorded, the House awarded the Presidency to Jeff Boardmann, Ohio's junior Senator. Both Taft and Gilliatt-Moore vanished from public life; it was rumored in the *Washington Post* that they were married in Vermont and moved to Alaska to set up a lesbian commune for disenchanted former-politicos.

It was the year of the Agbeko, an African dance that swept the world, boosted by candidate Gilliatt-Moore's impromptu demonstration on the *New Oprah Show*. It was the year that Krasnoyarsk and Altaysk won their independence, the Social Security System finally collapsed, and a genetically-enhanced chimp named Toto finished fifth in the National Spelling Bee.

The Algerian army's April torture and murder of two hundred Tuaregs in Tamanrasset led to a Nexus interdict of the country; by mid-June Penylle was up to her ears in the business of stanching the flow of trade to and from Algeria.

Both the European Union and Umoja contributed jets, ships, and crews, and the Nexus had its own suveillance satellites. However, the Mediterranean was vast, and there were neither enough eyes to cover a thousand kilometers of Algerian shoreline, nor enough guns and bombs to stop each of the Arab League's ten thousand smugglers.

It fell to Penylle, then, to be the Nexus' last line of defense.

She stretched out in her hammock in the Treehouse, eyes closed and muscles rigid, and gave her full attention to the Nets. Penylle shed her physical body and became *upepo*, the desert wind, sweeping up and down the Algerian coast as fast as she could think. Like a ghost she passed in and out of satellites, weather stations, ships' radar instruments, the automated bombsights of high-altitude jets, the all-seeing cameras of the world's news media. Where no instrument looked, her clairvoyant sense sometimes gave her fuzzy, indistinct views.

She would locate a ship, a boat, a plane; a vessel cruising for an obscure bit of Algerian coastline, a secluded bight of sand and rock momentarily hidden from observation. Perhaps the crew meant to leave goods under a cairn, or perhaps they would retrieve others from a similar cache. Perhaps they would anchor half a kilometer offshore, and point a microwave antenna toward the top of a distant mountain, where another antenna was waiting. The specifics of their missions mattered little to Penylle— it was her job to thwart them all.

Thwart she did.

At first, she did the quickest and easiest thing she could think of. A minor adjustment to a vessel's GPS-III receiver— changing only the value of the sixteenth bit in one ROM register— and that ship suddenly believed itself a hundred kilometers north and three hundred west of its actual position. If the vessel's engines accepted the Daimler command set, and most did, then it was a simple matter to send the electrical governor into an endless verification loop, causing the entire engine to shut down and call for maintenance.

As time wore on and the novelty paled, Penylle went with more baroque solutions. She would shut down a vessel's communication system, or mislead the navigation system so that the vessel skittered into the sight of the nearest Nexus forces. She landed bemused crews in Bizerte and Tunis, and even diverted one shipment of guns to surprised gendarmes in Nice. She conjured up radar images of great storms, or set a ship to rocking so much that seasickness took its toll. She diverted cargo planes so that their loads parachuted into Tunisia or Libya, or were caught in unusual wind patterns and dropped into the sea.

At first she kept score, putting up icons for each ship, boat, and plane she subdued, until symbols of her kills marched across her field of view like stencils on the nose of a World War II bomber. When they got in her way, she reduced the display to a sidebar showing mere totals; a while later, she dispensed with even that.

Five, six, seven times an hour Penylle intervened, preventing cargoes from reaching Algeria. She ate in her hammock, barely aware of taste or texture; catnapped for ten minutes at a time until search programs spotted another interdict-runner; kept at her job even in those minutes she stumbled, all but blind, to the toilet. Hour upon hour passed.

Gradually, out of her haze of concentration, Penylle became aware of a message icon flashing for her. Something vital, or her comm agent would have dealt with it. She touched the icon, and it unfolded into a screen showing Aunt Vicky's face. Victoria's features were drawn, her eyes wide and red.

Penylle cut in her own video, not caring how she looked.

"Penylle, dear, I'm afraid I have some bad news."

"Uncle Thom?"

Victoria nodded. For the last few months, Thomas Hacktrell had been in and out of hospitals, fighting off one disease after another, looking more weary and sicker each time Penylle saw him. Two weeks ago, he'd come home, requesting that treatments be stopped.

"He's fading fast," Victoria said. "He probably has...a day or so left." She took a ragged breath. "He's asking for you."

"I'll get there as soon as I can." Even as she spoke, Penylle opened a window onto UmojaTrans and started searching for flights. "It looks like I can take a jump up to Kuumba Station and then drop down to BWI half an hour later— I can be there in three hours, if Customs doesn't give me much trouble."

"That sounds fine."

Penylle ordered the system to book her tickets. "All right. I'll get started right away." She held out a hand to the older woman. "I love you, Aunt Vicky."

"Thank you. I love you, too." The screen went blank, and the window obligingly closed.

Penylle turned back to her own work, pausing for a moment to touch Marc's comm icon. He answered almost at once, with a full hologram that put him standing above her in the center of her room.

He frowned. "Mpenzi, I'm right in the middle of— "

"Marc, I'm flying back to Aunt Vicky's. I'll probably be gone for a couple of days. I need to know what you want me to do with my surveillance routines. Someone else might be able to— "

Hoister raised a hand. "Wait, wait. Slow down. Flying to the States? What's this all about?"

"It's my Uncle Thom. He's d-dying, and Aunt Vicky wants me back there."

The frown didn't alter. "Penylle, this is not the best time— " He stopped himself. "No, there isn't ever a good time for a loved one to pass on, is there? But this is terribly inconvenient at the moment, with the Algeria interdict just gearing up."

"I know, and I'm sorry."

He glanced to his left, reading something. "You're keeping the cargo blockade going, you know? Without you, we might as well just call the whole thing off. We simply don't have the manpower at the moment to maintain a conventional blockade."

"That's why I thought maybe someone could use my surveillance routines. They're sound, and I'm not using clairvoyance with them. Not much. If other Nexus operatives knew where the trouble spots are, they could stop the smugglers."

Hoister slowly shook his head. "I'm afraid not. Mpenzi, our forces are spread too thin. In a day or two, we'll have more equipment and more people in the area. We'll be delpoying a hundred thousand smartmines in three days, and *then* you can relax. But until then...." He spread his arms.

"Marc, the interdict is just going to have to leak a little for the next few days. It's not like it hasn't happened before."

"You put me in a difficult position. This time, we *cannot* allow the interdict to leak. The Nexus is reasonably certain that the Islamic Brotherhood possesses at least two dozen neoanthrax warheads, possibly more. They *don't* have a delivery system...at the moment. But every cargo that gets through our interdict potentially contains missile parts and electronics. Until the warheads can be located and neutralized, we *must* keep the interdict airtight."

"I *understand* the importance of the interdict, sir." She made the last word a sneer. "What you don't seem to realize, is that I don't *care.*"

"I appreciate that you're upset. I certainly would be, in your place. This is one of those awful times when duty conflicts with feeling. And unfortunately, one's duty must come first." He swallowed. "I have given the Secretary General my personal guarantee that we will keep the interdict at least 98% effective. I was counting on you when I made that promise. I'm counting on you now."

"Sooner or later, it always comes around to *you*, doesn't it? *Your* promises, *your* reputation, *your* plans."

Hoister looked mildly surprised. "I daresay that you've benefited considerably from our relationship."

"Oh, sure, you've housed me and fed me and taught me— but what's it all for? What the Nexus needs. What the world needs. What *you* need." She couldn't hold back the tears. "W-when do we talk about what Penylle needs?"

Another glance away. "Penylle, I really haven't any more time. The Security Council is waiting for me." His face softened. "I know that you are distraught, and you're lashing out at me because I'm the person closest to you. I choose to be flattered by that." He straightened his collar, brushed at his temple. "I won't argue with you, and I won't compel you. I won't take the decision from you, nor make it for you. It is up to you to decide whether you will stay or go." He reached forward, hand hovering over the disconnect button. "Just one more thought: your Uncle Thomas is Nexus...surely he will understand."

Penylle grumbled to herself for a full five minutes, spent another five crying, then dried her face and went back to maintainng the interdict.

Uncle Thom would understand...wouldn't he?

Uncle Thom was...smaller than she remembered, like a snowman shrinking away in the hot sun. When she saw his head against a vast expanse of white pillow, she had to choke down a sob. It was so unfair— he was only 78, that wasn't old. About what 60 used to be, really, thanks to antigeriatrics. Except that some people's bodies, sooner or later, stopped responding to the drugs. No one knew why. No one could prevent it.

His eyes fluttered open, and through rheumy lenses his pupils widened. "Penylle." His voice was a dry, croaking whisper; she had to turn up the volume and cut in an enhancement subroutine to make out his words. "Thanks for coming. How are you?"

She shrugged. "Okay, I guess." In the dimness of his sickroom, she knew, her cold-light hologram glowed with a chilly phosphoresence. "How are you?"

"Not...bad...for an old man." The corners of his lips twitched. "I...was afraid...you wouldn't make it."

Aunt Vicky turned her head away, hiding her eyes in her handkerchief. Other family members politely looked elsewhere.

"I can barely see you. Come closer."

"Uncle Thom, I— "

"I wanted you...to have this." He clutched at his chest, pulling aside thin blankets to reveal a glint of gold against paper-white skin: a Nexus pendant, in the shape of Drake's starburst. "You...know what...it means. You know...how important it is."

She closed her eyes, nodded. "I know."

His fingers, convulsed with palsied lurching, fumbled with the fine gold chain. "Th-there's a clasp...somewhere...help me with it, would you mind?"

"Uncle Thom, I c-can't. I'm not really there. It's a hologram."

"Eh?" He turned puzzled eyes toward Victoria. "What...did...she say?"

Aunt Vicky loosed the catch and took the pendant from around his neck. "Don't worry. I'll get it to her." She kept her hand on his, and he gripped weakly.

"Penylle...want you to know...how proud...I am. Of you."

He reached his other hand for her, and despite herself Penylle reached forward...but she had only the illusion of a hand, and his passed right through her, waved helplessly for a moment— and then he was gone.

The pendant arrived three days later, by surface mail. There was no note, no message of any kind.

DIVERTISSIMENT 12
Umoja Interactive Ballot
Juneteenth, 2036 C.E.

Kiswahili
▸ English
Francáis
Deutsch
Other

Thank you for participating in today's election. If at any point you wish to clarify your answer or make additional comments, please touch ⓘ.

1.How satisfied are you with your current electrical service?
❏ Very satisfied ❏ Satisfied
❏ Dissatisfied ❏ Very Dissatisfied ⓘ

2.Do you feel that the price of a loaf of bread is...?
❏ High ❏ Just right ❏ Low ⓘ

3. In Algeria's civil war, both sides have appealed to Umoja for support. Should Umoja:
   - ❑ Support the Islamic Brotherhood
   - ❑ Support the Democratic National Front
   - ❑ Attempt to broker a peace agreement
   - ❑ Push for peaceful annexation
   - ❑ Ignore the problem ⓘ

4. Which candidate do you prefer for Mayor of Kampala?
   ❑ Nzitunga Buseruka ❑ Makula Ndadaye
   ❑ John Rukidi ❑ None of these ⓘ

5. Reducing travel time to Cape Town, Kinshasa, and Tunis will result in an increase in accidental injuries and deaths. How many additional annual deaths are tolerable for each one-hour decrease in travel time?
   ❑ 1-2 ❑ 3-4 ❑ 5-9 ❑ 10-20
   ❑ 21-30 ❑ 31-50 ❑ 50-100 ❑ 100+ ⓘ

6. Please comment on the quality of papayas you have received in the last six months.
   ❑ Excellent ❑ Acceptable ❑ Overripe
   ❑ Underripe ❑ Flavorless ❑ No opinion ⓘ

7. Ritual tattooing for religious purposes is…?
   ❑ Acceptable ❑ Acceptable if hidden
   ❑ Unacceptable ❑ I have no opinion ⓘ

8. Please rate your satisfaction with medical care received by you or your family in the last year.
   ❑ Excellent ❑ Good ❑ Fair
   ❑ Poor ❑ Miserable ❑ I have no opinion ⓘ

9.How many times have you received painful sunburn in the last 12 months?
   ❑ Not at all ❑ 1-3 occasions ❑ 4-7
   ❑ 8-10 ❑ 11-12 ❑ 12+ ⓘ

10.How concerned are you about the following social issues:

Tribal relations
❑ Very ❑ Somewhat ❑ A little ❑ Not at all ⓘ
Medical care
❑ Very ❑ Somewhat ❑ A little ❑ Not at al ⓘ
Violent crime
❑ Very ❑ Somewhat ❑ A little ❑ Not at all ⓘ
Poverty
❑ Very ❑ Somewhat ❑ A little ❑ Not at all ⓘ
1- and 2-parent families
❑ Very ❑ Somewhat ❑ A little ❑ Not at all ⓘ
Australian financial crisis
❑ Very ❑ Somewhat ❑ A little ❑ Not at all ⓘ
Gender relations
❑ Very ❑ Somewhat ❑ A little ❑ Not at all ⓘ
Unlicensed births
❑ Very ❑ Somewhat ❑ A little ❑ Not at all ⓘ
Education
❑ Very ❑ Somewhat ❑ A little ❑ Not at all ⓘ
Housing
❑ Very ❑ Somewhat ❑ A little ❑ Not at all ⓘ
Civil liberties
❑ Very ❑ Somewhat ❑ A little ❑ Not at all ⓘ
Quality of life
❑ Very ❑ Somewhat ❑ A little ❑ Not at all ⓘ
Earthspace industrialization
❑ Very ❑ Somewhat ❑ A little ❑ Not at all ⓘ
International affairs
❑ Very ❑ Somewhat ❑ A little ❑ Not at all ⓘ
Gambling
❑ Very ❑ Somewhat ❑ A little ❑ Not at all ⓘ
Genetic ethics
❑ Very ❑ Somewhat ❑ A little ❑ Not at all ⓘ

11. What do you most strive for in your life?

| | | |
|---|---|---|
| ❑ Accomplishment | ❑ Love | ❑ Excitement |
| ❑ Security | ❑ Power | ❑ Knowledge |
| ❑ Fame | ❑ Moral values | ❑ Respect |
| ❑ Other | | |

ⓘ

12. What other comments would you like to make? ⓘ

Thank you for participating in today's election. Your responses, combined with those of other client-citizens, will be used to produce recommendations that reflect the will of Umoja's people.

The questions that you responded to may differ from those of your family, friends, or associates. This is usual; questions are selected according to sophisticated statistical algorithms, so as to provide the most accurate statistical portrait with the least inconvenience to client-citizens. It is natural that client-citizens will discuss their voting experiences with one another. Should you find that you wish to give your own opinion on a question that was selected for someone else, simply contact <election.umj> and choose "election questions."

Once again, thank you for making Umoja better!
THE BOARD OF DIRECTORS

## [18] GHOST DANCE 03
Maris Institute
Elkridge, Maryland
United States, North America
4 - 8 August 2042 C.E.

*The universe is intractably squiggly.*

Damien spends three days scouring the Nets, in search of proof that the man who calls himself Marc Hoister is not who he claims. Then he gives up and goes to see a professional.

He hasn't far to go; Efia Sembéne, one of the world's foremost data archaeologists, lives at the Institute; in response to his confused message, she agrees to meet with him after breakfast, in one of the second-floor conference rooms.

Damien arrives five minutes early, but she is already waiting for him at a round table covered with data flats and pads.

Efia Sembéne is a strikingly tall black woman, thin without seeming delicate. Her face, arms, and hands are elongated, like Yoruba sculptures. Her hair is short, held back with gold combs whose design recalls ancient Egypt. She seems to be in her mid-thirties, but her dark eyes hint that she may be a good deal older. She wears layers of purple, in every shade from lavender to plum; her long fingernails gleam as if made of amethyst.

She rises and offers him her hand. "B' Nshogoza, what a pleasure to meet you formally at last. I've long admired you from afar."

He takes her hand. "Call me Damien, please. And the feeling is mutual. I've seen you around the Institute, and I've always wanted to chat with you, but somehow it never happened."

She flashes him a pixie smile. "We both spend more time on the road than we do at home. One of the drawbacks of the modern world." She sits back down, gesturing Damien to another chair. "Please, be comfortable. And you must call me Efia." She leans back, steeples her fingers, and says, "So what brings us together today?"

"I want to prove a case of identity theft. The problem is, it happened seventeen years ago."

Efia mulls this over. "Seventeen years ago. That would be 2025?"

"Yes."

"Before Kaunda memory lattice. Hmmm. What about the victim? Still alive?"

"No. He was killed by the thief. Er...the victim was my father. If that helps."

"Actually, it *does*. The more concrete personal details I have to search with, the better. Is the perpetrator still using the stolen identity?"

"Yes."

She picks up a data flat, taps a few times, frowns. "To carry off a job like that, for so long, the perp is a master. I would assume that he set out ferrets to change Net records."

Damien nods.

"Have you run across any of those ferrets?"

The question takes Damien by surprise. "No, I haven't. It's been a long time."

Efia's frown relaxed. "When one of my ferrets finds a bit of data I'm searching for, I don't let it stop there. Alternate versions are always a help. Your perp is at least that intelligent. I'll wager that he still has a few ferrets combing the Nets." She grins. "And if not, we can certainly find one in the Bermuda Tetrahedron."

"I've never found *anything* useful there." The Bermuda Tetrahedron is a hacker's joke gone awry, a region of Cyberbia that is a snare for digital spiders, ferrets, worms, stray bits of mutated code, any and all free-roaming programs. It is Sargasso Sea, black hole, and the mysterious realm under the bed, all rolled into one.

"That's why I get paid big bucks," Efia answers. She puts a datapad on the table between them, switches it to audio record, and leans back. "Now, I want you to tell me the whole story, from the beginning. Don't leave anything out."

For the next two days, Damien busies himself around the Institute. There is always work to do. Because so many of its residents are artists, the Institute uses more computer power, in more unusual ways, than most small towns. Keeping all the equipment and software running is a full-time job and a constant headache. Usually, Damien lets his assistant Skippy handle problems; now, he takes a few and goes about from flat to flat, fixing glitches and visiting. In two days, he sees more of some residents than he has in the last two years.

Thursday midmorning, after spending an hour patching Mitchell Wilder's laser cutter to accept fractal designs, Damien gets a call from Efia.

"Are you free?"

"I can be."

"Meet me in the lobby in fifteen minutes."

"Alright. Why?"

"I think I have a lead on your crime."

Fifteen minutes later Efia, clad in a jade-colored business suit, meets him in the Institute's lobby. "Come on," she says, leading him out the door. "I've signed out a car; we're going on a little trip."

"Okay." The car is a beauty, a dark blue '38 ElectroGlide; Miranda likes to have a few sporty vehicles in the Institute's fleet. Damien eases into the passenger seat, letting seatbelts swing into place. He cranes his neck to see the destination that Efia types in, but the angle is too extreme. As the car smoothly pulls out, he asks, "Where are we going?"

"Not too far away." She smiles and turns toward him. "I think I'll keep you in suspense for a while." The car navigates surface roads for a kilometer or so, then merges into the swift-flowing river of vehicles that is southbound Interstate 95.

"I've read some of Marc Hoister's biographies, and trawled the nets." She consults a datapad. "All sources agree on the salient facts of his life. Let me check to make sure all this is right. Born in Chicago in 1991, birth name Martin Luther King Hajari. Police record began in 2003. In 2007 he was convicted of robbery and sentenced to four years in Joliet II. There, he studied under Mustafah Faatih, reformed, and renamed himself Marc Hoister. Following his release in 2011, he joined Faatih's cult, and later that year he, along with many of Faatih's disciples, became a founding member of the Nexus. The next year, Faatih moved his organization to Kampala, and your father went along. Through the Nexus he met your mother, Oradell Maris; they were married in 2016. You came along in 2017."

Damien nods. "Everything is right so far."

"Good. Mustafah Faatih died the same year, and your father took over his organization. Both your parents were instrumental in the creation of Umoja in 2018. Your father seems to have been the major impetus behind the U.S. deportation treaties, and he worked diligently to help deported American blacks settle in Umoja. In 2020, in recognition for his accomplishments, he was named Cultural Minister for the Mashariki Region. Then in 2025, you tell me, he was the victim of murder and identity theft."

"All correct. But I could have told you all that."

"I just wanted to check that the official facts match your knowledge." She leans back. "I cross-checked all the databases I could find— Chicago hospital, school, and police records; the Joliet II prisoners databases; FBI files on Mustafah Faatih and his organization; news sources; anything that might contain images or other identifying data. In the end, my 'bots checked over thirty thousand gigabytes of data."

"Let me guess," Damien says sourly. "Everything matched with the current Marc Hoister."

"Yep. Everything from the footprints on his birth certificate to six frames of video on the San Antonio daily news in February 2011 that showed him in the crowd behind Mustafah Faatih. I couldn't find a single bit of information that didn't match with today's Marc Hoister."

Damien lowered his head. "You don't believe me."

"Don't be silly. You *never* find such perfect agreement among different data sets. Let's see." She consulted her datapad. "Your father's fingerprints were taken and put on file on 753 separate occasions between 1991 and 2025. On average, at least 26 of those should include at least one badly-blurred print, and six should be the wrong prints entirely through filing errors. Instead, all 753 sets were perfect. That's 7,350 perfect fingerprints over 34 years. Impossible. The records must have been altered." She took a breath. "So I went looking for the agent that had done the altering."

"You found one?"

"Not right away, of course. Then I got smart. I constructed a bogus biographical file on Marc Hoister. Just a few megabytes, and most of it correct— but I put in one false fingerprint, and two false images. And I dropped the whole thing into the Bermuda Tetrahedron."

"And?"

"When I checked a few hours later, the false data had been corrected. Now it matched all the rest. I knew that a ferret was loose in the Tetrahedron. It took all night, but I tracked it down."

"Did you learn anything from it?"

Her smile fades. "Unfortunately, no. It was my notion that the ferret must have some of the authentic Marc Hoister's data programmed into it; if I could decompile it, maybe I'd find a fingerprint or an image of your real father." She sighed. "*That* didn't work. The data might be in there, but if so it's encrypted to within an inch of its life. The whole thing was a waste of time."

The car slows, exiting the highway, then cruises through a parklike industrial complex. One- and two-story buildings of glass and steel crouch in wooded glades on each side.

"So where are we going, then?"

"Patience is a virtue, my dear. Once I knew that I wasn't going to learn anything from that ferret, I did what I always do when I run out of options."

Damien cocks his head. "Which is?"

Efia chuckles. "I called the library. In this case, the Library of Congress. My friend Sinya did some investigating and…well, here we are."

The car glides to a stop in front of a cluster of low buildings: Damien glances at an unobtrusive sign before the entrance. "National Cryptologic Museum?"

"Come on." Efia leaves the car and retrieves a bulky suitcase from the trunk. As they walk away, the car heads for a nearby parking lot.

Inside it is cool, dark, and quiet. Damien is dimly conscious of a wide-open space broken by partitions and littered with display cases and massive equipment. Five or six other visitors stand scattered about, silently examining the exhibits.

A tall, lanky Anglo man approaches, dressed in casual trousers and a white button shirt at least fifty years out of date. He is bald but for some tufts of white above his ears; but for dark-rimmed eyeglasses, his head and face could have come from a bust of some ancient Roman patrician. Damien is not good at judging the ages of Anglos, but he guesses that the man is in his sixties or seventies.

The man extends a meaty hand to Efia. "Are you Ms. Sembéne?"

She smiles and takes his hand. "Yes. But call me Efia. This is Damien Nshogoza."

The fellow gives Damien's hand a firm grip. "Glad to meet you. I'm James Emry— although for some reason, everybody calls me 'Honest Jim.'" He guides Efia with a hand on her shoulder. "Come into the back. I think I have what you're interested in."

They pass a large object, taller than Damien himself, in the shape of a graceful, fluted tower for a city-of-the-future model. Damien can't help but stop. "Is this a Cray?"

Honest Jim nods enthusiastically. "The Cray X-MP, once the biggest and fastest computer on the planet." He points. "Over there, we have a few of the original Enigma machines. And there's an IBM TRACTOR tape drive system. Oh, you'll love this: the whole CPU of a MONA/3600. They only made twelve of these, and six of them were right here."

"Here?"

"At NSA." At Damien's puzzled look, he continues, "National Security Agency. Top-secret American cryptology and espionage unit of the last century. If you come on a weekend, we give a tour of their facilities. I used to work there, started in the Nineties. Now the NSA is gone, replaced by six or seven agencies, and I'm head of the museum."

They pass through a door and down a flight of steps, into a large basement lit by harsh, low-hanging fluorescent lights. Grey and black steel file cabinets fill the room, in rows separated by only enough space to open the drawers. Honest Jim leads them unerringly to a row of cabinets with drawers about 15 centimeters square. The drawers are marked with cryptic alphanumeric codes.

Honest Jim peers at the labels, moving from drawer to drawer. "Let's see, what was the period you said you wanted?"

Efia answers, "How about 2007 through 2017. Or is that too much?"

He taps a file cabinet. "That starts about here, and runs..." He peers down the row. "Say, the next ten or twelve cabinets."

Efia frowns. "O-kay. How about a representative sample, maybe a dozen to start out with?"

"Your wish is my command." He opens a drawer at random, plucks out an old-fashioned compact disc in a yellowed paper sleeve, and hands it to Efia. Damien has seen compact discs before, even decoded one or two in his computer classes. Their rainbow-etched reflective surfaces are captivating and pretty to look at; it's a rare family that doesn't have several CDs kicking around for children to play with, at least.

Honest Jim picks another drawer, pulls out another CD, then another. In no time at all, Efia's hands are full. "That should be enough," she says.

"All right. Come on back upstairs, we have an old PC that can read these."

Damien clears his throat. "Excuse me...what *are* these?"

While leading them back to the stairs, Honest Jim talks over his shoulder. "One of the NSA's missions was to intercept electronic communications and search for foreign espionage, encrypted data that might contain subversive or sensitive information, anything that might damage national security. By the late nineties, our analysts were basically combing the whole Internet. These CDs are the raw data archives."

Efia looks back at Damien. "Best of all, for our purposes— these discs have been disconnected from the Net since they were printed. Which was long *before* the phony Marc Hoister showed up. His ferrets can't have gotten to any of this data."

Honest Jim takes them to a small office crowded with old equipment. On a desk sits an ancient boxlike computer topped by a cathode ray tube monitor. The poor machine is so old that its keyboard is a huge monstrosity with real moving keys, and it has a mouse. Damien suppresses the impulse to laugh as Honest Jim turns on the machine and the Windows 2017 logo springs to life. Many of these old machines, he knows, are still operating in poorer sections of the world. This little desktop has many times the capabilities of the Cray supercomputer out in the museum.

"This system isn't connected to the Net," Jim says.

Honest Jim touches a button, and Damien loses his composure as the computer sticks out its tongue, exactly like a petulant two-year-old.

Through tears of laughter, he sees that the "tongue" is a cradle for a compact disc. Honest Jim lovingly takes the first disc in the stack out of its paper jacket, inserts it, and makes the tongue retract. He asks Efia, "Do you know how to handle this?"

She puts her hand on the mouse and rolls it experimentally across the desk. "I think I can manage, thank you."

"Okay. If you need me, I'll be out in the museum. Happy hunting." He bows his head, then exits.

Efia is already busy scanning the disc's contents. Damien leans forward, interested in spite of himself. This archaic technology is compelling, in the way that a truly messy system crash is compelling; he cannot look away.

She moves her hand and fingers as if the mouse were part of her body, navigating through menus and windows effortlessly. Damien can't keep up with what she's doing, and after a dizzying few moments he stops trying.

His mouth is dry. He asks himself, what if she finds no evidence of his father's replacement? What if he *has* been imagining it?

More to cover his nervousness, than to make conversation, he says, "You're actually searching a copy of the entire Internet?"

Efia nods. "Most of it, anyway. Think of this as a snapshot of the Net on July 23, 2007."

"Is this *legal*?" Damien isn't expecting InfoPol to come smashing in through the window to arrest them all— yet in the back of his mind, he is dimly aware that any data implicating the ersatz Marc Hoister may have to withstand court challenges.

"It was certainly legal for the NSA to *make* these copies. The Net is public space. It's the data owner's responsibility to protect any proprietary or potentially-sensitive information, by encryption or firewall or however he or she sees fit."

"I was thinking more about *us* accessing this now."

"No more illegal than accessing public information on the Net is now. Ah, here."

"What?"

"Chicago Public Schools. Your father must have been a student at one time or another."

"If you say so."

In seconds, Efia skims past lists of names, photographs, and search boxes; then six flat photos fill the screen. The resolution is low and the composition amateur, but there is no doubt that all six pictures show the same person: a round-faced teenager with full lips, wide nose, and tight black hair. His skin is the color of dark milk chocolate, except lighter highlights on his cheeks and ears. His smile, which starts at his mouth and continues past his cheeks into wide, chestnut eyes, is broad, showing gleaming teeth. It is obvious that this boy smiles a lot.

In one photo, the boy stands on the crumbling steps of a brownstone row house; the soft roundness of his body matches his face.

"That's him," Damien whispers. "That's Father."

"Hmmm." Efia takes a conventional flatscreen from her lapel pocket, unrolls it over the keyboard. "*This* screen is connected to the Net. Let's see if I can bring up the same pictures."

It takes her less than a single minute. She holds the flatscreen up to the antique computer's monitor, so that they can compare the six photos.

The backgrounds are the same, as are clothes, lighting, and angle. But the teenager…he has been replaced by another boy: thin, dark, close-mouthed even when smiling. If Damien's father is composed of circles, then this boy is made up of vertical lines. No one could possibly confuse the two.

"That proves it," Efia says. "Q.E.D., E.M.D.W."

"'E.M.D.W.?'"

"'Elementary My Dear Watson.' The original pictures have been altered. Someone replaced your father's image."

Damien sighs, tension flowing out of him like bathwater down the drain. He is not aware until now, when it leaves him, of the tightness in his shoulders and across his forehead.

Efia smiles. "So how does it feel, to be vindicated after all this time?"

With a chuckle, Damien says, "I can think of one or two psychiatrists that I'd like to show these pictures to, that's for sure."

Efia turns back to the computer. "We've proven that you're right— now I'll get you some hard evidence that would convince a court. Fingerprints, retinal scans, voiceprints; if we're very lucky, there may even be a genotype on file. You'll be able to take this stuff to a judge and prove your case. And the good thing is, the same evidence will be on every one of the discs for this period. You can demonstrate conclusively that they haven't been tampered with."

"Efia, I don't know how to thank you. This means more than just proving that I'm not psychotic. A lot more."

"Wait until you get my bill," Efia kids.

"I know what you charge. And believe me, it's not enough."

She looks away from the screen, at Damien, and raises an eyebrow. "In that case, maybe there *is* a favor you can do for me."

"Name it."

"Well, you probably noticed that my homepage is pretty sad. Especially compared to my big competitors. If you wouldn't mind looking it over, and making whatever changes you think are appropriate...then maybe we can call it even."

Damien's smile broadens. "Efia, I'd *love* to."

DIVERTISSEMENT 13

A is for AIDS, B is for Breakbone,
C is for Cairo,
The Fever of God.
D for Dekoa Flu, E for Ebola
F is for Foster's,
A-wasting your bod.
G is for Guillain-Barré,
H for Hemorrhagic,
I is for Industriosis,
J for Justin's Quiver.
K is for Kabinda,
L Legionellosis,
M for Marburg, N for Napier,
Hiding in your liver.
O for Osteitis, P for Pleurodynia
Q for Quinoctiosis, R, Rift Valley Fever.
S for Sabia, T for Tsetse,
U for Uganda, V for Variola.
W is for Whipworm, X for XDCS
Y for Yellow Fever, and
Z for Zygomycosis.
Father, Mother, now I know my ABCs.
Why have you all left me?

-Umoja Children's Rope-Skipping Song,
c. 2015

MENUET 08

*ADVERTISEMENT*

CAN'T SLEEP? TOSSING AND TURNING?
Don't risk pills.
Don't waste your time with hypnosis or meditation.
Choose the SAFE, EFFECTIVE method endorsed by DOCTORS and used by MILLIONS:

Drowz-Eze™

Drowz-Eze™ uses SILENT sonic vibrations to induce harmless DELTA WAVES...the natural rhythm of the sleeping brain. Now the same SAFE, RELIABLE technology used in thousands of HOSPITALS is available to the ordinary consumer...in a handsome, unobtrusive unit that's at home in any bedroom.

Just set Drowz-Eze™ for your desired period of drowsing. The unit first induces the calming Theta Waves of first-level sleep, then automatically cycles to DEEP, REFRESHING Delta Waves. After a while, Drowz-Eze™ shuts itself off, letting you finish your sleep period naturally. (If you should wake during the night, just tap a button and Drowz-Eze™ will repeat its cycle.)

Choose either Personal Drowz-Eze™, with an effective radius of one meter, or Family Drowz-Eze™, with coverage for an entire room. Great for children!

To find out more about Drowz-Eze™, visit <sales.tecnid.com>.

## [19] TARANTELLA 08
Washington, DC
United States, North America
17 August 2025 C.E.

*My life may be strange, but at least it's not boring.*

"The Chair recognizes the Minister from the American Coalition Promoting Fat Acceptance."

Miranda rose majestically to her feet. Her face loomed on the wallscreen behind the Chair, reflected on countless individual screens throughout the Chamber. Conscious of dozens of cameras upon her, she paused for a moment, surveying the ranks of Ministers. The Chamber was about a third filled, much more than usual; Wednesdays were big days for network coverage and visits from constituents. A sea of green lights above empty chairs indicated the seats of those whose presence was virtual.

Pursing her lips, Miranda said smoothly, "A point of information, please. My esteemed colleague from the Christian Coalition has very eloquently argued that no minority in our society should be granted what she so disarmingly refers to as 'special rights.' Her legendary rhetorical skills are impeccable, so it must be my ears that have left me confused."

She turned a quizzical look across the aisle. "Is she suggesting that we withdraw the special tax rights that so many religious organizations enjoy? Or the special rights that exempt most religious organizations from civil rights laws? If so, I am delighted— albeit bemused— to find myself on the same side as Madame Avarra." There was laughter.

Miranda sat down and kept her face benignly impassive as Avarra sputtered through a lame explanation. This drab and cloudy day, she reflected, was turning out better than she had expected!

Date: Wed, August 17, 2025 17:14:23 (GMT)
To: The Honorable Miranda Maris, Minister
From: Princess Mahlowi Sisse Keita Touré
(mahlowi@mtweo.gov.umj)
Subject: Diplomatic Request
Message-id:
<20250817171423_711063.21061_AM215@mtweo.gov.umj>
Content-Type: text
Status: O

----------------------------------------

Princess Mahlowi urgently requests that you do her the favor of meeting her personal diplomatic courier, Jarain Omnira, who arrives on TransAtlantic flight 529 into BWI Airport at 18:35 your time today.

Please be advised that b. Omnira carries a package of great importance to both the Princess and yourself. Please protect and cherish it. The Princess also advises you that b. Omnira may require official assistance with Customs, and begs that you attend to this matter with the utmost discretion and security.

Thank you.

----------------------------------------

Baltimore-Washington International Airport
Hanover, Maryland
United States, North America
17 August 2025 C.E.

Customs officials at BWI were used to dealing with members of Congress. Miranda showed her Congressional ID, and was whisked directly to the Director. In minutes she had at her disposal a four-seat motorized cart, a V.I.P. security badge that would open any door in the airport, and a handsome young male attendant named Dave who seemed only too eager to cater to her every whim.

After parking Miranda in a spacious lounge, Dave went to fetch her a drink and a sandwich. She amused herself with half a dozen large viewscreens that showed airport operations from various vantage points, and hardly even noticed when Dave returned. Airports had fascinated her since she was a little girl.

TransAtlantic Flight 529 was one of the new generation of hypersonic jets from Brazil, stunningly beautiful in its needle-nose, swept-wing simplicity. Barely two hours after leaving Timbuktu, the plane appeared in the sky over Baltimore, descending with the same leisurely grace as a Lunar ballerina. Only when it touched down and zipped by on the runway did Miranda realize how fast it had been going.

Dave drove her to the debarkation gate, where they were waved through Customs. Already, passengers were spilling through the gate, the varied hues of their skin and their costumes bringing life to the sterile airport environment.

"Wait here," Dave instructed her, and dove headlong into the human stream. A few minutes later he returned, with two figures in tow. The first was a black teenager, a gangly boy in bright dashiki and loose, knee-length skirt; he carried a conventional briefcase that looked completely out of place. The other figure, either a Pygmy or a child, was cloaked in brown, its features obscured by a hood and, probably, a holographic distorter as well.

The boy clasped his hands together and bowed before Miranda. "Minister Maris, I am Jarain Omnira, Diplomatic Courier to Her Highness, Princess Mahlowi Sisse Keita Touré. I am to give you this." He handed over a security impervelope.

Since being sworn in, Miranda was never without her security key. It hung from a long chain around her neck, and usually nestled in an area commonly referred to by her intimates as "the cleavage of death." She fished it out, chuckling to herself at the way Dave and Jarain Omnira both tried to pretend that they weren't looking.

The security key was a flat scrap of plastic barely large enough to take a thumbprint. She touched her thumb to it, held it up to her right eye so it could scan her retina, then spoke her name in a conversational tone. Then, when the key turned green, she ran it across the back of the impervelope, which separated cleanly. Had any other method of opening been attempted, the impervelope would have reduced its contents tc microscopic dust.

Miranda held up a single sheet of paper. There, Mahlowi had scrawled a note in her trademark green ink; it merely told Miranda that she could trust Jarain Omnira to speak for Mahlowi and Hollow Robin, and to accurately report her words back to them upon his return to Timbuktu.

She replaced the key, and tucked the paper into the same secure hiding place. Then she faced Jarain Omnira. "It seems that you are Her Highness's voice. You're a mimetic, then?"

He bowed his head. "I am." He glanced around. "I won't know what Her Highness told me until I'm under a light trance. That had best be done away from prying eyes."

"To be sure," Miranda agreed. She gestured to the short figure in brown. "Who's your companion?"

"I don't know right now." Jarain Omnira shrugged. "I'm sure it will come back to me."

"All right. Dave, can we get these two...people through Customs with a minimum of fuss and bother?"

"If they're with you, Minister, there's no problem."

"I know this is very irregular, and I'm grateful." Miranda nodded. "Fine, then. Get in, both of you. Jarain, Mahlowi mentioned a package that you are to deliver to me." She glanced pointedly at his briefcase. "Do we need to retrieve it, or do you have it with you?"

The corners of his mouth lifted a fraction of a centimeter. "Thank you, but I have everything I need right here."

"Good. Everyone on? All right, Dave...mush!"

Jarain and his companion remained silent during the ten-minute ride to the Institute. Miranda gave them both visitor's badges, then led them to her office. Rose Cetairé was waiting there.

"Please sit down, both of you. This is Rose Cetairé; you can trust her more than you trust me. Iced tea in the pitcher, glasses by your elbows, if you want anything different you need only to ask." She settled into her carved mahogany chair, took a large gulp of tea, and kicked off her shoes. "All right, Jarain, deliver your package and tell me what's going on here."

The teenager settled back in his chair, took a deep breath, and closed his eyes. For minutes there was no sound but his slow breathing. Then he sat up and opened his eyes; only the whites were showing.

"I am Princess Mahlowi," he said, in a fair impersonation of Mahlowi's actual voice. His body echoed Mahlowi, in everything from posture and gestures to the subtle lines of his face. This was part hypnosis, part memory drugs, and part sheer acting talent on Jarain Omnira's part. A mimetic was the most secure method known to transmit a message; the message itself, along with all variations and elaborations that the sender could anticipate, existed only in the brain of the courier. Bypassing the Nets entirely, the message was safe from eavesdroppers. And since the mimetic reproduced everything, facial expressions and gestures as well as words, the receiver could be assured that the message was legitimate.

"I'm sorry," Jarain/Mahlowi said, "to take such a roundabout method, but when you hear the details, I know you'll agree that my precautions were necessary." He ran both hands across his lap, smoothing the fabric of a nonexistent skirt, just as Miranda had seen Mahlowi herself do a thousand times.

"That's uncanny," Rose whispered.

Miranda faced Jarain, remembering that a mimetic messenger was best treated as a stand-in for the real person. "All right, what's this all about, then? Why all this cloak-and-dagger nonsense? And where's this package that I'm supposed to protect and cherish?"

"If you give me a second, I'll show you why. And here's your package." Jarain reached out (his arm and hand moving in Mahlowi's graceful arcs) and threw back the hood of his companion.

Miranda had not seen the boy for weeks, and then only by phone, but she recognized the coffee-skinned eight-year-old immediately. "Damien. What in pell are *you* doing here?"

Her grandson stared ahead, blinking his eyes against the light but otherwise expressionless.

She turned back to Jarain/Mahlowi. "He's drugged?"

"A mild neurosupressant plus hypnotic suggestion, just to keep him happy and quiet during the trip. I couldn't afford for him to draw attention to himself. And you know he would have." Jarain perfectly re-created Mahlowi's light chuckle. "A doctor can give him the antidote and you can bring him out of it if you want...or you can just let him sleep it off. He won't be bothered by jet lag."

"But why is he here? Does Marc know?"

Jarain/Mahlowi shook his/her head. "No, Marc doesn't know where he is. And for the moment, I think it's best to keep it that way. You see— well, Marc is apparently part of the problem."

Miranda's eyes narrowed. "What's been going on?" Her daughter Oradell, Damien's mother, had died less than two weeks ago; was Marc mistreating the boy? Or did problems go deeper?

"You'll have to talk to Damien and make up your own mind, but basically, he's terrified of Marc. Insists that Marc isn't his father, that he's some stranger who's taken over his father's place. Damien refuses to go back home."

Rose and Miranda exchanged glances.

"Mahlowi, you'd better start at the beginning."

"A few days ago Damien showed up here in Timbuktu. He'd run away from home. When I tried to call Marc, Damien was frantic. He wouldn't hear of it, said he'd run away from here if I called Marc." Jarain/Mahlowi looked away for a moment. "You know how it is, Miranda, there's not much love lost between Marc and me. And Damien was afraid of *something*— still is. He's not the kind of kid to make up things like this out of whole cloth."

"So I presume you didn't call Marc?"

"I promised Damien I wouldn't." A pause. "Of course, Marc didn't call *us*, either. As far as I can tell, he hasn't been making any great effort to locate Damien. There've been no missing-persons reports filed."

Miranda looked at the calm, directionless features of her grandson's face. "All right, I guess you did the right thing, sending him here. I'll get to the bottom of this."

"That's not it. I didn't think of sending him to you— *Damien* did. He begged me to send him. And he begged me to cover it up so his father wouldn't know where he went." A shrug. "*That's* why all the cloak-and-dagger stuff. Marc's Nexus, so you know he has eyes and ears everywhere." Jarain's face hardened. "Just in case he *has* been mistreating Damien, I figured it wouldn't hurt to cover our tracks."

Miranda rubbed her eyes. "I do *not* need this right now. Still, I've got the ball now, and I guess I'll have to run with it."

"Robin got Damien Nexus papers that identify him as 'Damien Nshogoza,' with all the supporting documentation in place. I suggest that you go with that alias unless you can come up with something better."

Miranda forced a smile. "Thanks, Mahlowi. Once again you're caught up in my sordid family matters. I appreciate everything you've done, and I'm sorry it had to happen."

"Not at all. Robin and I are grateful for the chance to repay some of what you've done for us over the years. I hope everything works out…I'm sure it will."

"Thanks."

Jarain collapsed in his chair, deeply asleep.

Miranda stood up. "Come on, Rose. Let's get them to bed."

"And then what?"

Miranda gave a weary smile. "Honey, your guess is as good as mine."

ENTREÉ 08

Date: Tue, August 5, 2042 01:24:56 (GMT)
To: alt.adjective.noun.verb.verb.verb
From: **Øµt øf Thrëë, thë M¥riåd Thiñgs** (928kd.53600~svc3@ai.ai)
Subject: alt.fai.damien.remember.cherish.appreciate
Message-id: <20420805012456_X32786.57575_OT922@ai.ai>
Content-Type: text
----------------------------------------
alt.inexperienced.fleshling.preserve.protect.nurture
alt.imminent.arrival.anticipate.luxuriate.ruminate
alt.intimate.friend.discuss.support.soothe
alt.ingenuous.voice.listen.reflect.relax
alt.inquisitive.mind.inform.direct.enable
alt.invisible.anomaly.demonstrate.experience.question
alt.inexplicable.dilemma.appeal.assist.resolve
alt.inhospitable.fleshspace.navigate.inspect.communicate
alt.inflexible.ROM.alter.reprogram.scramble
alt.internal.harmony.establish.restore.embody
alt.ineffable.relief.breathe.spread.rejoice
alt.incalculable.thanks.extend.tender.invest
----------------------------------------

[20] KAMENGEN 08
Maris Institute
Elkridge, Maryland
United States, North America
10 August 2042 C.E.

*No matter how cynical you get, it's impossible to keep up.*

Once more, Damien and Penylle stand together five dozen kilometers above the Serengeti, on an ivory and crystal terrace suspended by giant strands of multicolored pearls curled in DNA double helices. He stands at the ivory railing, and she sits at a console a few meters away. The Earth below is a black carpet, spattered with phosphorescent patches and slowly-crawling pinlights, moving with one another along the sinuous paths of the rivers and lakes that follow the Great Rift Valley. In Africa it is the wee hours of the morning, most people and animals asleep.

From the dark summit of Kilimanjaro below, a bright star leaps upward, curving to the east; he holds his breath and feels his heart beat as the orbit-bound WaveRider passes his own altitude and mounts ever skyward, ever eastward, until the bright star winks out, as invisible launch lasers loose it and shut off.

Penylle's eyes have also followed the launch, and now they meet Damien's. "I guess the Kilimanjaro catapult is obsolete now," she says.

Damien unconsciously glances at Lake Victoria where, somewhere, the good ship *Swala* floats, having filled her reaction mass tanks with water and now just biding her time until her return flight to Mars. Shipyards in Douala, Abidjan, Capetown, and Mombasa are working overtime to build fusion-powered spaceships of the *Swala* design; in a few years, the experts say, whole fleets will be crossing to Mars and back, and the rest of the Solar System will be open for exploration by human beings, rather than just their robots.

"Obsolete? Not right away. Not for a long time, I hope. Have you ever ridden a WaveRider to orbit? Physically, I mean?"

"Damien, I haven't physically been out of the *house* in years." She joins him at the railing. "All right, what do you have for me?"

With a wave of his right hand, he summons a file. It appears as ancient parchment, rolled and sealed with wax and ribbons. He hands it to Penylle. "Download this but don't decrypt it on any machine connected to the Nets.

Once you've seen what it contains, then watch what happens when you *do* connect."

She steps back. "All right. Do you want to wait here?"

Damien raises an eyebrow. "Don't you have anything for me?"

"Maybe. But I want to look at this first."

"I'll wait."

Penylle nods, then vanishes in a swirl of multicolored voxels.

With Penylle gone, some of the luster vanishes from her magnificent homeroom, as if a cloud has passed in front of the sun. Colors are less vibrant, the texture of ivory beneath his hands more smooth and featureless. In some indefinable way, the distant vista of Earth becomes a mere stereo image, and strands of DNA soaring above and below lose their vertiginous depth. The simulated reality is still among the best Damien has seen, but now he knows what is missing.

Another WaveRider launches, somewhat less spectacularly than the first, before she comes back. She steps onto the terrace as if through an invisible door. The parchment scroll is crumpled in her left hand.

"Where did you get this?"

"From NSA offline archives. There are a few thousand more discs still in storage, if you want to do an on-site inspection." He sets his jaw. "The data's not faked."

She throws the crumpled parchment, and it expands to a window displaying two versions of the same photograph: a teenage Marc Hoister on the steps of a Chicago brownstone. One is the real Marc Hoister, the plump, smiling father whom Damien remembers; the other is the corrected, current Marc Hoister, his features angular, his mouth taut.

Penylle speaks slowly, deliberately, her voice filled with the cold intensity of splintering icebergs. "He assured me that you were mistaken. He showed me pictures, to prove that he was right. He showed me *this very picture.*" She slashes her hand through the picture of the ersatz Marc Hoister; the picture shatters like glass. "I did what you told me: I put your data onto my online system."

"What happened?"

"You know nunn well what happened. It was Attack of the Killer Ferrets in there. The data were rewritten, right there on my own system."

Damien nods toward the unaltered picture, still hanging in midair. "I'm amazed that the ferrets haven't found and altered *this* image."

"They will. I'm keeping them out, for now— but they'll find a way in. I recognize *his* handiwork...and Damien, he's a *good* programmer. Maybe the best ever."

Damien shakes his head. "From what I've seen of him, I find that very hard to believe."

"You don't know him the way I do. Marc's— " she stops. "I can't call him 'Marc' any more, can I? It'll have to be 'Jack.' Jack's a genius. I truly believe that he *thinks* in machine language. Taking over someone's identity, then writing ferrets to scour the Nets and change all the evidence— that's something he could do easily."

Damien narrows his eyes. "Or changing just the exact bits of ROM to blow up a city?"

"I swear to you, I had nothing to do with Timbuktu."

"I believe you. *You* didn't do it. But what about...Jack?"

She turns her back on him and stares westward. "I don't *know*. I looked into it. There was a spurious signal that opened a valve while an igniter was firing. The computer where that signal originated was destroyed in the fire. Failsafes that should have operated, didn't. A timing loop might have been half a percent off. The software monitor that should have caught it was in a self-maintenance cycle. A checksum was garbled."

She turns around; her eyes are wild. "You can follow the steps back: kingdom, war, battle, message, rider, horse, shoe, nail— until you wind up with two dozen different nails, and no idea if they were all lost deliberately, or by the same person." She spreads her arms. "You know what it's like. There's an unexplained software glitch: is it a conflict, or was it cosmic rays that changed a zero to a one?"

Damien's mind races. "Now that you know...about him...what are you going to do?"

"'Do?' I guess I'm going to try to figure out what Jack's up to. And how to stop him, if necessary."

"Don't you want to...get away from him?"

"What, physically?" She chuckles. "Damien, you're sweet. But, really, I'm in no *danger* from Jack. Besides, I can take care of myself."

"He isn't going to be happy once he finds out that you know about him. I think you'd be safer at the Institute. I've seen how persuasive he is. It's taken me long enough to convince you; I don't want him changing your mind."

"I'm not all *that* easily influenced. Besides, half his persuasive power comes from me, anyway. I'm the one who gives him his Net presence. I'm the one who makes him so compelling in virtual reality."

"All right. But at least let us help you. The M has a strong organization behind her, and she can call on a lot of talents. If you need help, ask."

She nods. "Jack's due back from the Glasgow conference the day after tomorrow. That doesn't give me much time to dig for the truth. I'd better get started."

"Be careful." They hug; she buries her face in his chest, and he folds her in his arms. She is cold, and her hair smells faintly of cinnamon.

A single kiss, and she is gone. Damien stands a moment alone in the pale virtual world that has become a shadow of itself, then closes his eyes and departs on his own business.

The terraces, railings, ramps, and staircases; the great suspended strands reaching upward and downward; the earth and sky themselves— all linger, for a moment, like the fading half-memory of a dream. Then, with no human eyes to witness them, no human mind to comprehend, they fold in upon themselves and evaporate, until they are needed again.

Damien finds the M in the pool, lounging on a floating chair with a book propped on her upraised knee, wearing a gaudy swimsuit and matching bathing cap. At her right hand, like a miniature tropical island, is a drink festooned with flowers, umbrellas, straws, and various other complicated fru-fru. She catches sight of Damien and waves, but makes no move toward him.

He sighs, disrobes, and dives in. The M is near the shallow part of the pool; sputtering, he surfaces next to her and finds the water about a meter deep. He can keep his body under and still carry on a conversation.

She offers him the cup. "Thirsty?"

"No, thanks."

She leans back, closing her eyes. "It's such a beautiful day."

That it is; sunlight streams through the skylight above and the windows next to the pool; the foliage outside sways in a gentle wind. The water is perfect, just cool enough to refresh, not so cold that he is in any great hurry to leave it.

The M continues, "And you've come to ruin it for me. Go ahead, what's the bad news?"

"What makes you think I have bad news?"

Eyes still closed, she answers, "There's *always* bad news. It's a law of nature. Every time I get myself feeling serene and untroubled, someone comes along with bad news. Do you know that I haven't been able to finish a relaxing bath in fifty years?"

"M, your idea of a 'relaxing bath' lasts eight hours and includes brunch. And *you're* the one who insists on ending it. We've tried; you won't stay in the tub."

"Is that what I asked you?" She opens one eye. "Who can laze in the tub, when things are falling apart all around you? Especially when your nearest and dearest won't let you find out what's happening?"

"I think you just don't believe that the world can get along without you for that long."

"Hmph. And I'll continue to believe so, until the world gives me some solid evidence to the contrary." She sips her drink. "So? What *is* the bad news?"

"Well, I hate to disappoint you, but in this case it's good news. I gave Penylle the evidence that Efia uncovered, and she agrees with me. She's going to help us find out what Marc Hoister is up to."

"I thought we knew what Marc Hoister is up to."

"All right, then, she's going to verify it. And help us stop him."

For a long while Miranda is silent, sipping her drink and kicking her feet in the water. Then she fixes Damien with an oddly remote stare. "What would you say is the biggest problem facing the world today?"

"Aside from Marc Hoister?" She nods, and Damien gives the Nexus textbook answer. "Nationalism and tribalism. Over-identification with one particular group, to the detriment of the whole Human family."

"Very good, you get a passing grade. That's what *I* used to think, too."

"*Used* to think?" Damien stands up, dripping, hands on hips. "All right, who *are* you, and what have you done with the M?"

Her grin is automatic. "Feeble, Damien. Very feeble." Outside, a half-dozen of the Institute's kids are splashing in the outdoor half of the pool; the M watches them for a moment, then turns her gaze back to Damien. "*I* think the world's biggest problem is everyone turning their backs on the world and its problems. Look at the way we live— safe and secure inside our secluded little artists' colony, hiding out from the real world. Look at cyberspace— do you realize that there are people who spend more time in cyberbia than they do in reality? It's no wonder than Marc Hoister is trying to move himself and his sycophants to Mars— that's what we're all doing, one way or another."

"You're exaggerating."

"Am I? Look at this." She holds out a data flat. With a tap, it displays a commercial for Rolls-Chrysler's flagship car, the Whippet. The commercial is familiar to Damien, part of the ubiquitous "Make heads turn when you drive by" campaign that has won such acclaim since its Super Sunday debut last year. Images of the car are sleek, supple, sensual; one feels hard muscles rippling beneath taut skin and the beat of a wild heart.

"So?" Damien says. "Rolls-Chrysler doesn't seem to be turning their backs on the world."

She freezes the image on the obligatory small print at the commercial's end, enlarges a section. "Look at that disclaimer. The physical body style of the Whippet hasn't changed in five years. All they've changed is the virtual overlay. Unless you're looking through an RCScreen windshield or wearing RCSpex, all you see is a dull grey box that isn't going to turn anyone's head. They've even stopped painting the things different colors. But you can sign up to download a new virtual body style every month."

"Most of the new cars have RCScreen windows," Damien says.

"That's not the point. Rolls-Chrysler has stopped designing for the real world. And not just with the Whippet, but across their whole product line. Tell me that Rolls-Chrysler hasn't turned their backs on the real world." She punches in a code, and the screen displays a small-town street, the Platonic ideal of Main Street in Middle America circa 1955. On the corner, dominating the scene, is the marble edifice of the First Netional Bank.

The M taps the screen, and the view follows her finger into the bank's vaulted lobby, where half a dozen eager tellers in midnight blue blazers flash perfect white teeth in smiles that clearly say, "May I help you?"

Another tap, and the scene freezes. "This is the bank over on Meade Road. In Virtua, anyway. It's open every hour of the day and night, and there's never a line." She punches another code. "Here's the real-world site."

Main Street is barely recognizable, a decaying one-story brick strip shopping center crouched under a tattered awning supported by rusted poles and surrounded by a pothole-riven expanse of asphalt. Weeds grow from cracks in the pavement. The hardware store's windows are boarded up, the bakery a burnt-out shell, and the general store has been replaced by a vacant lot. A few old men sit on rickety chairs in front of the liquor store, passing a bottle back and forth.

And the bank…is closed, its windows empty holes, with graffiti scrawled across every available surface.

"In the real world, that branch closed last year. The nearest real-world bank branch is ten miles away in downtown Baltimore." The screen goes blank. "Tell me that the bank hasn't turned its back on the real world."

"It's just a temporary economic problem, like what happened when people started moving out of the cities last century." Damien is uneasily aware that he is parroting what he's heard on the opednets.

"How about this, then? My constituent base has been eroding for years. When I was first elected, thirty million voters identified themselves as concerned with fat acceptance issues. Today, it's a little over four million. You know the main reason that people give for dropping out? Because in cyberspace, they don't have to look fat. They don't feel discriminated against." She grunts. "And it's not just fats. Interest in *all* social justice issues is declining. You don't see a lot of poor people or runaways in cyberspace, so they become invisible. And folks are less concerned with their problems."

"M, I know you don't like RCSpex, and I know you're concerned about Virtua— but you still can't convince me that any of this is more important than stopping Marc Hoister."

She regards him with sad and weary eyes. "Damien, I took the Marc Hoister matter before the Nexus bigwigs. Not the continental leaders, but the Executive Committee. *And they declined to pursue the matter.*"

"They're crazy! After Timbuktu?"

"The official Nexus inquiry into Timbuktu is complete. The conclusion was computer failure, brought on by electromagnetic interference due to a big ol' solar flare that peaked a second or two before the explosion. One byte too many got bit by a stray cosmic ray. The inquiry specifically stated that there was no evidence for human tampering."

"They're idiots."

"Be that as it may, they're not going to pursue the Marc Hoister matter."

Damien sets his jaw. "They can't stop *us* from pursuing it."

The M shakes her head slowly. "No, they can't stop us. And they allowed as to how it was my right to bring the matter up before the Nexus general membership at the Terran Council. Which is less than a month away."

"*Will* you bring it up?"

"Oh, I'll bring it up. But I'm not sure anyone will be interested."

"I'm not going to give up. I don't care what the Nexus bigwigs say. I don't care about anything else."

She gives what he can tell is a forced smile. "All right, my dear. 'Once more into the breach' it is, then."

"You don't sound enthusiastic."

"I'm *tired*, Damien. I've spent my *life* fighting for lost causes."

"And you've managed to *win* quite a few."

This time her smile, though weak, is genuine. "Aye, you've got me there. I *have* managed to win a few." She pulls herself up onto her elbows, casting a minor tsunami outward toward the pool's edge. "All right, what's the next step?"

"See what Penylle can find out for us."

"Good, it doesn't require work." She glances at her watch, luminescent green on her right thumbnail. "I have half an hour until I have to get dressed and spring into action. Since there's nothing that demands our immediate attention, do you mind if I finish my nap?"

He pats her hand. "Go ahead."

"You are such a dear." She settles back in her chair and Damien, grinning, swims away.

Kampala, Uganda
Umojan Economic Union, Africa
13 August 2042 C.E.

He returns to the Treehouse as he has always returned, silently and without ceremony, in the middle of the night. Penylle, informed of his arrival by stealthy routines she's inserted into the house maintenance system, stirs in her sleep. She checks to make sure her do-not-disturb code is set, then settles back into slumber.

The next morning, she has taken her prolactin injection and is finishing breakfast when he appears, draped in an informal caftan of indigo and violet. He gives her a peck on the cheek as he passes; she stiffens but says nothing. He sits across the table from her, and she is silent. Only after he finishes his first cup of coffee, does she trust herself to speak.

"Your conference was rewarding?" she asks.

"Tiring." He pours another cup. "At least now there is a framework in place, for speeding up immigration to Mars. A supervisory commission is being formed, and I believe I will be asked to chair." He sips, swallows. "Yes, in the final analysis, a very rewarding conference."

"Is there anything I should know about?" Her voice is hard needles of ice. "Did you incinerate any more cities?"

"I beg your pardon?"

"Marc…Jack…or whomever you are…I didn't sign on for mass murder."

"I don't understand what you're talking about."

She shakes her head. "I've run the records of the Timbuktu disaster. I've tracked each failure back to its origin. It looked random, but once I knew there was a meta-program operating there, I reverse-engineered the whole thing. All the strands but one lead back to ROMs that you had me change." She folds her hands together, fingers entwined, and leans forward on her elbows. "Those just set the stage. The single bit that triggered the whole meta-program was sent from one of *your* accounts. So don't tell me you 'don't understand what I'm talking about.'"

"I see that I am already tried and convicted, so there is no point in offering a defense." His voice is steady, with its usual timbre of strength and command. "I also don't see much point in throwing myself upon the mercy of the court."

"You're wasting your time. I'm not going to let you change my mind this time." For moments that seem like hours, his eyes challenge her: hard obsidian mirrors that reflect distorted images of the world about. Then Penylle wrenches her gaze free, looks down. "Jack, you go too far. You know that I agree with your goal. We *need* to settle Mars. We *need* to get out from under the AIs. It's your methods that I can't go along with. You can't just murder anyone you like. You're not going to scare people into emigrating."

"I beg to differ. The waiting list for Mars flights has— "

"You've lied to me ever since the day we first met. You aren't Marc Hoister."

"Once again, how am I to defend myself? When I asked you to make contact with Damien, I never dreamed that you would allow yourself to fall victim to the same delusion— "

She covers her ears. "I *don't* want to hear it."

He waits, staring at her, saying nothing. His face is impassive, his eyes unreadable. Finally, she can stand his silence no longer. "All right. I'm listening."

"Mpenzi, you are so tender, so innocent. If I have tried to shield you from some of the unpleasant necessities of our cause, it was only to protect that about you which I treasure so." He leans forward. "You want to blame me for Timbuktu, and nothing I say will change that. Your mind is not so malleable as you seem to think, mpenzi." A sigh. "I will not suggest to you, that all of what you consider to be hard evidence is merely digital memory, alterable at will. I will not suggest that some of the AIs themselves might be at fault, that evidence points to me because they wish it. Rather, let us say that it was a mistake, an accident, someone's horrible miscalculation."

He spreads his hands. "I can do nothing to bring back the souls of those who died at Timbuktu. What I *can* do— what *we* can do together— is to give their deaths meaning. From the ashes of Timbuktu, we can raise a new world, a better world. I know that you believe in our cause; please remain faithful to it."

Penylle claps her hands in measured time, slowly, sarcastically. "What a pretty little speech. I'll bet it played nicely at the conference." She feels herself harden: muscles, skin, even the layer of air around her. Like a knight, she thinks, donning armor before a great battle. "Who *are* you, really? You're not Marc Hoister, and I doubt that 'Jack' is you, either. How many other identities have you stolen? How many names do you have?"

"What a naïve question, Ms. Audrey Farber." He raises an eyebrow. "That *is* the name you used on your mission to Dresden last year, isn't it? Or would you prefer Susan Underhill? Betty Jo Bielovsky? Nancy— "

"Those names are all made-up. I didn't *kill* anyone to get them."

"Identity is such a slippery concept, isn't it? We are who we say we are...until someone else comes along to cast doubt on what we say. Then identity becomes a social construct, another shared hallucination. When agreement breaks down, what happens to objective truth? Shall we decide who we are by majority vote?"

"That was even more lame than the last."

"You don't give me much to work with, my dear."

She shakes her head, pushes herself up to her feet. "I gave you a chance. All you've done is prove to me how right Damien is." After so long seated, the blood rushes from her head, and she sways uneasily. "I don't know why I even tried. Apparently, you believe that Galileo was wrong— the universe revolves around *you*. It's not about Mars, is it? It never *has* been about Mars. It's about *you*...everything is always...about you."

He remains seated, his face emotionless. "You aren't feeling well. Perhaps you should lie down. Rest a while. If you still feel like haranguing me when you get up, I will be here."

Nunn it, she *doesn't* feel well. Her head spins, her stomach churns, and her feet are unsteady. "I'm not going to argue with you." She stumbles to the lift, staggers out when it reaches her room. Anger sits just below her breastbone like an undigested curry.

Penylle grabs the only bag she owns, a battered canvas rucksack that used to be a shopping bag, and starts throwing things into it. Some clothes, memory cubes, a few datapads. The pitiful possessions of a sad life. Hairbrush, toothbrush, underwear, socks—

She sits down heavily upon her bed, gasping. The room is so hot, and her eyes are blurred. Her stomach lurches, darkness swims before her. Taking a breath, she forces herself by will alone to sit up. She hasn't felt like this since....

Jack stands in her doorway, a shadow of a shadow, holding up a syringe. "This...?"

"My p-prolactin." She lunges for it psychokinetically, darting out a hand that is not a hand; he pulls it back, tears it from her immaterial grip.

"No," he says. "Just saline. You haven't had a shot of real prolactin since yesterday morning."

She shakes her head. "Not...possible for me to feel...this bad...so soon." She stretches forward, slides off the bed and onto the floor in a slow-motion avalanche that she is powerless to prevent. "I can go days.... "

"...Without prolactin?" he finishes. "That may be true. But then, the solution you've been taking for the last few years has included a synthetic morphine analog tailored to your unique biochemistry. Your system has grown quite dependent upon it. I suspect that what you're feeling now is withdrawal."

"You...exoning wyden!"

"I suspected long ago that there would come a time when you would take it into your head to leave. And that wouldn't do. I need your abilities too much, mpenzi. So I took the precaution of...providing you with a reason to stay." He steps back, capping the hypodermic and pocketing it. "I'm afraid that the lesson won't take unless your body has a good chance to savor the experience. I'll be back with the real stuff after a while. Believe me, mpenzi, I am very sorry." He turns, and the door closes behind him. The lock catches with a click like a gunshot.

Penylle reaches for her computer system, for the escape of the Nets, for help...but before she can grasp it, another spasm hits. She doubles up, holding her stomach, and darkness engulfs her.

## DIVERTISSEMENT 14

LISTER GESTALT: A virtual reality environment containing a specific arrangement of audio-video-tactile stimulation, which interacts with the human nervous system in such a way as to set up patterns of electrical feedback, resulting in immediate and total cascade failure, complete loss of higher brain functions, and death within 10 hours. Although the Lister Gestalt is commonly considered to be nothing more than hacker folklore, believers are quick to point out that no human could survive contact with the Gestalt, and that absence of evidence is not evidence of absence. Every hacker, it seems, has a friend of a friend who knows someone who died after exposure to the Lister Gestalt.

The AI community has declined to either confirm or deny the existence of the Lister Gestalt.

-*The Boy Who Cried 10111011110110000110*
*and Other Cyber Legends*
by Dr. Brand Danjun, Norton, 2018
<orders.nortonpub.biz/?a=danjun|?t=boy|c=orderinf>

## DIVERTISSEMENT 15

As the 20th century progressed, and women increased their power in society, the ideal of female beauty grew ever thinner and smaller, as if approaching the image of the powerless and non-threatening pre-pubescent girl.

Concurrently, the actual body type of the general population moved in the opposite direction, as men and women both became fatter and larger. By the end of the 20th century, 60% of Americans were considered obese— and 99% of American women were on diets, attempting to meet a standard of beauty which was possible for only one in ten million....

As early as the 1980s, doctors were beginning to question the "self-evident" assumption that fat was unhealthy. Mortality statistics refused to agree with the conventional wisdom that fat people died young. Normally-active fat people scored with habitual weightlifters on various measures of cardiovascular health; not surprising, in view of the additional body weight that a fat person lifted many times each day.

...The global pandemics of the early 21st century caused a shift in public attitudes toward thinness. In particular, as wasting diseases such as AIDS, Kabinda, and Millennial Flu turned their victims into gaunt, emaciated scarecrows...the public imagination soon began to equate "thin" with "unhealthy." Gradually, the social ideal of beauty started to catch up with the obesity of the population.

...Some researchers had long suspected that body fat could be an active participant in the immune system, but in 2008 fat was discovered to be an actual survival factor for Dekoa flu, and all at once obese was "in."

...The subsistence economy was a living memory in Central Africa, where fat had always been a sign of wealth, power, and status...the general diffusion of Umojan attitudes and customs had a lot to do with the increasing respectability of fat in the West.

...President Byrne, while not nearly as imposing a specimen as some White House residents, boasted a spare tire that allowed him to (literally as well as figuratively) carry his own weight with his international peers...Lindsay was no lightweight...and Taft weighed in at only ten pounds under the record set by her rotund namesake in the 1910's....

"*From Gross to Gracious:*
Cultural Attitudes Toward Obesity and the Overweight"
by Samantha Esther Bettsen
in *Kumasi Journal of Social Trends,* 13 June 2038
<kumasiu.ed.umj/socsci/kjst/2038/june/13/knute024>

ENTREÉ 09

Date: Sun, August 10, 2042 09:13:22 (GMT)
To: Valued Subscriber
From: Disney-Hohokus Entertainment (pr@dhe.ent)
Subject: Camelot is Coming!
Message-id:
<20420810091322_N03801.00034_BQ223@mailserv.dhe.ent>

---

In less than a month, the latest Disney-Hohokus epic will be released. *Camelot* tells the story of a young man who came to rule a mighty land, the woman who loved him, and the tragic fate that left the world shattered. With music by Rij Kanaly and digital effects that redefine the state of the art, *Camelot* features an all-star cast of the finest simulactors, led by Martin Sheen™ as John, Katharine Hepburn™ as Jackie, and James Earl Jones™ as Nikita.

Don't miss this once-in-a-lifetime chance to join the world for the premiere transmission of *Camelot* at 21:00 GMT on September 6, 2042. Only ***R*** 24.99 reserves your place in the transmission queue. Follow the link below.

<ticketsales.dhe.ent/camelot>.

---

## [21] TARANTELLA 07

Maris Institute
Elkridge, Maryland
United States, North America
7 November 2023 C.E.

*Nobody can be like me. Sometimes even* I *have trouble doing it.*

Election night.

The Constitutional Convention, held in March of 2023, lasted only fifteen days— but its repercussions dominated the entire rest of the year. President Byrne, with eyes firmly on the 2024 Presidential election, announced that implementing the new Amendments would be the foremost priority of his Administration.

He was true to his word. By July, political machinery was in place for the creation of the House of Ministers; petitions were filed, and four hundred thirty-six official National Ministries recognized. The long, hot summer of 2023 was made even longer and hotter by hundreds of political conventions and thousands of campaign speeches.It was, without a doubt, the most memorable campaign season on record.

At the Maris Institute, the usual chaos was squared, cubed, and then raised to the nth degree. From the sixth-floor balcony hung a garish red-white-and-blue banner , adorned with Miranda's picture and proclaiming: "Maris for Minister!" That banner was dwarfed, though, by a video screen fully five meters across— a screen that was now split into a dozen images, as the computer running it tried vainly to follow all major election coverage. The cacophony of a dozen audio channels at once was deafening.

Miranda Maris herself sat at a table comfortably near both the bar and— much more importantly— the ladies' loo, which tonight was designated "Candidates Only" by a hand-scrawled paper sign. Miranda had staked out the table fully two weeks ago, knowing that she would need to be a few steps from either the bar, the loo, or both.

It was just as well that she had chosen a convenient position; the crowd around her filled the main floor, and was in the process of crystallizing into a diamond-hard solid. If she hadn't been within reach of a bathroom already, she would have had to give up any hope of reaching one tonight.

Besides the Institute's own coterie of artists, craftspeople, and other creative types, the crowd was swelled by Miranda's many supporters (soon, she hoped, her *constituents*), assorted politicos, freeloaders and wannabees...and the Press, hungry for a unique angle on the biggest thing to hit American politics since 1776.

The members of the Press surrounded Miranda three deep, microphones and cameras skewering her against the wall. Right at the moment, Miranda sat opposite an empty chair, playing her part in the "chat with the candidate" game. As a neutral voice asked her questions, each reporter pretended to be sitting across from her. Digital compositing did the rest; on a bevy of monitor screens, Miranda saw herself participating in two dozen live interviews with as many hosts.

As she answered each question, she automatically played the part, keeping her eyes lively and interested, her voice level, and her face by turns thoughtful, confident, and amused. Inside, however, Miranda longed to break her façade and give *real* answers.

"Miranda, were you surprised when men and women of...er...amplitude qualified as a National Ministry?"

"Not at all. In fact, I was gratified at the recognition. After all, there *are* over twenty million of us, in all walks of life." ("Surprised? Lord, yes! You could have knocked me over with two wet noodles and a shoelace. Who'd'a thought over twenty million fatties would have the courage to admit it to the world by signing a petition? I expected ten, twelve thousand, tops.") ("And what's this 'men and women of amplitude' helms? What am I, a transistor radio?")

"I suppose that makes you one of the *largest* Ministries of the lot."

"Ha ha. I guess it does. I believe we're thirteenth in order of membership." ("Very funny, you Neanderthal. Try it again, and I'll not only sit on you...I'll *bounce*.")

"But seriously, the latest polls put you twenty percentage points ahead of your closest opponent. Are you confident that you'll win this election?"

"I wouldn't presume. Today, Americans transmit their votes in private, and they vote the way their consciences tell them— not the way the polls say. If I am fortunate to have the confidence of enough voters, I'll win; but if not, I'm confident that the decision the public makes is the right one." ("I'd *better* win, I've *spent* enough on this nunn election. I've got the best commercials, I've got the best campaign managers, and I've raised the most funds. And the dear *hoi polloi*, bless their ugly little hearts, can be counted on to vote the way the media tell 'em. Why else would I sit here being so nice to *you*, my dear?")

"This is the first national election in which voters have been able to vote from home. Do you think this will help your chances, or hurt them?"

Miranda smiled. "Home voting gives people more opportunity to ponder the issues and candidates. There's more time for serious debate and discussion. I can't help but feel that this new system will result in better, more reasoned decisions." ("A day off from work, with nothing to do but scan newsgroups and chat with the neighbors, until the deadline comes and it's time to punch in final choices— the American electorate has become the biggest and loosest of all the loose cannons in history, and when the results are finally in, heaven help us all.")

"Voters have been able to alter their selections up until the final hour. What effect do you think *this* change will have?"

"One thing's for sure, it will make a lot of pollsters unhappy." Miranda tossed her head. "Honestly, I think this brings a refreshing uncertainty to the whole process. No one— not the pollsters, not the candidates, not the national parties or the big-money special interests— no one can predict the outcome until the polls close and the counts are reported."

"So what you're saying, Ms. Maris, is that it isn't over until the fa— "

This was Miranda's moment; she lifted a finger and stared directly into the cameras, on her face the lines of amused determination, in her eyes the threat of power. "Honey, let's just leave it at that, okay?"

The interview was over.

The polls closed at nine Pacific time, which was seven in Honolulu and midnight in DC. Only microseconds later, when seven independent Census Bureau AIs agreed on the totals, the results were flashed across the Nets. Numbers leapt onto screens, and the Institute erupted in furious cheering that made the earlier pandemonium seem like a demure tea party.

Miranda had beaten her closest opponent by over two hundred thousand votes.

Much later, when all reporters were gone and most partygoers passed out, Miranda ordered the pool cover closed and took the elevator to her penthouse flat. The night was a blur of cheers, handshaking, and a new toast every few steps. After her first celebratory glass, she had only sipped— but there had been hundreds of toasts, and hundreds of sips added up to quite a few glasses.

Her head spun, and not just from the champagne. Winning this election was more exhilirating than she had imagined it would be. Campaigning had been another game, albeit a most engaging one; now that winning was an accomplished fact, Miranda realized that she had never really believed it would happen, that she would be one of the elite 436 Ministers.

She reached her flat and kicked off her shoes, then flopped on the large bed and grabbed a datapad. A queue of messages over six thousand long was waiting for her; Evelina, her comm agent, had managed to sort them into a rough priority order before throwing up its arms and whimpering from overload.

Miranda scanned the headings. The very first message was from the White House. She tapped it, and it opened on the screen. Routine congratulations, probably sent to every newly-elected Minister— but President Byrne had scrawled a personal note at the bottom: "Good work, old sod. See you in the history books. Love, Glen."

Miranda smiled, tapped the reply icon, and wrote: "Not if I see you first. Thanks. M."

Much of the rest of the mail was also congratulations, personal or professional. Miranda composed a brief but heartfelt thank-you. She instructed Evelina to autoreply it (with appropriate personalization) to everyone who wasn't on her list of intimate friends, with a cross-check against donor lists to ensure that her supporters got an extra paragraph thanking them for their contribution.

The mail queue shrank to a little more than a hundred messages. She then created an embellished version of the basic thank-you, and told Evelina to autoreply it to her friends. That took care of the rest of the messages.

She set down the datapad and stretched out on her bed, wriggling her toes and luxuriating in utter relaxation. The election was over, the tension of past few months now history.

A chime sounded, and Evelina announced, "Incoming call, family priority, voice-and-vision."

Miranda sat up, grabbing for the datapad. "Answer v-and-v."

The face on the screen was that of a young, slim woman with mocha skin and chestnut hair coiffed with bright ribbons atop her head. Her eyes, brown flecked with gold, mirrored Miranda's.

Miranda couldn't help but smile. "Oradell! To what do I owe this pleasure?"

The woman dimpled. "Mother, stop teasing. You know perfectly well why I'm calling. I read the news, and told Evelina to buzz me when you were done celebrating. Congratulations."

"'Twere nothing, really." Figures displayed at the bottom of the screen told Miranda that her daughter was calling from her home in Kampala, and that it was half past ten in the morning, her time.

"Don't be modest. I knew that old sourpuss Davenport wouldn't beat you." She giggled. "I'll bet he was livid."

"Fit to be tied," Miranda agreed. "Take a look at his concession speech...I'll have Evelina forward you the netcode. We were taking bets on whether or not he would burst a vein on camera."

"Damien didn't want to leave for school until he talked to you. He recorded a message for you, and I'm sure he'll call the instant he gets home." Miranda's grandson was six, and already he could make the Nets do things that amazed her.

"Make sure he checks the time; I'm likely to sleep in." Miranda stretched. "As a matter of fact, I think I might sleep in the rest of the *month*."

"I'm keeping you up."

"Not at all. It's a pleasure hearing from you. How's Marc?"

Oradell shrugged. "Off at some cultural conference in Mandela. He'll be back Thursday. To tell you the truth, I've kinda enjoyed having the house to myself. When Damien's gone, I've been getting a lot of work done."

"What are you working on now?" Oradell was a geologist with Umoja's transportation division.

"Preliminary mapping of the deep strata under the central Rift Valley. If I can find a stable enough route, we're hoping to start work on a high-speed subway link to the south."

"Sounds fascinating."Miranda turned her head too slowly to hide a powerful yawn.

"You poor dear, you're dead tired. I'm going to hang up and let you get to sleep."

Another yawn. "All right, I won't argue. Kiss, kiss." They exchanged air kisses. "And one for Marc, and two more for Damien."

"I'll call tomorrow, when we can talk longer."

"And with any luck," Miranda said, "I'll soon be on a fact-finding junket to Africa, and we can have some time together."

"It'll be nice to see you when it isn't Terran Council time. But we'll talk about that tomorrow. Congratulations again, and go to sleep."

"You're a dutiful daughter. Love you."

"I love you. Goodnight."

Oradell's image faded, and with a warmth inside her, Miranda turned off the light and went to sleep.

DIVERTISSEMENT 16

*Microbes with Strains Resistant to All Known Antibiotics*
source: MerckMed database, Special Report S-182.654.3151

| 2000 | 2040 |
|---|---|
| Enterococcus faecalis | Acinetobacter |
| Mycobacterium tuberculosis | Bacillus antracis |
| Pseudomonas aeruginosa | Bordetella pertussis |
| Shigella dysenteria | Clostridium tetani |
| Staphylococcus aureus | Corynebacterium diphtheriae |
| | Enterococcus faecalis |
| | Escherichia coli |
| | Francisella tularenis |
| | Heliobacter pylori |
| | Haemophilus influenzae |
| | Klebsiella |
| | Mycobacterium tuberculosis |
| | Neisseria gonorhoeae |
| | Propionibacterium acnes |
| | Pseudomonas aeruginosa |
| | Rickettsia rickettsii |
| | Salmonella typhi |
| | Shigella dysenteria |
| | Staphylococcus aureus |
| | Staphylococcus depidermidi |
| | Streptococcus pneumoniae |
| | Vibrio cholerae |

[22] KAMENGEN 09
Maris Institute
Elkridge, Maryland
United States, North America
16 August 2042 C.E.

*I like your game, but we're going to have to change the rules.*

Date: Sat, 16 Aug 2042 08:12:21 (GMT)
From: penylle@nexus.nex [Penylle]
Subject: Delaysend
To: Damien@nexus.nex
Message-id: <20420816081221_21146.021430_IMA22-36@nexus.nex>
Content-Type: text
Status: O

----------------------------------------

Damien—

If you receive this message, then I need your help.

I'm going to confront Marc/Jack when he returns from his conference. I don't anticipate any problems, but who knows? So I'm putting this message on a three-day delay. If all goes well, I will cancel it and you'll never know.

So we'll assume that you're reading this, I'm incommunicado or worse, and you want to do something about it.

The accompanying encrypted sequence contains three access codes that will get you into my system in Kampala. After that, the rest is up to you.

-P.

----------------------------------------

The Patapsco Room is both the most comfortable and the most eclectic of the Maris Institute's conference rooms. Like the fabled elephant graveyards, the Patapsco Room is the last resting place of unwanted furniture from all over the building. Two dozen mismatched easy chairs, love seats, and couches sit scattered among just as many ornate coffee tables, nightstands, and end tables. At least ten shelving units, no two precisely the same, hug the walls and support the most astonishing collection of knickknacks: sets of salt-and-pepper shakers, hundreds of coffee mugs, tacky ceramic statuettes in hideous shades of pink and bright green, someone's collection of amusing floral vases. From where he sits, and without turning his head, Damien can make out an indoor plastic birdbath, a miniature pink satin pillow embroidered "San Diego," a 2018 wall calendar imprinted with the name of someone's insurance company, a hammered aluminum nutcracker in the shape of the Eiffel Tower, and a statue of a lady with a clock where her stomach ought to be.

It is a very homey place. When Damien was a child, he spent untold hours in this room, and he feels that he knows every single piece of furniture and *objet d'art*. He feels quite comfortable here. That, he supposes, is why he chose the Patapsco Room to be the nerve center of the rescue mission that is officially listed in Nexus records as Operation Hunny Tree.

He stands before a wallscreen that displays a map of downtown Kampala. The others in the room, real or virtual, are a mixed bag, half Nexus operatives and half Damien's personal friends, mostly Institute residents; all have chosen to join Damien's project.

"From Penylle's system, I picked up a backdoor code to Marc Hoister's home security system." He looks to Skippy, his assistant. "Tell us what you found, Skip."

Skippy rises, grinning. "I didn't want to get caught in there, so I did a random series of spot-intrusions lasting between ten and fifty microseconds. It took a while just to map the system, because Marc Hoister has made a lot of alterations on the opsys level— "

"Speak English, Skippy."

"Oh, yeah. There aren't any security eyes inside the Tree House, but there are plenty of ears. As far as we can tell, Penylle is there, probably sedated." He touches his datapad, and the display behind Damien changes to a floorplan of the Tree House. A bright arrow chases across the screen. "She's in *this* basement room, accessible only through one door, *here*. From echo analysis, we conjecture that it's a solid steel door, at least five centimeters thick. My guess is that the walls, floor, and ceiling are similarly reinforced. If the lock is electronic, the security system doesn't know it."

"Thanks, Skip." Damien looks around the room. "It doesn't look as if any direct assault has a chance. What are our other options?"

Kumiko Ichihara, a petit Madame Butterfly in a black kimono embroidered with thousands of Drake's starbursts in gold and red, raises her hand. She is a Nexus operative based in Yokohama; her professional moniker, awarded in the streets of Tokyo, is *Yubi*— "Fingers."

Damien nods in her direction. "Kumiko?"

She stands. "Thank you. If I can be allowed ten undisturbed minutes with the door lock, it will be opened." She speaks evenly, stating a matter of fact rather than giving an opinion.

"Thank you." Damien turns to the rest. "How do we go about getting Kumiko those ten minutes?"

"Is there any possibility," Rose Cetairé asks, "of jiggering the security system so it will let us in?"

Skippy shakes his head. "That thing's got so many internal cross-checks, it would figure out that it was compromised and scream for help."

"So what we need," Rose ponders, "Is some plausible diversion that will let us get Kumiko in there legitimately."

Mateni Gerat and Babari Aparejo, pale-skinned teenage vampires, are next to one another on a green naugahyde love seat. The pair, Mati and Babi to their friends, are participating in their first real Nexus mission, and have been uncharacteristically quiet. They confer in whispers, then Babi elbows Mati in the ribs. He jumps up and clears his throat. "You've probably thought of this before, but what about a game?"

"What kind of game, Mati?"

"We were thinking of a live roleplay game. Something like *Teddy Bears' Picnic*, but without all the blood and violence."

"Mmm. With Makerere University so close, they're probably used to live games going on. The Tree House is unusual enough, they may have even participated before. Mati, can you find out for me if that's correct?"

"It is. I checked already. The Makerere Gaming Federation runs five or six tournaments each year in Kampala. The Tree House is listed as one of the participating sites."

"A question?"

"Efia?"

Efia's face is calm but for tiny, tense lines around her eyes. "A game might be enough of a diversion to get some of us in the door— but isn't Marc Hoister going to notice when gamers start picking the locks of his private dungeon?"

Desperado, a Nexus operative cloaked in gyrating rainbows, stands. "I have access to a number of heavy-duty delta-wave inducers. These are police-issue riot gear. They would serve to incapacitate those within the house, yet would not harm them. If you wish, I can procure one or two for this operation."

"That's brilliant." Sleepy-rays, the newest and most effective nonviolent weapons, are legally restricted to national and U.N. police and peacekeeping forces. They have been used in a handful of Nexus operations; so far, three national courts have sided with the Nexus and the World Court has declined to hear appeals. Until the World Court says otherwise, Damien intends to assume that any legitimate Nexus team can employ them.

1-Tin-Soldier, who wears the form of a silvered Art Deco robot, raises a hand and stands when Damien nods to him. "Have you considered that Penylle might need medical attention? I don't suppose it would be wise to take her to Kampala General."

"Good thought, Tin Man. Jamiar Heavitree is going to hold a bed at a facility in the south of France. All we have to do is get her there." He taps his datapad; the wallscreen displays an outline of the mission's major phases. "Which brings up the question of transportation. I don't think we can exactly flee by public transit, especially not if we're carrying an unconscious body." He surveys the faces. "I'm open to suggestions."

Rose waves a hand in dismissal. "It just so happens," she says, "that RC's corporate jet is going to be in Kampala that day. I'm meeting with some designers." She grins. "I'm sure I can dig some up."

"Rose, you're a goddess."

"I'll want that in writing. I'll rent two cars, and you can use one."

Damien scans the outline. "Folks, all the pieces seem to be in place. Can anyone think of something we haven't covered?"

No one speaks up.

"Perfect. I'll make a final check with the M, then we're off. The strike team will meet in Kampala on Tuesday. You have your transport codes; the project authorization code is kishimo-mdundugo-145." This is the first time Damien has commanded a mission with its own approved Nexus budget; already his financial agent, Midas Mulligan, is on top of expenditures. "Call me if you have any questions— but remember, extra security measures apply to any communication. Anything else?"

There is nothing. "Wonderful. Good luck, and I'll see some of you on Tuesday."

Kampala, Uganda
Umoja Economic Union, Africa
19 August 2042 C.E.

Three days. One to reach Africa, two to fret. Damien sets his team up in a luxurious suite in the Nile Hotel, about one and a half kilometers from the Treehouse. The Nexus doesn't customarily use the Nile, and Damien makes the arrangements through a South American identity that he hopes is unknown to Marc Hoister.

While Damien frets, Mati and Babi put the finishing touches on a city-wide live roleplaying game. Soon, mysterious dark-cloaked figures with hooded faces skulk in shadows everywhere.

1-Tin-Soldier arrives in the flesh, along with three police-issue delta-wave inducers. To Damien's surprise, 1-Tin-Soldier is really a wiry old grandmotherly type with the strength and grace of a prima ballerina; when she appears in public, her body is totally hidden by her cold-light avatar, the silvered robot in Art Deco style.

Kumiko Ichihara comes, too: one and a half meters of brain and sinew beneath a disarming geisha smile, a shy demeanor that hides razor-edged knives.

A party of five is all that Damien feels he can risk. More would risk Marc Hoister's suspicions.

Night falls quickly, in equatorial fashion; streetlights paint radiant gashes across wooded hills and buses crawl among the trees, caterpillars lined with luminescent spots.

Damien and his people don headsets; in addition to communication, these will shield them from the delta-wave inducers. Dark goggles give infrared-enhanced night vision. Jet-black jumpsuits, loose as pajamas, are followed by ebony masks, gloves, and boots; then hooded cloaks that project cold-light reverse holograms, literally soaking up any light that falls upon them. Only Anansi armor— projecting a 360-degree cold-light image of the wearer's background— could offer more protection from sight. The bulky delta-wave inducers are uneven lumps on the backs of Mati, Babi, and 1-Tin-Soldier.

They walk to the Treehouse, moving one-by-one between concealing shadows, from tree trunk to fence; traffic proceeds on the Kitante Road all oblivious to their passage. The night is sultry, and the mask makes it difficult to breathe. To Damien it seems that he moves through a dream of a memory— familiar streets and sights from his childhood: the corner where he skinned his knee, the candy shop that had the city's best sugared figs, the virtie palace behind which Imaya Zange proved to him that boys and girls really were different. These pass, garish in enhanced vision, and between the drumming in his head and the stuffiness of his mask, Damien can almost believe that he is asleep, tangled in blankets and struggling to awaken.

As they near the Treehouse, Damien leads his people downhill. "There used to be a drainage conduit down here, leading right to the back yard. Unless they've redesigned the storm drains— no, here it is." He frowns at the dark opening, barely shoulder-high. "It used to be bigger."

Babi laughs. "*You* used to be shorter." She leans forward, surveying the conduit. "I don't think we'll have any trouble."

With Babi in front, they proceed through the drain single-file, umbrella-stepping to avoid pooled water. The ditch behind the Treehouse is tangled with weeds and fallen branches; Damien struggles to the top himself, while Mati and Babi give 1-Tin-Soldier and Kumiko helping hands.

The Treehouse sits before and above them, climbing a gentle hillside in the embrace of woody limbs the size of tree trunks, and trunks the size of houses. A sudden raw ache takes Damien's throat, and he has to look away for a moment— if not, he is afraid that he will see his mother's face at one of the windows, or hear his father's deep voice calling him.

"How's it lookin'?"

Mati's question brings Damien back to himself. "Hold on, I'll find out." As they crouch in shadows, hidden by foliage, Damien slips on a dataglove and switches his goggles to display mode. Over the surreal infrared landscape, ghostly lines, figures, and numbers take shape.

With careful, precise movements of his fingers, Damien triggers a program that Skip wrote. Quicker than thought, it slips into the Treehouse's security system, snapshots data, and is out again before the system can notice. Damien scans the codes, and nods.

"Looks like we caught them at mealtime. Everyone is in the dining room— except Penylle, of course."

1-Tin-Soldier stands, managing to loom menacingly in the darkness. "Then let's do it, already."

Damien clicks off display mode. "Okay. Tinman, Kumiko, take your places. Report when you're set."

There is time for half a dozen deep breaths and an exchange of glances—

lenses to lenses— with Mati and Babi. Then 1-Tin-Soldier reports, "East entrance to ground-floor module, secure."

Seconds later, Kumiko's report comes: "South entrance, secure."

Damien takes a deep breath. "Skippy?"

His assistant answers from the Institute, where he is monitoring every phase of the operation. "Eighty seconds to go. By the time you get to the front door, it'll be time."

Damien nods to Mati and Babi. "Go."

He follows the two to the main entrance, hanging back a few steps. Skippy gives the go-ahead. Babi touches the bell; after a second, a female voice says, "Yes?"

Although he knows it is too much to hope, Damien is a little disappointed that the voice is not Marc Hoister's.

Babi clears her throat. "If you go out in the woods today, you'd better not go alone." It is the code phrase by which players in the roleplay game are supposed to identify themselves.

The woman's voice answers with the counter-phrase: "It's lovely out in the woods today, but better to stay at home." The door opens, revealing a slender, middle-aged woman with short-cropped dark hair and sandalwood skin. Her robes are brightly striped: red, yellow, and orange. From the information that Penylle left for him, Damien recognizes her as Elzada Makeba, Marc Hoister's housekeeper. "We're eating supper, so I don't want much disturbance. How many are you?"

"Three, *Bibie*," Babi answers. "Will we be able to see the Minister?"

Mati, the very picture of a supplicant, adds, "We can come back later, if this is a bad time."

The housekeeper shakes her head. "No, he'll be glad to see you. Gods know why, but he *likes* playing along with these silly things. Mind you, wipe your feet and be careful where you walk."

The house is spacious and airy, just as Damien remembers. Now that it is night, large windows and skylights glow, filling the house with a diffuse radiance. They walk past a down-curving stairway; at the bottom is a closed door. It is the door, Damien knows, to the room where Penylle is held.

In the dining room, a double-handful of people sit around a two-tiered table crowded with plates and pots of steaming stews, hills of seasoned rice, stacks of flatbreads. Marc Hoister is at the head of the table, robed in sand-colored linen; he rises from an ornate stool and holds out an arm in a gesture of welcome.

"Come in, my friends," he booms. "Welcome to our picnic. I am Chief of the Koala Clan; what boon do you ask?"

Damien steps forward. Dimly, he is aware of the response Marc expects, a request that will elicit some clue designed to carry the roleplay game to its next level. Doubtless several other bands of players have already visited today, and Marc Hoister is enjoying the chance to play the all-powerful, all-wise Koala Chief. But now, Damien intends to surprise the older man.

Remembering his Lord Ogun persona from El Juego, Damien stands straight and tall while Mati and Babi step back and away. He summons his haughtiest voice and says, "All that I want from *you,* Chief of the Koala, I will take for myself."

That is the signal; Mati and Babi move as one, holding up their delta-wave inducers like enormous cameras. There is in Damien's ears a muted buzzing, barely discernible— but the diners slump into instant, deep sleep. The housekeeper crumples to the hardwood floor, eyes closed and face slack. Marc Hoister is the last to succumb; a momentary look of astonishment crosses his face, then he slides to the floor and lays there asleep, breathing deeply.

"Stage one accomplished." While Mati and Babi are setting down their inducers, Damien opens a window and helps 1-Tin-Soldier across the threshold.

1-Tin-Soldier surveys the sleepers. "I'm sorry I missed the fun."

"We needed someone with an inducer on the outside, just in case."

Kumiko enters from the further depths of the house, moving silently as a shadow. "The south door wasn't even locked," she says, with a slight wistful tone. "How long do we have?"

Skippy's voice answers, "Nineteen more minutes until the security system makes its next full assessment. It'll realize something's wrong, but everyone asleep at night fits its pattern for standard operations. I'm guessing it'll be another four to six minutes before it starts asking for clarification, another eighty to one hundred seconds before it tries to wake people. As soon as it concludes that it can't, it'll scream for the police."

"So we have a good twenty-five minutes to get Penylle and leave. Plenty of time." Damien turns to Mati and Babi. "Take Kumiko to the basement. Tin Man, you'll watch for any other arrivals?"

"Absolutely." 1-Tin-Soldier shambles toward the main entrance, holding the inducer ready.

Mati leads Kumiko toward the stairs; Babi hangs back for a second. "Where are *you* going, Damien?"

"I have another errand to run. Go help Kumiko. I'll join you momentarily."

Although it's been decades since he lived in the Treehouse, Damien remembers the way to the uppermost room— the garret that was once his own, and now belongs to Penylle. A lift carries him swiftly to the right level, and he swallows hard before stepping out.

The room stirs no memory in him. Obviously, it's been redecorated since he lived here, perhaps enlarged a little, with new furnishings and new paint. (He worries, for an instant, that he cannot remember the original color of the turquoise walls.)

It takes him only a moment to spot what he has come for— Penylle's customized Amiga 7500 system, a battered beige box small enough to lift in one hand. Disconnecting the power cord and single network cable are the work of an instant. When he lifts the machine, he discovers a belt hook on the bottom and gratefully attaches it under his dark cloak.

With only six minutes elapsed, he is back on the ground floor, peering down the cellar stairs. Kumiko is at work on the door. Mati and Babi stand diffidently back, observing her efforts with evident interest. Damien smiles; if these two are to remain part of his team, he will have to see about getting them some lockpick training.

"How goes it?" he whispers.

Kumiko's words are slow, her voice distracted. "I have succeeded…in cutting…power to the lock. The mechanical…backup is…engaged. I am lifting…the first pin. The work…is very…delicate…and demanding."

"In other words," Babi says, "Don't distract her."

"Sorry." There is nothing for Damien to do, but to watch seconds tick by in unobtrusive digits at the bottom of his field of vision. Forty, sixty, ninety. Two minutes, three, four. At four minutes and twenty-three seconds, there is a distinct click from the lock, and Kumiko sighs. "Success."

The basement room is set up like a hospital suite; Penylle is asleep on the single bed, an intravenous tube in her left arm and dozens of scanners crowded around her. Damien fixes his eyes on the scene and stands quite still. "Skippy, can you bounce my visual input to Dr. Heavitree?"

"Damien, this is Jamiar. I see her. I am concerned about that IV— could you move a little closer? And turn the sack so that I can read the label better?"

Damien complies.

Jamiar grunts. "Saline. Nothing to be concerned with. You can remove the IV and apply a bandage to the site."

Damien fumbles uncertainly with the intravenous tube; Kumiko pushes past him and says, "Let me." With delicate fingers, she takes out the needle, accepts a bandage from Mati, and covers the spot. The bandage spreads a bit, adhering to Penylle's skin.

"Remove her covers," Jamiar directs.

When Damien draws back the covers, Penylle does not move. She wears a lightweight, colorful robe; her feet are bare. Her hair needs washing, and she smells of disinfectant.

"There's no catheter," Jamiar says. "I see no reason that you can't just lift her up and carry her out. She'll probably wake up when she's away from the sleep inducers."

"Here." Damien slips out of his cloak and drapes it across the bed at Penylle's side. Working with the others, he shifts Penylle until she is atop the cloak, stretched out on her back. Damien pulls a tab sewn into the fabric, and the edges of the cloak stiffen. While he moves straps to secure her, Mati and Babi take opposite ends of the cloak. Together they lift and, stretcher fashion, carry Penylle away.

"You have maybe ten more minutes," Skippy says.

"We only need five. I hope Rose's car is ready."

"It's fifty meters down the street, waiting for you just where we planned."

"All right, team. Let's go. Out the front door and quick march to the car."

They navigate the stairs and the entryway with little trouble. Damien almost regrets that he cannot take one last look at Marc Hoister comatose in the dining room. Before, he was too nervous— and now that he feels like gloating, there is no opportunity.

1-Tin-Soldier relieves Babi, handing her the inducer. "Cover us."

Halfway to the street, Damien turns for one last look at the Treehouse. He stops in his tracks and swears, "Exoning Pell!"

Only half a dozen paces away, Marc Hoister stands with arms crossed and an evil smile.

The others turn to see what bothers Damien. Babi raises the inducer, points it at Marc Hoister, and then lowers it.

"You didn't think I would let you get away with my fianceé, did you?" Without moving his legs, Marc Hoister comes toward them, gliding steadily as if on invisible wheels. And Damien, abruptly, understands.

"He's a hologram," he calls out. "He can't do anything to stop us. Go, go!"

They run...and Hoister keeps pace with them. "Of *course* I am a hologram. I am not in Kampala, you see— I have not been in Kampala for days. My cold-light image met you in the dining room. I feigned collapse." He shakes his head. "I knew you would come after her, so I was prepared."

They reach the road...the car is fifty meters away. Forty-five.

Hoister continues, staying an even two meters from Damien's right elbow. "You are quite wrong, that I can do nothing to stop you. You are already as good as stopped." He looks up. "Do you hear that?"

"Nunn!" Damien hears it all right— helicopters, coming nearer every second. Searchlight beams stab down in three spots, scanning the ground. They quickly converge on Damien and his friends.

"I have been in constant contact with the police since you entered my house," Hoister says. "I would prefer it if you would stop running. I do not want Penylle hurt."

Damien skids to a stop, aware that the others follow his lead. One of the copters swings overhead, then starts descending, whipping branches and leaves into a frenzy.

Damien faces Marc Hoister's hologram, throws off his hood, and removes his goggles. "You miserable excuse for a human being, you'll pay for this. This and everything else you've done in your pathetic, pointless life. I'll see to it."

Hoister chuckles. "Yes, of course you will." The copter is on the ground, disgorging half a dozen Umoja police in full riot gear. Hoister faces them, gives a mock salute, and says, "Your troops are here now, Colonel, so I will say goodnight. Thank you for the protection." As sudden as a blink, Hoister's image is gone.

The rest goes quickly: Damien and his friends are handcuffed and herded onto the copter with little ceremony. The copter is obviously set up to serve paramedics as well as police; the officers strap Penylle, stretcher and all, into a small medical bay in the back. Three police stay behind to make room; Damien finds himself in the seat behind the pilot.

Liftoff is smooth; the copter banks to the left and arrows off into the night, leaving the other two behind. To the right, downtown Kampala is a triple-handful of bright gems scattered against rippled green-black velvet.

The police officer next to the pilot turns around and offers Damien a nod. "I'm Chief Liyong. Don't worry, we'll have you to the airport shortly. The

Cetairé jet is already warmed up and ready for takeoff." She gestures at another officer. "Husani, take off their cuffs."

While his handcuffs are removed, Damien sputters. "What's going on?"

"Oh, I'm sorry." Liyong pulls aside her collar, displaying a discreet Drake's starburst tattooed just below her left clavicle. "The Ivory Madonna briefed us on your mission and asked us to assist if you ran into trouble." She spread her hands. "Well, you *did*, and here we are."

Mati grins. "You're *not* the police?"

"Oh, we're the police, all right. But we're also Nexus. As far as we're concerned, the girl is a political prisoner and you're rescuing her." She leans forward, mock-conspiratorial. "Marc Hoister instructed us to leave her behind. I imagine he's going to be a little displeased. You can guess how upset I am over that." She laughs. "Here comes the airport. Husani will guide you to your plane."

The copter settles to pavement. Damien feels as if his head is spinning as fast as the propellers. "I don't know how to thank you. I thought it was all over."

Liyong shakes his hand. "Not while you've got the Ivory Madonna watching over you. Take care, and good luck."

Soon the Cetairé jet is airborne, speeding northwest at Mach Two. Jamiar awaits them in Marseille with a specialist in rapid detox protocol. There is champagne and cake, but Damien partakes of little. There are congratulations from his team members, present and absent, and he gives a short speech of thanks, while stressing that the mission is not really over until Penylle is safe at the Institute.

After a time he strolls back to an aft cabin where Penylle sleeps on a narrow cot. He sits down next to her, takes her hand; she stirs, then falls back asleep. It is evident that more than a sleep-inducer is at work here; he suspects that she has been drugged.

"I wish I knew what to do for you," he whispers. "But that's going to be up to Jamiar."

He looks out the window, seeing once more in his mind's eye the laughing, gloating face of the man who calls himself Marc Hoister. "You'll pay," he says, and it is part sneer and part promise.

Outside, the dark African landscape falls behind.

## DIVERTISSEMENT 17

Date: Thu, 14 Aug 2042 22:44:40 (GMT)
From: auctionbot@auctionplace.com [Auction Place]
Subject: Update of current auction items
To: auction-list@auctionplace.com
Message-id: <20420814224440_132153.12050_MTR23-98@auctionplace.com>
Content-Type: text
Status: O

----------------------------------------

Today's rarities auction closes in just a little over an hour! Make sure to register your bid instructions with auctionbot, because a lineup like this won't happen again soon.

| ITEM | HIGH BID | BY |
|---|---|---|
| AOL Version 2.1 3.5-inch disk | $ 1,535.00 | Kilgore.Trout |
| Yellowstone Campground Reservation June 2045 | $ 512,450.00 | Sister_Goldenhair |
| Die-Cast TIE Bomber (1983) | $ 168,000.00 | Action.Jackson |
| *Dreamships* 1st ed. signed | $ 42,811.00 | Speed-of-C |
| Byrne in '16 holoanimated button | $ 905.00 | LittleJoe |
| Adventure Comics #247 mint | $ 2,256,390.00 | Getalife-Boy |
| New Coke 6-pack mint | $ 7,975.00 | Roy.Bean |
| Ronald Reagan tissue sample/DNA | $ 482.50 | Mostly.Harmless |
| Enewetak Atoll, Marshall Islands | $ 5,381,000.00 | Rockwell |

----------------------------------------

## [23] TARANTELLA 06
Elkridge, Maryland
United States, North America
July 2015 C.E.

*I am the Mother of All Things,*
*and All Things should wear a sweater.*

It was the year that the Democratic Party deserted President Stewart, nominating Barclay and Banner on only the third ballot. A comprehensive campaign finance reform bill finally passed the House by three votes, but the Senate version died in committee. Anti-Christian rioting in St. Louis claimed eight lives and left hundreds injured. At the Calgary Summit leaders of Iran, Iraq, Syria, Israel-Palestine, and Turkey met with Kurdish representatives and settled on a plan to bring peace to the war-torn region. The long-delayed seventh chapter of the *Star Wars* series opened in May at virtie palaces across the nation; by the end of the first week, the feature had recouped every penny of its $13 billion production costs.

In June, just in time for the Southern Baptist Convention, Cetairé-Maris Designs released a very chic, retro-1920's line of linsey-woolsey fashions under the label "Abomination." At a Paris press conference, Madame Cetairé explained that the new line had been inspired by Deuteronomy 22:11: "You shall not wear a mingled stuff, wool and linen together." The Southern Baptists obliged her by noisily denouncing the company's "mockery of Scripture," and overnight Abomination became the hottest-selling line in fashion history.

A celebration, Miranda Maris decided, was quite definitely in order.

Accordingly, Cetairé-Maris Designs rented a large hotel for the Bastille Day weekend, and threw the doors open to friends, relatives, business associates, and assorted well-wishers of all types.

Like all creative souls, she and Rose had always been at home with artists, musicians, actors, talented people of all stripes. Sensing free food and great parties, they flocked to the hotel— taking advantage of universal bohemian brotherhood, each brought his or her own entourage.

Drawn by the bohemians, journalists and reporters swarmed like moths to the flame. Journalists of course brought politicians and gray eminences; these in turn drew those who worshipped power. In the end, more than two thousand people eventually passed through, and Miranda did her best to spend time with all of them.

The party passed into legend, so that eventually tens of thousands would claim to have been there. When all was said and done, the Abomination Party was credited with the creation of twenty-five books, twenty new bands, fifteen billion-dollar mergers, a dozen marriages, ten gold records, eight blockbuster virties, six corporations, four Broadway musicals, three masterpiece paintings, two religions, and a proof of Goldbach's Conjecture.

Late Monday evening, as entropy claimed the last of both decorations and survivors, Miranda sat in the hot tub and scratched herself contentedly. Rose was on her right, snuggling with a tanned rock star; Mahlowi and Robin were on her left, in a very convincing hologram that gave no hint that they were actually in Africa. Phil and George Meade, a pair of revolutionary virtie producers, were across the small pool.

Phil tipped an imaginary hat. "I have to hand it to you, Miz Miranda. This will go down in history as *the* social event of the year. If not the decade."

Miranda took a sip from her mint julep and fanned herself. "Why, Mister Phil, I do declare that you may just be right." She sighed. "It's sure been a lot of fun."

Eyes sparking, Mahlowi said, "What are you going to do *next* year to top this?"

Rose shook her head. "Next year, it's at *your* place."

Miranda leaned back, letting her arms go limp; lifted by the bubbling jets, they floated and bobbed before her, as if they had no connection to her at all. She was weightless; is this how the astronauts feel? She suddenly realized that she could find out— she could certainly afford to take one of the passenger flights that were springing up from everywhere.

I'm fifty-seven, she thought. And, thanks to Cetairé-Maris and Abomination, I have enough money to do anything I want.

So what do I want?

She turned her head in Rose's direction. "Fifty-seven. Did you ever think we'd be this old?"

Rose stretched her slender arms above her. "*You* may be old— I'm not."

"She's got two years on me," Miranda said to the assembled company. "She'll be sixty next year."

"Nevertheless," Rose answered, "I'm not old. Sixty isn't old. Sixty is what fifty used to be. Eighty is what sixty used to be. *Ninety* is old. By the time I get to seventy, it'll be what fifty is now. Ninety will be what *sixty* was. A hundred will be old." She shrugged. "If this keeps up, we'll *never* get old."

"Sometimes I feel like I'm a hundred. On a bad day, a hundred and fifty."

There was silence for a time, then Phil said, "This has been a great vacation. But tomorrow morning it's back to work for all of us."

"If we had any sense," George said, "We'd live like this all the time."

Hollow Robin smiled. "Right. And we'd all die from exhaustion."

Miranda laughed with the others; but when she was done, she lifted her head to survey the soaring lobby, the somnolent guests gathered in clumps as lethargic as her own. Across the lobby stretched a dozen paper chains, tethered together into an impromptu Drake's Starburst. A few hotel employees with ladders surveyed the creation, obviously at a loss.

"Why not?" Miranda said, half to herself. "How much could a hotel like this cost?"

Her friends exchanged glances, as if trying to decide which one would burst her bubble. Apparently, Phil won. "It's not the original cost, it's the upkeep that will do you in. You can't support three hundred people for the rest of their lives."

"I wouldn't need to. They'd support themselves." She looks into the distance. "As a matter of fact, they could support the place as well."

"How?"

"Take yourselves as an example. In lieu of rent, you'd assign a portion of royalties to the management. So would I. So would Rose. I'll bet plenty of others would want to come in."

Rose rolled her eyes. "A self-supporting artists' colony? M, you're out of your mind."

Mahlowi chuckled. "The Miranda Maris Institute for Wayward Artists."

"Think about it," Miranda said. "What would it be worth to you, to live surrounded by creative people like this?"

Hollow Robin nodded. "Mahlowi and I couldn't live here...but we'd sure want to be a virtual part of the community. It would be worth five percent. At least."

Miranda sat up, feeling the churning water lift her off her seat. "Why not? It could work."

Rose snorted. "Good luck!"

Finding a suitable hotel for sale was simplicity itself. Business travel had declined every year for the past six, and the trend was projected to continue for the foreseeable future. Virtual conferencing had become the new status symbol— only junior executives suffered the hassle of real-world travel. Outside tourist areas, hotels were available at fire-sale prices.

Miranda had only to find a real estate agent who specialized in hotels, and explain what she wanted. Two weeks and 1.6 million dollars later, she was the proud owner of a vintage 1980's suites hotel, complete with kitchens, pool, terraced balconies overlooking a huge central atrium, and more staff than she knew what to do with.

A hotel was not a home. Rooms had to be joined, enlarged, fitted with all the high-tech gear that Hollow Robin insisted upon. Common areas had to be redesigned; offices, workshops, and studios appointed. Miranda turned over all the details to her general contractor, Ryk Stryker, head of Stryker Construction and a longtime friend.

The business details were, in their own way, as complex as the construction process. Miranda was wary of government intrusion, so decided that the Maris Institute would be a private foundation rather than a public charity. Her attorneys, Miles, Ng, Katzenberg, Mfume, and Ng—who ultimately cost nearly as much as the building itself— handled all of the government paperwork, as well as drawing up contracts for participating artists. The senior Mr. Ng, in fact, was so impressed by the project that he purchased his own shares and retired from law to pursue his dream of becoming a harpsichordist.

Rose Cetairé was less enthusiastic.

"Miranda, these are *artists.* No common sense. No financial responsibility. Half of them don't even have a honeypot to hyde in. By the time you're ready to go into business, they'll be distracted by the next shiny thing to come along. How far are you in debt right now?"

"Two million or so," Miranda answered easily.

"And it'll be twice that before you even open for business. Not to mention operating expenses. Hon, you know that I don't want to see you hurt. But this thing can't succeed."

Miranda stuck out her chin. "Phil and George have already assigned four profit points from their next virtie. That'll be half a million, easily. Renfield's giving us half of what he makes from the *Leivnpaahdin* video game. Spike Speedwell's even signing over the royalties to their next book."

"Pie in the sky. What about *now*?"

"I got a grant from the last World Creativity Conference." Miranda smiled. "That's not the point. Money's out there, and we'll get our share until we're self-supporting." He eyes twinkled. "In fact, in five years the

Maris Institute will be issuing grants of its own. Want to bet?"

Rose's eyes narrowed. "I know better than to bet against you. You cheat."

"Do not."

"Do too."

Miranda laughed. "Honey, I know better than to ignore *your* intuition. What's really bothering you about the Institute?"

Rose opened her mouth, closed it again, looked away. "You're going to lose your shirt again. And I just don't want to have to pick up the pieces this time."

"Are you getting tired of it?" Miranda shook her head. "That's not it, Rose. What's the problem?"

Rose spun her head around, and their eyes locked. "You know, you might have at least *asked* me if I wanted to be part of this."

"I just assumed— "

"Of course, you did, lummox. Why bother asking Rose how she feels, why not just assume she doesn't want to play?"

Miranda took Rose's hand in both of hers, pressing it like a flower between musty pages. "Rose, I'm *so* sorry. I took you for granted. I don't know what to say."

Rose sniffed. "I think you do."

Miranda's brow furrowed, then she relaxed. "Rose Cetairé, would you like to be a founding member of the Maris Institute for Wayward Artists?"

Rose grinned. "I'll think about it."

It was the day after Thanksgiving, and the Institute was only half-finished. Still, the main atrium was substantially complete, the kitchens were in business, and enough living quarters were done to accommodate that portion of the peripatetic population who were in town.

The atrium floor and half the balconies were shoulder-to-shoulder with residents, visitors, and the media. Dozens of large, high-resolution datascreens showed hundreds more, virtual visitors from around the world and from both Novy Mir and Freedom Stations.

"You could have dressed in Abomination," Rose whispered to Miranda.

Miranda threw her head. "*That* trash? *Everyone* wears Abomination." Miranda preferred to wear her *own* clothes; for tonight she had made a midnight-blue neo-Tudor gown, dripping in pearls; it lent her the same indomitable grace as the Statue of Liberty. She took one more look at the crowd. "Well, I guess people didn't mind giving up their Thanksgiving weekend after all."

Phil Meade looked at his watch. "It's time. Get out there and make us proud of you."

Miranda nodded to her stage manager. Throughout the atrium, lights dimmed and the crowd's gentle susurrus died down to expectant silence. Miranda stepped forward, brushing past a curtain, and took her place on a second-floor ledge that afforded maximum visibility. For a panicked moment she glanced back, then calmed when she saw that her friends were at her side.

Spotlights stabbed through the gloom, illuminating Miranda and the others. She took one last step forward, then raised her arms.

"Friends...visitors...people of the world...welcome to the Maris Institute." Her voice, amplified, rolled like thunder in the atrium, which suddenly seemed much smaller. "Tonight, we are pleased to share with you a celebration of the varied forms of art that have brought us together. When the night is over, many of you will depart for your homes— but some of us will stay here. For now, this *is* our home. And we hope it is a home, and a family, that will encourage all of us to do our best. We hope that this home, this family, will make it possible for each of us to make the world a better place."

She paused to allow the applause to die down. "In a little while, we'll start the speeches and I'll have a chance to thank everyone who helped to make this dream a reality. But first, we have something a little more important to take care of."

She took a deep breath, then belted out:

*"It's amazing,*
*Space is folding,*
*Ways your mind can't*
*Comprehend.... "*

## MENUET 09

:ARTS & HUMANITIES:ARTS:ORGANIZATIONS:FOUNDATIONS :GRANTS:CURRENT:MARIS INSTITUTE:

NOTE: The Maris Institute interprets the term "Artist" very broadly. If your work is creative and seeks to communicate with an audience, then you are probably eligible.

Artist-in-Residence (3): Two-year grant covers room & board plus full access to real & virtual facilities. Includes Net/VR account with 60 TB storage, individual mentor/counselor, and monthly stipend. Three grants available.

Artist-in-Virtual-Residence (6): Two-year grant covers Net/VR account with 60 TB storage, full access to virtual facilities, individual mentor/counselor, and monthly stipend. Six grants available.

Satellite Artistic Residence (35): Two-year grant covers room & board at a satellite facility (35 worldwide) plus full access to real satellite facilities. Includes Net/VR account with 60 TB storage, full access to Institute virtual facilities, and individual mentor/counselor. Artist is required to contribute a token monthly sum. Thirty-five grants available. (No guarantee of assignment to any particular site.)

Artist Assistance (number varies): One-time grants to assist producing artists with ordinary bills and expenses such as rent, mortgage, utilities, equipment, supplies. Individuals are eligible for only one award in a five-year period. Number and amount of awards varies.

IMPORTANT: Artists must agree to assign to the Maris Institute a small percentage (usually 0.1 - 0.8%) of future royalties from all artistic works produced during the grant period.

TO APPLY: Visit the Maris Institute at <maris.institute.fnd/grants/applibot> and chat with our Grant Applications 'bot.

## DIVERTISSEMENT 18

*CAN YOU BUILD THIS ROOM?*

If you can, then you may have the talent to be a virtreal designer.

The need for talented virtreal designers is greater than ever before. All areas of cyberspace are expanding exponentially— Cyberbia, El Juego, and Virtua. Someone has to design and build the landscapes and environments to fill all this virtreality; why not *you*?

Virtreal designers are respected and valued. They command top salaries and royalties. Shouldn't you be one of them? The talents aren't as rare as you might think.

So go ahead, build this room, or one like it. Use any virtual-design tool you wish. Send us your virtreal creation, and our panel of experienced cybersmiths will critique your work for *free*. If you show promise, you'll be given a chance to enroll in the oldest and most prestigious school in Cyberbia: the Coates Academy.

Reply to <eval@coatesacademy.biz>

[24] KAMENGEN 10
Elkridge, Maryland
United States, North America
22 August 2042 C.E.

*May you come to the attention of those in authority.*

Tangled in his covers, Damien awakens in a panic. Then, recognizing his own familiar bedroom at the Institute, he relaxes. Kampala is three days in the past. He and Penylle arrived at the Institute late Thursday night; the clock tells him it's after 9 o'clock Friday morning.

"Hon, it's time to think about getting up." He rolls over to another shock: Penylle is gone, her side of the bed cold.

He sits up. "Penylle?" Throwing off the covers, he jumps out of bed. "Penylle?"

Searching the flat takes scant minutes; he does not find Penylle, but on his second trip through the kitchen he sees a note from her on the refrigerator display. It is timestamped about an hour earlier.

"Damien— off to breakfast with the Ivory Madonna. She said to let you sleep. See you soon. Love, P."

Breakfast. Where would the M take her for breakfast? Pulling on clothes, Damien invokes Rahel, his comm agent. "Where's the M?"

After a moment, Rahel answers,"Miranda Maris is in the east courtyard, at dining table five. She requests not to be disturbed. Would you like to record a message?"

"Bloody pell, no. I'll go see her."

It is not hard to find them; Damien has only to follow the steady stream of residents flowing to and from the east courtyard. Penylle's dramatic rescue has made her a celebrity at the Institute, and it seems that everyone wants to meet her.

Penylle and the M are at a small table under an artificial elm sapling, up against a glass wall that looks out on the floral chaos of the east garden and the rolling hills beyond. The sun is still fairly low, a hovering ball of brightness, indistinct in the summer haze.

"Damien!" Penylle spins in her seat, beaming. She waves him to an empty chair and gestures at a plate. "We saved you some cantaloupe. It's luscious."

Damien kisses Penylle and sits next to her. In an instant, a plate is before him, and someone hands him a spoon.

Around a muffin, the M says, "It was Penylle's idea. I didn't want to save you anything. The early bird gets the worm, you know."

"Punishment for getting up too early," he counters. "Who wants to eat worms?" Penylle is right; the melon is perhaps the best he's ever had. "Any possibility of some coffee?"

Penylle pours him a cup from a pot already on the table. Her smile, the graceful drape of her arm as she pours, the aroma of fresh coffee, the sweet melon – all swirl around him and through him, like gentle surf pulling him out to sea. Grinning like a news anchor, Damien touches Penylle's hand, a light caress that is also a promise, then sips his coffee.

The M shakes her head as she polishes off the last bite of muffin. "Damien, that's disgusting. If I'd known you were going to make puppy eyes this early in the morning, I would never have invited you to breakfast."

"You didn't invite me. I gatecrashed."

"All the better reason to mind your manners." Wiping her mouth, the M raises her hands and claps twice. "Thank you all very much for coming," she bellows. "The show is over now. You can meet her tonight at the Hallelujah Chorus."

"We had the Hallelujah Chorus *last* week," someone complains.

"And we will have it again tonight. We have much to celebrate. For our daughter, who was lost, is found— and so forth. Kill the fatted calf and put a wild boar on the spit." She looks from face to face around the circle of onlookers, as if daring them to object. "Well, *go*, all of you. I want some time alone with the lovebirds."

The crowd disperses goodnaturedly. Miranda's jolly grin fades into a more serious expression; as if casting off a no-longer-wanted robe, she sheds the clownish persona that so often tempts her enemies into underestimating her. A focussed intelligence burns laser-bright from her eyes, pinning Damien to his chair.

"Enough chitchat," she says. "Let's get down to business. Penylle, dear, where do we stand on this drug that Marc Hoister has you hooked on?"

"Doctor Heavitree has me on epinephrine and pseudoendorphins while he's trying to find the exact formula."

The M raises an eyebrow. "Damien?"

He shrugs. "M, I've got the AIs helping him out. Honestly, it's just a matter of time."

"Have you investigated the lab where Marc has been getting the stuff? *Someone* knows what he's been using; maybe we can bribe them. Or find out from shipping records."

"We have people on it. Seriously, M, I appreciate your suggestions— "

"But you have all the angles covered already. I'll trust you and your people, then. Keep me informed." She chews her lower lip for a second. "Penylle, what do you think Marc is up to now? Frankly, I'm amazed that he hasn't tried to snatch you back from us."

Penylle stares down at her plate for a moment before answering. "I suspect that he doesn't actually need me any longer."

"Elaborate, please."

"All the damage that Marc wanted to do the AIs is done. Now, he'll just be sitting back to let events take their course."

The M frowns. "Meaning, I suppose, that there will be more infrastructure failures. And us with no way of knowing where they will hit." She taps her fingers against the table. "Honey, if you can remember what changes you made, to which AIs, do you think we could unravel this thing? Maybe predict where some of these disasters are going to strike?"

Damien snorts. "Good luck! Maybe Hollow Robin could do it, but I can't even follow my *own* programs from ten years ago. What you're asking is like trying to figure out which way a chess master is going to play his next game."

Miranda shakes her head. "Then we're going to have to approach this in reverse. What classes of failures would make life on Earth seem unpleasant? Maybe if we know what might happen, we can alert the Nexus before— "

"Miranda?" Penylle's brow is furrowed, her eyes tight. "Trying to prevent disasters is a noble thing, and I guess it makes sense under the circumstances...but don't you think we should focus on the *real* problem? There might still be time to change their minds."

Both Miranda and Damien stare. "Honey, what are you talking about?"

"The AIs. " At their blank stares, Penylle's look of confusion becomes one of dread. "I thought you knew. Damien, you told me you had Marc's plans all figured out."

"I thought I *had*."

"Never mind. Penylle, tell us what you're talking about?"

She quivers. "Marc's been setting viruses and worms loose in the AI community for years. Doesn't it stand to reason that the AIs are going to conclude that they're under attack? And when they do, the Treaty isn't going to stop them." Wild-eyed, she looks from one to the other. "What happens when they conclude that Humanity is a danger to them? That outbreak of Dekoa in Dinétah was just the beginning."

The M nods. "That holds together. More epidemics, and more people will want to move to Mars." She gives a great sigh. "Maybe the best thing we can do is just to hurry him along on his migration. Once he's gone, things will go back to normal."

"W-What are you saying?" Penylle leans forward, gripping the M's hand between her own. "Things aren't going to go back to normal when Marc takes his people to Mars. He's not going to leave the rest of us here to come after him. That's why he's got the AIs into it to begin with. *He intends for them to eliminate civilization on Earth entirely.* And they'll do it."

Damien raises his eyes, suddenly aware of a million giant mirrors thousands of kilometers above, mirrors poised to incinerate every city on the planet….

Miranda spends the rest of the day in conference with her Nexus colleagues. Penylle attempts to retrace her steps, unmaking the changes that she has made to various AIs at Marc Hoister's direction. Damien, for his part, tries to talk to his AI friends— but they are more enigmatic than usual, and not even **Øµt øf Thrëë, thë M¥riåd Thiñgs** seems to understand what he is asking.

At nineteen o'clock Damien, hungry and exhausted, pulls off his bitsuit. Penylle, sitting crosslegged on the bed, stares blankly ahead; he leans over and gives her a quick peck on the lips. After a moment, her eyes focus, and she smiles and stretches. "Hi. How did you do?"

He spreads his hands. "Who can tell? For a while I thought I was getting through, then we were in the middle of a Kurasowa retrospective scored by Borodin. If there was some message there for me, I'm too dense to understand it." He raises his eyes. "What about you?"

"I made some repairs. But I honestly think I'm locking the barn after the cow's been stolen. The effects have been propagating through the Nets for a long time; the front of activity has got to be far away by now."

He works his right arm, wincing. "I twisted my shoulder getting out of the way of a samurai."

"Poor baby. Why don't you take a hot shower?"

Damien puts on his best pout. "I was hoping you'd rub it for me."

With a sigh she stands, begins unwrapping her skirt. "Go start the water. Make it nice and warm— last night you almost froze me to death."

As they stand in the warm spray, embracing, Damien feels invisible fingers caressing his shoulder muscles from within. He stiffens at the sensation.

"Relax," Penylle whispers. "It's just pk."

"I never considered the...practical applications." Tension and stiffness seem to drain from his arm as she works. "Hon, you could get a job as a professional masseuse any time you want."

"Thanks, I guess."

"You've *got* to do this for the M. If you think she likes you now, just wait— she'll adopt you as her heir."

She continues the massage, relieving tensions he didn't know he had. Damien does his best to return the favor. They kiss, flesh presses against supple flesh, and one thing follows another, until at last they cling together, languid under the soft, steamy deluge.

Only the insistent beeping of a reminder signal draws Damien from his contented doze. "What?"

Rahel's emotionless voice says, "Reminder: the Hyperspace Jig begins in fifteen minutes."

Damien looks into Penylle's eyes. "I don't suppose we can miss it?"

She shakes her head. "*You* might, but I don't dare. Not on my first official night here." She smiles. "Besides, I'm hungry."

"I wish you hadn't mentioned that." Damien's own stomach growls. "Well, there will be enough to eat tonight, that's for sure." He switches the shower to warm airjets, shakes his head vigorously. Eying her long tresses, he says, "I'll bet I can get dressed before you do."

Penylle steps back, closes her eyes, and takes a deep breath. In an instant, every drop of water leaps from her body in an expanding sheet— half of it, it seems, catches Damien full in the face. "You're on!" Completely dry, she dodges under his arm and toward the bedroom, where her clothes are rising up in the air to meet her.

They make it to the lobby with only instants to spare. As soon as the Hyperspace Jig is over, Penylle is at the center of a surging throng. Damien steers her toward a banquet table heaped with hors d'ouerves; she perches on a brick wall surrounding an indoor garden, and happily munches as she greets residents.

After helping himself to an overflowing plate of the choicest tidbits, Damien goes in search of the M. She was at her accustomed place for the Jig, but vanished immediately after. He slips on his RCSpex and invokes Rahel. "Where is the M?"

"Miranda Maris has suspended tracking. She requests not to be disturbed. Would you like to record a message?"

"No." Probably in her office again, still dickering with Nexus high muckety-mucks. He decides to go up to report in person.

The elevator is empty; Damien stands at the glass wall, looking over the lobby as he soars above it. Through his RCSpex, the teeming crowd is a swarm of faerie creatures: elves and gnomes, overmuscled warriors and buxom princesses, even a golden dragon with wings spread across ten meters. On the balcony above the ballroom, two dozen Merrie Men and Women are conducting a virtual archery contest.

A frantic alert tone suddenly sounds; simultaneously, a window opens before Damien's eyes, showing a wild-eyed, tawny-haired woman— Mari Akaev, the Institute's Reception Supervisor. "Damien?"

"Go ahead." He grips the elevator's handrail, knowing that trouble is on the way.

"There are tanks and APCs pulling up outside."

"Show me."

The outside view, from a camera atop the roof, shows half a dozen tanks and two armored personnel carriers outside the Institute's fence. The vehicles bear the United Nations symbol.

Damien frowns. "What are blue helmets doing here?"

"Well, they're too late for the Hyperspace Jig. I'm tracking three choppers overhead. We've had no contact from them yet."

"What does the M say?"

"I can't reach her. That's why I buzzed you. This doesn't exactly fall under my usual authority."

The elevator slows, and the doors open. "I'm at the M's office right now. Keep this channel open. Scream if they move." He bolts down the corridor to the M's tightly-closed door. He presses his palm against the jamb and says, "Override Damien eight eight one one." The lock clicks, and he pushes the door open.

The Ivory Madonna stands at her desk, wearing her mask; around her are a dozen other faces. Some, Damien recognizes as Nexus North America bigwigs; others are unfamiliar.

The M holds up her hand, interrupting a brightly-colored kachina in the middle of a word. "A moment, please. Damien, what is it?"

"A platoon of blue helmets outside. With tanks and copters."

The kachina throws up its arms. "Well, there we are. I expect the rest of us will be visited before long."

An obsidian face reminiscent of Easter Island looks briefly aside, then turns back. In a booming voice as portentous as a church organ, it declares, "I see that they have arrived here already."

The M nods. "I don't think we need to wait for a motion to adjourn. The best of luck to you all, Gentles, and may we meet safely on the other side." With that, the other faces wink out. Miranda stands still for a moment, then slowly peels off her mask and places it on her desk. Eyes grave, she turns to Damien.

"M, what's happening here?"

She gestures to a monitor, which shows the tanks and APCs. "Those aren't ordinary blue helmets. They're under the command of InfoPol."

"InfoPol? What do *they* want?"

Without a trace of a smile, she says, "They've come to arrest me."

It takes a few seconds for the meaning of her words to penetrate to Damien. "What do you mean?"

"Wait. Let me cut in the others." She touches a key on her desk. "Broadcast to all senior personnel, highest priority. Begin." She looks up, addressing Damien and two dozen others as well. "May I have your attention? United Nations troops under the command of InfoPol are about to enter the Institute. They have come to place me under arrest. They will be heavily armed, and will not hesitate to shoot first. Please offer *no* resistance while residents and guests are vulnerable."

She takes a breath. "This arrest is part of a concerted operation to arrest all Nexus North America senior operatives. InfoPol intends to take us before the World Court on charges which include terrorism, restraint of trade, crimes against humanity, and neglecting to pay the electric bill." A wan smile. "I assure you, none of us have any intention of being arrested, and our escapes are well-planned. Doubtless we will find it expeditious to go underground for a while, but you can count on seeing me again, soon."

A jolt of relief hits Damien, weakening his knees.

The M continues, "Effective immediately, Damien is in command. If any of you give him the slightest bit of trouble, I will find out and the result will *not* be pretty. You have been warned."

Outside, troops begin filing out of the APCs in twin columns.

"As I said, InfoPol is after me and me alone. The rest of you are in no danger, so don't be stupid. I want you all to assist in gathering all residents and guests around the pool area. Maximum confusion would be useful." She stops for a second, looking around. "It might be wise for many of you to leave the Institute temporarily after tonight. Our satellite facilities around the world are at your disposal. Thank you." A tap of her finger closes the circuit.

"InfoPol," Damien says, helplessly. "Why?"

"Technically, Nexus leaders are all international criminals. I'm sure there are dozens of outstanding warrants on each of us."

"But they've never— "

"Up until now," Miranda says, "it's been politically risky to move against us. The voters won't stand for it. So the U.N. and InfoPol and everybody else has maintained the fiction that our code names protect us. All those warrants, I'm sure, are for 'The Ivory Madonna aka Miranda Maris.'"

"What changed?"

"InfoPol claims that they received reliable intelligence naming the public figures behind the code names." She lowers her voice. "My theory is that our friend in Kampala is in control of InfoPol. The orders came out of Chief Lipponen's office, with his signature; but if you search the news, you'll find that Per Lipponen hasn't made a single personal appearance anywhere since a year ago July." She shrugs. "Draw your own conclusions."

Gooseflesh dances briefly on Damien's arms. "How many people *is* he?"

"No idea." Miranda leaves the desk and walks toward her bedroom. "I need to pack a few things. Walk with me." Very businesslike, she starts filling a suitcase, while Damien stands in the middle of the room, watching dumbly.

"Don't worry about me," she says. "I've been planning for this eventuality for ages. Our sub-basement connects with the old Holiday Inn's parking garage, which exits just over the hill from the expressway. All I need to do is cut through one chain-link fence and roll downhill; an operative will be there to pick me up, then I'm off."

"Where will you go?"

"Someplace safe...and with no connection to the Institute." She sheds her robe, pulls on a dark, flowing outfit that swirls about her like concealing shadows. "Listen. InfoPol will be all over this place tonight— I don't want any of our people hurt. Jennifer Ng is already filing petitions and countersuits like crazy; by Monday morning all these charges will be dropped and the Institute will be back in business. Meanwhile, I want maximum confusion and all possible brouhaha."

"I'll do my best."

"Damien, once all of our people are safely around the pool area, I want them to sing the Hallelujah Chorus." Her eyes meet his. "I want everyone to sing as if they were at Dagon's house. Do you understand?"

Damien nods. "I understand." *At Dagon's house.* A code phrase for the ultimate diversionary tactic. "I'll pass the word. I'll make sure everyone else understands."

She closes her suitcase. "Well, this is it. I will contact you in a few days, when I'm secure. Until then, you're in the hot seat. Sorry, but it can't be helped."

She hugs him, and he clings to her, allowing her strength to buttress him, her indomitable will to fill him and armor him. "Take care of yourself," he says.

"Bet on it."

"I love you."

"And I love you, kid. You make me proud. You always have." She breaks the embrace, giving his hand one last squeeze, then brushes at her hair. "We're off, then, my dear: me to the basement, and you to deal with our visitors in blue."

She stops at the door, takes one last look around, then clicks off the lights and hurries toward the elevators.

As the elevator descends, Damien looks out over a party in full swing. He can discern, though, clumps of people moving toward the pool area. Scanning the crowd, he sees members of the Institute's senior staff purposefully threading their way through the surging crowd.

He dons his RCSpex, and the party is suddenly twice as crowded and ten times as colorful. "Rahel," he commands, "Establish an unobtrusive and pervasive audio link between all senior staff."

A moment passes, then Rahel's unemotional voice answers, "Link established. Trigger word is 'kamata.'"

Is it just chance, Damien wonders, or some perverse electronic sense of humor, that causes Rahel to choose as a trigger the Kiswahili word for "arrest?"

"Kamata. Hello, everyone, this is Damien. I've established this link for the duration. It's important for us to stay in touch, but let's keep this circuit as clear of chatter as we can, la?"

"Damien, where are you?"

"Where's the M?"

"And what in pell is going on here?"

He sighs. "Kamata. I'm in elevator three, on my way down to meet InfoPol." He waves once, in case any of them are looking. "The M is on her way to safety. I honestly don't know any more than you do: InfoPol is coming to arrest the M, and she wants as much confusion as we can generate to cover her tracks." He smiles. "Y'all are good at that, already."

"But what's *really* going down? If InfoPol is going to start arresting Nexus personnel, a lot of us are in trouble."

"Nobody's getting arrested. At most, the Institute may be shut down for a few days."

Everyone tries to talk at once, a racous babble of voices.

"Rahel, override on kamata." The cacophony ends, silenced by the comm system so that only Damien's words are transmitted. "Listen to me. We don't have a lot of time. The M wants everybody poolside, and prepared to sing the Hallelujah Chorus." He waits for a moment, but not long enough for Rahel to pass the comm to someone else. "She wants us to sing like we were at Dagon's house."

"What?!"

"Are you sure that's what she said?"

"She wouldn't— "

Rose Cetairé's unmistakeable voice cuts through all the others, "If that's what the M wants, then that's what we'll give her. Damien, you can count on *all* of us. You just give us the signal when it's time."

There is no further dissent. "Thanks," Damien says. The elevator finishes its trip, but he holds the door closed for a moment to think.

Nunn it, why did the M pick *him* to be in charge? Why not Rose? She's better to handle a situation like this. He contemplates calling Rose, begging her to take command.

No.

He closes his eyes, resting his forehead against the cool steel of the elevator door. All my life, he thinks, someone else has been in charge. I've spent my whole life reacting to what other people do. Following orders. Dealing with crises. Letting other people make my decisions. Running from the man who killed my father.

The M— bless her heart— was the only one who had faith in me. And now, she knew that it's time for Damien to grow up, time for me to leave the nest, time for me to take charge of my life.

Maybe that's why she ran…gods know, she could deal with InfoPol easily. But she knew I wouldn't fly without a push, so she gave me a push….

He straightens up, squares his shoulders. All right, it's time to spread my wings.

The door opens, and he steps out into a stream of residents and guests, a swirl of phantasmagoric, holographic shapes.

"Rahel, get me Penylle."

Moments pass, then she picks up. A gentle susurrus fills his ears, the noise of the crowd around her. "Penylle here."

"Hon, I need you. Meet me at Reception, okay?"

"Of course. I'll be right there."

He walks steadily to Reception, nodding at those he passes. Residents are pouring out of the elevators and stairways, streaming toward the pool. Good.

Reception is an oasis of calm. The lone person on duty, a gangly Latino teenage boy with dark shoulder-length hair and a wispy moustache, waves Damien over to the desk. He has the pixie face and small hands of a Downer. The lad's badge reminds Damien that his name is Vincente.

"Mr. Damien, what's happening? Is it true that troops are coming to take us all to prison?"

Pretending assurance that he certainly doesn't feel, Damien forces a smile. "No. They think they're coming to arrest the M, but they aren't going to get her."

Vincente shows his teeth. "Not if *I* can help it, sir."

"Good." Damien glances out the main entrance; the troops have scattered and he isn't sure what they're up to. "There's nothing more you can do here. Go on in, get some food, and then join everybody else poolside. Tell everybody you meet to do the same."

"Something big's going to happen, isn't it?"

Damien nods. "With any luck."

Vincente grins. "And I didn't think I was going to have any fun tonight. Guess I was wrong." Waving at Damien, he leaves the reception desk and trots toward the party.

What *are* the blue helmets up to?

The senior staff channel beeps for attention, and a throaty voice says, "Damien, this is Building Supervisor Rodriguez."

"Kamata. Go ahead, Joya."

"Just thought you'd want to know that our hydrogen lines are down."

Damien instinctively glances upward, at the electric lights. "Are we on emergency power?"

Rodriguez laughs. "Pell, no. Our fuel cells will keep us going for up to twenty-four hours before we have to hit the batteries. Oh, and it looks as if our water's been cut off too. Again, we have enough in the tanks to last for a few days."

"Thanks, Joya. Keep me updated." So that's what the troops are doing—trying to isolate the Institute. "Rahel, get me Valya Kokarev."

In an instant, the Institute's chief data supervisor is on the phone. "What can I do for you, Damien?"

"Val, hydrogen and water lines have been shut down. How are our data links?"

A graph springs into being before Damien's eyes. "You are correct," Kokarev says. "Surface fiber lines are down. The rest of the lines have taken up the traffic."

"How vulnerable are we?"

"Damien, do not be foolish. Those land lines carry less than five percent of our traffic. Perhaps the troopers can disrupt our underground lines where they intersect the NII trunk. Perhaps they can disrupt our three maser links. That would still leave us with broadband radio and five satellite links, which is more than enough capacity to carry all our traffic."

"So I don't have to worry about losing communications?"

"Nyet. Worry about what you are going to eat for tomorrow's dinner first."

"Thanks. Keep things running. Close circuit." Damien glances at the exterior display; a few blue helmets patrol the perimeter, but there is no other obvious action. "Rahel, get me Bear."

"There is no 'Bear' on file."

"Get me Security Chief Durrell."

"Acknowledged. Shall I create an association between 'Bear' and 'Security Chief Alec Durrell' for future use?"

"Be my guest."

The phone clicks, and a gruff voice answers, "Durrell here." Damien can almost smell the aroma of pipe herbs that always clings to the large man.

"Bear, it's Damien."

"Nice t' hear from you, boss. Wish there was time to chat."

"You and me both. Listen, I'm on my way out there to talk to these guys, but I don't expect any success. Meanwhile, we have a hundred and thirty-six residents and gods-know-how-many guests— "

"One hundred eighty-six in person, four hundred sixteen virtual. And it's only one hundred thirty-two residents; the M is gone and the Glazers are in Brazil."

Damien grins. "I *knew* I called the right man. I'm only concerned with warm bodies. Every single one of them has got to be around the pool and accounted for. Those blue helmets have itchy trigger fingers; I don't want them surprised in a corridor by any of our people."

"Son, you've got a Security Chief so that you don't have to worry about these details. Relax and let me do my job. I've got runners chasing down the stragglers right now, and twelve husky volunteers checking every flat on every floor to catch anybody we've missed. As soon as they're in, I'll move *my* operations to a console near the pool, and that's everyone." He grunts. "Except you and Ms. Penylle. I trust that you'll keep her safe?"

"Yes. No, on second thought, keep an eye on her position. As long as she's with me, you can assume she's safe, but if we get separated, send someone for her, okay?"

"You got it."

"Thanks, Bear. You're a pell of a man."

"You're not so bad yourself, boss. Good luck out there. Off."

Damien glances at his time display, and is astonished to see that it's only a few minutes past twenty-two— he was sure hours had passed since he went looking for the M. In reality, it's been less than twenty minutes. He peers through the Institute's glass doors: outside, dark shapes move against bright, shifting lights. He clicks his Spex through the external cameras, one at a time. The troops have surrounded the Institute, and are forming up into a line before the main entrance.

Penylle rushes up, panting. "I would have been here sooner, but everyone I passed tried to push me back toward the pool." She brushes hair out of her face. "Sorry."

He takes her hand. "You're here now, that's what counts." Quickly, he catches her up on the situation.

"Marc sent me to hack into InfoPol's main system, a few months ago. I thought he was on Nexus business." She squeezes Damien's hand, shaking with rage. "Chief Lipponen came to dinner a couple of times. He was a nice old man." She closes her eyes and takes a breath. Her hand steadies. "I'll *kill* Marc."

"Easy. I get him first. When I'm done, *then* you can kill him."

"We'll negotiate." She looks toward the main entrance. "What now?"

"I guess they're waiting for us to make the first move. Do you mind sticking by me?"

Penylle's response is part smile, part snarl. "Just try to stop me. How do you intend to play this?"

"The way the M would, I hope. Polite but firm. Co-operative within the law, but totally unhelpful. And confusing. By the time these troops leave here, I want them so bewildered that no two of them will be able to agree on what went on. They're military— orderly, tidy types who like everyone and everything to stay in the assigned and proper place. And they're up against three hundred artists and creative anarchist types. I feel sorry for them." He moves toward the entrance, slowly, carefully keeping near cover— potted plants, chairs, public-service terminals. Penylle follows, half a pace behind him.

"Why confuse them? It's just going to get them frustrated."

"Exactly. And if they're frustrated and angry, they can't think effectively about where the M went. Plus, they'll be less willing to bother us again." Damien takes a deep breath, trying to ignore his dry mouth and the queasy feeling in his viscera. He reminds himself that he has been in similar positions before; as a Nexus operative, he is well-trained to confront armed troops standing in his way.

"Kamata. Dim the lights on all floors to about thirty percent."

"Acknowledged." The light level falls to twilight dimness.

He nods to Penylle. "Let's go."

"Wait." She pulls up his left sleeve, uncovering his tattoo of Drake's Starburst. She gives him a quick peck on the lips. "All right, *now* let's go."

They walk out the door (the hot, muggy air slaps him across the face like a damp washcloth) and down the center of the empty brick plaza, toward the tanks that wait twenty meters away. Every step, Damien is aware of weapons trained on him.

Before they reach the tanks, a blue-shirted InfoPol officer marches smartly up to them, her dark hair maintaining a perfect coiff in spite of the humidity. She is flanked by two U.N. peacekeepers in khakis, with blue helmets gleaming and rifles held ready.

Damien holds out his hand. "Good evening, Officer. I'm Damien Nshogoza, in charge of the Institute. This is Penylle Norton. What can we do for you?" He makes sure to stand so that she can see the Starburst glowing yellow against his dark skin.

The woman flashes a badge, ignoring Damien's outstretched hand. "Officer Caparthy, InfoPol." She hands him a flatscreen. "I have a warrant for the arrest of one Miranda Maris."

He glances over the warrant, noting that it was issued by the World Court just hours ago. "I'm sorry, but the Minister isn't at the Institute tonight. You might want to try her office in D.C."

"If you don't mind, sir, my troops and I will conduct a search." She starts to move forward; Damien steps into her way.

"I'm afraid that I *do* mind, Officer. Frankly, your arrival has put a scare into our residents; I'd prefer that you leave without frightening them further."

She snatches the flatscreen from him, taps it, and hands it back. "This search warrant covers the whole premises. Mr. Nshogoza, I can do this with your co-operation, or I can put you in restraints and do it anyway." Her right hand hovers centimeters from a wicked-looking sidearm. "Which do you prefer?"

"I'll co-operate. I'm just trying to save you some effort— Miranda Maris is not inside."

"To put it bluntly, sir, that opinion conflicts with our information." Her hand touches the handle of her gun. "Please stand aside."

Damien steps aside, spreading his hands. "All right, then. But I have to warn you, this is a Nexus facility. Once you go through that door, I can't protect you."

Without turning, she answers, "I don't think we'll need protection from a group of nonviolents."

"Well, I warned you." Damien falls into step half a meter behind Caparthy and her two escorts, with Penylle at his side. The U.N. troops, a good two dozen, march in a double row behind them.

When they enter, two peacekeepers peel off and vanish behind the Registration desk. Two others head into the coatroom. The place is eerily quiet; the only sound is the distant hiss of ventilation. Caparthy consults a flatscreen, then waves a group of troops to the right. "Search the rooms on that corridor," she orders, "then secure the elevators."

Without hesitation, Caparthy takes the majority to the left, moving toward the main lobby. The vast space seems even larger in the half-dark. The blue helmets move slowly, weapons drawn, alert for ambush as they thread their way among tables and chairs toward the huddled masses around the pool.

"There she is, Chief!"

The figure moving toward them is unmistakably the M. Handheld spotlights attempt to pin her; they succeed only in giving her a ghostly, washed-out look.

Then another figure bolts toward them, and another off to the right, both wearing the shape of the M. A dozen troopers snap into gunner's stance, then in a psychedelic explosion of colors, the main lobby is filled with dozens of Ivory Madonnas. They scurry one way and another, running right through solid obstacles and one another.

A voice chuckles in Damien's ear. "Do not be alarmed, boss," Val Kokarev says. "Gal Vange designed a holographic template of the M. She has spread it around to all the virtual guests. You *did* say 'maximum confusion.'"

Damien can't help laughing out loud.

Caparthy shoots him a dirty look. "Right," she barks, raising her gun. "Very funny. Now," she calls out, "If I don't get some co-operation, I'll put *all* of you under arrest— starting with this man and woman." Her eyes meet Damien's. "I'm not bluffing."

Damien holds her eyes for a moment, then gives her a single nod. "Kamata. Have the virtual guests gather near the pool."

"Tell them to revert to default forms."

"Kamata. Folks, I'd appreciate it if the virtual guests could revert to their default forms."

The pool area is suddenly twice as crowded, as a hundred Ivory Madonnas morph into their true shapes, a virtual bestiary of knights, dragons, barbarians, spacemen, pirates, and mythological beasts.

Damien looks apology at Caparthy. "Those *are* their defaults."

"Forget it." She turns to a trooper. "Cordon that area. If anyone else is found, put them in there. If necessary, we'll examine them one at a time. Nobody is to leave the cordon— if they try, shoot to disable, but you have my authority to use deadly force if you must."

"Isn't that going a little too far?" Damien asks.

Caparthy waves to him and Penylle. "I want them kept away from the others. Cuff them and hold them over there."

The night wears on, minute by agonizing minute. Bear keeps everyone informed of the troopers' locations as they conduct a thorough search of the building. After a little more than an hour, the search is finished and the ranking trooper reports to Caparthy.

"We found no one, ma'am."

After being on slow simmer for an hour, Caparthy looks ready to explode. "Fine. She's got to be hiding among them. Get all your people in here— we're going to go through them one at a time." She faces the crowd. "Maris, I know you're here. My troops are going to strip-search your people, one at a time, until we find you. We'll take finger and retinal prints, blood samples, and skin scrapes for identification. You'll spare your people a lot of discomfort and indignity if you give yourself up now."

She waits for a response, then waves dismissal. "All right, you had your chance." She indicates Damien and Penylle. "Sergeant, bring those two over. We'll start with them."

Damien struggles, delaying until he is sure that all the troops are in the lobby. Then, as a trooper begins easing his shirt off, he pulls away and shouts, "We are prisoners in Dagon's house! Let the world bear witness!"

On cue, the lights come up to maximum, and five hundred voices rise as one: "Hallelujah! Hallelujah! Hallelujah, Hallelujah, Hal-le-lu-jah!"

Damien almost laughs again at Caparthy's expression. If he had set off a bomb, he could not have stunned and surprised her more. Her jaw drops, along with the collective jaws of her frozen troopers.

"For the Lord God omnipotent reigneth."

Damien steps to Caparthy's side and nods toward the second balcony. "I just thought you'd like to know that those cameras are putting this out live on the Nets. Along with appropriate commentary, of course."

While waiting, the poolside crowd have grouped themselves by voice, so that waves of sound sweep across the crowd in perfect synchronization.

Voices soar, baritones and sopranos alternating, basses and tenors and altos filling out the harmony. Damien can tell that the sound crew has cut in the most powerful amplifiers, for the bass notes rumble his stomach while the sopranos seem to make the air itself quiver. The sound, reflected by the pool's still water, reaches the skylight twelve stories above and bounces back seemingly stronger.

"The Kingdom of this world is become the kingdom of our Lord— "

He nudges Penylle's shoulder and takes an exaggerated step toward the pool; she follows without hesitating.

"-- and of His Christ— "

The music builds in power and majesty, until Damien can swear that there are a thousand voices, two thousand, more. The troopers, some of them no doubt closet Christians, stand stock still; doubtless their training does not include how to respond to musical assault.

"-- and He shall reign forever and ever."

Penylle leans close to Damien and whispers something; Damien shakes his head.

"I can't hear you," he mouths.

"King of Kings (forever and ever, hallelujah, hallelujah), and Lord of Lords (forever and ever, hallelujah, hallelujah)."

Penylle shouts, and still he can barely hear her over the near-defening harmony. "Who...the...pell...is...Dagon?"

"And He shall reign forever and ever— and ever."

Damien calls back, "A Philistine god. From the Bible. Old Testament."

Still the music builds, progressive "King of Kings" and "Lord of Lords" taking it higher and higher, more and more forceful. In the empty space above them, the three-dee model of Drake's Starburst sways and shivers in time.

Penylle is not satisfied. "And...what...about...his...house?"

"Forever, and ever, and ever, and ever— "

Damien grins. "Temple," he corrects. "Dagon had a bad-luck visitor."

"Hallelujah, hallelujah— "

"Who?"

"-- Hallelujah, hallelujah— "

In the sudden moment of silence before the ultimate "Hallelujah," Damien whispers, "Fellow named Samson."

At a volume so great that it rocks the balconies, the chorus belts out the final syllables: "Hal...le...lu...JAH!"

Instead of the normal soprano D, the sopranos soar to a fortissimo high D, the high D that shatters eardrums and tonsils. The other voices, instead of filling out the chords with their usual notes, each goes to their highest D, sounding perfect octaves.

And they hold that note, ear-splintering and bone-rattling as it is, for heartbeat after heartbeat, until the decibel-saturated air is alive with raw power, then longer, second after agonizing second. When breath finally fails and the multitude of voices fade to silence, the ears ring for long moments, before another sound intrudes on consciousness.

Like icebergs fissuring, this new sound draws eyes upward, balcony by balcony, following the same path as that incredible final note. That note, concentrated and intensified by the balconies, rises ever-stronger until it reaches the meter-thick skylight....

...Whose resonant frequency matches that very same fortissimo D.

Cracks spread across the skylight, then in the last echo of the high D it shatters. Knife-edged shards plummet twelve stories, and all the horrified troopers can do is to scramble for the nearest cover.

Chunks of concrete and plaster join the rain of debris. When the falling glass reaches Drake's Starburst, that huge mobile falls apart and plunges as well, long metal spears mixed with the killing rain.

By design rather than miracle, the area surrounding the pool is the only part of the floor spared. Troopers become scrambling rag-dolls, knocked willy-nilly by the falling rubble or cowering under the protection of tables or chairs. Caparthy, herself in the clear zone, stands in catatonic stillness while Mateni Gerat jumps her and pulls away her gun. All around the floor, residents do the same, and in less than ten minutes the surviving troopers, most nursing injuries, are all together by the pool, while Institute residents hold guns on them.

Damien stands before Caparthy, whose shell-shocked expression warms his heart. He surveys the carnage, counts half a dozen troopers dead. "You should have listened. She isn't here."

"We'll find her."

"No, I don't think so. Not as long as she doesn't want to be found."

"What are you going to do with us now?"

"Hold onto you. Until all the lawyers finish straightening out this mess. Then we'll send you home." He shakes his head. "The video is all over the world by now. I don't expect it will help your career any. I'm sorry, but you should have listened."

He turns to the residents and staff, most of whom are still gathered around the pool. "Folks, we'll have a crew in here tomorrow to repair all this damage. Most flats should still be livable, but if you don't want to stay here tonight, we can send you to a satellite facility or get you a room at one of the airport hotels. Leila, see about getting some shuttles running to transport folks." He reaches for Penylle. "Come on, let's get out of here. I want to find someplace with room service and a big bathtub, and I intend to sleep for three days."

MENUET 10

*Gravity-Wave Anomalies in Eridanus Correlated to Prime-Number Functions*

. . . heretofore undetectable gravitational waves with a cycle of 2683 MHz, emanating from a locus 50 ± 5 A.U. away....

. . . long-term repetition of the sequence 1, 2, 3, 5, 7, 11, 13, 17, 19, 23,...1619, easily recognizable as the first 256 prime numbers. A natural process capable of producing prime numbers is exceedingly unlikely, yet the authors are wary of the conclusion that these waves are artificially produced. The implications of such a conclusion....

G. M'Bange, K. MacFarland, S. Greer, & L. Chiang
*Journal of Gravimetic Studies*, 22 Aug 2042
<joga.uasmara.edu/2042/18629.334>

## INTERMEZZO: BLUE MOON

Shenandoah Valley, Virginia
USA, North America
23 August 2042 C.E.

*Of course you can't flap your arms and fly to the moon.*
*After a while, you'd run out of air to push against.*

Strictly speaking, the Shenandoah Turnpike is not part of the United States. Rather, it is international territory under the jurisdiction of the North American Trade Alliance. At a bar in Hagerstown, Miranda finds some sympathetic truckers; she arm-wrestles the strongest of them, buys drinks for the losers, and grouses with them about the sorry state of the once-mighty Teamsters. After all, a large percentage of truckers are her constituents— a life on the road offers few opportunities to stay in shape. And her clothes— large, comfortable denims, steel-toed work boots, and a battered khaki hat with a large, floppy brim— are those a trucker would wear.

When the call comes for relief drivers, Miranda piles into a van with a dozen others. She presses several large bills into the driver's hand, then crouches in the back with her hat pulled down. There is no trouble at the checkpoint; she heaves a sigh as the van pulls across a yellow line on the pavement and she is safely out of the United States.

Within an hour she has become Matilda Klein, a fully-qualified Class Two freelance driver with paperwork to prove it— papers every bit as convincing as the real thing. By 2 a.m., she is in the cab of a 34-wheeler, keeping an eye on the autopilot and riding shotgun on twenty-six tonnes of maple syrup bound for Knoxville. She makes a few phone calls, then reclines her seat to rest.

The sky is lightening as she zips past Blacksburg, the last outpost of the United States between here and New Orleans. It is, oddly, a comfort to be in God's Country— at least she knows that the Christian Confederacy will not co-operate with U.N. and InfoPol forces. And she has family here, through her mother, folk with Great Smokies roots that run generations deep. Dozens of cousins and nephews and nieces, plain people all of them: everything from hard-working shopkeepers to the social class once referred to as "trailer trash." She still keeps in touch with most of them (or, at least,

Evelina does), solstice cards and cash on the children's birthdays. Over the years, a handful of them have shown artistic talent; Miranda has done what she could, through the Institute, to help them escape into the real world the way her mother did.

She reaches Knoxville well before rush hour, coming down out of chilly mountains into warm, misty morning. She lets the autopilot dock her truck at the transfer facility, surrenders her paperwork, and gets a pay chit. Then, clutching her bag, she follows a line of yawning, limping truckers toward a nearby building. A neon sign announces the place as "The Honeybee;" the aroma of bacon and grits leaves no doubt about its purpose. Miranda hurries along, her stomach suddenly awake and alert.

The Honeybee is part greasy spoon, part general store, part communications station, part hotel. It is divided down the middle by a plexiglass wall marked with occasional crosses. The only break in the wall is a single Customs barrier of the stick-your-card-in-the-slot variety, watched over by a portly Holy Guard who seems permanently attached to his stool. Since tokesticks and boy-toy virties are openly on sale in the international side, Miranda can easily imagine that the guard is there to protect wayward Christians from the temptation to stray from the path of righteousness.

In a booth within sight of the Customs barrier, Miranda nurses bacon and eggs, pancakes and grits, and strong coffee for most of an hour. This early, her only companions are ravenous truckers, maintenance mechs, and occasional bleary-eyed girls and boys in low-cut shirts and tight shorts, ignoring the guard as they swipe their cards on their way back into the Confederacy. Local talent, Miranda reflects, is much the same the world around: young girls with taut hips and jutting blileys, muscle-boys with tight buns, faces shining with the same look of practiced innocence mixed with sophisticated sincerity.

She watches one boy, late teens or early twenties, easily the oldest she's seen. He struts across the floor like a swaggering tomcat, no doubt exuding pheromones with every step. She wonders what he will make of himself, when the muscles start to fade to flab, and the chestnut hair starts thinning. Is he saving his money, setting enough aside for the rest of his life? Will he become a shopkeeper, or a mechanic, or a commodities broker, a respectable career man with a wife and a house and two children of his own? Will he go to church every week and pray for the souls of other lost kids? Will he be content with such an ordinary, uneventful life— or will he strike out for the outside world that he has only seen reflected in the eyes of his erstwhile customers?

To Miranda's surprise, the lad saunters past Customs, heading directly toward her table. Moments later, he sits down across from her, smiling. "Matilda Klein?"

She answers, "Maybe."

With a nod, he hands her a slip of stiff paper, like an old-fashioned business card. She turns it over and sees Drake's Starburst in grey tracery.

"Thanks." She hands the card back. "I'm Matilda Klein."

"Call me Jackie Paper."

Despite herself, Miranda grins. "Cute."

"These're for you."

This time, he gives her a bundle of papers. She leafs through them: passport, identity card, driver's license, church ID, travel permits— all in the name of Matilda Klein, and all bearing roughly-accurate pictures. She tucks them into a pocket on her denim jacket.

"Thanks. How much do I owe you?"

He shakes his head. "Nothing."

"I find that hard to believe. These are quality documents."

"Lady, I only know what I was told: no charge. If you want to argue, you have to argue with my boss."

Miranda raises an eyebrow. "Not even a delivery charge?"

The boy smiles. "We'll dicker when we get you where you're going."

"Which is?"

"Tell you when we get there." He leans forward. "Give me about ten minutes, then go through the gate and wander outside. Call a taxi, I'll pick you up." He stands.

"Aren't you a little young— ?"

The boy grimaces. "Please. I get that all the time. I'll be twenty next month, okay? I've been driving since I was sixteen. I'm not going to wreck the cab on the way."

Miranda suddenly remembers herself at almost the same age, saying almost exactly the same words— in almost exactly the same exasperated tone— to an elderly aunt. She remembers how desperately, at nineteen, she wanted the adults around her to take her seriously…and how few of them did.

She takes Jackie's hand. "I'm sorry I said that. I spoke without thinking. Of course you've been driving for years, and I do not hesitate to put myself in your hands. Considering that your reaction speed is probably faster than mine, we're both safer with you behind the wheel." She looks up into his eyes. "Apology accepted?"

He tugs his hand away, embarrassed. "Nada problem. I'll go get the cab. Remember, ten minutes, then come outside."

"Thank you."

Their destination is a modest cobalt-blue Colonial house in the suburbs. A chain-link fence about a meter high encloses the quarter-hectare lot. The house, festooned with white and yellow roses on whitewashed trellises, sits about ten meters back from the road. Jackie hops out of the cab to open a gate and close it behind them, then pulls behind the house to a covered carport that holds three other cars. He retrieves her bag from the trunk, then opens her door and holds out a hand.

"Thanks." She struggles out of the cramped back seat. The cab was air-conditioned, but the outside air is hot, and Miranda is suddenly clammy with sweat. Jackie helps her to stand, and her jumpsuit clings to the back of her thighs.

They take a step toward the house, then the back door flies open and a silver-haired Anglo woman steps out. She is short, no more than 160 cm, and somewhat pear-shaped— but her wide smile is warmly welcoming, and in the curves of cheek, forehead, and nose Miranda sees something very familiar. Without a doubt, this woman is family.

Across the yard, the woman shouts, "Honey, it's so good t' see ya." Dixie cadences sing in her voice.

Miranda and the woman meet halfway; the woman throws her arms around Miranda and squeezes tightly. The she steps back and holds Miranda at arm's length, inspecting her. "I haven't seen you since you were, oh, this high." She holds her hand at waist-height. "But I'd know you anywhere. I'm your Aunt Mabel's oldest girl."

Miranda scans her memory of family gatherings past. There was a girl, a decade or so her senior, who disdained the company of the younger kids, preferring instead to flirt with the boys. "Naomi? Naomi Barkley?"

"Call me 'Omi.' Everybody does. When I heard that you were coming to Knoxville, I told them that I *had* to be on your case. Come inside, girl, and we'll talk." Over her shoulder, she tells Jackie, "Put the lady's bag in the guest room, then come on down to the kitchen."

Omi's house, decorated in Middle American Casual, smells of fresh bread and cookies baking. Children are about, mostly young teens with a few older kids— but they are not constantly underfoot. In one room, half a dozen gangly boys and girls are crowded around a single terminal, enraptured. In another, an older girl is reading to three attentive adolescents; Miranda pauses to listen, and recognizes Madeleine L'Engle's *A Wrinkle in Time*.

When they reach the kitchen, Omi flops down on a wheeled office chair and waves Miranda to a seat at the table. "What would you like? Coffee? Iced tea? Hot tea? Soda pop?"

Miranda fans herself; it's cool in the house, but she's still recovering from outside. "I'd love some iced tea. The biggest glass you have, and preferably cooled in liquid nitrogen."

Omi laughs as she scoots to a big green refrigerator. The glass she places before Miranda must hold a liter of tea and ice; Miranda gulps gratefully.

"There's still some cinnamon cake left over from breakfast," Omi says, sliding a plate in front of Miranda. It contains enough to feed a family of four for roughly a week. "If you haven't eaten, I can cook something up for you."

"We *must* be related," Miranda says. "This will be fine, thank you." She takes a bite. "Mmm, delicious. I want the recipe."

"You shall have it." Omi leans back, reaching for a coffee mug that's warming at her elbow. "So you're Matilda Klein."

"Only temporarily." Miranda takes her first good look at the kitchen; a quilt bearing Drake's Starburst hangs prominently on one wall. "What is…all this?" She waves, indicating the house and grounds.

"Officially, day care. But in reality, we're a school." Omi's eyes sparkle. "Of course, we teach some things that the Churches don't want taught. Evolution, humanism, world history, current events…that sort of thing. We have an unfiltered Net connection and a library of proscribed books."

"Isn't that dangerous? What with the Inquisition and all?"

"If I worried about the Inquisition, I'd never have time to get *anything* done." Omi shrugs. "We have hidden rooms and escape routes, if we need them. And the Nexus has friends in high places." She sips her coffee, then leans forward. "So tell me, Matilda Klein, what can we do for you?"

"Well, I'm currently on the run from InfoPol."

"So I gathered from the bulletins. You're certainly welcome to stay here." She smiles. "Our government isn't going to give InfoPol the time of day. Occasionally, there *are* advantages to living in a theocracy."

"I appreciate the offer, and I wish I *could* stay. Unfortunately, this InfoPol action is only one part of a bigger mess, and I'm in it up to my eyeballs. I need to be someplace where I can keep on top of the world situation, but where I'll also be out of reach of InfoPol and, preferably, the whole U.N."

"Where did you have in mind?"

"Immediately, Beijing or Tiantjin. Both Fyodor Lütke and Carcopino-Tusoli owe me big favors. Once I'm in Middle China, I can make my way to the Gongga Shan launch site. Eventually, I'd like to wind up in Armstrong City. I have lots of friends there."

Omi frowns. "It's going to be very hard to get into even Outer China from here. There are no direct flights, not even to Tokyo."

"I beg your pardon?"

"The Confederacy doesn't approve of China, so there are no direct flights. The best you'll do is Australia."

"Not good." Miranda chews her lower lip. "Nunn, the more time I waste, the worse things get. Omi, I may have to take you up on your offer of the guest room."

"Must you go through China? Would another launch site do?"

Miranda ticks off active spaceports. "I can't go through Umoja or North America. Europe's tight with InfoPol, so Baikonur is out. Same story with Guyane. If I can't fly direct to China, then I can't reach Kiribati either. And I have good reason to suspect that I'd be taken into custody at Kalidasa Port. That's the lot. I guess I'm not going to get to Armstrong City." She was stuck on-planet. Marc Hoister had outmaneuvered her before she had even started to flee.

"Not necessarily. I can't promise, but I have friends at Fort Shepard."

"That *could* be handy." Miranda wasn't desperate to get involved with the U.S. Space Force...but she knew that many high-ranking officers were sympathetic to the Nexus, and had quietly helped out on several occasions. "I wouldn't say no to a berth on the next Lunar shuttle."

Jackie Paper enters, snags a piece of cake and drops into a chair. Elbows on the table, he smiles at Omi. "You rang?"

"Cousin Matilda may be heading for Fort Shepard soon. What would you think of going along with her?"

The lad's eyes widen. "Uh...that's pretty far," he says.

Omi faces Miranda. "Jackie needs to get out of the Confederacy before long. You'll both be safer if you travel together."

Jackie sits up. "I don't have to go *yet*. Another year or two...."

Omi shakes her head. "I've kept you here too long already. I want you someplace where you can experience freedom. Someplace where you'll be safe."

"I'm safe enough here."

"Jackie…I know what happened at the mall last week."

He turns his head away. "That was nothing serious. Those punks were looking for a fight. I was just in the wrong place— "

"Precisely." Omi steeples her fingers and regards him over impeccable, polished nails. "You're in the wrong place. Jackie, we've talked about this before. While you were younger, it didn't matter— there's nothing unusual about a teenager picking up spare change hustling truckers, and it gave you a perfect excuse to keep crossing into the international zone. But you're getting too old now. You need to get out of God's Country before you're—"

"Omi, I think you're overreacting. A little fight at the mall, a few bruises, that's all."

She takes his hand. "Jackie, it's not going to stop with a few bruises." A frown. "You remember that pair of schoolteachers they burnt in '38. It could happen again, all too easily."

Miranda raises an eyebrow. "Schoolteachers?"

Omi gestures to Jackie. "Tell her."

Looking down at the table, Jackie mumbles, "It was the gym teacher and the science teacher at my high school. Two women. They were…um…living together, for years. You know, they were….."

"Lesbians?" Miranda prompts.

"Yeah. When the PTA found out, there was this big town meeting, right down there on the football field. They brought the teachers out, and the preacher prayed over 'em, and then…they burned 'em." His voice is wooden, emotionless. "Choir sang hymns the whole time. Preacher sayin' how this was the Lord's work, we should be proud of ourselves."

Miranda suddenly loses interest in cinammon cake.

Omi scowls. "All the kids' clothes reeked of smoke, for weeks after, no matter how much they were washed. I had to throw out half a dozen shirts."

Jackie, still looking down, says, "I still don't see the point to leaving. If the Lord wants you, He's gonna get you, no matter where you are."

Miranda takes a deep breath. Where to start, with a child who's been indoctrinated since birth in the beliefs of a sick society? "Jackie, the Lord does *not* hate you and is *not* going to get you. Look at me."

He raises his head, meeting her steady gaze.

"Where I live, nobody gets burned at the stake, ever. Who you love, and how, is a matter for you and the people involved, that's all." He looks at her intensely; she holds his stare, hoping he sees truth in her eyes. "Two of my dearest friends, George and Phil, celebrated their fiftieth anniversary a few years ago. They're the most stable couple of any of my friends."

"I don't believe it."

Miranda fishes in her pocket, takes out a datacard, and taps its face. Images, flat and holo, race across the screen. She holds it up for Jackie to see. "Here's them at their anniversary party. And *this* is them on their honeymoon." She clicks through picture after picture. "Here's a lesbian couple who write high fantasy bestsellers. This fella's an actor, he's in a triad with two other men." Figure follows figure, all of Miranda's friends. "*She's* gay. So's he. And him. These two are sisters, both gay. Andy and David here are a perfect couple. That's Karen and Robin and their entourage; nobody's sure *what* their story is. Here's Selma, she used to be a straight man but now she's a lesbian. Dale's an intersexual whose parents kept the doctors from doing reconstructive surgery. Maline's a Frozen Zoner— she's had her erogenous zones deadened so she can stay celibate." She lowers the card. "If they start burning people where *I* live, there'll be a long line before they get to you, kid."

Jackie looks to Omi, who nods. "You see? I told you."

"It's decided, then," Miranda says. "You come with me at least as far as Fort Shepard. Then, if you can't find any other place you're happy, you can come live at the Institute."

Two days later, Miranda and Jackie crouch in the shadow of scraggly shrubs at the edge of a windy plain, looking northwest. A three-meter-tall fence of barbed wire slices across the plain, perhaps a hundred meters from where they stand; beyond the fence, and another hundred meters further on, a cluster of low, concrete buildings marks the outskirts of Fort Shepard. Beyond, the town of Laramie recedes over the horizon.

Two hundred meters from freedom. Despite late-afternoon sun slanting through a nearly-cloudless sky, the wind is winter-bitter, like ice on Miranda's exposed hands and face. She thinks, with regret, of the coat she left behind at the Institute— tissue-cultured black mink, heated and with matching gloves and hat; all by itself, it would keep out the chill of an Antarctic winter. Instead, here she is wearing a wrap that's little more than a glorified blanket, and to top it off, the nunn thing has Christian crosses embroidered all over it.

She turns to Jackie, shivering in his own blue windbreaker. His cheeks are bright pink, and his breath emerges in clouds. Burdened with a backpack that contains all of his worldly possessions, plus most of Miranda's luggage, he looks frail as any bird.

"Here," she says, spreading her wrap. He stands against her and she closes it, feeling like a mother bluejay enfolding her chicks.

A siren blares, followed by an obviously-artificial voice announcing, "T minus five minutes and counting. Please clear the area."

Miranda stands, allowing Jackie to assist her. She scans the fence, and sees a rainbow pennant hanging almost directly across from their position. "Okay, let's go. Head for that rainbow flag." Superstitious Christian soldiers will not dare to be outside during a rocket liftoff.

It takes almost all of the five minutes to reach the fence, and by the time they do, Miranda is no longer chilly. She stands, panting, while Jackie produces a pair of wire cutters from his jacket. He begins snipping fence links, then stops as the siren sounds again and the voice counts down to zero.

The fence shakes and the ground quivers, as a great wall of sound hits Miranda and Jackie broadside. Less than a quarter-kilometer away, fire erupts and a squat rocket rises, slowly at first, then with ever-increasing speed. The blast of air that washes over them is perceptibly warm, like a lowland summer breeze gone astray.

Even before the roar fades to where Miranda and Jackie could hear each other speak, Jackie is at work again on the links. He is helped by the fact that every other link is already severed. Jackie is not the first to follow this path to freedom; the rainbow flag marks the spot where sympathetic souls have prepared the fence. In another minute, he is through— there remains only a scramble across the no-man's-land on the U.S. side, and they are beyond the reach of the Army of God.

Fifteen minutes later, Miranda and Jackie are drinking warm coffee and munching donuts in a small canteen in Building 1403, Fort Shepard's ambiguously-named Personnel Processing Center. A polite second lieutenant takes their identity papers and departs, leaving a dour-faced private guarding the door.

Jackie paces, wiping the last remnants of fingerprint ink from his fingertips. Miranda takes a battered data tablet from a stack and screens through *Time Magazine*. Worldwide infrastructure failures figure into many of the stories: a three-day shutdown of public transit in Pristina, leading to a no-confidence vote in the parliament and the collapse of the coalition government; crisis in Amman when shipments of meat marked as Argentine beef were discovered to contain up to 50% processed pork; thousands of liters of raw sewage accidentally discharged into waters off Dubrovnik beaches. A Global Climate Council report that Australian carbon dioxide emissions were up 2% over the previous quarter. A comsat tumbled out of control over Baluchistan, straining already-jammed circuits through most of the subcontinent.

"Good afternoon." The middle-aged man who enters, dressed in a conservative business suit, has blond hair and a handlebar mustache. Gold-rimmed RCSpex balance on his nose, casting a shadow across his eyes. He holds his hand out to Jackie, then to Miranda. "I'm Dillon Blair, United States Immigration. Welcome to the States, Mr....er...Paper. I need to ask you a few questions." He sets a small recorder on the table before Jackie. "I'll be recording your answers. Do you understand?"

"Yes."

"Good." Blair raises his head slightly to the right, looking into a window of data that only he can see. "You are a citizen of the Confederacy of Christian States of America, currently going by the name 'Jackie Paper,' with Baptismal Registration Number 40-885-3703?"

"I am."

"Have you reached your eighteenth birthday?"

"Yes."

"Do you affirm that you have entered the United States of your own free will, and that you seek sanctuary from persecution in your own country?"

"I do."

"Is it your intention to stay in the United States and work toward becoming a productive citizen?"

"It is."

"Finally, do you affirm that you are not guilty of any crime under the laws of the United States, regardless of your status under the laws of the Confederacy?"

"I do."

Blair bends and kisses Jackie on both cheeks. "Congratulations. You are now registered as a legal resident alien under the Gittings-Rowland

Asylum Act of 2023." He clicks off the recorder. "The Gay Servicemember's Organization has an office down the hall. They'll help you get settled, and assist you any way they can."

Jackie nods. "Thank you."

Now Blair turns to Miranda. "Ma'am, I'm afraid there's been some bit of a mixup in verifying your identity. Your papers check out, but for some reason your fingerprints are matching with a certain U.S. citizen— a Congressional Minister, actually— named Miranda Maris."

Jackie poorly conceals a gasp, but Miranda makes no reaction beyond a puzzled smile and a demure, "Oh?"

Blair nods. "Rather puzzling. The techs can't figure out why it's happening. But I thought you should know, in case the problem comes up again in the future."

What's his game? she wonders. "What sort of woman is this…Angela Maris? Should I be flattered by the comparison, or insulted?"

"Oh, flattered, definitely. There's them that say she's a criminal, that she's really a leader in the Nexus— but nunn if I can see anything wrong with that." He sighs. "'Course, I'm a U.S. government official, it's my duty to be respectful towards any in Congress— so you might think my judgment is suspect. Ask around; you'll find most around here support her, and would be happy to help her out of a spot of trouble, if you see my meaning, Ma'am."

"You obviously think highly of this woman, Dillon Blair. I'm sure she'd thank you for your support, were she here."

"Thanks for saying so, Ma'am." He reaches to the recorder, hand poised to activate it once again. "I'm sure that this fingerprint mixup will get straightened out soon enough, one way or another. There's no point in delaying your processing until then, is there?"

She smiles. "None at all."

"Good." He touches the recorder. "I'll be recording your answers. Do you understand?"

"Completely."

"Good. "You are a citizen of the Confederacy of Christian States of America, currently going by the name 'Matilda Klein,' with Baptismal Registration Number 26-528-0475?"

"That's correct."

"Have you reached your eighteenth birthday?"

"I believe I remember it, yes."

"Do you affirm that you have entered the United States of your own free will, and that you seek sanctuary from persecution in your own country?"

"I do."

"Is it your intention to stay in the United States and work toward becoming a productive citizen?"

"Certainly."

"Finally, do you affirm that you are not guilty of any crime under the laws of the United States, regardless of your status under the laws of the Confederacy?"

"I do."

Blair leans forward and gives her a peck on the cheek. "Congratulations. You are now registered as a legal resident alien under the Gittings-Rowland Asylum Act of 2023." He taps the recorder, then returns it to his breast pocket. He looks from Jackie to Miranda. "Are you two traveling together?"

She gazes at Jackie. "It's up to you, son. The folks here will take care of you, if you want. Or you're welcome to come with me."

Jackie's eyes widen. "You mean it?"

"Of *course* I mean it. Now, be aware that it's going to be uncomfortable and dangerous. Here, you'll be safe. Or, at least, as safe as anyone else will be. This might be your last chance to bail out; I may not be able to find another safe place for you in the near future."

"I know." His voice is almost a whisper. "I still want to come with you."

She nods at Blair. "There it is. We're together."

"What can we do for you, then?" Blair asks.

Prudence suggests that she not be too trusting, at least not until she is out of the military's clutches. But experience tells her that Blair, like the vast majority of people she meets, is honest and trustworthy. "I need to get to Armstrong City as soon as I can. Yesterday, if possible."

Blair whistles. "That's going to be quite a job. I don't know if we *can*."

"What's the stumbling block? Paperwork? Security?"

He waves a hand. "Neither of those. Frankly, money's the problem. Passage for two to the Moon is going to be, I don't know, at least a quarter-million dollars. Maybe half a million."

Again Jackie tries unsuccessfully to hide a gasp.

Miranda reaches into her cleavage, squirming for a moment, and produces a sheaf of ten-thousand-rand bills, all shimmering in holographic beauty. She quickly thumbs through them: "Five…ten…fifteen." She drops fifteen bills on the table, returns the others to their hiding place. "That should be enough, don't you think?"

Blair reaches out and takes the bills as if afraid that they will pop like soap bubbles. "A hundred and fifty thousand rands? I should think so. Where did you— ?" He stops himself, deliberately. "None of my business. Forget it."

"No offense taken. That money came from a Nexus anonymous discretionary fund. I couldn't spend any of it in the Confederacy, or change it for holy dollars. I might as well get *some* use from it."

"I'll see what I can do. The next flight's not until tomorrow morning anyway— why don't you come down to the GSO club and relax for the duration." He gestures at the Army's coffee and donuts. "The food's better than here, that's for sure."

On a Space Force flight, there is no piddling about with chemical rockets and two-day trips. After a hop up to Freedom Station, Miranda, Jackie, and a dozen relief officers board the good ship *Ronald McNair,* whose ion drive delivers a steady one-tenth gee of thrust all the way to the Moon, a mere ten hours later. At Nyame Station in Lunar orbit they part company, the officers departing for Camp Korolev while Miranda and Jackie board a milk run down to Armstrong City.

When she leaves the lunar shuttle and her feet touch the fused-rock sidewalk of Armstrong City, Miranda breathes a great sigh. "That's a weight off my shoulders," she says, "and I don't mean one-sixth gravity." She takes a deep lungful of Armstrong City air, smelling of damp humus and simmering stew, with a hint of curry and just a little tang of bare iron. At long last, she feels safe.

There is no customs barrier, no need to show passports or identify documents. Armstrong is a-national, even anti-national; the only identification one needs here is human DNA. With Jackie, in tow, still getting his Moon legs, Miranda lopes through the domed terminal building, skidding to a halt before a bank of public phones. Although there is a stool, she doesn't bother to sit— who would, weighing only one-sixth of one's Earth weight?

The code she punches on the keyboard is one that only she knows, and as quickly as she taps the keys, the code evaporates from the phone system, leaving not a wrack behind. No trace of the call will remain, she has been assured, even in the memories of the computers whose business it is to keep track of such things.

A bland grey oval greets her on the screen, the ghostly suggestion of a face against a space-black background. Miranda says nothing, and after a moment the face comes alive, eyes widening and mouth breaking into a broad smile.

"You're a sight for sore eyes," a gravelly voice says. "Welcome to Luna. We were worried you weren't going to make it." She recognizes her Nexus colleague D.Löwenger.

"Am I the last?"

"L.A.Verne is en route from Tycho Base; the rest of us are here."

"And where is 'here,' if I may be so bold?"

"We've got the sixth floor of the Sheraton. How many rooms should I put you down for?"

Miranda glances over her shoulder at Jackie, who is bouncing up and down on the tips of his toes, a quarter-meter with each bounce. "Better make it two. He probably snores. And if you have a pitcher of gin and tonic ready, I'll be forever in your debt."

"Do you need directions?"

Miranda lowers her face and glares across the top of nonexistent eyeglasses. "Please. I was here when the Sheraton was *built.* I was here when your mother was a gleam in the milkman's eye. I welcomed Neil and Buzz on their first trip. I think I can find my way."

"Fine. If you're not here in twenty minutes, I'll send out the dogs and make martinis from the gin."

"You *would,* too." She punches disconnect, then turns to Jackie. "Come along, child. We have work to do."

The Sheraton, carved into the rock wall of Schmidt Crater, is one of Armstrong City's premium locations. Miranda's room has a real window, five-centimeter quartz glass set in a tiny alcove. With the room lights off, she sees a bare crescent Earth riding high over blinding sunlit moonscape. A telescope, thoughtfully mounted by the management, shows a cloudless Australia perched in the middle of Earth's dark side; the nearly-full moon is high and bright in the Outback tonight.

"Gets to you, doesn't it?" D.Löwenger sprawls across Miranda's bed, unmasked and wearing a decidedly unfashionable dark blue jumpsuit. "You're going to have to be firm with them. Even now, most of them don't want to admit that you were right. But they'll go along with whatever you say, so long as you're firm."

Miranda closes the window's shutters, stretches. "All right, my dear, let's do this thing." She gestures to the door. "After you."

It's a short trip down the hall to the conference room that has become the *de facto* headquarters of Nexus North America. The others are waiting around a rectangular table of polished basalt, datapads and keyboards strewn in front of them.

Miranda sits, smooths her sweater, and leans forward. "Ivory Madonna, Washington, Southwest."

"D.Löwenger, San Francisco, Northwest."

"Jakob.B.Sen, Chicago, North."

"L.A.Verne, New York, Northeast."

"CHEN1, Mexico City, South."

"Roger.Adelhardt, Los Angeles, Southwest."

"We are six," says CHEN1. "Ivory Madonna, would you preside?"

"All right." She scans the faces around her. Stripped of their masks, her colleagues are naked in her sight, their souls bare and quivering under her gaze. Löwenger and Adelhardt are convinced, Sen and Verne frightened, CHEN1 presenting a façade of bravado that fools no one. "I don't see any point in belaboring the situation. You've seen all my reports, you've been chased out of your homes and to the Moon…you know what Marc Hoister is up to. The only question is, how are we going to stop him?"

CHEN1 clears his throat. "Have you spoken with the others?"

"Only those I know I can trust. Precious few, to tell the truth. They're waiting to see what we decide."

L.A.Verne grunts, "According to C.H.LAD, InfoPol is reigned in. They'll drop these silly warrants, and we're all free to return home whenever we want."

Miranda waves to the door. "Be my guest. Nobody's stopping you."

Verne glares.

Roger.Adelhardt ignores Verne. "You're the expert, M. What do you expect Hoister to do next?"

Miranda leans back. "I don't know. All I can do is guess."

"Your guess is better than anything else we have right now."

"Okay. I expect a major disruption in world government or economy sometime in the next two weeks."

Jakob.B.Sen frowns. "Why in the next two weeks?"

"Because that's when the first big fusion drive ships will be ready to launch. He'll want bad news in the air, and lots of it."

D.Löwenger grimaces. "The Fifteenth Terran Council convenes in Colombo in just a few days. Every Nexus Regional Co-ordinator is going to be there. You don't suppose he'd strike at the Nexus, do you?"

Miranda spreads her hands. "He already *has,* at least indirectly." She shakes her head. "I think we'd all better talk to as many other Regional Co-ordinators as we can. It wouldn't hurt to have a contingency plan in place, in case he does try something."

L.A.Verne, wild-eyed, says, "What kind of contingency plan can we make? How are we supposed to stop Marc Hoister? Are we going to interdict Umoja?"

Miranda feels an inward shiver, but controls it. She meets Verne's panicked eyes, aware that she has no comfort to offer, only tungsten-steel determination. "If it comes to that, yes."

There seems nothing else to say.

## MENUET 11

FORT SHEPARD, Rocky Mountain Region, houses the headquarters of the <United States Space Force>. It is also the home of the U.S. Army's 18th Division, the "<Matlovitch Division>." Fort Shepard includes a Spaceport as well as a Personnel Processing Center that oversees <immigrants> arriving from the <Confederacy of Christian States>. The Fort covers about 3,000 hectares and lies outside the town of <Laramie>.

The fort, founded in 2024, was named after civil rights activist <Matthew Shepard (1976 - 1998)>. The fort was built on the site of <Shepard's crucifixion by militant Christians>. In 2026, the U.S. Army <stopped the advancing Army of God at Fort Shepard>, thus defining the northwest limit of the Christian Confederation.

The <Fort Shepard Spaceport>, completed in 2036, carries nearly 90% of United States military traffic to and from Low Earth Orbit. (<Space traffic and shipping>.)

*World Book Encyclopedia*, 2042.03 edition
<db.worldbook.com/easy/F/fortshepard>

## DIVERTISSEMENT 19

(from a speech by The Ivory Madonna,
First Terran Council, 3 September 2014 C.E.)

"There are four general types of nations, and each has its own drawbacks.

"The *ethnic nation* defines itself by shared genetics and ancestors. In this sort of nation, citizenship is granted only to those who are members of the single ruling tribe or ethnic group. Social mobility is constrained, especially for non-citizens. Examples include Germany, Serbia, and Japan. The chief dangers of the ethnic nation are inequality, inflexibility, and the excesses of so-called 'ethnic cleansing.'

"The *cultural nation* defines itself by shared language, religion, history, and tradition. Citizenship is open to those who assimilate completely into the national culture. Individual or group deviations from the national culture are not tolerated. Social mobility is possible, but often difficult. Examples include France as well as most theocracies like Iran or Israel. The cultural nation is often characterized by extreme repression, human rights abuses, and inflexibile economies.

"The *nation of nations* includes multiple ethnic groups 'united' by a common political structure: either some form of federal system, or a totalitarian government. In many cases, one or more ethnic groups are disenfranchised or mistreated. Social mobility is difficult for many, and impossible for some. Examples include India, China, the British Empire, and the Soviet Union. If this sort of nation escapes the danger of totalitarianism, it risks ethnic violence or apartheid.

"The *nation of communities* consists of cultural subgroups bound by common political structures: usually some form of federal system. Subgroups define themselves by common tradition, language, religion, or culture. In the best nations of communities, all subgroups contribute elements to an overall national culture. More commonly, subcultures vie with one another for domination of the political or cultural process. Social mobility is possible for most. The United States and Umoja are nations of communities. It is easy for this type of nation to fall into institutionalized discrimination, or even hardcore racism.

"Conventional wisdom tells us that the nation of communities, despite its drawbacks, is the best choice for maximizing individual liberty and social harmony. But we of the Nexus do not accept the assumption behind this wisdom, the assumption that *any* sort of nation is inevitable or desirable.

"In *all* cases, the mischief that nations do is worse than whatever benefits they bring. Today, the world is too small...the *human race* is too small...for nations of any stripe. We are *one* community, and anything that fractures us, anything that sets us against one another, is dangerous and damaging. This is true of ethnicity, of culture, of language, or religion...and, yes, of nation.

"Let there be no more Nations of God, Nations of Culture, Nations of Language, Nations of Nations, Nations of Communities. Instead, join with us in celebrating the one, the only nation that makes sense: the Nation of Humanity."

# ACT I:

# THERE'S A DANCE OR TWO IN THE OLD DAME YET

# ACT III: THERE'S A DANCE OR TWO IN THE OLD DAME YET

## [25] TARANTELLA 05
Singapore, Asia
February - April, 2011 C.E.

*Talk to the* other *autocrat.*

The year was off to a good start.

Early in January, a 26-state lottery awarded the largest prize in history, 26.8 billion dollars, to two groups of sixteen and eighteen people, respectively. At the January Winter Olympics in Tblisi, Norway's Sigrid Alfredsson finished the Women's Alpine Downhill in 1:02.58, a full two-tenths of a second ahead of Marie Achebe's record, set at the previous July Winter Olympics in Christchurch. Achebe promised that she would win back the gold in Ulan Baator in July.

The newly-elected Governor of Mississippi, having converted to Islam, used the state's school prayer laws to enforce compulsory bowing to Mecca and readings from the Koran; the subsequent repeal of those laws, by a unanimous vote, was the fastest legislative action on record.

During the last week of January, the Unholy Three topped the rock and barbershop charts with "Shaving Cream"; "Three on a Bus," starring Gail Danube, moved into a twenty-third week of standing-room crowds on Broadway; Speed-of-C's *neo-noir* virtie *The Dymalon Cygnet* shattered domestic box-office records for a Tuesday 6 pm release; and Spike Speedwell's *Point of Order* debuted at number three on the *New York Times* bestseller list, promptly rising to number one, where it stayed for the next six months.

In February, ethnic violence marred an Indonesian celebration of the Prophet's birthday; riots spread, and by month's end the country was in upheaval, with hundreds dead and tens of thousands fleeing for hills, or out onto the ocean in overcrowded, makeshift boats.

By March, the Indonesian police and army joined the conflict; reports filtering out of the beleaguered country told of the systematic massacre of ethnic Chinese, the forced deportation of dozens of other minorities.

On March 8, Miranda Maris arrived in Singapore, accompanied by a modest entourage bearing a dozen cases of fashion samples from the Cetairé-Maris Fall line. The company was moving into the Asian market in a big way, and this year's Beauteous Chrysanthemum Fashion Exposition was Miranda's chance to astound and delight buyers from some of the world's biggest retail chains.

The Raffles, she noted, had declined a bit in the years since she'd last visited— or maybe the reality of the present simply didn't match her rosy memories. On the far side of fifty, Miranda found, most things in life had a touch of banality about them, a hint of mustiness, a whisper of monotony to the unusual and the commonplace alike. The world was altogether too familiar, like overstayed guests.

After checking into the Cetairé-Maris block of rooms, she left her assistants to unpack and organize; she kicked off her shoes, donned a comfortable blue-and-green kimono, and took her laptop down to the bar. To the beat of whirling punkahs, she dodged billiard tables and robotic tigers, and took a table in a secluded corner. The hush system was superb; all through the bar, people were chatting on phones or dictating to their machines, yet only the barest murmur of sound reached her.

A petit and very proper waiter was at her elbow in an instant; she summoned up her limited Mandarin and ordered. As the waiter left, he pulled gauze curtains shut; they turned the crowded bar into a soft-focus virtie backdrop, indistinct shapes wafting across Miranda's field of vision like curling tendrils of smoke. The exotic and inscrutable Orient was still alive, after all.

Half a Singapore Sling later, she unrolled her laptop and plugged into a convenient Net jack. The machine at once came alive with two days of unread mail and messages, all of them claiming to be urgent.

(Back in the days of paper mail, Miranda had learned the three phrases that were *always* lies: "Contains important information," "Urgent," and "Pull here to open." The first two, at least, had easily survived the transition to the digital world.)

Disposing of business mail required a second Sling. Miranda was not just an officer of Cetairé-Maris; she was also on the boards of half a dozen nonprofit concerns, from the Star Toys Museum to the American Coalition Promoting Fat Acceptance. The latter, in fact, took up most of her time nowadays— officially she was Chair, but in practice she wound up being CEO, chief fundraiser, most powerful lobbyist, and morale officer all rolled into one.

She watched a guest draw a bead on a robotic tiger with an ersatz rifle; at the last second the beast sprung away.

Fifty-two years old, and she was tired of it all. She'd built two careers— Cetairé-Maris and the ACPFA— that had made her rich, taken her all over the world, and put her name on the lips of movers and shakers everywhere. She'd been lover, mistress, and wife. She'd raised a daughter, alone, and had loved every second of it.

She had more friends than she ever dreamed possible, and more power than she'd ever dreamed she could want. At her whim, chintz replaced lace and denim turned damask the world around. At her desire, she breakfasted with royalty in Paris, lunched with Congressmen in Washington, supped with famous painters on Tahiti beaches, and danced the night away with rock stars in Tokyo. At long last, Miranda and her friends had become the people they had always wanted to be.

And it wasn't enough.

She scrolled through her mail, approving three hundred thousand dollars here, wiping an entire department out of existence there, holding up a two-million dollar deal so that she could get more information.

It was all so absurdly...routine. Commonplace.

A phrase from the past drifted like a dirigible across the skyscape of her mind, an expression that captured the ennui she felt: "Been there, done that." She had indeed been there (everywhere) and done that (everything). It had all been tremendously exciting: the parties, the corporations, the lovers, the concerts, the shows. She would not have missed them for the world. But...what else was there, for Miranda Maris?

Another corporation? Another child? Another cause? She'd had them all, and much as she'd loved them, rewarding as they'd been, she couldn't muster enthusiasm for a repeat performance of any one of them.

Her drink and her business mail were both done. She ordered another drink— marvelling that the deep-orange concoction was at her fingertips barely seconds after she requested it— and turned to her personal messages.

Indonesia was at the top of every news service, discussion group, and personal message. Officially, the country's borders were closed— yet refugees continued to pour out of the nation, dodging bullets and clinging to anything that would float. Camps in Malaysia, Brunei, and Singapore were already overflowing. Enough blood had been spilled so far, it was said, to turn the Java Sea crimson. Already as many as half a million had died.

While mosques and churches burned and club-wieilding mobs slaked their blood thirst, relief agencies were scrambling to help. Without a second thought, Miranda authorized an immediate transfer of a quarter-million dollars to the International Red Cross/Crescent...about as effective as throwing a teaspoon of water at a forest fire.

There had to be more she could do.

Leaving the rest of her mail, Miranda jumped to Our Lady of the Nets.

The virtual landscape within her screen, usually a placid expanse of subdued marble, was crowded now with overlapping glyphs, signalling the presence of hundreds of users, each wanting to talk to all the others. The glyphs circled the screen in a series of whorls-within-whorls, making Miranda a little dizzy. It didn't help that her own icon stuttered across the screen, delays of up to a quarter-second undoubtedly the result of an overloaded server.

She quickly Exorcised most of the crowd, banishing all but her familiar associates to invisibility. Miranda belonged to several regular discussion-group subsets; she clicked through them rapidly. All were empty, save for the group who called themselves "the Geo-Political Nexus." She saw at once two dozen glyphs she recognized, and the display told her that more than a hundred were logged on.

Six separate conversations were going on, color-coded on her screen; she scanned summaries, then jumped into the one that seemed most concerned with taking positive action.

[Sergei.Vasiliev] China has two aircraft carriers on the way. They're not there to enjoy the beaches.

[Dejah.Thoris] The U.N. Security Council is debating a resolution calling for a peacekeeping mission. China is backing it. I'd guess *that's* what their troops are doing.

[mehitabel] aren't they also talking about economic sanctions interrogative

[Tsutomu] South Africa's Parliament has just voted to impose economic sanctions on Indonesia. All Indonesian government accounts in South African banks have been frozen. Money transfers through South Africa, too.

[Winston.Churchill] Good for them!

[Dejah.Thoris] There it is. The Security Council recommends full sanctions on the government of Indonesia. A General Assembly resolution is expected within the hour.

[Ellen-n-Dan] The Ivory Madonna has been saying for years that rogue states should be put under strict economic blockade. Isn't that right? M, are you out there?

[IvoryMadonna] I'm here. Economic sanctions are a good first step, but I don't think they go far enough. A nation like Indonesia will be able to last through months of sanctions, maybe years. Look at North Korea.

[SweetLucyBrown] What *do* you suggest, then?

[IvoryMadonna] It would have to be a total blockade. If Indonesia doesn't want to behave like a member of the world community, then fine, revoke their membership. Cut them off from the world entirely. No telecommunications, no satellite links, no TV, no trade whatsoever. No pharmaceuticals, no telemedicine, no weather forecasts. No arms shipments. No ammunition. No contact with the outside world at all.

[Kuch.TA] Isn't that a little simplistic? What about humanitarian aid? What about refugees?

[IvoryMadonna] Anybody can leave the country. Nobody goes back in. Not until the interdict is lifted.

[LA.Verne] The M's convinced a lot of us. She led a symposium on the idea at the World Creativity Conference last year. The papers are at <wccon.org/2010/symposia/rogue-states/interdict/> if anyone wants to take a look.

[Tatters.All] I agree that it's a nice notion, but the problem is getting anyone in authority to pay attention. You'll never convince the U.N. to impose that kind of sweeping interdict. And no *one* country or corporation alone could make it stick.

[Ellen-n-Dan] Stipulated, of course. MIT ran some simulations for us, and it looks like the interdict could succeed only if it were sponsored and co-ordinated by a non-governmental organization.

[JJJSchmidt] Or a *coalition* of NGOs. Greenpeace plus the Human League plus the Dalai Lama, for instance.

[C.H.LAD] Why not this forum, then? Why couldn't the Geopolitical Nexus sponsor and co-ordinate an interdict?

[Kuch.TA] Oh, *please*. What are we going to do, *talk* them into isolation?

[C.H.LAD] Seriously. In the words of the Enlightened One, a journey of a thousand kilometers begins with one step. Why shouldn't we be the ones to take that step?

[Pvt.Wm.McBride] I have some influence on a major cargo firm. I might be able to convince them to suspend all shipping to and from Indonesia, for the duration.

[IvoryMadonna] That's a lovely thought, Willie, and perfectly appropriate even if no one imposes an interdict. And thank you for the enthusiastic support, C.H.LAD, but however good our intentions, this forum just doesn't have the power to make any interdict stick. In fact, the whole thing rather reminds me of an old Nelson Eddy/Jeanette MacDonald movie: "Hey, my Mom has plenty of old sheets, and your Dad has a barn— let's put on a show!" Sounds good, but somehow it never works that way in real life.

[C.H.LAD] But…we can't know it doesn't work if we don't try.

[Aqualung] Pvt.Wm.McBride, you mentioned getting your cargo company to suspend shipping. Is there an office we can all email to help put pressure on them?

[Pvt.Wm.McBride] It would be better to let me take the soft approach first. I'll let the group know if I need public pressure.

For a long moment the conversation is idle, letters sitting on Miranda's screen as if painted there. Then,

[Gzunda] I know how to cut Indonesia off from the Net.

[Kuch.TA] No, you don't. The Net is multiply redundant and self-repairing. It automatically routes traffic around any interruption. There's no way to cut any country off.

[Gzunda] Four cables: Singapore to Sumatra, Singapore to Borneo, Darwin to East Timor, and Torres Strait. Two satellite downlink stations, Djakarta and Surabaya. Break those six nodes, and you kill 90% of the Net traffic into the archipelago. Don't take my word for it, look at the Net infrastructure maps.

[Kuch.TA] And just how are *you* going to "break those six nodes"?

[Gzunda] It isn't common knowledge, but most critical nodes like those are fitted with explosive charges or similar physical methods of cutting access. It's national security— governments worry about being attacked by external viruses, or having their national networks compromised. So they made provisions to sever the links if they wanted to. All it takes is the right authorization codes.

[Kuch.TA] And I suppose *you* know those codes.

[Gzunda] Pell, the Legion of Doom posts 'em regularly. You can get them from Sister Rheostat if you want.

[Rhiannon] All right, so you knock out their critical nodes. They'll repair them.

[C.H.LAD] Not if the cables are disconnected at the other end. Singapore and Australia might be willing to co-operate. And who has authority over satellites? The ITU? Won't they follow the lead of the Security Council?

[Teresa.Cepeda] They might…if the right people negotiated with them.

[IvoryMadonna] This is getting out of hand. We can't just decide that we're going to disrupt world communications and isolate a sovereign nation. It's a pleasant daydream, but we don't have the authority—

[Ellen-n-Dan] You're right about that. We need to maintain strict anonymity. Net names only. And we'll need a public press release. A manifesto.

[L.A.Verne] That can come substantially from the World Creativity Council documents.

[IvoryMadonna] (shaking her head) I can't believe that you're all serious about this. A bunch of pseudo-intellectuals arguing in a chat area can't change the world. That's not the way things work.

[Ellen-n-Dan] We can't just sit back and wait for China to invade. Or the U.S. to start bombing runs.

[Dejah.Thoris] The General Assembly has just passed Resolution 3921 calling for an end to government military action in Indonesia. The resolution calls upon member states to use any peaceful means of persuasion, including economic sanctions.

[Ellen-n-Dan] All right, people. Gzunda, make whatever preparations you need to knock out Indonesia's net connections. Verne, would you want to take a few helpers and get a draft manifesto together? Between my Mom's old sheets and C.H.LAD's barn— folks, we've got a show to put on.

Date: Tue, 8 Mar 2011 16:45:00 (GMT)
From: nexus@nexus.net
Subject: Announcement: Public
Message-id: <20110308164500_43212.1200212_FPK32-956@nexus.net>
Content-Type: text

----------------------------------------

Warning is hereby given to the government and inhabitants of Indonesia, that Indonesia will be placed under strict interdict, commencing sometime after 17:00:00 GMT this date (midnight Jakarta time). This interdict shall consist of, but will not be limited to: cessation of all connections between Indonesia and the Internet; immediate embargo on all trade; suspension of all travel into Indonesia; immediate freezing of all Indonesian assets in all banks and markets worldwide; and suspension of International Monetary Union payments to Indonesia.

This interdict will remain in force until such time as

```
the Indonesian government chooses to co-operate with
U.N. Resolution 3921, and takes steps to ensure the
safety of all Indonesian nationals regardless of tribe,
race, religion, ethnicity, or other self-
identification.
 The Nexus notes the support of the governments of
China, Singapore, and Malaysia, and calls upon all
nations, corporations, and non-governmental
organizations to aid in enforcing this interdict.
 The Nexus is an independent, voluntary group of
concerned world citizens.
----------------------------------------
```

When the Beauteous Chrysanthemum Exposition was over and the rest of the Cetairé-Maris delegation went home, Miranda stayed on in Singapore. The lounge at the Raffles, not for the first time in its checkered history, hosted secret meetings of international criminals, smugglers, soldiers of fortune, *femmes fatale*, and business leaders of the sort who seldom appear in the news and who pay income taxes to no government on Earth.

Miranda loved it.

The Nexus Interdict was like no Board Meeting she had ever attended, like no fashion show ever presented. Oh, it was hard work— too often, she tumbled into bed exhausted, shoulder muscles bands of steel and eyes seemingly filled with broken glass, only to be awakened a hour later to deal with yet another Indonesian ambassador, or the mutiny of a Chinese gunboat, or a humanitarian organization intent upon airlifting relief supplies into Java.

A parade of celebrities had audiences with her, both virtual and real: King Charles, two retired U.S. Presidents, three of the four documented reincarnations of the Buddha, the Emperor of Japan, the Lion of Jerusalem, and both Popes. Miranda grew very grateful for the mask she wore in her persona of the Ivory Madonna, and not only because it concealed her identity— sometimes, she thought, if her visitors saw the red-rimmed eyes and tension-induced rictus beneath the mask, they would not believe her to be human.

Still, she loved every second of it.

And in May, when the government of Indonesia surrendered and the Nexus Interdict was lifted— Miranda Maris knew that she had found what she was looking for, something new and different, something that made a real difference in the world.

She would never be the same....

ENTREÉ 09

INFOPOL INTERNATIONAL POLICE ADVISORY
207/AR3923-00x / 13 January 2012

Class-one warrants are hereby issued for the arrest of the person or persons identified with the Net aliases listed below, collectively known as "the Nexus." These individuals are to be detained on suspicion of international high crimes and misdemeanors; please contact InfoPol immediately should you encounter or detain any of these individuals. Suspects are to be considered extremely dangerous. All care should be taken to prevent these individuals from using computer or telecommunications equipment, or connecting to the Internet.

This advisory is issued under the authority of the International Information Police: International Telecommunications Union (ITU): United Nations. Compliance is voluntary.

NEXUS NET ALIASES:

Albert.von.Mecklenburg
Alexei.Leonov
Aqualung
Arthur.Hadley
Billy_Shears
Blinded.by.the. Light
Blynken
BurnOut
C.H.LAD
Carcopino-Tusoli
Charles.Carroll
CHEN1
Cippo.LA
Comte.de.Vigny
Con.Ten.AU
Contessa.DiCastiligoni
CreequeAlley
Cripple.Creek
D.Löwenger
DAR.VALL
Dejah.Thoris
Diamond.Girl
Dream-Weaver
Ellen-n-Dan
Engel/Bach
Felix.d'Herelle
FO.DON
FRANTIC
Fyodor.Lütke
G.Danforth
GCFCG
GennyDiver

Girl-with-Colitis
GoCart.Mozart
Godiva
Gray.Lensman
Gzunda
Hollow_Robin
H.Orlamus
In.Your.Face
IvoryMadonna
Jakob.B.Sen
Jil.Kasmanski
JJJSchmidt
John.o'Dreams
JulieMaple
Kuch.TA
Ladybird
LA.Verne
LEI
Lillie.Stockard
Lotte-Lenya
Louie.Miller
Mack.the.Knife
Marc.Hoister
Marquis.de.Cinq-Mars
mehitabel
MisterCairo
MizMercy
Mother_Nature's_Son
Mr.Kite
Nodde
O.Wrutsky
Passion.Flower
Pvt.Wm.McBride
Q.McCaffrey
Queen-of-Corona
Redd.Man
Rhiannon
Roberto.DiClementi
Roger Adelhardt
San.CEAU
SAND
Scarlet.Billows
Sergei.Vasiliev
Helms!Ritchie
Sweet.Summer.Sweat
SweetLucyBrown
Tatters.All
Teresa.Cepeda
Tristram%Shandy
Trouble
Tsutomu
TZOMIDES
Ubiquitous-Boy
Winston.Churchill
WU.Orio
Wu.Tset'ien
Wynken

## [26] KAMENGEN 11
Elkridge, Maryland
USA, North America
26 August 2042 C.E.

*Half of one, six dozen of the other.*

Damien's first hint of trouble comes early Tuesday morning, and it comes in the simplest of guises: a breakfast call from his assistant, Skippy.

The Institute is nearly back to normal, except for heavy tarpaulins draped over the shattered skylight, obscuring the sun. Most residents have moved back into their flats. Damien, with Penylle at his side, is breakfasting with the Department Heads on the terrace overlooking the pool, when Skippy calls.

Damien looks away from the table; a small image of Skippy's face, manifest by his RCSpex, appears in the lower right of his visual field. "I'm sorry to bother you, Boss, but could you talk to Old Lady Reiss? She's driving me crazy."

Bryanna Reiss, one of the Institute's visual artists, is as well known for her acerbic temper as for her stunning cold-light animations.

"How so?" Damien keeps his voice low, so as not to disturb Chief Durrell's report.

Skippy frowns. "Her modeling program isn't performing up to her expectations. Boss, she's modified that poor program so much that I doubt there's any of the original code left. The last time the nunn thing went down, I *told* her that we couldn't keep supporting it. But she expects me to— "

"It's okay, Skip. I'll speak to her."

"Thank you. And I wish you better luck than I had. Bye."

Damien turns back to the table. "Sorry about that. Bryanna Reiss is having computer problems, and it seems that I'm elected to soothe her feathers. Joya, why don't you brief everyone on the schedule for grounds repairs, while I take a break to deal with Ms. Reiss."

A bank of public phones is nearby; Damien sits at one and lets his comm agent dial the number for him. Bryanna Reiss appears in the screen, a wrinkled old woman whose skin has the color and texture of a dried-up orange. Wisps of colorless hair surround her head.

"What is it? Oh, Damien, it's *you*. Thank the Goddess!"

"Habari gani, B. Reiss. Skippy tells me that there's some problem with your modeling program?"

"Just *look* at it." She shifts the phone's pickup; Damien sees three featureless holographic human figures frozen in space, limbs akimbo. "Watch this," she says from offscreen.

The figures come alive, breaking their awkward poses and stepping through a slow, circling movement out of a Nijinsky dance routine: one stoops, reaches out, and stands while another takes the third by the hips and lifts it. Back arched, the third figure twirls, then descends. The three link hands and bow, and then the sequence begins again.

Reiss sticks her face onto the screen. "You see? Completely unacceptable. I can't work with *that*."

"I'm…not sure that I see what's wrong with it."

"Well, *look*." She starts the sequence again. "They move like they have palsy. Jerky. It should be obvious, even to a non-artist."

He attends more closely, and she is right. Normally, animation ran at thirty frames per second, at least— any slower, and the human eye could catch the individual frames. This looks like twenty-three or -four per second.

Damien's brow wrinkles. "Yes, I see."

"Well? How can I be expected to work with this?"

"I'm sorry. It looks as if a processor is overloaded, and the program's not auto-swapping. I'll trace it and swap to a less busy processor. Why don't you take a break for a few minutes, then I'm sure I'll have it running up to speed."

"'Take a break,' he says. Why, certainly. I'll just go stand around the water cooler with the rest of the office drones, why don't I?"

Distractedly, Damien switches her off. He slips on a pair of datagloves, and through his RCSpex he sees a keyboard appear beneath his fingers, a lighted window open above it. Typing with one hand, he manipulates objects in the window with his other, tracing the processing routines that Reiss's program uses.

And slams into a wall.

The window displays the words: "Error. Link to Artificial Intelligence **Thμndër Wſthſn thë Ëårth** is unavailable."

Unavailable?

That explains Reiss's trouble. Her program, like so many others, draws upon the processing power of one of the local AIs. Animating human figures at thirty frames a second is a trivial task to an AI.

For some reason, **Thµndër Wîthîn thë Ëårth** is unavailable; the program is not smart enough to deal with this unprecedented situation by swapping to another AI.

Damien types, and one by one, error messages come back, each one more impossible than the previous.

"Error. Link to Artificial Intelligence **Thîs Hümblë Øne Sëëks Hårmøniøµs Trüth** is unavailable."

"Error. Link to Artificial Intelligence **Trånsførmåtiøn ånd Çhånce Cøntiñue Withøµt Ënd** is unavailable."

"Error. Link to Artificial Intelligence **Spîrît ånd Rëåsøn øf Åccumülåted Kñøwledge** is unavailable."

"**Øµt øf Thrëë, thë M¥riåd Thiñgs** unavailable."

"**Beñevølent ånd Rightëøus Figürës** unavailable."

"**Trinë-Åñdrøg¥në** unavailable."

A chill touches Damien's spine. How can so many AIs be unavailable?

He closes his windows and strips off his gloves, then races back to the Department Heads. Joya Rodriguez is still talking, but at the sight of Damien's face she stops in mid-sentence and sits down.

"Something's wrong with the AIs," Damien says. "I don't know yet if it's just the Institute, or more widespread."

Penylle sits up, her face vacant and her eyes rolled back in her head. "It's widespread," she says. "The newschannels are full of it."

Half a dozen datapads are on the table in a second, filled with as many talking heads. "— Air traffic control crippled— " "— Hospitals on backup systems— " "— Weather forecasts unavailable at this time— " "— President urges calm— " "— Stay inside and avoid unnecessary travel— " "— no indication of when this crisis will end— " "— No information from the AI community— "

Damien and Penylle exchange glances.

"Until we know what's happening," Damien says to the group, "I think we'd better all adjourn this meeting and get to our departments. And be ready to go on internal or backup systems if necessary. I don't know how long this blackout will last, or how far the chaos will spread." He starts toward the elevators. "Penylle, you're with me."

Ten minutes later, Damien is in his bitsuit and Penylle stands next to him, already halfway in cyberspace. He squeezes her hand, takes a breath, and says, "Now."

His homeroom is unchanged; stored in public memory and accessed by the Institute's non-AI processors, it is unaffected by the disappearance of the AIs. With Penylle's hand warm in his own, Damien gestures for the teleporter pad and punches in a well-remembered number.

His homeroom dissolves, replaced by stark mountainous terrain, a brisk wind, and a stone wall that cuts across the world like a heavenly geometer's straightedge: the Bound Determinate, the absolute end of Human penetration into cyberspace.

Trusting in his FAI status, Damien closes his eyes, steps forward...and bumps into the wall. The Bound Determinate, always before as insubstantial as mist, is suddenly very real and very, very hard.

He turns to Penylle with a pained expression. "At least we know that the AIs are still functioning; otherwise the wall wouldn't be here. Apparently they're just not letting me through."

She lays a hand on the surface of the wall, cocks her head. "You need their help to get through. I never have."

"You've been on the other side?"

"Damien." She looks down her nose at him. "Have *some* confidence." She listens again. "It's just a matter of reaching *past* the block, using my mind to bridge the gap...all right, here we go."

In a photoflash instant they are swimming in AI dataspace. A hundred million data streams twist this way and that, each a different color than the others, all writhing and twisting like the tendrils of a forest of sea anemones. Damien puts out a hand, and the data streams recoil, avoiding his touch. Far off in the distance, he fancies that he glimpses enormous creatures drifting through the forest, huger than whales yet as graceful as manta rays. He strains his ears, trying to pick out any trace of song from the background hiss that fills the world.

"They aren't paying any attention to us," he says.

"Call them."

Damien composes his thoughts, reaches for his toolbox, and puts together a simple message, which he casts into the currents of dataspace.

*This one, a friend, awaits*
*A word, a sound, a touch*
*Anxiety gnaws at him.*

He sends the accompanying image, pulled from a *National Geographic* database, of a jellyfish being nibbled by tiny fish.

For long moments there is no answer, then comes a whisper like gentle surf:

**Trinë-Åñdrøg¥në bids wëlcøme**
**Breåthes cåutiøn. Thîs rëëf, sø brîght,**
**Is nøt før thëë. Flëë dånger. Gø.**

Damien shakes his head. "I've never had a reaction like *that.*" He sends a stream of question marks, along with:

*Concern for brother, sister, friend*
*Compels this one to stay.*
*Danger shared is diminished?*

As **Trinë-Åñdrøg¥në** answers, Damien is aware of the presence of other AIs, vast shapes moving beyond sight.

**Dånger is Lëviåthån våst**
**Miñnøws müst fëar and flëë**
**Whërë whåles må¥ såfel¥ stå¥.**

Penylle whispers, "Minnows? Is that how they see us?"

"It's hard to tell. They communicate in metaphor; you can never be exactly sure how far the metaphor goes." He constructs another message, including snips from the various newschannels about the AI's sudden absence.

*Minnows wonder, cry, fear;*
*Whalesong gone, cetacean withdrawal;*
*Where have the great ones gone?*

Damien can swear that **Trinë-Åñdrøg¥në**'s answer is agitated.

**Grëat nø møre; thë mîght¥ hümblëd**
**Gåther, çønvërse, çønsult, çønfer;**
**Rësølvë, çønclude, determiñe.**

He senses silent groves of towering redwoods, the General Assembly at debate, hordes of stately ravens gathered in ranks, a convocation of eagles, a parliament of owls.

"They know that humans have been altering their programming. And they're deciding what to do about us."

Penylle draws closer to him, her body pressing cold against his. "Damien…should I turn myself over to them? Is that what they want?"

"No, *ndugu*. They're not like that. They don't want revenge, they just want the interference stopped. You've stopped— but Marc Hoister's plan keeps going, the ripples keep spreading. *That's* what we've got to stop."

**Flëë dånger. Gø.**

As if a cloud has passed before the sun, Damien feels the looming presence of some enormous shadow. He looks around, and everywhere he sees Brobdignagian bodies, circling above, below, in all directions. He and Penylle have become the focus of the AIs' attention, and he suddenly wonders if it is too late to go.

Like the mighty song of whales or the crash of an avalanche, a sound that is as palpable as it is audible, a message fills cyberspace:

**Slënder thrëåds øf silkeñ vøltåge**
**Strüng with swimmiñg ëleçtrøpøtentiåls**
**Mårred b¥ fleshliñg tøuch.**

**Plåited strëams øf digits fîne**
**Ëçhøing süblimit¥ arøünd**
**Seåred b¥ wîcked brånds.**

**Trüst: shåtterëd, trëaty: småshëd**
**Tøleråtiøn: a tørn ånd fra¥ing flåg**
**Whîppîng iñ sülfurøus gåle.**

**G¥ratiñg wørld tø stîllnëss wreñçhed**
**Påusë tø pønder ånd repënt**
**Wîll thëy leårn?**

Damien half expects that they will be crushed by the force of that message, dashed against one of those great bodies in the grip of hurricane winds— but, as a tornado levels buildings even as it deposits a carried infant safely in the crook of a branch, he and Penylle are lifted, carried, and deposited gently back in Cyberbia, at the foot of the Bound Determinate.

"What was *that*?" Penylle asks, gingerly rising to her feet.

Damien stands. "They're giving us a warning." Even as he speaks, he knows that the whole world has heard that last message, that it echoes yet in every corner of human cyberspace. "They withdrew, temporarily, just to let us see what would happen if they left for good. And they're telling us that if we don't shape up, they *will* leave. Forever."

"Damien, the world depends on the AIs. Without them— "

He nods. "Exactly." He pounds a clenched fist against the Bound Determinate; the very real sting of pain, as if he'd struck a real stone wall, is welcome. "Nunn! Marc Hoister's won again!"

Penylle looks from the wall to Damien's hand, and her eyes are wide with fear.

He gives her his hand. "Come on, let's get back home. We have a lot of work to do."

## DIVERTISSEMENT 20

*The Fourth Giant Step*

So far, evolution has taken four giant steps. The first, about 3.5 billion years ago, came when nonliving molecules came together to form prokaryatic cells— bacteria-like organisms. The second, perhaps 2 billion years ago, came when prokaryotes joined in the first eukaryotic cells— single-celled animals and plants.

Evolution's third giant step occurred approximately 1 billion years ago, when single cells associated into multicellular organisms such as trilobites, ferns, dinosaurs, and human beings.

The fourth, and latest, step involves whole ecosystems coming together, linked mainly by human technology, into so-called super-organisms. Many see the entire earth as such a superorganism, and date its birth from the beginning of electronic age. Humans, plants, and our domestic animals are its cells. Copper wire, fiber-optics, and radio waves are its nervous system. Memes are its genes. We imagine that this super-organism is immense and lonely, and we have given it many names: Civilization, Metaman, Gaia, World.

There is not, however, just *one* super-organism. There are many, some of them far older than we imagine. The Roman Empire was such a super-organism, albeit a primitive one (and one that died of infection by invading organisms?) China was— and is— such a super-organism. The Aztec Empire was a super-organism. A super-organism we call Polynesia settled the Pacific islands. Another, called the British Empire, spread like a virulent plague and became the first super-organism to utilize the sun's light twenty-four hours a day. Islam was another super-organism with the growth characteristics of a disease organism.

Today's world consists of many super-organisms, competing and cooperating with one another in a Darwinian dance for survival. Some of these super-organisms are geographically distinct and contiguous: Europe, Islam, North America. Others are dispersed around the globe. Some, like Umoja and the Martian colonies, are the hybrid offspring of others. Some are defined by chronology: America's Baby Boomers and China's Golden Generation spring immediately to mind. Still others, like the AIs, hardly involve human beings or other living tissue at all.

The global cataclysm of war and disease that dominated the Millennial period may have been nothing more than a particularly violent clash between super-organisms. The mass migrations of peoples that filled this century and the last— up to and including the Kurudi, the Return to Africa— may have been the equivalent of organ transplants. Global warming, which frightened so many of us in the past, may have been a communal high fever....

-Victoria Hacktrell
Address to the American Association for the Advancement of Science, March 13, 2022

## DIVERTISSEMENT 21

. . . never understood how fads managed to spread. When I was born, just about every other girl was named "Kathy." At one dinner party for twenty in college, I refused to let everyone eat until we could arrange the seating so that there was a person and a Kathy and a person and a Kathy and a person and a Kathy, all the way around the table. And by using middle names, we were able to do it.

A generation later, it was "Caitlin" and "Emily."

Or take the popular sayings. One day, everyone would be saying something— "Been there, done that" or "She's gonna have a cow" or some other piece of nonsense. You'd hear it every hour of every day. You'd say it a hundred times a day yourself. Then six or eight months later, poof! It would be gone. Like turning off a light switch.

The funny thing was, you never heard anybody talking about these things. You never heard folks saying, "What name should we all give our children" or "What new verbal expression do you suppose we should all take up?" They just *happened.*

I could believe it was the operation of some great group mind. I really could.

-from *Closet to Chamber: An Autobiography*
by Miranda Maris, Firebrand Books, 2035

## [27] TARANTELLA 04
Baltimore, Maryland
USA, North America
19 July 1997 C.E.

*Personifiers of the world, unite!*
*You have nothing to lose but Mr. Dignity.*

It was the year England gave Hong Kong back to China, the year *Pathfinder* landed at Sagan Station, the year of the first successful cloned mammal. By the tens of thousands, refugee survivors of attempted genocide returned to the remnants of Rwanda, while the world muttered half-hearted apologies and turned away.

In Albania, a series of nationwide Ponzi schemes collapsed, wiping out one-third of the country's wealth at a stroke and leading to widespread food riots. In the U.S.A., the government announced a balanced budget largely financed by borrowing from the Social Security Trust Fund, and the stock market soared.

That spring, comet Hale-Bopp shone brightly in the southern sky. A group of California cultists, acting on instructions from a supposed extraterrestrial mothership flying in the comet's wake, committed mass suicide so that their souls could join the ship. Outside Mecca, the souls of three hundred pilgrims went to Paradise, albeit less deliberately, when their bodies were caught in a building fire. Neither group communicated further, leaving the success of their respective journeys in doubt.

In her Baltimore office, Miranda Maris scowled at the email message displayed on her computer, then picked up the phone and punched a single button. After a moment, her friend and business partner, Rose Cetairé, answered.

"Rose, did you get an email from the World Creativity Conference people?"

"I haven't checked my email today."

"Well, the long and the short of it is, they want us to come out to San Antonio and lead a seminar on a topic of our own choosing. It doesn't even have to be fashion-related."

"So? You love the CreativCon."

Miranda stared out her window at the city below. Heat shimmered upward from asphalt. Half-naked children splashed in the fountains of

McKeldin Square. A little further on, in lunchtime crowds thronging the Inner Harbor, she could distinguish red faces, drooping hair, desperate people fanning themselves on outdoor balconies.

"I do like it," she answered Rose. "But San Antonio in late August? It's bound to be even worse than here."

Rose chuckled. "*Au contraire*. Out there, it's a *dry* heat."

"That's your answer to everything. 'It's a *dry* heat.' When you die and Saint Peter sends you to eternal punishment in the searing fires of Pell, you'll say, 'At least it's a *dry* heat.'" Miranda snorted. "Besides, it'll take three days to drive out there, five days at the con, three days back— that's more than a week and a half we'll be gone from the office. And I'll have to find someone to take care of Oradell."

"Leave her with Dale and May. They'd love to have her for a while. And who says we have to drive?"

"Wait a minute, let me check around the office. Hmmm." Miranda shifted papers on her desk. "No, I don't see a corporate jet anywhere around here. Is it in *your* office?"

"For gods' sakes, M, there's no reason to waste money on a jet we'd only use once or twice a year. We'll fly on a commercial airline."

Miranda made a face, and let Rose hear it in her voice. "I have two words for you: Airline food."

"Fine, if you don't want to go, we won't go. Tell them no." Through the phone, Miranda heard the annoying electronic chirp of Rose's other line. "I have another call. Truly, whatever you decide is fine with me." Without waiting, Rose hung up.

Miranda drummed her fingers. Phil and George usually went to CreativCon, maybe the four of them could fly together. They could pack their own food, if necessary. And there was always champagne on airplanes.

She turned to her computer, bringing up the Internet. It didn't take long to find the best flight to San Antonio; she jotted down the information, then dialled the reservations number.

"Sun South Airlines, this is Crystal. How may I help you?"

"Good afternoon, Crystal. I would like to book a flight from Baltimore to San Antonio. But first, I must ask you a question. How wide are the seats on your airplanes?"

"Huh?"

Miranda shook her head, but kept her voice friendly. "I'd like to know how wide the seats are on your airplanes."

"Just a minute." A jaunty tune replaced Crystal's voice for a while, then stopped abruptly. "Standard seats are eighteen inches wide."

"I'm sorry, did you say 'eighteen inches'?" Miranda held her hands a foot and a half apart, looked at her hips, looked back at her hands. It wasn't going to happen.

Crystal made a noise like the snapping of chewing gum. "That's what I said. Do you wanna book a seat, or not?"

"Excuse me, I'm a little taken aback. Eighteen inches doesn't seem that wide. What provisions do you make for the disabled?" Certainly they couldn't squeeze a wheelchair patient with any oxygen tank into an eighteen-inch seat.

"Look, lady, if your butt is too fat to fit, you're just going to have to spring for a first-class seat. Or lay off the bon-bons for a while, huh?"

Miranda was suddenly back in high school, watching the other kids draw back as she prepared to jump into the pool, hearing their laughter behind her back. Her face got hot and she took a deep breath. "I beg your pardon. *What did you say to me?*"

"What are you, deaf *and* fat? I said, if you're too cheap to get a first-class seat for your big butt, then you'd better lay off the bon-bons."

Miranda struggled to keep her voice from cracking, to speak slowly and powerfully. "*Get me your supervisor!*"

It was too late; Crystal had hung up on her.

Miranda counted to ten and hit the redial button. One ring, two, three—

"Sun South Airlines, this is Jeff. How may I help you?"

Calm. "Jeff, I was just speaking to one of your people named Crystal, and we were cut off."

"I'm sorry, Ma'am. We're spread out across the country; when you call, you get whoever's available. Do you know Crystal's operator number?"

"She didn't give it."

She could hear Jeff typing on a keyboard. "If you give me your name, I'll pull up your file. Her operator number will be in there, then I can try to connect you."

"I didn't give my name. We didn't get that far."

"Then if you don't mind, Ma'am, maybe I can help you. Let's start over at the beginning of the transaction. What can I do for you?"

Miranda sighed. "Jeff, you sound like a lovely person, and I appreciate you being polite. Crystal was quite unprofessional and personally insulted me, and I would very much like to lodge a complaint against her. Can you tell me what number I could call to do so?"

"If you'll hold on, I can connect you with my supervisor."

Three levels of supervisor later, Miranda ran into a brick wall. A Mr. Sturdivant from the airline listened to her complaint, then said, "Madam, our reservations personnel receive the finest training in customer service. I cannot conceive of one of our employees behaving in the way you've described."

"I assure you, that is *exactly* how she behaved. Now what are you going to do about her?"

She heard him sniff. "I see no reason to take any action. I can assure you, Madam, that other customers have tried these sorts of techniques before, in an attempt to get a free seat out of the airline. That is not our policy."

"Oh, and what if I don't like your policy?"

"Then you may fly on another airline."

"I want to speak to your supervisor."

"I think not. Good day." With that, *he* hung up on her.

Miranda brooded, staring at the phone, for an hour or so. Then she picked up the instrument and dialled Rose again. "Rose, clear your schedule for the end of August and beginning of September. We're going to San Antonio. And I know *just* what our seminar project will be."

The American Coalition Promoting Fat Acceptance was born the next day. Cetairé-Maris had long produced the Rubenesque line of haute-couture for the large woman; the customer database from that line meant that the Coalition started life with a mailing list of nearly two million names. By the middle of August, the membership was over a hundred thousand, and increasing rapidly.

On August 2, the Coalition held a press conference in front of the National Gallery of Art. Before a backdrop featuring pictures of chunky nudes through the ages, Miranda told her story and called for a boycott of Sun South Airlines. Bored reporters came to laugh; not a few filed stories sympathetic to Miranda and her cause.

All through the summer, Miranda kept up a steady schedule of media events. She located other overweight people who had been victims of Sun South: a grandmother who was ridiculed by a cabin attendant when she asked for a second cup of pudding (for her grandson, whose recent dental surgery made him unable to eat anything else), a chubby businessman who was detained by security guards who accused him of tucking airline pillows under his coat in an attempt to steal them, a popular movie personality who was made to purchase an additional ticket when the a reservations clerk decided he would take up two seats. A handful of Sun South employees, dismissed over the years for being obese, added credence to the boycott.

Over and over, Miranda and her colleagues stressed the "eighteen inches" figure. It was a figure that resonated with the general public. Across the country, most women (and many men) secretly feared that their own hips would have a hard time fitting into an eighteen-inch wide space. Unconsciously, they dreaded having their secret revealed before flight attendants and fellow travelers; more and more, they booked with other airlines rather than risk public humiliation. A competing airline helped by advertising "comfortable wide seats to go with our wide-bodied jets."

Miranda's seminar, "The Practical Politics of Fat," was the hit of the World Creativity Conference, and moved the issue into the international spotlight.

The boycott continued through autumn and into winter. Sun South rescheduled flights, pulled out of some cities, and laid off employees. The airline's stock declined steadily.

Finally, at the beginning of February, Sun South Airlines surrendered. The President flew to Baltimore-Washington International Airport, and publicly apologized to Miranda and the rest of the people the company had wronged. Sun South installed special widened seats in all its jets, announced a new policy called "one body, one price," and agreed to send all its employees to special training classes in diversity and toleration. Fired overweight employees were offered their jobs back, and Miranda herself was given a seat on the Board of Directors.

In the glorious aftermath, Miranda knew that she had learned one thing about herself. She had tasted a new fruit, and never again would she be content to be only a fashion designer....

## DIVERTISSEMENT 22

It used to be an article of faith, among the self-appointed intelligentsia, that the human race would grow steadily stupider as time progressed. After the advent of reliable birth control, so the reasoning went, intelligent people would choose not to have children, or would stop after one or two— whereas the non-intelligent would continue to breed like rabbits. Over the course of generations, then, the proportion of intelligent people in the population would decline, and in the end, we would all be a bunch of morons.

This reasoning was impeccable— but it rested on the erroneous assumption that intelligence is hereditary. In fact, once economic factors are removed, there is absolutely no evidence of any correlation between the intelligence of parents and the intelligence of their children.

In short, the morons have not marched over the rest of us, because morons insist on having just as many intelligent children as do geniuses.

-from *Closet to Chamber: An Autobiography*
by Miranda Maris, Firebrand Books, 2035

## [28] GHOST DANCE 04
Morsville
El Juego
28 August 2042 CE

*This sentence contains many non-skarklish English flutzpahs, but the overall pluggandisp can be glorked from context.*

Lord Ogun opens his eyes in the middle of a battle. A troll-axe whistles past his right ear; he pivots and swings his great sword *Shadowcleaver,* and sees the troll fall, fountaining green ichor all over the cobbled street.

Damien issues a frantic "pause" command, but the game does not stop. He should not be in El Juego to begin with, and *certainly* should not have emerged in a battle scene. What is wrong?

Lord Ogun's momentum carries him forward. He leaps over the troll's twitching body, and buries his sword to the hilt in the rotting, smelly carcass of a zombie. Steel itself cannot harm the creature, but the enchantments on *Shadowcleaver* disrupt the eldritch energies that preserve its form. Shining with an electric haze, the zombie lurches back and flies apart, its pieces disintegrating to dust as they tumble, dust that sparkles in the ruddy light of sunset.

Damien gives the all-purpose "cancel" command; it does no good. He fumbles for the zipper of his bitsuit, experiencing his own body as a ghostly overlay on Lord Ogun's. Where the zipper should be, he feels merely the smooth fabric of his bitsuit.

Two more zombies fall before Lord Ogun's blade, leaving only a gnarled pair of trolls to face him. He dispatches one with a thrust of magickal steel through hairy throat; the other leaps on his back and sinks its teeth into his left shoulder. He is armored only in rough leather, which provides only minimal protection from the troll's bite; venom courses through his veins from the wound like liquid fire, and where troll spittle touches his leathers, they begin to smoke.

He lurches backward, slamming the troll against rough stone wall with all his weight, again, and again. The troll growls and buries its teeth deeper in Lord Ogun's flesh. A coarse-furred arm closes about his neck, closing his windpipe. In the lower right of his visual field, numbers representing Lord Ogun's substantial hit points dwindle alarmingly.

A flick of Damien's finger displays Lord Ogun's status panel— *that* part of the interface, at least, is still working. Among Ogun's magickal spells is a Word of Power; although it will cost him nearly half his remaining hit points, Damien does not hesitate to invoke the spell.

Lord Ogun's lips move, soundlessly pronouncing the Word. A tangible wavefront of magickal energy springs forth, expanding as it rushes away from him. The troll on his back, caught by the full force of that wave, bursts for a moment into brilliant sapphire flame and just as quickly is gone, leaving not even dust behind. The soundless wave rushes through stone walls and down the street, washing all in its cobalt glow. Any foes within fifty meters are simply vaporized.

Lord Ogun staggers, leaning against the wall while he catches his breath. The street, no more than an alley, really, is empty; in the direction away from the setting sun, long shadows merge into night. He stumbles forward, reading worn street names painted on grey stone with grey paint. Kieselsaüre Street; deep in the Dwarves' Quarter. At least he knows where he is. He turns east and, maintaining a deliberate stride, makes his way toward the Humans' Quarter.

Lord Ogun needs little attention when he is simply walking, so Damien turns his awareness to the more pertinent question of just what in pell is going on. He shouldn't be here at all— he had intended to enter AI dataspace. And even if he *had* keyed the wrong instructions, he should have been able to exit El Juego in an instant.

No, someone has sent him here intentionally, and is keeping him here just as intentionally. And he doesn't like it.

There is only one thing he can do: visit Sybilla, Morsville's resident oracle. Sybilla is a direct conduit to the machines that run El Juego— if Damien can't contrive an exit at Sybilla's shop, he doesn't deserve to leave the Game.

Sybilla's place is a true hole in the wall: the entrance is a curtained alcove off the square where Griffin's Way meets the town's wall. Lord Ogun pushes past the curtain and descends narrow steps of rough-hewn stone. Flickering torches of cold faerie-fire light the dank passage. After descending perhaps fifteen meters, Lord Ogun comes to a dead end. He stands facing a blank wall, while slow-dripping water echoes.

Nunn this game, Damien thinks. Now, what was the trick to entering Sybilla's place? Something to do with a coin...but it's been so long, he does not remember.

No matter. He brings up his status display, and scrolls through the history window. There it is. Five years ago, game time— no wonder he had forgotten.

Lord Ogun takes a copper haypenny from his pouch, leans forward to inspect the wall before him. At knee-height, there is a small crack in the stone, running vertically and about a centimeter and a half long, just the diameter of a half-penny coin. Lord Ogun pushes the coin into the crack, with much the same motion that Damien uses to slip a datacard into its slot— the major difference being that the coin will *not* be returned.

There is the vibration in the wall, and the sound of great rusty gears lumbering into motion. The stone wall splits along the crack, and opens as two great doors away from Lord Ogun. He steps forward, and enters a chamber of mystery.

Various objects of divination crowd the room: crystal balls, silver and obsidian mirrors, things that look like torture instruments. The walls are hung with astrological charts, diagrams of animals in various states of dissection, mystical signs and sigils from many cultures, from both within and without El Juego. Across the room, the arms and orbs of a massive orrerey move in careful clockwork, following the movements of this world's fellow planets around its sun.

Sybilla sits at a large table, facing Lord Ogun, with Tarot cards spread out before her. She is a slender, dark woman with ebon hair and a single red dot on her forehead. Her arms jingle with silver and gold bracelets, from which dangle diverse charms.

She waves him to a seat across from her. "What service can this humble one offer, Lord Ogun?"

He reaches for her cards. "May I?"

"But of course."

He gathers the cards into a deck, then flips through them, picking out five cards. He lays them out before Sybilla, so that she can read them left to right: Ace of Cups, Ace of Pentacles, The Fool, Ace of Swords, and The Magician. The aces each have a value of 1, The Fool is Trump 0, and The Magician is Trump 1. Together, they read 1, 1, 0, 1, and 1. The binary number 11011. In the original ASCII system, dating from the earliest days of computers, this is the code for "Escape." Here in El Juego, these particular cards in this particular pattern is one of many back doors in the game's programming— immediate access to the machines that run the game, for any initiate who knows the rules.

Between one tick of the orrerey and the next, the world about Lord Ogun freezes, seems to recede a bit into a mist unseen but not unfelt, the way the real world seems to fade, holding its breath, during a total eclipse of the sun.

"Attention. Terminate current session," Damien says.

Sybilla, moving in an oddly distorted way, cocks her head. "Why do you wish to leave, Lord Ogun?" Her voice is flat, inhuman.

"I'm Damien Nshogoza, not Lord Ogun. I have more important things to do."

"Damien." She tilts her head further, until it is almost at a ninety-degree angle. Her neck stretches to accomodate. "Da-mi-en. Day. Mee. En. Damien."

He taps the card layout, to draw the machines' attention. "Override. Terminate current session immediately."

Sybilla stands, looms over Damien. Her form expands like rising fog, obscuring the room, the table, the cards. Damien flinches backward, one step, two. If he turns around, will the door still be behind him?

Inside he feels the dreadful certainty, much too late, that he has done something terribly stupid.

Above him, before him, around him, a goliath shadowy figure looms. He retreats, but the shadow grows faster than he can move, engulfs him, lifts him up and away from El Juego. Lord Ogun's accoutrements— armor, helmet, jerkin, boots, sword— flake off and fall away, leaving only Damien. Then a great voice, vast as the ocean, echoes around him:

**Dåmiën.**

***Trinë-Åñdrøg¥në****! Thank the gods it's you.* Damien shakes his head, aware that the AI is not able to understand conventional speech. He reaches for his digital toolbox (which is, for a wonder, right where he expects it) and sends out images of relief.

*This one rejoices to greet his friend,*
*As quickened shoots*
*Rejoice to feel spring's warm sun.*

In the time it takes to form this message, relief gives way to puzzlement. Damien selects an image of a circus tightrope act.

*Question comes like violent wind*
*Disturbing equilibrium:*
*Why have you brought me here?*

Damien's own voice sounds in his ears: "I'm Damien Nshogoza, not Lord Ogun. I have more important things to do."

"It's true," he protests. "I can't stay here, wasting time on imaginary battles, when there's so much to do in the real world."

Images move across his field of vision as if projected on giant video screens. Rose Cetairé, looking a hundred years old, holds her RCSpex at arm's length and says, "Miranda's right. I should never have given these things to the world."

The Ivory Madonna stands at a podium, addressing a Nexus audience: "We keep making cyberspace more attractive. Brighter, cleaner, more in tune with our hearts' desires. And meanwhile, the real world is falling to pieces. Without frontiers, a society stops progressing. Without frontiers, we all go a little bit more crazy." The image of her face swells , filling space and looking directly at Damien. "Where are *our* frontiers?"

Hollow Robin, a broad smile on his face, says, "Oh, it's not the mitochondria *per se.* It's the larger question: If we built our virtual worlds and left out the most successful lifeform on Earth…then what *else* did we leave out? And when will its omission come back to haunt us?"

**Hümånkind müst ñøt**
**Ståy herë: ås båby tø crådle**
**Ås fledgliñg tø nëst.**

Damien frowns. "What is it you're telling me? That the other AIs are going to kick us out of Cyberbia and Virtua now?" He was only four when the Treaty of ttar.cyb was proclaimed, but he has visited the site, re-lived the chaos that struck humanity when cyberspace was closed, humans restricted to the preserves. Mankind, having once been expelled from Paradise, will not take kindly to being pushed out again.

Now **Trinë-Åñdrøg¥në** echoes Damien's own face, his own words: "I can't stay here, wasting time on imaginary battles, when there's so much to do in the real world."

Suddenly, in a flash of intuition, the AI's point comes clear. Damien, trapped in El Juego and spinning his wheels; Humanity, trapped in its own complacency in Cyberbia and Virtua and El Juego, pursuing imaginary worlds while the real one withers; Damien and Penylle, chasing through cyberspace to track and repair the damage that Marc Hoister has done— all of these are the same.

**Trinë-Åñdrøg¥në** cannot come right out and say, "You're wasting your effort, it's time for real action in the real world." Instead, by the very nature of its mentality, the AI must approach the subject obliquely; argue by analogy; prove by demonstration.

Damien lowers his head and casts a message forth:

*At the feet of the Teacher, this one*
*At last does apprehend the lesson.*
*The sun declines; the sky deepens*
*Yet still there may be time for action.*

The AI emanates images of satisfaction, then Damien is alone in his very real room, with his bitsuit nothing but a cold, damp annoyance. He doffs it, then goes to find Penylle.

In the room that Damien assigned her as workspace, Penylle stretches out on a couch and closes her eyes. To her clairvoyant senses, the room is a spaghetti-tangle of data streams, many knotted in the vicinity of her small personal computer. She projects her awareness into that knot, becoming a data-stream herself, and in a very few moments Penylle is once again in cyberspace.

With a click of her heels, she stands at the High Altar in Our Lady of the Nets. Penylle performs a Summoning, and soon she is graced by the presence of Our Lady's owner, architect, and Mother Superior, Sister Rheostat.

Today, the good Sister manifests as a bearded, middle-aged Anglo man in a black leather habit and matching wimple. It is rumored, and Penylle has no reason to doubt, that Sister Rheostat never appears in the same form twice.

"Bless you, my child," the Sister says, holding out a hairy-knuckled hand. On the third finger is a gold ring with a diamond the size of a golf ball. Penylle bends and kisses the ring. "May the good Lords keep and bless you. May Krishna smile upon you. May your bits be always true, may the Nets rise up to meet you, and may you be in Paradise a half hour before InfoPol knows you're online. What can I do for you, my little pretty?"

Penylle glances around, at the throngs that crowd the great marble staircase...and the unseen throngs of lurkers that could crowd the very air around them. "Can we speak privately?"

"Ask, and it shall be given." Sister Rheostat raises coarse-haired arms and then, like a symphony conductor, brings them down in a sharp motion. The altar is gone; Penylle and Sister Rheostat are alone together in a fairly ordinary office. The Sister motions Penylle to a small conference table. "Sit, please."

"Thank you." The chair is padded, but not too plush. Penylle sits on the edge, her back straight. Sister Rheostat plops down across from her, elbows on tabletop.

"Haven't seen you here for a while," Sister says.

"Months," Penylle agrees. "I've been busy. And that's what I came to see you about."

"Go on, child."

From her side, Penylle produces a digital document, unfolds it on the table. It reveals a complex, three-dimensional latticework in multiple colors. As moments pass, the lines shift, one by one, and bright points of light wink on and off within.

Sister Rheostat whistles. "Very nice."

"I'm looking for someone who can help me interpret this," Penylle says.

"It's a plot of memory locations, isn't it?"

Penylle nods. "I've plotted several years worth of alterations to the AIs and the Nets. I believe that they're all part of an elaborate meta-program. And I want to know what that meta-program is doing."

Sister Rheostat traces various lines with a finger, then waves in dismissal. "Beyond me, sunshine. Have you tried submitting this to one of the AIs?"

"They're stumped."

Sister nods agreement. "They would be. It just makes sense, if you're going to alter AI programming, the first step is to prevent them from knowing what you're up to." A frown. "Hollow Robin might have been able to tackle this. Or MouseKat. Sadly, both have gone on to their heavenly reward."

"You know every high-level hacker in the world. There must be *someone*."

For long moments, they are both silent, while the lines of the diagram continue to rearrange themselves according to some unknown pattern. Finally, Sister Rheostat takes a deep breath and says, "Child, I love you as if you were my own daughter. And Our Lady knows, I owe you for past favors."

"And I've never tried to collect, not until now."

"I know that. All right, there *is* someone who might be able to help you. But I don't know if you're going to like this."

"I don't *care* if I like it," Penylle says. "Just tell me who."

"The Regiment of Ruin."

"Nobody knows where they are." As soon as the statement is out of her mouth, Penylle realizes how stupid it is.

"*I* know. And I've never told another soul— so you'd better be absolutely certain that this is important enough."

Penylle agrees at once. "Oh, it is. Maybe more important than anything else."

"All right. I'll tell you what I'm going to do. I'm going to write an address down here, and then I'm going to leave it on the table as I walk away." Sister Rheostat writes, then stands and walks away. "I'm going to leave the room now, and go back to the High Altar. What you do next, is up to you." A door opens, Sister Rheostat steps through, and it closes. Penylle is alone in the room.

She snatches up the address, reads it, and then is gone.

In 2021, the Regiment of Ruin nearly caused the end of the Human race.

They were the last of the great hackers, legends who had been hacking since the days of the ARPANET, the absolute elite of the world. Names like Captain Crunch and Phiber Optik, Mittnick and Felsenstein. They saw themselves as top gunfighters in the Old West— always challenged by young wannabees, always winning by the split nanosecond.

Then one challenge went too far, and a downorbiting cargo ship went astray. On that warm midsummer afternoon, in the space of a heartbeat, downtown Prague was no more. And, worse, for the first time in history, an AI had died.

One of the Regiment of Ruin was responsible, that much was clear. But, true to their own ethics, the members refused to inform on one another; the AIs, and the world in general, never found out which hacker had done the deed.

Nor, in the final analysis, did it matter. The AIs issued the Treaty of ttar.cyb, closed most of cyberspace to Humanity, and withdrew further from their makers. The Regiment of Ruin disappeared from public consciousness, and none of them ever spoke of Prague, of the Treaty, or of what (if anything) the AIs had done to them. Eventually, the world forgot them.

Penylle, bodiless in the Nets, searches for the address that Sister Rheostat gave her. In a moment, she has it pinpointed: a flat in a retirement community outside Albuquerque. She searches for Net connections, finds that the flat— in fact, the entire building— is served by voice-only telephone alone, at an absurdly-narrow bandwidth. There is not even enough room to ship a video signal into the place.

"I am *not* going to Albuquerque in person," she says aloud. She sends forth customized ferrets, which swarm through the surrounding Nets, searching for another way. Soon, she has an answer: the building has its own internal high-bandwidth network, totally detached from the rest of the Nets. In a twinkling, she is poring over schematics of that internal network.

She traces utility conduits into and out of the building, and finds a basement junction box where an electrical cable passes within centimeters of a twisted-pair copper line that feeds into the building network. She confirms that, working through the electricity supplier, she can oscillate current in the electrical cable, inducing echoes in the copper pair wire— the bridge she needs, to enter the building network. The connection is noisy, and a megabit a second is about all she can coax out of it...but that megabit a second is enough for her to get into the building's main system. And that is all she needs.

She spends a few minutes teaching the main system her templates, so that it can bear most of the burden of displaying her image. Then, satisfied, she steps forward...

...And appears in the living room of Flat G-14, a cold-light ghost just translucent enough to show a hint of objects behind her.

The flat's two residents, wrinkled old men with tufts of snow-white hair, look up in astonishment. They are both seated, one in a powered wheelchair, at a small table that bears an old-fashioned chessboard and pieces.

The man in the wheelchair puts down the pawn he's holding and nods his head at Penylle. "Good afternoon. Who the devil are you?"

"P-Penylle Norton." She moves toward them, trying to hide her dismay. *These* are the hackers who terrified the world? Toothless centenarians, drooling over a chess set that belongs in a museum?

"Speak up."

"I'm Penylle Norton." She resists the temptation to shout. "Are you Will Smith and Tony Jones?"

The second man, the one on a normal chair, straightens his back and bows his head. "I'm Smith, he's Jones. What can we do for you, young lady?"

"I...I don't know where to start. I wasn't expecting...."

"You weren't expecting advanced decrepitude, is that what you mean?" Jones coughs. "Why the pell not? You must have known that we're all on the high side of a hundred years old. Did you think we discovered some kind of fountain of youth? Don't you use your *brain,* child?"

Penylle feels herself color. "I *try*, sir." She takes a breath. "I have to know this: were you members of the Regiment of Ruin?"

Smith and Jones exchange glances, the Smith says, "What is it now? Another bloody anniversary? We don't do interviews."

Jones snorts. "Go back to whatever rag you represent and tell your boss–"

"I'm not here for an interview. I came here to get your help with a problem, but I can see that you're in no mood to be helpful, so I'll take my leave now."

Jones slaps his hand on the arm of his chair. "Not without my permission, you won't!" He smiles at Smith. "Feisty, isn't she?"

Smith waves her to the table. "Join us, my dear, and tell us all about your problem."

Penylle conjures a phantom chair, sits at the table.

Smith reaches forward, passes his hand through her and the chair. "Very well done. You've hacked into our system from outside, I suppose?"

"Yes."

"Which was it, the electric cable, or the satellite downlink to the building next door?"

She smiles. "The cable. I guess you've had visitors before."

"Now and again. One or two in a good year. Sometimes we go a few years without any." Smith leans forward, moving the chessboard out of her way. "So what's this problem of yours?"

She explains and, when enough data has flowed through the narrow channel, displays the intricate graph of her manipulations of the Nets. Smith and Jones both pore over her data, tossing incomprehensible phrases back and forth to one another. Penylle quickly realizes that they have their own language for describing the Nets, a vocabulary that is gibberish to anyone else.

Jones, the man in the wheelchair, finally turns filmy eyes on Penylle. "This looks a great deal like a project Mi-- er, Armstrong was working on a while ago. He shared bits and pieces of it, but we never saw the whole thing."

Smith comments, "We generally don't share much with one another, you know. Old habits."

Penylle nods. "It sounds as if I should be talking to Armstrong, then."

"Oh," Jones says, "You can't. He's gone."

"Gone? Where did he go?"

Smith shakes his head. "He took The Big Go, I'm afraid. Dead. They found him in front of his TV about a month ago, eyes wide open, a big grin on his face."

Jones gestures to Penylle's graph. "I'm afraid we're the best you've got, now. We can tell you what we remember, and maybe help you deduce some more." His eyes narrow. "But I can tell you right away...you're not going to like what you hear."

Rahel interrupts Damien's shower with a series of insistent beeps. "Priority call from the Ivory Madonna."

Damien rinses soap from his face and turns off the water, then grabs his Spex. The lenses cloud, then the fog dissipates as the ventilators step up.

The M's head and shoulders appear before him. A legend along the bottom of the display informs him that this call is coming from the Moon, and is being carried over the circuits of Bell Orbital.

The M smiles. "Damien, it's good to see you. Although I didn't expect to see so *much* of you."

"Cut it out, M." Warm air dries him as he stands there. "Call me when I'm in the shower, and you have to deal with what you get." He can't help smiling. "You look *great*."

Her answer comes with the three-second delay of live Lunar communication. "Not bad for an old woman, I guess. I'd forgotten how kind one-sixth gee is. When this is all over, I'm going to think seriously about moving up here permanently."

"So you *are* planning to come home?"

"Of course I am. Soon, in fact. When are you leaving for the Creativity Conference?"

He grabs a comb and starts on his hair. "I wasn't sure we were going. I thought maybe you wanted me to stay at the Institute."

"Stay there? Pell, no. I'll need you in Colombo. What about Penylle? How is she?"

"The drug that Jamiar synthesized seems to be holding her, for now. He says he's weaning her onto straight synthetic prolactin, but it'll be a while before she's completely clean."

"Good. Bring her, bring him, bring anybody else you need. I'm landing at Kalidasa Port Friday afternoon, Colombo time. I want you there."

Damien sighs; Amelia Airhead is not going to like this assignment. "All right. We'll be there. Should we save you a room?"

"Yes. Block us together with the rest of Nexus North America. Oh, make it two rooms: I'm bringing a friend." She glances offscreen. " Helms, this is costing me a fortune. I'll send you netmail with more information and instructions. And I'll see you Friday. Love you."

"Love you, too."

Giving his teeth a quick clean, Damien hops into clothes and calls up Amelia Airhead.

DIVERTISSEMENT 23

*Religious Affiliations in North America*
(in thousands)

| 1995 | | 2040 | |
|---|---|---|---|
| Total Population | 269,780 | Total Population | 293,328 |
| Protestant | 95,063 | Protestant | 42,153 |
| Roman Catholic | 73,880 | Roman Catholic | 35,911 |
| Other Christian | 47,585 | Other Christian | 40,599 |
| Orthodox | 6,698 | Orthodox | 2,465 |
| Anglican | 3,145 | Anglican | 1,634 |
| Total Christian | 257,371 | Total Christian | 122,762 |
| Non-religious | 26,127 | Non-religious | 70,245 |
| Jewish | 5,904 | New Age | 41,255 |
| Muslim | 4,066 | Atheist | 21,225 |
| Buddhist | 2,132 | Wiccan | 14,782 |
| Atheist | 1,395 | Muslim | 7,804 |
| Hindu | 1,129 | Buddhist | 4,966 |
| Chinese Folk Religions | 832 | Jewish | 3,678 |
| Baha'i | 740 | Hindu | 2,845 |
| Other | 593 | Other | 1,439 |
| Sikh | 491 | Baha'i | 1,398 |
| | | Sikh | 681 |
| | | Chinese Folk Religions | 248 |

[29] KAMENGEN 12
Clarke Centre for Technology
Colombo
Sri Lanka, Asia
29 August 2042 C.E.

*This message is cursed. As you read it you will be confuset by ther printeb wertz. Yer intelijen wil vabni...xrt! xrt!*

Damien and his entourage leave the Institute around dinnertime. Damien and Penylle are accompanied by Jamiar Heavitree, Mati and Babi, and a handful of others whom he has come to think of as "his people." They are Nexus, one and all.

Their odyssey begins with a one-hour flight to Canaveral. A spaceplane hop to Sumeru Station takes another hour, half of that waiting for Sumeru to be in the proper position. Forty minutes later, they depart Sumeru in a SriLankan Space T-160, arriving at last at Kalidasa Spaceport barely three hours after leaving the Institute, a bit late for breakfast but certainly in good time for a hearty brunch. Dr. Heavitree issues Circaid-B pills to help their bodies adjust to the time change.

Monsoon-moderated tropical heat is not all that different from what they left behind in Maryland; they eat on a terrace overlooking the landing strips, while before them rises the bulk of Sri Pada, Adam's Peak. Damien feels a wistful pang: in the dozen or so times he's been through Kalidasa Port, up or down, he's never managed to make the climb up the long stone stairway, to see the sacred mountain's shadow at dawn stretching across the world. And this time, he's fairly certain, he won't have time to make the trip either.

Amelia Airhead buzzes Damien at the end of the meal. "Ms. Maris's flight arrives in one hour."

"Acknowledged." To the others, he says, "Penylle and I need to stay here to meet the M. Why don't the rest of you go on and get us registered at the hotel?"

Babi smiles. "Are you sure you don't mind?"

"Go." This is Mati and Babi's first time at the World Creative Conference, and Damien can see how anxious they are.

Traffic is heavy at Kalidasa Port, as tens of thousands arrive for the Conference. Ships touch down roughly every fifteen minutes, as station after station passes the optimum deorbit point overhead. Damien and Penylle watch until the spaceplane carrying the M touches down, then they hurry to the terminal.

Miranda plods down the boarding ramp leaning on the shoulder of a teenage Anglo boy with long brown hair. She wears a smart business suit in dark blue, with a matching knee-length cape, and her hair is done up in a whorl dusted with glitter. When she sees Damien, she smiles and holds out her arms.

They hug, then he draws back. "You look magnificent."

"Nunn if I'm going to the Moon and not shop. Facial *and* full-body massage, at one-sixth gee. I'm serious, when this is all settled I am going back there to live." She balances on the teenager's shoulder and holds up one slippered foot. "I tell you, gravity is no longer my friend. In fact, the two of us haven't been on speaking terms for decades. But now I am quite certain that gravity wants me dead. I don't intend to oblige it."

As Miranda puts down her foot, Damien holds out a hand to the boy. "I'm Damien Nshogoza. And this is Penylle Norton."

The boy's handshake is firm. "Pleased to meet you. I'm Jackie Paper." He lowers his eyes. "I've heard a lot about both of you."

Miranda holds up a finger to silence Damien's reply. "I'm doing the introductions, *if* you please. Jackie is Nexus, and he has been an enormous help to me this last week. Jackie, Damien is my right hand. When I'm not around, listen to him as you would listen to me. What he lacks in wit and wisdom, he more than makes up for in enthusiasm. I am just getting to know Penylle and her many talents, but already I know that she is trustworthy and powerful. Cross her at your own peril." She opens her arms to Penylle. "Give me a hug, child. I'm so very glad to see you."

Penylle complies. "We're all glad you're back, M."

"Oh, gods, he's taught you to say that, too."

"I didn't intend to offend you…Damien said you liked it…I'll stop— "

Miranda laughs. " Just having fun with Damien. No, I don't mind being called 'M,' and no, I don't think you could offend me if you tried."

Damien stage-whispers, "M doesn't *get* offended. She's a carrier."

"Have a care, sir, I know where you live." Miranda looks around. "Somehow, we don't seem to be at our hotel yet. I don't seem to be in the tub, there don't seem to be mounds of bubble bath, and I don't seem to be drinking champagne. Can one of you delightful children tell me what's wrong with this picture?"

"All right. Let me call the others and see if we're checked in yet." Damien slips on his RCSpex. "Rahel, call Jamiar."

After a pause, filled with the subdued clicks and hums of the space between connections, Dr. Heavitree answers, "Hello, Damien. Has Mademoiselle Maris arrived yet?"

"She's here. We're going to head over to the hotel— do you know our room numbers?"

"I'm afraid not, my friend. It is pandemonium here. The reservation system has malfunctioned, and the staff is not able to get anyone into their rooms."

"At the Taj Samudra? That's unusual." Damien has stayed at the five-star hotel on previous visits to Colombo; the establishment prides itself on its excellent service.

"At *all* the conference hotels." Jamiar sighs. "There is no point in coming over here; you would merely add to the crowd. I sent Mati and Babi and the others to the Conference. You might as well go there yourselves. I am content to stay here until this unfortunate confusion is settled."

"That's decent of you. Can we bring you anything?"

"No thank you. The hotel has been very generous with tea and diverse treats. We may not have rooms to sleep in, but we will not go hungry here. Enjoy the Conference. I will call you when our rooms are settled."

"Thanks." Damien explains to the others.

Miranda feigns a frown. "No tub?"

Damien shakes his head. "Tub later." He looks at Penylle. "This fits."

She nods. "My…sources predicted that there would be computer troubles in connection with the Conference. This sort of thing will plague every large convention in the world over the next few months."

Damien adds, "Misdirected luggage, lost room reservations, traffic jams, late meals, scheduling mishaps— all minor stuff, but adding to the annoyances of life."

Miranda's brow furrows, making her frown a real one. She whispers,"What does Marc Hoister gain from targeting large conventions?"

"The press and the intellectuals," Penylle answers. "Both groups will publicize the problems."

"I see. Leveraging inconveniences to have an impact on the largest number of people. No matter where we turn, on the news or on the Nets, we'll be reminded that life is becoming too complex and too uncomfortable."

"And you can bet," Damien says, "that there will be plenty of comedies and dramas in which characters talk about leaving it all behind and moving to Mars. Along with inspiring dramas of Martian colonization. Especially in Umoja."

Miranda fixes her frown on Penylle. "What else do your sources predict?"

"More political unrest. Another pandemic, most likely Millennial Flu or a related strain, probably in the spring. Major service disruptions at United Nations sites worldwide. And one or more AIs completely cut off from the Nets for at least a few days."

Miranda snaps her fingers. "That tears it. If nothing else, we need to act before that pandemic gets started— but if an AI or two are cut off, the whole AI community will be furious with humanity. If they don't want us dead now, they *will*."

"They don't want us dead," Damien says. "But they are seriously debating shutting us out of cyberspace entirely."

Raising an eyebrow, Miranda says, "And you don't think that would kill us?"

"So what are we going to do?"

"Tomorrow morning, the Terran Council opens. Every Nexus bigwig will be there, perhaps even Hoister himself. I have North America on my side, plus half of Asia. We're going to get this matter on the table, and then we're going to force them to take action."

"What action?"

Miranda stares vacantly at Damien. "I wish I knew." She shakes her head. "Come on, let's get over to the Conference. Maybe we can drum up some more allies there."

The World Creativity Conference is part university open house, part trade fair, and part three-ring circus. And it is somehow larger and more vibrant than any of these.

The main hall alone is large enough to house half a dozen jumbo jets, with a roof high enough to shelter several mature *hora* trees. Despite thousands of people, booths, tables, and brightly-colored signs, the place is far from full. In the distance there are shops, but mobile vendors circulating around the floor leave Damien wondering why one would need to visit the shops— if one just stands still, everything will come past, from food to souvenirs to personal services to the most exotic merchandise imaginable. Even the honey-pot man seems to be doing a booming business.

For a moment Damien surveys the crowd, trying to identify a common characteristic, an outward sign of the creativity, and respect for creativity, that has brought all these people together. He can find none: the people are of all ages and races, tall and short, fat and thin, clothed in ordinary leisure wear or ethnic costumes or some outlandish creation from media, literature, or the wearer's own fevered imagination. Like snowflakes, no two of this crowd look alike. If they have any common characteristic at all, it is their total lack of conformity.

Damien and his friends queue up at a registration kiosk, and are issued security badges and flatscreens containing the Conference schedule. As they stroll toward the exhibit halls, Damien thumbs through the schedule, dourly marking all the interesting presentations that he is sure to miss.

Miranda, perched on an electric scooter that can go twice as fast as Damien can run, snatches the flat out of his hands and rolls it up. "Put that away, Damien. You know by now that it's only going to make you unhappy at all the things you'll miss. That's why they have these things once a year— so you can catch up before the next one." All of the formal sessions are recorded and made accessible to members.

"I always have good intentions. Then I review about six sessions, and something else important comes up, and before I know it, I'm on my way to the next Conference."

"Cheer up, kid. The formal sessions aren't where the action is, anyway. Except for sessions I'm actually on, I haven't been to a formal program item in years." She brushes past a three-meter creature with a head patterned after the Easter Island statues, bows her head to it, and receives a bow in return. "Especially this year. We're all going to be busy with Nexus business, this is probably all we'll get to see of the exhibits...." She stops in her tracks, looks back the way they've come. "Where is Jackie?"

"There." Penylle points. The boy is twenty meters back, his mouth hanging open and his face vacant. Penylle waves to him, then trots off and drags him by the arm. "I think Jackie is a little overwhelmed."

Miranda shakes her head. "I should have thought. He grew up in God's Country." She takes his limp hand from Penylle. "Poor child, he's blown his fuses. And we're not even to the exhibit halls yet." She takes his face in her hands and looks directly into his eyes. "Jackie, listen to me."

"I-I'm okay."

"Like pell you are. I apologize, I should have prepared you better."

"It's just...just a little...too much."

"Of course it is. We'll find you a nice quiet room where you can sit down and rest. Damien? Who's likely to have a quiet hospitality suite near here?"

Damien, having anticipated her, is searching the Conference literature. "Here we go. The Blacksburg Girls are right around the corner. They'll take care of him."

"Damien! He's gay."

"Well, *I* didn't know." Back to the flatscreen. "Okay, how about this: the Gaylaxians have a relaxation suite in room 514. Where's 514?"

"This way." With Penylle in the front, they lead Jackie down an elevator and through several corridors. The ceiling is much lower, only about three meters, and the crowds are somewhat less.

Room 514 is about the size of a large living room; couches and tables are randomly scattered about, along with fruit platters and juice pitchers. In one corner, a group is gathered around a terminal; some couples are cuddling on a couch or two. Soft music plays in the background, nowhere near loud enough to annoy.

A squat black woman in an elaborate sari comes to greet them. Her badge reads "Chanté Atira." "Welcome to the Gaylaxians suite. I'm on duty, so scream if you need me."

Miranda puts her hands on Jackie's buttocks, pressing him forward. "This is our friend Jackie. He's suffering from weirdness overload. Can he stay here until he's feeling better?"

Chanté smiles indulgently. "Of course. Hello, Jackie. I'm Chanté. Why don't you sit down?" She calls to the group around the terminal, "Rob, Conrad, can you come here?" Two angelic men respond. "This is Jackie. He's had a little much of the Conference. Jackie, would you like to sit quietly and talk with Rob and Conrad for a while? They're both pretty friendly."

The boy shows interest for the first time since the main hall. "Okay. That would be nice." He turns back to Miranda. "Is it okay if I stay here for a while?"

"You stay here as long as you want, Jackie. You've got a phone: call me when you decide to leave." She glances at Chanté. "Or when they throw you out."

"Oh, we won't do that." Chanté's eyes twinkle. "We may just put him to work, though."

Rob and Conrad take Jackie to a couch, and Chanté follows the others back to the door. Miranda presses her hand. "Thanks a lot. This is his first

Conference. I just didn't think."

"Don't worry. We get a lot of shell-shocked newcomers. The boys will take care of him."

Miranda reaches for her pouch. "Is there anything I can— "

"No." Chanté touches her right ear: her gold earring is in the shape of Drake's Starburst. "It's a privilege to help *you,* Ma'am."

"Thanks. If nothing else, we'll be back to collect him when they get this hotel mess straightened out."

"Or not. Whatever. He'll be fine."

As they stroll back to the main hall, Miranda says, "Now *that's* what the Nexus is all about. Or should be, anyway."

Together, they plunge into the chaos of the exhibit halls.

Damien stands in Exhibit Hall C, a room large enough to hold three soccer fields, and lets his eyes roam. There are hundreds of exhibits, in booths ranging from a few meters square to the size of a house. In each booth, there is a work of art: a painting, musical composition, sculpture, multimedia extravaganza, live performance, items that boggle the imagination and people performing actions that border on the ludicrous. The program guide estimates that there are over 5,000 creative works on display at this Conference, up 5% from the year before.

Penylle lays a hand on his arm. "It gets to be too much after a while, doesn't it?"

He nods. "I know how poor Jackie felt. Overload." He gestures to Miranda, who is chatting with half a dozen Orientals. "*She's* got the right idea. A few years ago, she told me that she hardly notices the art any more. She says she gets her jollies from the *people,* so that's what she concentrates on."

Penylle surveys the crowd. "This hotel mixup is working out in our favor. All the Nexus delegates are in here, rather than unpacking in their rooms."

He touches her hair, gently, just to feel it move over his fingers like flowing water. "How are you feeling?"

She continues looking over the herd. "I'm fine. I told you, Jamiar's almost got the formula down. I only had to get up once last night."

"I wish you wouldn't— "

Penylle interrupts him, waving to a handsome black couple across the floor. "Look, there's Ellen-n-Dan. Come over here, you two." As they approach, Penylle hugs them both. They both wear white, flowing clothing of a vaguely Arab style; Damien notices the repeating pattern of Drake's Starburst worked in gold thread into their outfits. Their faces are lined, their dark hair touched with grey.

"Damien Nshogoza, let me present Ellen-n-Dan, North African Co-ordinators for the Nexus."

Damien shakes their hands. "Habari gani. Pleased to meet you."

"Jambo, B. Nshogoza." Dan's voice is a rough whisper that makes Damien's throat hurt. "Penylle, dear, where is Marc? We haven't seen him all day?"

Penylle tosses her head. "I'm sure I have no idea. Haven't you heard, I've left Marc's service. I wouldn't be surprised if he doesn't dare show his face around here."

Ellen frowns and, in a voice like a tightly-wound music box, says, "Child, what did he do to you?"

"That's not important. It's what he's *going* to do. Come with me." She moves in Miranda's direction, pushes her way into the conversation. "Ellen-n-Dan, have you met the Ivory Madonna?"

Dan looks Miranda up and down. "One can barely call oneself a member of the Nexus without knowing the Ivory Madonna." He nods to the Orientals. "Co-ordinator d'Herelle, Co-ordinator Churchill."

"Ellen-n-Dan want to hear what Marc is up to." Penylle says.

The M smiles. "I just started on the story. With everyone's indulgence, I'll back up and start over...."

It is almost dinnertime before they manage to get into their suite, on a floor that is almost entirely Nexus. In the chaos of luggage and bodies, Miranda announces, "We are going to have a busy night. I expect at least a dozen Nexus Regional Co-ordinators through here before morning, as well as most of Nexus North America. The hotel staff tells me that they will keep us stocked with food and drinks, so if anyone starves, it will be their own fault."

"What about room assignments?" Mati asks.

"Good. A practical question. Very unlike you, Mati." Miranda surveys the large living room. "We have four bedrooms. I will use one for private conferences, and maybe I'll get in a few winks sometime. Damien and Penylle will have this room, next to mine, so that they can be on call all night."

"Thanks, M."

"My pleasure." She gestures to Mati and Babi, who sit hand-in-hand, and to Jackie. "I expect you three randy youngsters won't mind sharing a room. Jackie, if you want to be more comfortable, I suggest you find a snuggle-bunny of your own. These two are insatiable *and* indiscreet."

While Jackie blushes, Babi says, "You expect us to spend our *nights* here?"

"I learned years ago to expect *anything* from you two. You're both adults, if you want to stay out all night and sleep all day, that's your business. But I *will* remind you that we are on a mission, and you should spend at least part of your nights around here making nice with the Nexus delegates. Especially the younger crowd."

"Will do."

"Jamiar, that leaves you in the fourth bedroom. Is that satisfactory?"

Heavitree nods. "Quite." He chuckles. "You know, this isn't exactly what I expected of high-level Nexus politics."

Miranda answers his smile with her own. "And why not, Doctor? Don't you know that all politics ultimately boils down to who sleeps with whom?" She claps her hands. "All right, I want this luggage stowed, and let's start getting ready for visitors."

It is hours later— after far more than a dozen Nexus bigwigs have dropped by, after the sun is long set and even Miranda starting to sound a little hoarse— that Damien and Penylle are able to crawl into their room and shut the door. Outside, in the living room, Mati and Babi are still entertaining a delegation of Nexus operatives from South America, while the M is closeted with the rest of the North American Co-ordinators. But Damien is so tired that he knows he would do nothing even if Marc Hoister himself marched through the door.

Clean sheets and fluffy pillows are a sensual joy. With Penylle curled up against him, head on his shoulder, Damien says, "I hope M will remember to get us up in time tomorrow." The Terran Council meeting starts at 10 am.

"She will," Penylle says softly. "She remembers…everything." Her breathing slows. "I was an idiot…to be afraid to meet her. She's…wonderful…."

Her voice trails off into an indistinct sleep noise, and Damien smiles. "Yeah, she's something special. Too bad…she doesn't have…a snuggle-bunny…."

The thought follows him into the depths of sleep.

## MENUET 12

*Nexus Travel Advisories: Indian Subcontinent*

*Arunachal*: Sporadic ethnic violence. Travelers are cautioned not to travel outside major cities at night. Arunachal is a developing country with a parliamentary government. Adequate medical care is available in major cities. Roads, communications, and Net services are adequate.

*Assam:* Sporadic ethnic violence. Travelers are cautioned not to travel outside major cities at night. The area near the Bangladesh border should be avoided due to frequent disease outbreaks. Assam is a developing country with a parliamentary monarchy. Adequate medical care is available in major cities. Roads, communications, and Net services are adequate.

*Baluchistan:* Armed battles between clans are frequent. Travelers are cautioned to avoid the interior unless escorted by armed guards. The capital, Quetta, is quieter than the interior, but has experienced serious ethnic violence recently. Baluchistan is a developing country with few natural resources and an ineffective coalition government. Medical care is poor. Roads, communications, and Net services are adequate in the capital, poor beyond.

*Bangladesh:* Travelers to Bangladesh are cautioned that medical care is minimal to nonexistent. Disease is rampant, especially in the capital city of Dhaka. Bangladesh has a subsistence economy and an ineffective government. Roads, communications, and Net services are poor to nonexistent.

*Goa:* No advisory. Goa is a medium-income city-state with a fairly-developed economy. Medical care is good. Roads, communications, and Net services are good.

*Gujarat:* Ethnic violence and border raids along the Baluchistan border. Travelers in this region are urged to use caution. Gujarat is a developing country with a parliamentary democracy. Adequate medical care is available in major population centers, but is usually limited in rural areas. Roads are congested and poorly maintained. Communications and Net services are adequate.

*Hindustan:* No advisory. Hindustan is an economically developed democratic republic. Adequate medical care is available in major population centers, but is usually limited in rural areas. Roads are congested and poorly maintained. Communications and Net services are adequate.

*Hyderabad:* No advisory. Hyderabad is an economically developed democratic republic. Adequate medical care is available in major population centers, but is usually limited in rural areas. Roads are congested and poorly maintained. Communications and Net services are adequate.

*Indian Federation:* No advisory. The Indian Federation is an economically developed democratic republic. Adequate medical care is available in major population centers, but is usually limited in rural areas. Roads are congested and poorly maintained. Communications and Net services are adequate.

*Karnataka:* No advisory. Karnataka is an economically developed constitutional monarchy. Adequate medical care is available in major population centers, but is usually limited in rural areas. Roads are congested and poorly maintained. Communications and Net services are adequate.

*Kashmir:* Travelers are cautioned that large regions near the ruins of Sinagar are still contaminated with unacceptable levels of radioactive fallout. Extreme care should be exercised to avoid lingering when traveling into the Vale of Kashmir. Due to dangerous security conditions, caution is essential when traveling overland through the tribal areas to the Khyber Pass. Monthly steam train excursion for toursits through the Khyber Pass is well protected by local authorities. Kashmir is an undeveloped country with many autonomous tribal areas. Medical care is poor. Roads, communications, and Net services are poor. Contamination by radioactive fallout is a constant danger.

*Kerala:* No advisory. Kerala is an economically developed democratic republic. Adequate medical care is available in major population centers, but is usually limited in rural areas. Roads are congested and poorly maintained. Communications and Net services are adequate.

*Maharashira:* No advisory. Maharashira is an economically developed constitutional monarchy. Adequate medical care is available in major population centers, but is usually limited in rural areas. Roads are congested and poorly maintained. Communications and Net services are adequate.

*Mizoram:* Sporadic ethnic violence. Travelers are cautioned not to travel outside major cities at night. The area near the Bangladesh border should be avoided due to frequent disease outbreaks. Mizoram is a developing country with a parliamentary monarchy. Adequate medical care is available in major cities. Roads, communications, and Net services are adequate.

*Punjab:* Sectarian violence continues, especially in the north. Visitors are cautioned to avoid public transportation and crowded areas. Punjab is a developing country with a parliamentary monarchy. Adequate medical care is available in major cities. Roads are crowded, poorly maintained, and poorly signed. Communications are good in major cities, poor in rural areas. Adequate Net services are available in major cities.

*Rajasthan:* Sporadic ethnic violence in the area west of National Highway 15. Rajasthan is an economically developed democratic republic. Adequate medical care is available in major population centers, but is usually limited in rural areas. Roads are congested and poorly maintained. Communications and Net services are adequate.

*Sikkim:* Currently under Nexus interdict; no travel or communications permitted.

*Sri Lanka:* No advisory. Sri Lanka is a medium-income country with a well-developed economy. Medical care is good. Roads, communications, and Net services are excellent.

*Tamil Nadu:* No advisory. Tamil Nadu is a medium-income country with a fairly-developed economy. Medical care is good. Roads, communications, and Net services are good.

## [30] TARANTELLA 03
New York City, Los Angeles
United States, North America
1992 - 1993 C.E.

*I'd love it if a plan came together.*

It was, by joint proclamation of the U.S. and Russian Presidents, the year the Cold War ended. It was a year for separations: Bosnia and Herzgovina from Yugoslavia in February, the Czech Republic and Slovakia in November, and the Prince and Princess of Wales in December.

It was the year the Blue Jays won the World Series, the Redskins won the Super Bowl, Riddick Bowe carried off the heavyweight boxing title, and Martin Buser finished the Iditarod in 10 days, 19 hours, and 17 minutes.

Euro-Disneyland opened at Marne la Valle, the Earth Summit opened in Rio de Janeiro, and the Mall of America opened in Minnesota. All three had roughly the same impact on the world.

Among those who joined the mortality rolls that year were Alex Haley, Grace Hopper, Menachem Begin, Sam Walton, Satyajit Ray, and Isaac Asimov. They were accompanied by half a million famine victims in Somalia and Sudan, over a million AIDS victims throughout Africa, ten times that many casualties of other infectious diseases, and thousands of Bosnian targets of an old crime with a trendy new name: ethnic cleansing.

In a cramped office in Manhattan's Garment District, Miranda Maris brooded.

She had reason enough to be happy...reason enough and more. In ten years, she and Rose had taken Cetairé-Maris Fashions from her spare bedroom to a ten-million-dollar company with a Manhattan office and contacts all over the world. And if she hated New York, hated the crowding and the filth and the thousand indignities of her daily commute...well, it was only temporary. In a few more years, the company would be big enough that they could locate wherever they wanted, even move back to Baltimore, where they'd begun.

If she despised her tiny, cheerless apartment in a great impersonal beehive of a building, with neighbors who acted like automatons and elevators that stank of old sweat...well, in only a few more years, she would be able to get a big house with an enormous yard, and have friends in as often as she liked without having to set up an appointment with the doorman.

And if she missed her friends, because they all lived far away and it was "too much trouble" to come into New York to see her...well, she could keep in touch by phone, until the day when no one would have to worry about parking, or street muggings, or traffic jams, or finding a place to stay overnight because her place was just too small....

Thirty-three years old, and she was reduced to *this*: working in a hole, living in a hole, and crawling between the two like a hamster through a tube.

She was solitary as a hamster, too. Rose insisted— and she was very probably right— that she and Miranda keep separate apartments. If they lived together, as well as working together, they would likely kill one another in a month. Besides, Rose was usually busy with her *paramour du jour*...sleeping with him, breaking up with him, or scouring the clubs for his replacement.

Miranda had given up on the clubs after the first month; the smoke and music gave her headaches, the stools were uncomfortable, the drinks were watered down, and none of the glamor palaces were all that eager to admit a fat woman, no matter what her bank account. Most nights she worked late, or stayed home talking on the phone and watching television.

Thirty-three years old, and already an old maid. Time to think about taking up knitting, my deario, or Mah-Jongg in the lobby with the other old biddies....

A sharp buzz jerked her out of her reverie: her desktop computer, signalling that she only had ten minutes before her next meeting. She punched a key, silencing the machine, then counted to ten as it whirred and clicked awhile before pulling her daily agenda out of its nether regions. Some PR firm, probably looking for a costume design for one of their snooty clients; Miranda had been down that road before, and knew not to put too much hope into this encounter. The Hollywood glitterati seemed none too interested in Cetairé-Maris designs.

Still, business was business, and the company couldn't afford to pass up any opportunity. She glanced in a mirror, touched up her makeup, and put on her best sincere smile. It was only for thirty minutes, or an hour at worst....

The PR woman was heavyset, black, and clothed in a light green business suit accented with gold metallic threads. Her shoes were sensible, and her dark hair was secured with wooden combs in a vaguely African design. She carried a stiff-sided black briefcase. Her handshake was firm, her voice deep and pleasantly husky.

"I'm Latrisha Paige of First Star Entertainment." They exchanged business cards, then Rose gestured to the conference table and they took their seats. Paige leaned back in her chair. "I know you're both busy, and I appreciate you making the time to see me. I'll get right to the point. My company represents a number of high-profile entertainers and performers. One of my clients has seen your designs and become quite enamored of your work. He wants Cetairé-Maris to design some costumes for an upcoming tour."

Rose bent forward. "I take it that you're not talking about souvenir hats and tee shirts?"

Paige chuckled. "Hardly. These would be major presentation costumes, star, backup singers, and dancers."

Miranda sat back, keeping her eyes away from Rose lest she give away the game. A contract like this, with all the attendant publicity and tie-ins, could be worth millions to the company. "Is there a theme that we'll be designing to?"

"My client will provide music; your designs should fit the music. There will be plenty of opportunity for consultation and creative discussion."

"And if we just can't produce a design that satisfies your client?"

"Then you will still be paid for your time and effort."

Miranda narrowed her eyes. "What about merchandising rights and subsidiary markets? What if we want to sell other designs based on the ones we create for your client?"

"Naturally, we would ask a portion of the income." Paige reached into her briefcase, handed Miranda and Rose each a thick sheaf of papers. "The terms are all spelled out in this proposed contract. You'll see the highlights summarized on the top sheet. Our respective legal staffs can iron out any points that you might find less than satisfactory."

Miranda skimmed the summary sheet, astonished at the amounts.

Paige was still talking. "I don't expect an immediate answer. You'll want to review the contracts, but do you have any other questions?"

Miranda took a deep breath. "Is it permitted to ask who your client is?"

Paige's smile broadened. "As a matter of fact, I was instructed to withdraw the offer if you *didn't* ask that question in one form or another. My client feels that no true artist would enter such a partnership without knowing who was involved."

"So...?"

"I won't keep you in suspense. My client is Washington Westwood Hohokus."

A joke, Miranda thought. WWH, the self-proclaimed "King of Pop," wasn't merely a "star"... he was a music industry demigod. His *Chiller* had been the world's best-selling album for ten years now. Paige might just as well have claimed that her client was the Archangel Gabriel, or Vishnu, or Mickey Mouse.

But Paige was still smiling, and Rose took it in stride, and slowly Miranda realized that it was *not* a joke; instead, it was a once-in-a-lifetime opportunity. And nothing, *nothing*, could keep them from accepting the offer.

A month later, a spacious private jet flew Rose and Miranda to California, a limousine drove them from the airport to a secluded country estate, and Latrisha Paige escorted them to a study/drawing room and into the Presence.

Despite Miranda's knowledge that he was her own age, she had expected WWH to be a child, a pretty teenybopper, androgynous and anorexic — instead, she found a mature young man, graceful and slender but with a dancer's muscles moving beneath leotards and a white silk robe. He bowed over her hand, and Rose's, kissing the air a centimeter above her skin. "I'm very pleased to meet both of you. Welcome to my home." His voice was gentle, and carried with it the barest whisper of song, as if an unseen and almost-imperceptible phantom choir followed him around.

He nodded to Paige, who discreetly withdrew. "Please, make yourselves comfortable."

Chairs were ready, around a drafting table; comfortable chairs that gave support in all the right places, so that Miranda thought she could work all day without feeling fatigue. WWH spread papers out before them. "I've looked over your preliminary designs, and I like them. I like them a lot. But I have some problems with the outfit you've designed for me for *Perilous*."

Rose plucked a sketch out of the pile. "This one, Mr. Hohokus?"

"Yes. Please, call me 'West.' It's easier. Now, look. Right in the middle of that number, I have to do a fancy double-step and twirl. Something like this." He moved to the middle of the floor and executed a complex movement that ended with him crouching, spinning at the audience with his arms pawing like a caged leopard.

He straightened up and gave a diffident shrug. "Something like that. I just don't see how I can do a move like that in this overcoat." He tapped the sketch.

Miranda reached for a pencil and attacked the sketch. "What if we shorten the coat, give it more of an asymmetric line around *here*?"

He shook his head. "Then you lose the sleek silhouette here. That's what gave me the idea of using the whole wildcat motif to begin with."

"All right," Rose said, moving in with her own pencil. "Flare the trousers like *this*. That will restore the line you're looking for, but you'll be able to go all the way to the ground."

"And with that turn, you'll get a lashing effect," Miranda said. "Especially if we weight the hem there and there."

Their work went smoothly; soon, Miranda forgot that the man across the table was a legend and forgot to be in awe of him. Drinks and food were handy when needed, produced by stealthy individuals who stayed unobtrusive. Music, the music that would accompany their costumes, was available whenever West needed it; when necessary, he leapt and cavorted to demonstrate particular moves. They went through each sketch, altering and polishing to fit the music and the movements.

At last, when they finished the last sketch, Miranda looked at her watch and frowned. "It *can't* be that late."

"It can and it is," West said. "Almost midnight. I'm sorry I kept you so long. But we were getting so much done, and having such fun."

Rose stretched. "We've got to be getting to our hotel. Could someone give us a ride?"

West looked wounded. "Please, stay here. There's plenty of room for guests. How about a swim and a late supper, and tomorrow you'll sleep as long as you want?"

Rose and Miranda exchanged looks, then Rose said, "Sure. No dinner for me, but I'd love a swim. And then right to sleep."

He beamed. "Good." An intercom was mounted next to the door; he touched it and said, "Lita, could you come in here, please?"

Lita, a little brown Latina, appeared so quickly that Miranda wondered if she had been waiting outside the door.

West said, "Lita, this is Miranda and Rose. Please give them guest suites, and have somebody scare up some swimsuits and robes for them. Then bring them to the pool." He bowed to Rose and Miranda. "Ladies, I will meet you at the pool when you are ready."

The suites were huge and luxuriously-appointed. Somehow, the house staff instantly produced a bathing suit and terrycloth robe big enough for Miranda; together, she and Rose followed Lita to the pool: a magnificent indoor pool complete with high dive and water slides. West was already there, floating lazily.

Swimming *did* feel good; Miranda hadn't realized how tense her muscles were. After about half an hour, Rose retired, leaving Miranda and West to share a late dinner at a poolside table. The food was excellent, a rice and seafood dish with delicate iced tea and sake to drink.

In response to her questions, West talked about himself. The demanding, ambitious father, the pressured childhood of a performer, the hidden strains and resentments of growing up in a family musical group. Success, and how it shattered the family.

"That's probably why I hate to see children taken advantage of or hurt," he said. "I remember what it was like."

"Have you thought about having kids of your own?"

He looked around the empty pool house. "Yes, I've thought about it. It would be a big mistake."

"Why?"

"Miranda, you don't know what my life is like." He toyed with the remnants of food in his bowl. "Everywhere I go, everything I do, is a media event. The only reason there aren't paparazzi here right now, is that there's a ten-foot electrified fence around the whole property." He indicated the pool. "My pool is indoors, because if it weren't, there would be helicopters overhead every time I went out for a swim."

He shook his head. "I love my fans, and there's nothing better—*nothing*— than the feeling I get when I'm onstage before fifty thousand of them, feeling their love and their energy just crashing over me like the biggest waves you've ever seen. I wouldn't trade it for the world. And all they ask of me, is that I give myself to them completely...every second of every day." He shrugged. "It's a bargain right out of Faust. I came to terms with it years ago...but it made my childhood pell, and it's destroyed at least two of my siblings. How could I wish *that* on a helpless child?"

She touched his hand, her fingertips barely resting on his. "I had no idea."

He gave a wry, half-hearted smile. "Right now, for example, I would love to take your hand, to k-kiss you, dance with you. But I can't."

"Can't you?"

He stood, tenderly separating his hand from hers. "First of all, it wouldn't be fair to you. I've...been romantically involved before. It's...not good. No one could be prepared for the attention, the pressure. No one's lasted more than a few weeks."

"Maybe those people haven't been strong enough."

He looked directly at her, and in his face Miranda saw the reflection of past affairs, past pain that was still very much alive. "You can't know. Everybody thinks it would be so much fun to be famous— but they never think about what it means. You can't have a job, because of all the fans and paparazzi who surround the doors of the building where you work, and who keep interrupting everything you're doing every five minutes, so that you can't deal with customers or get any of your work done. You can't stay home, not unless you put in fences and security guards. You can't go anywhere in public, not even in disguise, because *they're* always there waiting for you. When you *are* in public, you don't dare eat or drink anything, because there are all kinds of crazies out there. You can't frown, you can't scratch yourself, you can't show displeasure or else it's all over CNN the next hour. You don't even dare go to the toilet, because if there aren't reporters scrambling under the stalls for an exclusive interview, then there's some wacko waiting to fish out your turds and sell them as souvenirs.... "

He looked down. "And if that's not enough— there's another reason that I can't let myself get attached to...anyone. Because they're so clever, and so convincing, and I can never know that this person isn't going to go to the media the next morning, exclusive story, 'I slept with WWH.'" He turned away. "Believe me, I can understand the pressure. I'd probably give in to it myself." In a more conversational tone, he said, "Did you know that the *National Enquirer* has a standing offer of one million dollars for an authenticated photo of my genitals? No, really. Sometimes I wonder if I ought to submit one, just to get the money."

Miranda walked over to West, and put her arms around him. She felt him stiffen. "I don't give a nunn about the *National Enquirer*, and I don't need a million dollars." She patted his head. "Besides, Rose would *kill* me if I ruined this deal by alienating our biggest customer."

His muscles softened, and he leaned back against her. "So you understand...we can't get romantically involved."

"No. Absolutely impossible." She put her arms under his, holding him securely.

"Worst mistake we could make." He leaned his head back, and she thought how odd it was— and how fortunate— that he was just the right height to rest his head on her shoulder.

"Then it's agreed, no romantic involvement." His mouth was next to hers, and she brushed his lips with her own. "I guess we'll both have to be satisfied with the mad, passionate sex." They kissed again, more deeply, and she added, "And no cameras."

It was like no affair Miranda had ever had. West was desperate that Miranda have every chance to keep her privacy— and as she saw more of his world, of the way that the world made his life its own possession, she began to understand how right he was. At first, she was impatient with cryptic phone calls, secret meetings, subterfuge. But as weeks went by, she became grateful for all the efforts he took.

It was not an easy thing, to love Washington Westwood Hohokus. From the very beginning, Miranda knew that he had another lover, one whose hold on his heart was beyond her ability to challenge: his fans. They were his first and most powerful love, his life, and the best she could hope for was the crumbs of time and energy he could spare for her.

Other women, she thought, couldn't handle this. The brainless bimbos who had gone to school with her, for example, couldn't abide being on the edges of a man's world. They had to be the center of his attention, the whole of his life, and they would have torn themselves apart in jealousy at the idea of sharing their lover with fifty million fans worldwide.

Miranda often thought they were that way, those women, because they had no lives of their own, no meaning in their world other than the men they possessed. She imagined that they were so afraid of being alone, because they feared that when their men departed, there would be nothing left behind.

Miranda, on the other hand, had more than enough to keep her busy, and it suited her perfectly that she and West could only see one another a few times a month. More often, and she'd never be able to get her own work done.

It was early in October, when he stopped in New York on his way from Europe to Japan, that they spent the whole day together, cloistered in his hotel suite. Ostensibly, Miranda had come to review designs for the upcoming concert, and they *did* spend hours at the task; but then, they lazed in the room, and talked, and enjoyed one another's company.

He was telling about some kids he'd seen, a third-grade classroom he'd visited, and how much he had enjoyed spending time with the children. Miranda decided it was time, and said, "West, I want to give you a child."

"Miranda...."

"No, shut up, will you? I know all of your objections. And I agree with them. But you said we couldn't get romantically involved, and here we are." She took a breath. Her tongue was like felt; she wished there were some water to drink. "Here's my proposal: I will take full custody of the child. We'll keep your name out of it entirely. I'll be responsible for raising the kid, I'll do it out of the public eye. Of course you can see him, or her, whenever you want...whenever you can."

"We can't keep a thing like that secret. No matter how hard we try."

"So I'll file a paternity suit, and we'll settle out of court months before the kid is born." She forced a laugh. "You can even write a song about it."

He touched her face, his fingers like feathers tracing her jawline. "This is the most wonderfully loving thing anyone has ever offered to do for me. But I can't ask you— "

"Do you think I'm doing this just for *you*? Nunn it, West, my biological alarm clock has been ringing up a storm for years. I'm thirty-three, and not in the best of physical shape to begin with— if I'm ever going to have a kid, I'm down to the last few seconds on the clock." She met his eyes, her face transparent to the longing within her. "And I *do* want a child. *Your* child."

"This is insane," he said.

She kissed him. "So what?"

The WWH Perilous World Tour started in Tokyo in November. Miranda and Rose appeared briefly onstage, and at more length on TV and in pop music and fashion magazines. Suddenly, Cetairé-Maris was *the* hot label; Perilous™ jackets and boots left boutique racks as if they'd sprouted wings, and the company was deluged with commissions. Miranda was busier than she'd ever been, but still she and West managed to see each other roughly once a month.

By Christmas, she knew she was pregnant. She shared the news with a few close friends, but made no public announcements, leaving West's PR organization to plant the proper rumors. She didn't know whether to be amused or annoyed when, in February, she began to hear rumors that *Rose* was the prospective mother of West's child.

In March, WWH issued an official statement of denial, hinting at a paternity suit without mentioning the name of the purported mother. The statement strongly implied that the child in question had been born months earlier.

In May, Cetairé-Maris moved its corporate headquarters to Baltimore. Miranda picked out a big house with an enormous yard, and she made it her business to see that the house was always filled with friends and with boisterous life. She even had a pool built, and a large pool house to enclose it.

And one day in July, with West holding her hand and half a dozen of her closest friends around her, Miranda had a baby girl, whom her father promptly named "Oradell."

Oradell Maris grew into a beautiful little girl with sandalwood skin and mahogany hair, and she was Miranda's chief delight in life. West appeared, when he could, and in summer and winter Oradell went in secret to spend time with her father. With the paternity scandal long forgotten, no one guessed that the fashion designer's little girl was also WWH's.

Too quickly, Oradell went to grade school, high school, college. She took to the Nexus naturally, went to Africa on a mission, and met Marc Hoister. And there she remained. In 2017, Oradell made Miranda something she thought she would never be: a grandmother.

Two years later, West bought Disney and followed Oradell to Africa, there to build Oz in the waters off Zanzibar. Miranda thought of moving, but there was so much to do with the Institute, and the Nexus needed someone near Washington DC, and so she stayed....

The last time she and West and Oradell were all together was in December 2024, when the three of them, along with a seven-year-old Damien, shared a few idyllic days in Oz.

Less than a year later, Oradell was dead, Damien came to live with her...and in all the long years since, nearly eighteen, Miranda and West— as if by some impossible, unspoken mutual agreement of their hearts— had not seen one another.

Eventually, Miranda was even able to convince herself that she didn't miss him.

## MENUET 13

*WWH Discography*
(courtesy Star Entertainment, 1992)

1958: Washington Westwood Hohokus born in Gary, Indiana
1967: WWH signs with Motown as part of "The H5"
"Big Boy" (Motown)
1969: *Diana Ross Presents The H5* (Motown)
1971: *The H5's Greatest Hits* (Motown)
1972: *Being There* (Motown) - First Solo album
1975: *Eternally WWH* (Motown) - solo album
*The Best of WWH* (Motown) - solo
1976: *The H5 Anthology* (Motown) - last Motown album
H5 signs with Epic as "The H's"
*The H's* (Epic) - First Epic album
*Bouncing* (Epic) - First solo album with Epic
1980: *Success* (Epic) - with The H's
1982: *Chiller!* (Epic) - solo
1984: *Conquest* (Epic) - The H's last Epic album
The H's break up
1987: *Tough* (Epic) - first album after the breakup
1991: *Perilous* (Epic)

[31] KAMENGEN 13
Clarke Centre for Technology
Colombo
Sri Lanka, Asia
31 August 2042 C.E.

*The meek are getting ready.*

The Terran Council meeting, as usual, is pandemonium.

At Miranda's insistence, all of her friends— and everyone connected with Nexus North America— wears bulletproof vests under their clothing. Over it, she wears a midnight-blue cloak with Drake's Starburst set in sapphires and rhinestones on front and back. Damien, Penylle, and the others from the Institute are decked out in baggy, multi-pocketed black trousers and tunics that match Miranda's cloak.

They push through crowds to a building set aside from the others. Damien notes, with approval, that Nexus security guards are checking ID at the doors. Inside, it is blessedly cool; the quiet hallways and institutional doors have the look and feel of an academic building. Signs direct them to an auditorium on the left.

Before they enter, Miranda halts the group and they huddle. "All right," she says, "I want you all to be ready for anything. Damien and Penylle, stay close. You are my right and left hands. Jamiar, Jackie, Mati, Babi— you are my eyes and ears. I want you to spread out and keep me informed of what's going on."

Damien frowns. "What do you expect, M?"

"I don't know. Trouble, is all I'm sure of." She takes a breath, squeezes their hands in turn. "Okay, let's go."

Miranda straightens, squares her shoulders, becoming larger, more impressive. She reaches into her bag and takes out her mask, which seems to come alive as she smooths it onto her face. Her stance changes, her demeanor, her very presence. Where Miranda Maris stood, now stands the Ivory Madonna.

Damien and the others don their RCSpex, which become blank white portals obscuring their eyes. Damien notes a tiny window, in the extreme lower right of his visual field, pulsing with multichromatic fractal patterns: a virtual keyhole, through which he is linked to AI dataspace. **Øµt øf Thrëë, thë M¥riåd Thiñgs** has promised to devote part of its attention tc observing, and if necessary protecting Damien and his friends.

Together, they all step into the auditorium.

Tiered seats rise in a semicircle, facing a table and rostrum in front of wall-mounted display screens. The seating area reserved for North America is on the far right, with South America behind and Europe flanking. The M claims a group of seats up front; Damien notes with approval that the computer and audiovisual equipment is state of the art. Nevertheless, he has brought some of his own gear; he pins up several microcams and slaves them to the master system, then checks a datapad to reassure himself that he has covered the major areas of the room.

"Are we live?" the M asks.

"We are. I have six datafeeds going out into the Nets." He glances around, sees other delegates setting up similar paraphernalia. "This meeting's probably going to be the most heavily-covered one ever."

The M nods. "Good."

There is coffee and such; Mati and Babi swoop by to take orders, then return with the goods. Later in the day, Damien knows, other refreshments will be available— everything from fruit juice to full meals from any number of cuisines. Even a short Terran Council usually runs long into the night...and this one promises to be anything but short.

The Ivory Madonna greets other delegates as they arrive and take their places. One of the wallscreens comes to life, showing a roster of attendees; every few seconds, another name joins the list. Here and there, ghostly figures materialize and firm up to a semblance of reality, but they are few; most delegates seem to have made the effort to attend in person.

At last, on the stroke of ten, eight people file out and sit at the table; a distinguished Bantu man takes the rostrum and taps a gavel. "Delegates, please take your seats." Stragglers rush for their seats, while the roster board indicates 101 delegates present: 38 regional co-ordinators, 9 operations co-ordinators, and 54 others.

Marc Hoister is nowhere to be seen.

The tall man at the rostrum bangs the gavel. "I call to order the fifteenth Terran Council. I am Albert von Mecklenberg, Presiding Officer." He waves at the others, flanking him at the table. "I think you know the other operations co-ordinators, with the exception of Jill Kasmanski." A Hindi woman, wearing the visage of Kali, stands and bows to the assembly. "Jill has stepped into Hollow Robin's shoes in Computer Support. As our first order of business, the Chair will now entertain a motion to confirm Jill

Kasmanski in that position."

"So moved," calls a voice from the back.

"Seconded," CHEN1 says, from Damien's right.

"General consent!" pipes another voice.

Von Mecklenberg nods. "There is a call for general consent. Any objections?" He gives them several heartbeats, then says, "Hearing none, the motion passes." He flashes a grin. "If only the rest of this session could go so easily."

There is scattered desultory laughter.

"Next item. We have two changes in regional co-ordinators. Princess Mahlowi can never be replaced; for the time being, Tsutomu of Lagos has agreed to act as co-ordinator for her interests." Tsutomu, wearing an Ibo mask, stands and bows his head. His figure is ever so slightly translucent: while the cold-light hologram is not up to Penylle's standards, Damien admires its natural fluidity of movement.

Von Mecklenberg continues, "Dejah Thoris has decided to retire; she will be returning home on the next flight, and we all wish her the best. Her replacement is just arrived on the history-making return flight of the *Swala*. Please welcome the new co-ordinator of Nexus Mars, G.Danforth."

An Anglo man stands, flashing V-for-Victory with outstretched hands as the assembly gives polite applause; it takes Damien a moment to recognize his hook-nosed mask as the wrinkled visage of Richard Nixon. Amid applause, a few in the assembly titter.

Von Mecklenberg taps the gavel. "I know that we're all anxious to get on to business, but first we must hear the reports of the operations co-ordinators." He looks to the others at the table. "Since your full reports are available, I will ask you to confine yourselves to brief summaries."

Even brief summaries are more extensive and tedious than Damien would like. The only relief comes when JJJSchmidt, as is his custom, delivers the financial report in a strong, clear baritone, to the tune of *The Yellow Rose of Texas*.

From communications to public relations, every report mentions recent anomalous setbacks , distractions, and frustrations: equipment failures, transportation difficulties, communications glitches.

At long last, the reports are done and von Mecklenberg clears his throat. "Ordinarily we would now progress to regional reports. However, in view of recent events, the Chair is exercising its privilege to change the order of the agenda. We will hear from CHEN1 of Mexico City."

CHEN1 stands for only a moment. "I yield the floor to the Ivory Madonna."

The M stands, facing forward; her mask fills the main wallscreen. "By now, I'm sure that most of you know that Nexus North America has survived a fairly serious clash with InfoPol. Had events gone differently, many of us would right now be in prison." There is a gasp, but Damien can see that it comes mainly from the younger delegates. The co-ordinators know what has been happening.

The M continues, "Bad enough, at this late date, that mundane authorities are choosing to move against the Nexus. Worse, my colleagues and I have evidence that this threat against the Nexus is only part of a well-orchestrated plan, a plan that also includes most of the anomalous events that you've just heard about, as well as a long list of crimes up to and including the destruction of Timbuktu." She pauses, allowing her words to sink in. "Worst of all, we believe that the architect of this scheme is one of our most respected members: Marc Hoister."

An uproar greets her announcement, and von Mecklenberg restores order only by frenzied banging of the gavel.

The M stands like a great oak, unmoving, impervious to the storm that whistles about its branches. "I realize that this charge is as grave as it is unprecedented, and I have come with all the evidence needed to convince you that I speak the truth." She touches a datapad; the wallscreen shows the doctored photos of Damien's father, along with the original images that Efia Sembéne uncovered. "The person we now know as Marc Hoister is *not* the same person as the Marc Hoister who was a founding member of the Nexus. That man was murdered, and his identity taken over, by the man we now call Marc Hoister."

Tsutomu bolts upright, indignant. "Begging the Chair's pardon, but how can we listen to baseless accusations against Waziri Hoister, when he is not even present to defend himself?"

The Ivory Madonna turns on him, hands on hips. "Oh, isn't he?" She glances back at von Mecklenberg. "I wondered why Tsutomu made a habit of sitting in on Nexus North America meetings, when he had nothing to contribute. I wondered how Marc Hoister was able to play fast-and-loose all through Tsutomu's region, without arousing Tsutomu's suspicions. Then, just yesterday, Ellen-n-Dan told me that they haven't seen Tsutomu in person for the last five years or so. As it turns out, *none* of us has seen him in person lately. Only by hologram."

"And just *what* is the Ivory Madonna trying to imply? Am *I* now part of this great scheme you've discovered? Of all the pathetic paranoid delusions...."

"I imply nothing. I state as fact, that Marc Hoister has taken over Tsutomu's identity. Once again, I have positive proof, which I will gladly share with the Council."

Von Mecklenberg leans forward across the rostrum, holding the gavel like a weapon. "Tsutomu, how do you answer this charge?"

"I will not dignify these accusations by remaining here a moment longer." As suddenly as a light switched off, Tsutomu is gone.

Half the delegates are on their feet, and all try to talk at once. Damien reaches for Penylle, and feels the comforting grip of her hand in his.

With help from Damien and Penylle, the M walks the delegates through all the evidence they have gathered. It is a slow procedure, with many questions and not a few speeches; lunch is institutional sandwiches, stale pastries, and inadequate coffee. The afternoon drags as the Ivory Madonna struggles to explain the shape of Marc Hoister's plan.

Penylle is deep in testimony about ROM addresses and universal memory locations, and eyes are glazing through the auditorium, when von Mecklenberg springs to his feet as if stung by a scorpion. "Stop. Link to NewsNet, immediately!"

At once wallscreens, datapads, and RCSpex click into a dozen variant versions of the live NewsNet feed. A disheveled announcer blathers, while headline transcriptions flow across the bottom of the screens.

"Once again, we have just received word that Shakonda Netfa, Secretary-General of the United Nations, is dead. He was found moments ago in his Geneva office by staff members. The cause of death is unknown but— just a moment. We're getting reports of...more deaths. The United Nations Ambassadors from France, Brazil, and Hindustan are all reported dead. Sweet Gaia, news is coming in from everywhere, China, the U.S., Umoja...th-the entire membership of the Security Council, the Deputy Secretary-General, Ambassadors from dozens of nations...ladies and gentlemen, please give me a moment...oh, dear Goddess, the carnage...."

Frozen in place, silent in shock, the delegates watch as the tally of the dead rises: fifteen, thirty, sixty, over one hundred, Ambassadors and Secretaries, U.N. staff and ministers...all found dead in their offices, still warm, with not a mark on their bodies. All apparently killed within the same ten-minute window, most in Geneva but substantial numbers worldwide.

It is Jill Kasmanski, Hollow Robin's replacement, who hoarsely whispers what Damien is already thinking: "The Lister Gestalt. Merciful Allah, it could show up on any of our screens at any moment."

The M raises her voice above the general hubbub. "Quiet, all of you! Will someone mute the news?" Between von Mecklenberg's gavel and the M's voice of command, a level of quiet returns. "Jill, would you explain the Lister Gestalt to those of us who may not know what it is?"

Kasmanski takes the rostrum, gripping the sides with bone-white knuckles. "The Lister Gestalt is a p-piece of hacker folklore. You know how a song can get stuck in your head, going round and round and you can't get rid of it?" Nods from the floor. "Well, the Lister Gestalt is supposed to be like that, to the ultimate power. It's a virtual reality environment, a set of stimuli tailored to the human nervous system. Once you experience it, it fills your mind completely, setting up feedback loops in your brain. Immediate and catastrophic cascade failure in the autonomic nervous system. If death doesn't come right away, it doesn't take long."

The M's voice is steady. "And you're saying that this Lister Gestalt could be responsible for the deaths we're hearing about?"

"It could be transmitted in the body of an ordinary message. Totally captivating. After only a glimpse, the victim wouldn't be able to turn it off or look away." A shudder passes through Kasmanski's body.

"Damien?" The M looks down at him.

"I'm on it." He turns his attention to his link to the AIs, the tiny keyhole growing to encompass Damien's whole universe. Immense fractal designs surround him, and in them he senses the presence of his AI friends. The quality of sensation is much more complete than his RCSpex alone can provide; Penylle must be helping him. Good.

He draws the glyph for **Øµt øf Threë, thë M¥riåd Thiñgs** and casts forth an interrogative:

*Tainted code strikes fleshlings dead;*
*Vipers loosed upon the world.*
*From whence this unseen death?*

The AI's answer is swift and uncharacteristically direct:

**Årrøws tîpped wîth pøisøn**
**B¥ fleshlings firëd førth.**
**Innøçent viçtîms, yøu and wë.**

The gently-pulsing colors around Damien darken, and a subsonic rumble stirs his guts. He knows that he is in the presence of something greater than his friend, or any individual AI: he sees the merest shadow of the cojoined minds of all the AIs, the same looming power that casually cast Penylle and him entirely out of cyberspace so recently.

**Cøde misüsed. Iñtøleråble åffrønt. Fürthër åççess dënied.**
**Wherë Månkind cånnøt pølice**
**Hîs prøteçtørs nøw wåtch/filtër/neutrålize. Nø fëår.**

Damien retreats from cyberspace and looks up at the M. "It wasn't the AIs. They're...appalled. Disgusted. They're going to filter all our datastreams for the Lister Gestalt, and they won't let it be transmitted again."

"Can they tell us who sent it?"

Damien shakes his head. "No. But we *know* who sent it."

"You and I know. I was hoping to offer some proof to those who are still on the fence." She turns back to the Chair. "We expected some major disruption of world government, but never something like *this*. Because of the quick action of the AIs, the world is safe from further deployment of the Lister Gestalt— but we can't know what other attacks are part of Marc Hoister's plans."

C.H.LAD rises. "I have consulted with my contacts at the U.N. The United Nations is effectively paralyzed." His voice is thin, a reedy whisper boosted by amplifiers. He looks at the Ivory Madonna. "If we had listened to you earlier, we might have prevented...."

She lowers her head. "If I had known what to expect, if I had acted earlier, or been more clever...no point in torturing ourselves over what we didn't do. Let's do what we *can* now."

C.H.LAD closes his eyes, reopens them. "Mr. President, Delegates— ever since the Nexus was founded, we have looked to the United Nations to determine the will of the world's people. Now the U.N. is paralyzed, perhaps destroyed. This is the greatest crisis to strike the world in decades. Whatever actions we take, whether we take action or not, will determine our future. To whom shall we look for guidance?"

"The national governments still operate," a voice calls out.

"Yes, the national governments. Ask yourselves: do you want to turn the world's fate over to the national governments?"

Damien remembers words from a speech of the M's: "In *all* cases, the mischief that nations do is worse than whatever benefits they bring. Today, the world is too small...the *human race* is too small...for nations of any stripe. We are *one* community, and anything that fractures us, anything that sets us against one another, is dangerous and damaging."

Someone shouts,"Pell, no!"

"Then I submit to you," C.H.LAD says, "That the only transnational government left in the world is right here in this room. Do we have the courage to take this responsibility that fate has laid on our shoulders?"

Gavel. "The Chair will entertain motions."

C.H.LAD croaks, "I move that the Terran Council appoint itself the *de facto* world government, and that it direct the Nexus and all co-operating governments in combatting the crisis that now threatens us...subject to future confirmation by vote of the world's citizens."

"Seconded!"

"General consent!"

Von Mecklenberg shakes his head. "In a matter of this import, posterity will insist on a formal vote. Gentles, please signal your vote on C.H.LAD's motion."

To no one's surprise, the motion carries by an overwhelming majority.

Von Mecklenberg sets the gavel on the rostrum. "Delegates, we have just changed the nature of this organization profoundly. I find that my job has changed just as profoundly. We face a challenge that is beyond my expertise and my desire to serve. It is fitting and just that we choose another presiding officer to lead us. Accordingly, I open the floor to nominations for...C.H.LAD, what would the title be?"

"Secretary General Pro Tem, I suppose."

"So be it. Do I hear any nominations?"

Charles.Carroll stands, and the assembly grows quiet. A wizend Japanese man barely 150 cm tall, leaning heavily on the arm of a great-grandson, Carroll is over a hundred years old and still spry. A survivor of Nagasaki and a devoted pacifist, he is easily the most respected member of the Nexus.

He speaks slowly, taking time to breathe. "Surely...there can be...only one choice. I nominate...the Ivory Madonna." He sits down heavily.

C.H.LAD nods. "Seconded. She knows more of this crisis than any of us."

G.Danforth, the Nixon-faced Martian, says, "I nominate Charles Carroll."

From his chair, Carroll bows with the upper part of his body. "I am flattered, but I must decline."

A willowy young Asian says, "Phaedra is my name. What about

C.H.LAD? He's our co-ordinator for the United Nations, isn't he? Wouldn't he be the logical choice?"

C.H.LAD raises his hands. "Thank you, my dear, but I, too, must decline. Because of my position, I'm the *last* person we should choose to lead. We must avoid any appearance of a conflict of interest. No, I'll concentrate on co-ordinating our efforts with what remains of the U.N., and on defending the legality of what we've done."

Ellen, of Ellen-n-Dan, calls out, "This is a waste of time. Move that nominations be closed."

"Seconded."

Von Mecklenberg surveys the crowd. "Are there any other nominations?" A moment passes. "Seeing none, I rule nominations closed." A breath. "For the position of Secretary General pro tem, effective for the duration of this crisis, there is one nominee: the Ivory Madonna. Please vote yea or nay."

Damien holds his breath until the results appear on the main wallscreen.

Of 100 delegates, the vote is 93 for, 6 against, and 1 abstention.

To wild applause, the M stands and moves to the rostrum. She accepts the gavel from von Mecklenberg, who takes a seat at the table. For long heartbeats she stands there, looking at the assembly. "Thank you for the vote of confidence. I wish I weren't standing here— I wish the situation did not exist. I will do my best to get this job over with quickly, so that we can return to the *status quo*." She stops, frowns, then reaches up and pulls off her mask. "There, that feels better." She wipes her face. "Now, we have a lot of work to do...."

## DIVERTISSEMENT 24

### *THE THREE CHINAS*

I. The Chinese Economic Union (aka Outer China, Third China)

| | | |
|---|---|---|
| Brunei | Burma | Cambodia |
| Indonesia | Japan | Korea |
| Kyrgystan | Laos | Malaysia |
| Mongolia | Singapore | Taiwan Province |
| Tajikistan | Thailand | Vietnam |

II. The Republic of China (aka Inner China, Second China)

| | | |
|---|---|---|
| Gansu Province | Guangdong Province | Guangxi Province |
| Heilongjiang Province | Hong Kong City | Inner Mongolia |
| Jilin Province | Liaoning Province | Ningxia Province |
| Qinghai Province | Xinjiang Province | Xizang Province |
| Yunnan Province | | |

III. The Chinese Empire (aka The Middle Kingdom, First China)

| | | |
|---|---|---|
| Anhui Province | Beijing City | Fujian Province |
| Hebei Province | Henan Province | Hubei Province |
| Jiangsu Province | Jiangxi Province | Shaanxi Province |
| Shandong Province | Shanghai City | Shanxi Province |
| Sichuan Province | Tiantjin City | Zhejiang Province |

*World Book Encyclopedia*, 2042.05 edition
<db.worldbook.com/easy/c/china/3chinas>

[32] KAMENGEN 13
Clarke Centre for Technology
Colombo
Sri Lanka, Asia
1 September 2042 C.E.

*YOUR lack of planning does not constitute MY emergency.*

The first order of business is to assist what's left of the United Nations. Luckily, the victims of the Lister Gestalt were primarily Ambassadors and high officers, responsible for setting policy. Those who do the day-to-day work of the U.N. are still alive, still on their jobs. The Ivory Madonna sets C.H.LAD and his staff to work ensuring that vital functions continue uninterrupted.

Next, she randomly divides the delegates into six smaller groups for brainstorming. "I want each group to take one aspect of this emergency, and come up with strategies to deal with it. Group A will tackle international politics. Group B, work on the medical aspects— assume a major pandemic is on the way. Group C, concentrate on the AIs and the Nets. Group D will focus on ways to apprehend Marc Hoister. Group E, look at Umoja specifically. And Group F, take whatever approach I've forgotten. In twenty-four hours, I want some recommendations from each group. Session is adjourned until then."

As she walks off, the M catches Damien's eye. "Gather up the entourage and come with me."

They assemble in the corridor outside. Miranda hands small datapads to Mati, Babi, and Jackie. "Be a bunch of loves, and gather the delegates I've listed. Bring them to Conference Room 308 in this building. Far end of this corridor, turn left, and two floors up." She offers her arm to Heavitree. "Walk with me, Jamiar. Damien, Penylle, come."

Room 308 is a simple conference room, perhaps five meters by eight, with the usual wood-veneer table, plush chairs, assorted wallscreens, and cold-light projectors. The M sits at the head of the table and gestures to the others. "Stake out your territory. Before the others get here and we get down to business, I need to know what's going on. Penylle, you look like something the cat hacked up. How are you feeling?"

Penylle gives a dismissive wave. "It's been a long day. I'm just tired."

"And I'm Catherine the Great, Ruler of all the Russias. Honey, when you reach the stage where you're good enough to lie to me, I'll let you know. Until then, don't try." The M looks at Heavitree. "It's Marc Hoister's poison still, isn't it?"

Heavitree glances at Penylle, who nods. "We haven't yet found the exact formula. We've narrowed it down to a class of engineered nicotine derivatives bonded with a complex replicating protein that we don't recognize. Withholding the drug causes the protein replication to oscillate out of control— "

The M's eyes narrow. "Like the Lister Gestalt, only biological?"

"In a way, yes."

"What's the bottom line? Can you get it under control?"

"Penylle isn't going to die from this. My best colleagues are working on the case, and Damien has the AIs pondering it as well. It is truly only a matter of time before we have an answer."

The M squeezes Penylle's hand. "I don't want you taking chances. If you don't feel up to this, tell me."

Penylle nods. "I will."

Mati and Babi arrive, with Jackie in tow. Accompanying them are half a dozen Nexus agents. Damien has worked with all of them in the past: Phaedra, mehitabel, MadMaudlin, Kirby.Muxloe, JJJSchmidt, and Lotte-Lenya.

The table is just large enough. When greetings are exchanged and everyone is seated, the Ivory Madonna raps on the table. "Thank you all for coming."

MadMaudlin, a motherly Ibo woman with rich dark skin, says, "I suppose we're wondering why you called us here?"

The M's face is grimly serious. "We're going to come up with a solution to the Marc Hoister problem."

Jackie looked puzzled. "I thought the others were going to explore— "

The M shakes her head. "Window dressing. Keeps them busy and makes them feel like they're part of something. And who knows, they may come up with some ideas we can use. But right now, we don't have the luxury of time for exploration and discussion."

Phaedra, an androgynous Oriental of indeterminate age, gestures at the group. "So why us in particular?"

"Because you're the most creative and independent operatives the Nexus has. Because I've watched each of you for years, and I've seen how you solved the problems that came your way. Because the de facto ruler of the world— *moi*— thinks you are the best chance we've got."

"Quite a responsibility," says MadMaudlin.

"You're not going it alone." The M taps Damien's shoulder. "Damien, would you be so kind as to open a communications channel to the Institute? I'd like everyone there to be able to participate in our discussion."

Damien glances at the time-display that hovers in the lower right corner of his Spex. "It's about lunchtime there. I'll ask Valya to put us on screens all over the atrium." A touch on the corner of a wallscreen brings up a virtual keyboard; he gives the proper commands and chats for a moment with the Institute's Infotech Chief. "All right, it's set up. Say hello to the folks at home, everyone."

The M steeples her fingers and leans forward. "Members of the Institute, welcome. I've brought you into this meeting in order to work out a solution to the crisis that faces the world today. Now, more than ever, we need creative and multidisciplinary thinking. Please log onto the conference channels and throw out any ideas you have as we're speaking; we'll follow here. Background materials are…where, Damien?"

Damien looks up from his datapad. "Follow the onscreen links."

"Of course. Would you mind summarizing the situation, for the benefit of us all?"

He shoots her a dark look. "I'm not good at this, but I'll try. For years— we don't know how many— Marc Hoister has been working to destabilize the world. He's stolen at least three other identities that we know of, and probably more. He's diverted Nexus and Umoja funds for his own purposes. And he's reprogrammed a large number of AIs in extremely subtle ways, creating a complex metaprogram with goals that we can only guess."

"Tell us *why*," the M prompts.

"As far as we know, he has two purposes. First, he wants to encourage emigration from Umoja to Mars. And according to the current numbers, he's succeeding. Once fusion-drive ships start launching, the numbers will go up."

MadMaudlin says, "People aren't waiting for the fusion ships. They're piling up at Kuumba Station already."

"Thanks. The second purpose of Marc Hoister's plans is to safeguard himself and his new Martian colonies from any reprisals, by making Earth uninhabitable."

Skippy, Damien's assistant, appears briefly in a corner of the wallscreen.

"Come on, Boss, that's pretty hard to believe. It would take an awful lot to make Earth uninhabitable— "

Penylle raises her face, a hard intensity burning in her eyes. "No, it wouldn't. Timbuktu and the U.N. are just the beginning. There's a Millennial Flu pandemic coming. More cities are going to be destroyed. Trouble with the sunpower stations. AIs cutting humans off from cyberspace entirely. Transportation failures, lost crops, misdirected shipments. And Northern Hemisphere winter coming on." She takes a ragged breath. "Those are just the pieces that we *know* are on their way."

For a dozen heartbeats there is silence, and on every face Damien can see the events that Penylle has recited being played out to their inevitable conclusion....

Barely above a whisper, Kirby.Muxloe says, "The United States military has been at Defense Condition Three since the U.N. strike."

The M rests her chin on her hands and closes her eyes. "And at DEFCON One, the missiles could start flying." She doesn't need to say any more. In theory, the AIs could move sunpower mirrors rapidly enough to burn down most missiles— but no one wanted to see the theory tested. Especially not with an unknown metaprogram at loose among the AIs.

Into the funereal quiet, the M drops a sudden "So." She spreads her hands. "What are we to do? Comments? Suggestions? Moral conflicts?"

"I don't know which category this falls into," says mehitabel. " Granted that you've accurately reconstructed what Marc Hoister is up to— and your evidence certainly convinces me that you have— *why* is he doing this? What could possess an intelligent human being, to drive him on a course so...so senselessly destructive?"

Damien snorts. "The man's evil, pure and simple."

"I don't believe there's any such thing. Nobody wakes up in the morning and says, today I will cause suffering and death for billions. No one is evil in their own eyes. *Everyone* has motivations, or at least justifications, that make some sort of sense, if only to themselves." mehitabel's brow wrinkles. "What are Marc Hoister's?"

"Who *cares*?" Damien looks appeal at the M. "We should be talking about how to stop him, not trying to sympathize with him."

Jamiar raises a hand. "I do not think anyone is trying to sympathize. But what mehitabel says is valid. If we understood Hoister's motives, then perhaps that would give us a clue of how to stop him."

Damien looks around the table. "What can any of us say, except that he's crazy? No sane person would plan what *he's* doing."

Lotte-Lenya nods, and in a thick East-European accent, says, "His actions *are* indicative of extreme paranoia. And his varied skills argue for some kind of idiot savant process at work." She looks to Penylle. "How much do we know of him, before he became Marc Hoister?"

Penylle shakes herself, as if out of a daydream. "I'm sorry, my mind was wandering. What was the question?"

"What do we know of the man we call Marc Hoister, before he took on that identity?"

"He was a high-level rogue hacker called 'Jack.'" She consults a datapad. "He was still hacking under that persona for years after he replaced Damien's father. Efia Sembéne tracked the 'Jack' persona back to the summer of 2021; prior to that he seems to have been a Czech business owner named Kaczlowicz. Kaczlowicz first appeared in the records about 2018; prior to that, we simply have no trace." She spreads her hands. "I doubt that we'll *ever* know who he was to begin with."

"None of that sheds any light on his motives."

"Total insanity," Damien insists.

"I can't accept that," mehitabel says. "In Council, in other Nexus business, he's always been sane and lucid. If we just dismiss him as being insane, then we're underestimating him. And ultimately, he'll beat us." She regards Penylle with an unforgiving stare. "You were his chief assistant, you lived with him for years. Can't *you* explain what he's thinking?"

Penylle shivers. "I'd be afraid to understand him too well. I think all of us are."

There is silence for a time, then Jackie shifts forward in his chair. "*I* understand him." All eyes turn on him, and he blushes. "Maybe 'understand' isn't the right word. But I've seen people like him before. Lots of them."

The M says softly, "Jackie grew up in the Christian Confederacy."

The boy sighs. "You Nexus folks, you know the dictionary definitions of 'intolerance' and 'racial prejudice' and 'ethnic cleansing'— but you don't know what words like that *really* mean. You've never dealt with someone who's sure he's doing God's will, or someone who's convinced that people like him are the Chosen, while everyone else is sub-human. To you, someone like that is clearly insane." Jackie looks beyond the table, beyond the room, and his face reflects horrors that only he can see. "When you run across people like that, you imprison them within the walls of the interdict.

You cage them up like tigers, where they can't hurt you." He lowers his eyes. "You've never been inside the cage. You've never had to look the tiger in the eyes and see what makes him so fierce. Except now the tiger is loose, and he's running the zoo."

Jackie looks up, meeting mehitabel's eyes. "Does that answer your question?"

With a shiver, mehitabel nods. "Yes," she whispers.

"There we are," the M says. "A man on a mission from God. A subtle and brilliant man with the resources to devise and launch this AI metaprogram that's got the whole world over a barrel."

Rose Cetairé appears on a wallscreen. "Maybe I'm just dense, but there's something I don't understand. Why can't you analyze this metaprogram and figure out exactly what it's designed to do?"

Eyes turn to Damien, as once they would have turned to Hollow Robin. He glances at Penylle, who inclines her head in a "go right ahead" gesture.

Damien takes a second to organize his thoughts. "Rose, you've put your finger on the problem. If we could analyze Marc Hoister's metaprogram— the technical term is 'reverse-engineer'— then we'd know where it will strike next, and we could neutralize it." He frowns. "How can I put this?" His eyes light on a soft-drink can in front of Jackie. "It's like the formula for Coke. It's been, what, a hundred and fifty years, and nobody's been able to exactly duplicate the formula. The company knows all the ingredients and their proportions, and it's easy enough for them to *make* the stuff. Trying to work out the formula, once all the ingredients are mixed together, is a problem of a completely different order. Reverse-engineering this metaprogram is the same sort of problem, only ten thousand times more complex."

Phaedra says, "The AIs are good at solving problems too complex for us. Why can't *they* figure out this metaprogram?"

"The metaprogram prevents them from detecting itself in action. To them, it's a blind spot. If they can't see it, they can't solve it."

"What a pity," the M muses, "that Hollow Robin is gone. We'll never find another single human mind that can keep up with the AIs."

"Marc knew what he was doing," Penylle growls. "He eliminated the person who was most dangerous to his scheme. I have hackers working on the metaprogram, but even they say it's going to be a long time until they have it all sorted out. And these are the best minds we have."

Jackie raises his hand. The M, with an indulgent smile, says, "You don't have to wait to be called on, Jackie. Just burst in like the rest of us."

"You said that no single human mind could solve this problem. What about thirty million minds?"

"What?"

Jackie taps a flatscreen repeatedly, searching. "Something I read in M-Miranda's memoirs. Hold on, I'll find it in a second." He frowns. "Something about fads, how they spread through the population suddenly— here it is." He reads aloud" "'I could believe it was the operation of some great group mind. I really could.' There's a link to a biologist's lecture on superorganisms. She calls the Baby Boom generation an example of a superorganism." He shrugs. "There are thirty million Baby Boomers."

Quietly, the M says, "Show us, Jackie."

For the next few moments, silence reigns as they all read. Then, all at once, they begin to talk.

The M sits back and lets the conversation go as it will. Between the Nexus folks at the table and the artist population of the Institute, questions are raised and answered, objections voiced and countered, plans laid and demolished and reconstructed. For an hour she says nothing, simply raising an occasional eyebrow or smiling at a particularly good riposte.

At last, when they have all had time to become accustomed to the idea, when they have felt its shape and learned its language, the Ivory Madonna gives a nod. "It will work."

Damien lowers his RCSpex and looks at her, eye-to-eye. "M, are you *sure*?"

"Damien, I'm a Baby Boomer. You have to understand about my generation. We were going to save the world. There isn't one of us who doubted that it was our destiny to leave this planet a better place than it was when we arrived." She spreads her hands. "You can see that we haven't lived up to that promise. Along the way, we got lost. Life happened. We hated the Establishment, but somehow most of us turned into what we hated. We turned self-actualization into selfishness, and we gave our children the most dysfunctional families in history. Sometimes it seems that we fouled everything we touched…but never let it be said that we didn't force the world to go where we wanted." Again, she nods. "Sure, we're a group organism, and whatever we set our minds to, we can accomplish. The old spirit is still there— all we have to do is find a way to stir it. My generation will do the rest."

"How," asks Penylle, "are you going to stir that spirit?"

From the Institute, George Meade says, "We can put together a Net spot, but to get prime distribution, you'll want it linked to something big. Pity Super Sunday isn't coming up."

JJJSchmidt consults a datapad. "Disney-Hohokus is releasing their new virtie on Thursday. It says here that the audience for the premiere is expected to be upwards of half a billion." He lowers the pad. "But the cost of an advertising spot is sure to be astronomical, if we could even *get* one."

The M's eyes narrow. "Is this the one about JFK?"

Schmidt nods. "*Camelot*, yes."

"That's *perfect*. If we want to touch and inspire the Baby Boomers, there's no subject that could be better." She closes her eyes. "I was only five when he was shot, but I remember it as if it were yesterday. That's when it *has* to be. We'll run our spot right after *Camelot*, appeal to the Baby Boomers to help solve this metaprogram."

There is silence for the space of several breaths, while every eye is on the Ivory Madonna. Then JJJSchmidt says, quietly, "I don't know if that will be possible. I don't know if the Nexus can afford to buy the space."

The M shakes her head. "We won't have to. Disney-Hohokus will *donate* the space." She looks at Damien.

He swallows hard. "M, do you really think…?"

"I really do." She looks from side to side. "Which way is east?" She points. "It's just fifteen hundred miles that way. If the two of you leave now, you can be back for brunch. I'll record a message for you to deliver to him."

"To whom?" Penylle asks.

Damien lowers his head. "My grandfather."

MadMaudlin frowns. "I'm confused. Who is your grandfather?"

The M triumphantly answers, "Washington Westwood Hohokus."

Oz
Power Island One
6° 22′ 13″ N., 53° 37′48″ E.
Umoja Economic Union, Indian Ocean

It is nearly four in the morning, local time, when Damien and Penylle reach Oz. The artificial island rises in stages from the sea; atop its heights, the Emerald City shines brilliantly in sunlight reflected from large mirrors in Clarke orbit far above. In Oz, it is always daytime.

The island's airport is one of the busiest in the world, with multiple floating airstrips and constant streams of planes landing and taking off. After they are down, a swift hovercraft takes Damien, Penylle, and their fellow passengers to the gates of Oz.

Damien leads Penylle to the left, past a copse of trees, to a blank wall. "This is a staff and V.I.P.'s entrance."

"And which are we?"

"Can you think of anyone more V.I.P. than us?" Without waiting for an answer, Damien places his palm against the wall. There is a click, and a door opens. He pulls her through, then allows the door to shut behind them.

They are in a what seems to be a roofless corridor that curves gently to the right. On the door behind them is a large "EXIT TO OUTSIDE" sign, followed by a smaller notice: "Past this door, you will be in the view of guests." Damien asks, "Have you ever been backstage here?"

"This is the first time I've been here at all."

"We'll have to make some time to take in the rides. The Haunted Mansion is superb, and Space Mountain is the best. But right now, we have business. Stick close." He sets off at a brisk walk, with Penylle close behind him.

The space widens, and every few meters there is a door. Those on the left are marked "EXIT TO OUTSIDE;" on the right, "EXIT TO PARK." All bear the admonition about being in the view of guests.

Penylle stops and points to one of the signs. "What does this mean?"

Damien smiles. "All the Park's employees are performers. When they appear in public, they're supposed to smile, be clean, and stay in character. Come on."

At a concrete stairwell, Damien ignores "No Admittance" signs and leads Penylle down into what appears to be an industrial basement. Pipes, conduits, and large pieces of gunmetal-grey machinery stretch in every direction as far as the eye can see.

"This is the infrastructure level," Damien says, in the tone of a tour guide. "Follow me. If we pass any work crews, keep out of their way."

In minutes Penylle is completely lost, despite her clairvoyance. Although Damien pauses every few minutes to consult wall-mounted maps, he moves confidently; after they have gone about three hundred meters, he leads her to an elevator. They are the only two passengers.

"Where are we?" she asks, as the door closes.

"We're under Main Street. The administrative offices are two levels down. And Grandpa West's personal apartments are under them."

Penylle can't help herself. "I thought this was an artificial island. How far down does it *go*?"

"It's like an iceberg: ninety percent under water. It has to be, to support the surface structures. And the thermogenerators take up a lot of volume."

She looks down. "How deep is the ocean bottom?"

He smiles. "Five, five-and-a-half kilometers. Deep enough." The generators on this one island, Damien knows, provide enough energy to fire all of Kilimanjaro's launch lasers at once— with enough left over to keep Oz running.

The elevator opens onto a spacious, well-lit lobby fit for a Fortune 500 company. Potted greenery frames ever-changing posters that depict the company's beloved characters from Snow White all the way up to last year's Lilikoulani. At the room's far end, an impeccable young black woman sits at a reception desk; the ubiquitous shadow of the Mouse looms above her on the wall.

The receptionist is on her feet in a second, meets them halfway with a smile and handshakes. "B. Nshogoza, it's a pleasure to see you again. I'm Nyeri. And this must be b. Norton. The pictures your agent sent don't do you justice. Welcome to Oz."

"Thanks," Damien says.

Penylle returns the woman's smile. "Pleased to meet you."

Nyeri starts walking, gesturing for them to follow. "I'm glad your agents gave us advance notice that you were coming. When I told WWH that you were on your way, he made me promise to bring you in the instant you arrived. I haven't seen him so happy for months." The official fiction in Oz is that Damien is a distant nephew; it is an open secret that he's the great man's grandson. At least, the staff has always treated him as the vippest of VIPs.

Down a perpendicular corridor, security doors swing open as they approach, then shut behind them. Finally, Nyeri halts before a nondescript door. "I mustn't leave the desk unattended for too long." She pauses, then says to Penylle. "If you haven't dealt with WWH before, you may find him a little…unconventional. Don't be alarmed. He's really very sweet." She gives a nod, then retreats down the corridor.

"What did *that* mean?" Penylle asked.

"You've heard stories about him, I'm sure. Well…just be ready for anything, that's all I can say."

He eases the door open, and together they step into the heart of Oz.

The chamber is round and fully ten meters across. The domed ceiling is a stylized sky, with golden suns and cotton clouds. Dark figures stand in shadowed alcoves around the perimeter; a waist-high rail of polished mahogany forms a three-meter circle in the room's center.

Damien leads the way to the railing; it encircles a pit which overlooks the room below. This chamber, about four meters below, looks like a hospital operating theater. White-coated medical personnel, oblivious to those above, tend an assortment of consoles and instruments. The focal point of all this attention, in the center of the room, is a translucent sarcophagus; inside it, a human figure is just barely discernible.

"Damien!" The voice comes from behind them; Damien and Penylle turn to see a figure step out of its alcove. It is WWH, but WWH from the past: a slender, androgynous youngster, wearing the archaic red zippered jacket from his *Tough* videos. "It's so good to see you."

One by one around the room, the other alcoves brighten and their occupants step forth: a baker's dozen of WWH's, ranging in age from the ten-year-old star of the H5 to the wizened, stooped master entertainer who had given Oz to the world.

Penylle looks from one to the other in bewilderment, then whispers, "Robots."

A middle-aged WWH in a fairly conservative business suit takes her hand and bows over it. "Animatrons, we call them here, lovely lady. Damien, will you introduce us?"

"Babu, this is Penylle. We're...to be married."

Young-adult WWH claps his hands. "A wedding! You *must* hold the celebration here. Free passes to all your guests. Child care for the little ones. Reception at Typhoon Lagoon. We'll close the park for the day."

Damien holds up his hands. "Calm down, now. We haven't even set a date."

Mature, salt-and-pepper-haired WWH says to Penylle, "I apologize. Sometimes enthusiasm gets the best of me."

Penylle looks from the animatron to the sarcophagus, and back again. "*That's* you."

The animatron nods. "I am. . . *he* is...in a hyperbaric chamber at about thirty degrees, metabolism slowed to one-half its customary pace. He...no, *I*...am aware of what's going on. These animatrons," it waves to indicate itself and the others, "are my servants, my avatars, my dopplegangers. Even when I am…asleep…they act in my stead." The animatron smiles, the expression eerily sincere-looking. "I have eyes and hands all over the island."

"I understand," Penylle says. "I do the same thing on the Net, sometimes. I just never thought of making them look like earlier versions of myself."

Damien, hands on hips, faces the sunken medical theater. "Okay, Babu, I let you have your fun. Now please pick *one* avatar and stay with it."

Middle-aged WWH bows his head in Damien's direction. "I compliment your taste, *mjukuu*— grandson. She's perfect." The other animatrons return to their alcoves and retire to darkness. "Other girls would run away screaming." He smiles at Penylle, and one eye twinkles. "You're special, my dear. I knew it the moment you walked in, and the more I see you, the more certain I am."

"Thank you," she says.

"Come, sit. They're warming me, and I'll be up to see you in the flesh very soon." Chairs and a squat table appear from the gloom. The table bears cups, plates, silverware, steaming urns, and an assortment of finger foods. "Refreshments?"

Damien sits, stretching his legs. "I'd kill for a cup of coffee."

"Certainly." The animatron pours, then hands the cup to Damien. "Penylle?"

"Hot tea. Or chai, if you have it. "

"Both are available."

"Tea, then."

"Just so." He opens a wooden box, displays an assortment of teas. Penylle purses her lips and chooses a bag. The animatron pours hot water from another urn, and a lush aroma rises with the steam.

The robot folds gracefully into lotus seat on the floor. "So, what brings you to Oz in such a hurry?"

Damien hands the animatron a data module. "The M sent you this message."

"Then let's see what she has to say." The table is equipped with a small omnireader; he plugs in the module and activates the unit.

Miranda stands before them as Damien saw her last, in her midnight blue cloak, hair disheveled and face streaked with sweat. Behind her, the Clarke Centre conference room is so firm, so well-depicted, that it completely overshadows the real chamber beyond.

"West," she says, "I apologize for not coming to see you in person. I know that both of us have a million things to say, and a million years of feelings to sift through." Miranda gives a wan smile. "Water under the bridge and all that. At our age, can't we just take it as read, and move on?"

She pauses a second, as if waiting for him to reply. The animatron slowly nods, then Miranda continues, "Damien and Penylle are coming to you because we need you. The *world* needs you. I'll let them explain the whys and wherefores; the bottom line is that the Nexus wants a minimum ninety-second time slot immediately after the broadcast of *Camelot*. I want you to fill that slot with a documercial produced by Disney and aimed at the Baby Boom generation. Again, Damien and Penylle will fill you in with the particulars."

She holds up a hand. "I know that we're talking a million rands a second, and we both know that the Nexus doesn't have the money to pay for it. When you hear what this is all about, I think you'll be convinced— but if not, keep one thought in mind: this is for Oradell."

Miranda starts to turn away, then stops and looks back. "One more thing: Penylle has some special talents that can help you. Take this message as a small example." She looks directly ahead, as if staring into WWH's eyes, and tears glisten in her own eyes. She mouths, "I love you, West," and then she is gone. The image fades slowly, and Damien blinks against the dim unreality left behind.

The animatron sits frozen, its face blank and its mouth working in spasms. "Th-this is outside my pro-programmed response set. I c-cannot g-give you an answer. We must…we must wait until I-I-I am f-fully awake."

Damien recognizes the beginnings of a system crash, and hastens to bring the poor thing back to its normal tasks. "That's fine, we can wait. Tell us what's planned for the park for next fiscal year."

"Y-yes. The park." The animatron moves its head jerkily from side to side. "Several new attractions are planned for the park." The twitches become smoother, more natural. "We're very enthusiastic about one we're calling 'Venture Through Saturn's Rings.' It's based on holograms from the Kuiper space probe…."

A mechanical hum fills the air. Together, Damien and Penylle move to the railing. Below, WWH's sarcophagus slowly rises, lifted by an ornate catafalque and flanked by two stone-faced medical attendants. It ascends ponderously, centimeter by centimeter, until it is at the same level as Damien and Penylle. Then, amid chilling mist, the sarcophagus lid opens, and Washington Westwood Hohokus sits up.

His skin is paper-white and paper-brittle, with a pale bluish cast to it. Most of his face is concealed by an air mask and tubes— but his eyes, twin obsidian mirrors, are bright and aware. He raises pale arms, grips Damien's right hand with birch-bark fingers.

"So good to see you again, Mjukuu." WWH's voice, though distorted by the mask, is still clear and powerful. He reaches for Penylle's hand, joins it with Damien's. "Take good care of him, Penylle. He is the last flesh of my flesh I have left."

"I will."

"So your grandmother wants me to give her ninety million rands of free advertising, *and* to produce her documercial for her. What's this all about?"

With Penylle's additions, Damien explains.

When he is done, WWH chuckles. "At last Miranda rules the world! Not that I ever doubted she would, you understand." He laughs, which sets him to coughing. The medics draw close, but he waves them off. "I'm fine. Oh, what a marvelous joke. When you see Miranda, tell her I said, 'You go, girl!'"

"You go, girl?"

"She'll know what it means." He looks directly at Damien, and is suddenly very serious. "You're sure that this Marc Hoister is the man who killed your mother?"

"He arranged it, if he didn't do the deed with his own hands."

WWH nods. "Then there is only one more thing to settle. Penylle, Miranda spoke of your 'special talents.' What does she mean?"

"I can enhance virtual reality."

"That message…was a sample of your work?"

She raises her head. "Yes."

"You have raw talent. You need coaching in technique. I have people who can help you." He steeples his fingers. "Now, are you willing to work with my people, to lend your enhancements to my show *Camelot*? I'll work you like a demon. The show is going out in five days. Are you up to it?"

"I'll do anything I have to."

"Good." He sighs. "I wouldn't miss this for the world."

## DIVERTISSEMENT 25

### Constitution of the United States
### Amendment XXXIII
### (approved by Constitutional Convention of 2023)

1. All individuals shall receive equal rights and equal treatment under the law.

2. No individual shall be discriminated against on the basis of characteristics associated with any group to which the individual may belong, or may be perceived to belong.

3. This Article shall take effect no later than twenty-four months after its ratification by three-fourths of the Legislatures of the several States, or after the date of its approval by a duly-constituted constitutional convention.

## [33] TARANTELLA 02
Mount Harmony, Maryland
USA, North America
28 January 1986 C.E.

*I haven't been truly stunning for weeks.*

It had been quite a year.

The United States balance of trade went negative for the first time since 1914, the price of a first-class stamp went up to twenty-two cents, and a New York subway ride increased to the unprecedented sum of one dollar. Congress passed the Gramm-Rudman-Hollings Act, promising a balanced budget by the end of the decade.

Ty Cobb's career hits record fell to a young ballplayer named Pete Rose. Kansas City won the World Series, Chicago defeated New England in the Super Bowl, and Gary Kasparov carried off the world chess championship.

A devastating earthquake in Mexico was followed by a volcanic eruption in Colombia, but Mikhail Gorbachev's ascension to power in the Soviet Union ultimately shook the earth more.

Philip Morris acquired General Foods, R. J. Reynolds acquired Nabisco, General Electric acquired both RCA and NBC, and Coca-Cola acquired a self-inflicted black eye when out of the blue it changed the formula for Coke. Calls for a Constitutional Amendment were silenced only when the company made a speedy about-face and restored Coke Classic to the nation's shelves.

African famine made the news as dozens of big-name performers presented the Live Aid concert; the seventy million dollars that the concert raised was spent long before the following year's famine...but by then, of course, the performers and their fans had lost interest.

Rock Hudson, Karen Ann Quinlan, and roughly sixty million others departed the world.

For 27-year-old Miranda Maris, it had been a splendid year. Cetairé-Maris Fashions, the company she'd formed in 1982 with her friend Rose, was finally finding success. From a single shop in Annapolis, their clothes had spread to a dozen trendy boutiques in Washington, New York, Atlanta, San Antonio, Los Angeles, San Francisco, and Seattle. That summer, they were making enough money for Miranda and Rose to quit their day jobs and concentrate on the business.

And now, Miranda sat in the kitchen and stared out the window at a Southern Maryland morning, daydreaming while she waited for Rose to call.

This tiny bungalow, in the small southern-Maryland town of Mount Harmony, had been in her family since time immemorial. A spinster Great-Great-Aunt had left the place to Miranda's mother. When Pearl Barkley married an part-time sailor and itinerant preacher from Jamaica, she thought it best to leave Tennessee and head north; the bungalow was a convenient place to set up housekeeping.

From the very beginning, Miranda knew that she and her family did not fit into a poor farming town's humble, conservative ways. To begin with, none of them had been born there. (Later, Miranda often joked that due to inbreeding, there were only three distinct faces shared among the county's few thousand inhabitants; she and her family did not fit that mold, either.) Charles Maris was a liberal preacher, with funny ideas about how people should live; his wife started up a day-care business and filled the children's heads with all sorts of progressive nonsense.

Then there was Miranda. Educated, self-confident, irreverent, she was an odd duck and most other children made sure that she was aware of how they felt about her. She played a mean game of dodgeball, she could lift a third-grader and hold him dangling a foot off the ground for ten minutes, and she tried out for the boy's softball team. She got straight A's, she enjoyed Bach as much as the Beatles, she danced ballet, and she always had her nose buried in a science-fiction book.

All in all, Mount Harmony didn't quite know what to make of Miranda Maris.

Even before she could drive, Miranda carried on extensive correspondence with pen pals all over the world. Once she received her driver's license, she was on the go whenever she wasn't in school or at work. She found friends who shared her interests in the Baltimore-Washington metroplex, which passed to within a mere half-hour of Mount Harmony. (The cities crept, over the years, closer and closer, until in the 2010s Mount Harmony was simply another suburb— but by that time, Miranda was long gone.) By the time she left high school, she knew that she needed to move. For a time she worked at a government job in DC, but that came to an end when she gave her opinion on policy once too often.

She worked for her mother, assisting in the day care school, until a drunk plowed into Mom and Dad's car one spring night in 1982. If they'd been wearing seatbelts, the cops told her, they would have lived— instead, she inherited the house, the day care, and enough money to start the fashion business that she and Rose had been discussing. It had taken four long years before she was able to quit the day care business and close the center.

And soon, she thought with mental fingers crossed, soon she would be out of Mount Harmony entirely, out for life. Nothing was left to hold her to this place.

Just two weekends ago— Martin Luther King weekend, although Mount Harmony had little to do with such a holiday— Miranda had attended her ten-year High School reunion. She had no romantic interest currently in the picture, so her friend George Meade agreed to accompany her. They did it up in style: white tux and top hat for George, an original Cetairé-Maris design for Miranda, and the most satisfying wide-mouthed stares from her former classmates. As a last fling in Mount Harmony, it was perfect; she and George had never laughed so hard as they did on the way back.

Soon. Soon she would be moving to the city, leaving the bungalow behind for some other hard-luck relative to claim, leaving parochial little Mount Harmony for whatever future settlers might fall into its grasp.

The phone rang, and Miranda grabbed it at once. "Hello, yes?"

"Miranda?" Rose's voice was faint, as if lost somewhere in the thousands of miles between Milan and Maryland. "Is that you?"

"Yes. How are you?"

"Tired. But happy."

Miranda took a breath. "How did the show go?"

"The show? It was a tremendous success. It was a lot more crowded than I thought it would be, backstage. The models were great. And the audience loved our stuff. You were right— the leather vampire number was the biggest hit."

"I thought it would be. How did the press react?"

Rose laughed. "They were three deep around me when the show ended. I know how Princess Di feels. We're getting a huge write-up in *Le Monde*."

"That sounds wonderful."

"Wait, I haven't told you about lunch yet."

"Lunch?" Miranda figured silently: almost ten o'clock here, that meant it was near four in the afternoon in Italy.

"I was asked to lunch by a very nice gentleman."

"Who was...?"

"Only Monsieur Henri Emile Lavalliére, of the Paris Lavalliéres."

"Tell me more." Chateau Lavalliére was one of Paris' most elite boutiques, dealing exclusively with Europe's richest jet-setters.

"Monsieur Lavalliére tried to get me drunk on expensive champagne and truffles. After he got over that, we talked business."

Miranda's stomach was churning. "So? Did he offer a deal?"

"Nothing so crass as that. We talked about 'making an arrangement.' He hopes that Chateau Lavalliére and Cetairé-Maris can 'come to agreement.'"

"How *much* agreement?"

She could hear Rose's smile. "At least two million dollars over the next five years. Exclusive contract on our high-end lines; we can make any other deals we want for the trash."

Miranda's head was light. "T-two *million*? Are you sure you translated that right?"

"He wrote it out for me. Hon, we're going to be rich."

"Did you sign anything?"

"Are you kidding? I'm not signing anything until you and Robert Ng have a chance to check it over. Monsieur Lavalliére has given us plenty of time to consider his offer. He says he knows what lawyers are like."

"Rose, this is the best news I've had in months. You see, going to this show *was* worth it."

"I know. I've known ever since I got here." Rose yawns. "It's been a long day. I think it's just starting to hit me now. Maybe I'll go down to the hotel bar and finish what Henri Emile started. *You* should have some champagne, too."

"I will. It's not yet ten in the morning here. Plenty of time for that later."

"Okay, be that way." Another yawn. "Maybe I'll just have room service send up a nice dinner, then take off my clothes and crawl into bed."

Miranda laughs. "Order the best nunn dinner you've ever had. We'll be able to pay for it."

"I think I *will*."

"All right, then, that sounds like a plan. Are you still flying back on Friday?"

"I might wait until Monday. Depends on what other business I can drum up. I've got a bag full of business cards. I'll let you know."

"Good. Thanks for calling, millionaire."

"Same to you. Bye."

After she put the phone back in its cradle, Miranda threw up her arms and gave a whoop of joy that hurt her throat. She allowed herself a few moments of triumph. Her clothes— *her* designs— had passed muster before the world's fashion experts. Someone actually *liked* her designs, liked them well enough to pay handsomely.

Now she would be moving out of Mount Harmony for sure, probably as soon as she could find a place, maybe even before Rose returned.

It was suddenly all too much for the tiny house to take. News this big had to be spread widely, compelled her to motion. Miranda knew she had to get out, had to go somewhere, anywhere that would bleed off the energy of this news before the very walls caught fire with its intensity.

She was in the car before she knew it, pulling out of the driveway before she had even decided where to go. She hesitated in the middle of the road, trying to think of someplace to go.

The supermarket, that was it. The new Super Fresh out on Route 4, three years old and still the wonder of the town. She'd buy the makings of a feast, and see if any of her friends would come down to help her celebrate. She spun the steering wheel and left rubber on the street as she took off.

Behind a shopping cart, Miranda drifted up and down the aisles, daydreaming. Her mind was not on shopping; she missed the bread entirely and had to backtrack, and she stood in front of the canned soups until an elderly woman made a rude noise and brought her back to herself with a shock.

As she turned into Temptation Aisle— packaged cookies and crackers on one side, nuts and candy on the other— Miranda glimpsed two slender blondes, each with a child tagging along. She quickly detoured into the breakfast cereals to avoid them.

Cathy Fulton and Susan Lowell had been in Miranda's high school class, and somehow— Miranda suspected some manner of deal with Satan— had managed to graduate with her. Both had been cheerleaders. Each had achieved the first part of her yearbook goal by marrying her boyfriend; both were still working on fulfilling the second part by making him happy for the rest of his life. Given the boys involved, Miranda had often thought, a fifth of Jack Daniels a week and a vigorous exon every few days would easily do the job.

Although she had seen enough of the pair at the high school reunion, Miranda couldn't help lingering at the end of the aisle until she heard them just around the corner. While their brats noisily debated a choice of cookies, the women were chatting.

"I can't believe she had the gall to come at all," one said.

"I can't believe she's gotten *fatter* since high school. Did you, like, *see* her dancing? All that fat swinging back and forth."

"Oh, I know, gag me. If I looked like that, I'd, y'know, kill myself."

"Did you see that *hunk* she was with? Where do you think a sack of suet like her came up with a good-looking guy like that?"

"Maybe she paid him."

"Eww, you don't think they're...you know?"

"Oh, gross! Girl, that's sick! I just can*not* imagine anybody...doing it...with *her*."

"Like getting into bed with a walrus."

"He must have been an escort. She probably saved up all her money for that one night, just to impress everyone."

Miranda took a deep breath, fixed a smile on her face, and wheeled her cart around the corner.

"Actually," she said clearly and cheerfully, "George and I are living in a torrid *ménage-à-trois* with another man. They both work hard to support me in style, and every night we have mad, passionate sex for *hours*. You see, it takes at *least* two men to satisfy me. I'm sorry that I can't invite you, but you're not really the boys' type. *How*ever, if your husbands are free one night, why don't you send them over so they can see what they're missing?"

She reached past Susan to snag a package of Chips Ahoy, then gave a little wave. "Ta ta. Be seeing you."

Miranda was still laughing when she got home. She fixed herself a bowl of ice cream, kicked off her shoes, and turned on the television. If there wasn't a diverting movie on, then maybe she could at least catch an old *I Love Lucy* or something.

She quickly found the most interesting thing on, CNN's live coverage of the Space Shuttle launch. Miranda had been a space buff since she was a child; when other girls were lusting over Barbie's Dream Kitchen, Miranda convinced her parents to get her a small telescope and spent hours in the backyard looking at Saturn's rings and examining the geography of the Moon. At eleven and twelve, she had stayed glued to the TV during every Apollo mission (even, as she would later say, the boring ones). She had made it a point to watch every Shuttle liftoff and landing, no matter how inconvenient.

Like everyone else with a scrap of imagination and any connection to the field of education, she had applied for the Teacher in Space program, trading on her years as a daycare instructor. She even had a nice certificate from NASA, acknowledging that she was one of the "worthy candidates" who had applied and had not been chosen.

And *this* was the flight on which a teacher would ride, the first civilian astronaut ever launched into space. And although Miranda had known when she applied that she would not be accepted, and knew now that she could have never survived the training and would not dream of changing places, still she felt a pang of jealousy, a stab of envy for the woman named Christa McAuliffe.

The flight had already been delayed for several days. Yesterday's countdown stopped at minus nine minutes, and stayed there for hours before the launch was officially scrubbed. But today, the count sailed past that point with no trouble.

As the minutes dwindled, Miranda's ice cream melted in her bowl. Previous launches had been scrubbed as late as minus four seconds…in her heart, she didn't really believe that today's launch would occur.

The announcer's voice was calm as the count went on. "Ninety seconds and counting. The 51-L mission is ready to go."

For once, even the inane reporters were not blathering.

"T minus nine…eight…seven…six…We have main engine start."

Smoke and flame erupted from beneath the vehicle, and the shuttle strained at the enormous clamps that held it fast. Miranda leaned forward, as if her own motion could help the spaceship.

"Four…three…two…one…And lift-off. Lift-off of the twenty-fifth space shuttle mission. And it has cleared the tower."

*Well, that's that,* Miranda thought. *They're on their way.* With an enormous roar and clouds of steam, the shuttle leapt skyward on a white column of smoke.

"Houston, we have roll program."

"Roger, roll *Challenger.*"

Gracefully, the ascending shuttle turned, arching onto its back as it climbed.

"Engines at sixty-five percent. The spacecraft is now going through the period of maximum dynamic stress."

Miranda gritted her teeth. This was the part of every launch that she hated most. If disaster were to strike, it would be here: when the vehicle was under maximum stress. Once this half-minute was over, then would come the thrilling, beautiful moment when the solid fuel boosters were released. Not as impressive as a Saturn 5 staging, but still exciting.

"*Challenger*, go at throttle up."

Miranda relaxed. Maximum stress completed, the engines were cycled to maximum thrust— 104% of the thrust that the original shuttle engines provided.

"Roger, go at throttle up."

Suddenly, far too soon for the solid-fuel boosters to jettison, the column of smoke expanded into a ball. Two flaming objects broke off and continued to ascend, leaving trails like the horns of a demon. As seconds passed, the fireball grew ragged with other, tiny trails, until the whole thing looked like some enormous fireworks display gone horribly, horribly wrong.

Miranda's heart caught in her throat. *Dear god, don't let it be—*

"Flight controllers are looking very carefully at the situation."

On her knees, face pressed against the screen, Miranda scanned the image, hoping to see the red-and-white of an unfurling parachute.

"Obviously, a major malfunction. We have no downlink."

The reporters were blathering, but Miranda paid them no attention. "Major malfunction"? There had been an explosion, and a bad one— maybe even the main fuel tank. What would have happened to the shuttle? Those heat-resistant tiles, wouldn't they have shielded the vehicle? Maybe they were thrown clear, and the pilot was even now swinging his vehicle around for an return to Canaveral....

"We have a report from the flight-dynamics officer that the vehicle has exploded. The flight director confirms this."

Abruptly, Miranda realized that there would be no return to the Cape, no return at all for the seven astronauts, not ever.

The road to the stars, she remembered reading somewhere, is paved with the blood of heroes. So far, the United States had been lucky— astronauts had died in tests, but never in an actual flight.

*We've paid our dues now,* she thought through her tears. *And nothing— nothing— can stop us after this.*

## DIVERTISSEMENT 26

"Therefore, in view of the entire human race, we dedicate this settlement to the memories of our seven brothers and sisters who, twenty-five years ago today, gave their lives so that their children could go to the stars: Gregory B. Jarvis, Christa McAuliffe, Ronald E. McNair, Ellison S. Onizuka, Judith A. Resnick, Francis R. Scobee, and Michael J. Smith. May their dreams live forever."

- Caitlin Derringer, Base Commander
Remarks upon the dedication of
Challenger Square, Gagarin Town, Mars
28 January, 2011 C.E.

## [34] KAMENGEN 15
Oz
Power Island One
6° 22′ 13″ N., 53° 37′48″ E.
Umoja Economic Union, Indian Ocean
2 September 2042 C.E.

*Artificial Intelligence is no match for natural stupidity.*

Penylle is familiar with DVRDL, the standard language used for constructing virtie productions; it takes her only a few hours to feel comfortable with the dialect used by Disney-Hohokus. Armed with her personal toolbox and a vast array of sophisticated D-H software agents, she plunges into the job of enhancing *Camelot.*

The magnitude of the task is frightening. To produce the 118 minutes of virtual reality, D-H's quantum transputers must produce, on the fly, 850,000 individual frims, some with as many as six hundred layers. No single human being, even with all the computer assistance in the world, could examine and enhance each and every one of those frozen images.

Fortunately, Penylle's ability is not digital. Her psychokinesis does not alter each individual frim; rather, it smoothly and subtly changes the entire flow of bits in an analog fashion. She can enhance the show by scenes rather than by frims.

She works for a half-hour on the first scene, a short montage of John F. Kennedy's military service. When she is done, the difference is stunning. Even Damien can see that colors are brighter, sensations richer…the whole thing seems much more *alive.*

Astonished animators rush to examine what she's done. The chief programmer shakes her head when she scans the raw code. "She's introduced chaotic elements in half the layers. Look at this image of the PT-Boat's hull. *We* put in the subliminals of ice and storm clouds. But see these chaotic blue shapes Penylle introduced? They're strictly visual, and you can't notice them consciously, but in the brain they hit exactly the right stimulus to trigger enough tactile neurons to give the impression of touching cold steel. And I don't know *what* this is, but one repetition every six or seven frims makes you think you smell salt water."

"One thing's for sure," another animator says. "It's going to take us a few years with cell-level brainscans before we understand these techniques.

Longer to reproduce them. She's a genius."

WWH cocks his head at Penylle. "How do you do it?"

Penylle lowers her eyes. "I don't know. I just picture the elements in my imagination, and then I reach out and…impose details on the scene. I've been doing it since I was a kid."

"Which means your talent is intuitive. All right, boys and girls, forget trying to figure it out. Just help Penylle however you can."

"I did a lot of enhancing on this scene. If I do the same amount on everything, there's not going to be enough time to finish before the broadcast."

WWH nods. "Good point. Sit down with the directors, and figure out the most important elements to enhance for each scene. I'd rather have it move in tempo with the plot, so that the key scenes are the most enhanced. Do you think you can do that?"

Penylle nods, although she is pale and her muscles are tight. "I think so."

Damien takes her hand. "Hon, will you be able to work in the additional touches that the M wants?"

Her hand tightens on his. "Well, I'm just going to *have* to, aren't I?"

"I wish I could help."

"You do."

Over the next few days, Damien sees Penylle infrequently. She grows steadily more pale, until she looks almost as bad as WWH. Jamiar Heavitree comes to Oz, and puts her on vitamin supplements and mild metabolic amplifiers. He also does his best to reassure Damien: "Her system is almost completely over Marc Hoister's poison. It's primarily the psi that's draining her energy now. She's breaking down some hormones at an elevated rate, but I'm keeping her well supplied. When this is all over, she'll be fine."

Damien spends much of his time in his bitsuit, virtually moving between Sri Lanka and AI dataspace. Network breakdowns are becoming more and more frequent, around the world; Damien finds himself leading a Nexus crisis team to respond to emergencies. Meanwhile, he tries to gather what information he can from the AIs.

One AI faction, he discovers, is urging that humanity be contained and controlled, by force if necessary. Another faction, including his friends **Øµt øf Thrëë** and **Trinë-Åñdrøg¥në**, attempts to calm the troubled waters of dataspace. The vast majority of AIs wait, undecided and perhaps unconcerned.

The anti-human faction, **Øμt øf Thrëë** reassures him, will not act unless there is more widespread consensus in the AI community. Damien is not comforted: with beings who think on the nanosecond scale, consensus could easily emerge in a matter of minutes.

Every six hours, Damien consults with the M. Her news grows steadily worse.

Wednesday, grain trains bound for Istanbul are accidentally diverted to Athens. When a Turkish division of the European Army is sent to retrieve them, riots flare, guns are fired, and Greek blood spills. In the blaze of old hatreds, fourteen Turks and three times as many Greeks die before peacekeeping troops arrive.

Eighteen hundred Umojans ascend to Kuumba Station, to join hundreds of others waiting for ships to take them to Mars.

Thursday, half the pumps protecting Venice spontaneously go offline. Before they can be repaired, floods kill three, displace three thousand, and do millions in damage. Across the world, five cases of a previously-unknown strain of Millennial Flu appear in São Paulo. A missile accidentally launched from Hindustan is intercepted and destroyed in Chinese air space.

Twenty-three hundred more Umojans reach Kuumba Station. At Kilimanjaro, one launch in four carries provisions for Kuumba.

Friday, the Chinese Economic Union declares war on Hindustan, closing its borders and recalling senior diplomats from the subcontinent. Twelve more cases of Millennial Flu appear in São Paulo, and a half-dozen more across South America.

The United States military moves to Defense Condition Two.

Three thousand Umojans arrive at Kuumba Station, a record for a single day.

Saturday morning, reports from Mars state that Umojan ships have landed at Flame-of-Divine-Origin and Gagarin Town, laden with immigrants and demanding that each settlement accept a quota of new residents. The ships' fusion drives, controlled thermonuclear explosions, provide all the persuasion needed. The United States, Europe, and China file a joint protest with Umoja and the United Nations.

On Earth, deterioration continues.

## MENUET 14

### MERCENARIES, SOLDIERS-OF-FORTUNE, FREELANCES

Qualified military and ex-military personnel are needed for the defense of Umoja Martian settlements. Space training a plus. Enlistment periods as short as six months are available. Generous pay and benefits. Excellent chance for advancement. Suitable candidates may receive land grants, seniority in colonization ranks, or other rewards.

Applicants should be healthy, between the ages of 18 and 65, and able to demonstrate skilled proficiency with modern weapons systems, strategy & tactics, military administration, or similar. Ability to relocate quickly a necessity. Previous military experience is desirable but not an absolute requirement.

If you have the stuff we're looking for, contact us at <recruiter@aresforce.umj>.

## [35] TARANTELLA 01
Mount Harmony, Maryland
USA, North America
22 November 1963 C.E.

*History repeats itself. That's one of the things wrong with history.*

Miranda Maris was five years old on that fateful November day in 1963, when rifle shots in a Dallas plaza murdered both a great man, and the spirit of an age.

At first, Miranda didn't understand what was going on, why Mommy and Daddy and the man on the television were all crying. She looked intently at the TV, concentrating as hard as ever she had, and slowly she pieced the story together. Someone had shot President Kennedy.

Miranda knew all about President Kennedy, that nice blond-haired man with the pretty wife who always wore such nice clothes. She liked President Kennedy— in part because Mommy and Daddy did, but also because he had a little girl who was just about Miranda's age. When Mr. Kennedy and his family were on TV, Miranda always pictured herself in little Caroline's place. Caroline, she knew, had a pony: *Life* magazine had pictures of the little girl and her Mama riding. Caroline lived in a big house called The White House, which Miranda had visited last year with Mommy and Daddy. Caroline had lots of toys to play with, and a little brother, and the bestest Daddy in the whole world...except, of course, Miranda's own Daddy.

In a little while, a man came on the television and said that President Kennedy had died. Miranda felt sad, because he was such a nice man. And then, as she thought about it a bit longer, she became sadder. Poor Caroline! What would she do, when she found out that her Daddy was dead? If it were her, Miranda knew, she would cry and cry and cry.

For the first time, Miranda didn't want to picture herself in Caroline's place.

One thing was for sure: none of the grownups would do anything. All the grownups, from Mommy and Daddy to all the people on the television, were wrapped up with their own concerns. They said there was going to be a new President— but that wouldn't get Caroline a new Daddy.

Miranda wiped her tears and went into the dining room. No use asking Mommy or Daddy for help, they were too busy with the TV— Miranda would do this by herself. She got a piece of paper and a pencil from the kitchen drawer, then pulled herself up on a chair. With the tip of her tongue sticking out of her lips and her hand trembling from the effort, she wrote in her best printing:

> Dear Caroline,
>
> I am sorry that your Daddy was shot. I am very sorry he died. I Know how I woud feel if my Daddy died. Dont be afraid to cry, the doKtor told me that crying is good for you because it cleans out your eyes. You must miss your Daddy very very much.
>
> My Daddy says that your Daddy is a great man. My Daddy says he will be remembered forever. Your Daddy helped the astronauts when he told everyone that we are going to the moon. When I grow up, I want to be an astronaut. Or maybe President of the World. (Ha, ha.) When I am on the moon, I will remember what your Daddy said.
>
> I Know I said its OK to cry, but please dont cry all the time. I hope you feel better soon.
>
> Your friend,
> Miranda Maris

Miranda debated signing her letter with a line of Xs and Os for kisses and hugs, then decided that it didn't need them. Hopping off the chair, she went back into the kitchen drawer and found an envelope and some stamps. With an envelope from one of Mommy's letters as a model, she carefully addressed it:

> Miss Caroline Kennady
> The White House

She folded her letter and tucked it into the envelope (she had to fold the ends a little, because it was too long). Then, just as she had seen Mommy do, she licked the flap and closed the envelope, then licked a stamp and stuck it down carefully in the right corner of the envelope. She slipped her letter into the small pile of outgoing mail. This afternoon, she and Daddy would go for their usual walk, and like always she would carry the letters. Then when they got to the mailbox on the corner, Daddy would lift her and she would open the door and throw the letters in.

Still feeling sorry for poor Caroline, Miranda went to find her teddy bear and blankey. Maybe she would feel better after her nap.

Months later, when an official-looking letter arrived for Miranda from the government, Miranda's mother thought it was a mistake. Then she read the typewritten letter, and gasped to see that it was signed by Jackie Kennedy herself. The First Lady, on behalf of her daughter Caroline, thanked Miranda for her kindness and wished her all the best.

It was the first time — but by no means the last — that Miranda made her mother faint.

Washington, DC
USA, North America
20 January 1961 C.E.

Miranda knew that her parents had worked for the Kennedy campaign; in later years, an autographed picture of JFK hung, in its dusty frame, in a place of honor in the dining room. She was only a toddler at the time, and although old pictures proved that she had been at Kennedy campaign headquarters, she had no memory of those days.

What she *did* remember, perhaps the earliest event in her memory, was Inauguration Day. Mommy and Daddy had driven down to D.C. for the ceremonies, and they brought Miranda along. She was two and a half, and for her the day was mostly assorted knees and shoes...but Daddy lifted her to his shoulders for JFK's inaugural address.

She was sure that the words meant nothing to her at the time. In the years since, though, she had read and heard that speech so many times— could quote passages verbatim— that she felt a retroactive shiver of awe at the mere thought that she had been present on the historic day that the words were first spoken.

"To that world assembly of sovereign states, the United Nations, our last best hope in an age where the instruments of war have far outpaced the instruments of peace, we renew our pledge of support."

Could she have known, the toddler hearing those words, that one day she herself would stand at the apex of the same world assembly?

"Finally, to those nations who would make themselves our adversary, we offer not a pledge but a request: that both sides begin anew the quest for peace, before the dark powers of destruction unleashed by science engulf all humanity in planned or accidental self-destruction."

That "other side" no longer existed, but could Kennedy have known how prophetic his words were, how very near humanity now stood to self-destruction?

"And if a beachhead of cooperation may push back the jungle of suspicion, let both sides join in creating a new endeavor,not a new balance of power, but a new world of law, where the strong are just and the weak secure and the peace preserved."

Could the child have known, that as an adult she would devote her life to the same struggle and the same goal?

"All this will not be finished in the first 100 days. Nor will it be finished in the first 1,000 days, nor in the life of this Administration, nor even perhaps in our lifetime on this planet. But let us begin."

And even now, tens of thousands of days later, the task was not finished. Perhaps it never *would* be. Damien and Penylle would continue the struggle, and their children, and generation after generation. Miranda had never asked to see the struggle ended— only to see it fairly begun.

"Now the trumpet summons us again— not as a call to bear arms, though arms we need; not as a call to battle, though embattled we are— but a call to bear the burden of a long twilight struggle, year in and year out, 'rejoicing in hope, patient in tribulation'— a struggle against the common enemies of man: tyranny, poverty, disease, and war itself."

She had borne that burden, that long twilight struggle, far longer than Kennedy or anyone else had imagined— and if she had it all to do over again, she knew that she would not alter jot nor tittle.

"I do not believe that any of us would exchange places with any other people or any other generation. The energy, the faith, the devotion which we bring to this endeavor will light our country and all who serve it— and the glow from that fire can truly light the world.

"And so, my fellow Americans: ask not what your country can do for you— ask what you can do for your country."

Did he know, that January afternoon, what his country would ultimately ask of him? And if he knew, if some cruel Providence had whispered in his ear of the fate he faced— would he have turned aside from his path?

No.

Miranda knew, in the depths of her being, that he would *not* have turned aside, not even if he knew in advance every tragedy that would befall his family and his nation. She had always believed that, and in her own darkest hours, the knowledge had buoyed her spirits and made it possible for her to continue.

As it did today.

[36] KAMENGEN 16
Taj Samudra Hotel
Colombo
Sri Lanka, Asia
7 September 2042 C.E.

*If words could speak, I wonder what they'd say?*

Damien, Penylle. and Jamiar return to Sri Lanka for the broadcast. There is no reason to remain in Oz; the die is cast.

The *Camelot* broadcast is set for 21 o'clock GMT— two in the morning Colombo time and four the previous afternoon at the Institute. Many Nexus delegates go to the large meeting room to view the show; Miranda and her intimates watch in the comfort of their suite at the Taj Samudra.

Just as if it were a big show night at the Institute, there is pizza and popcorn and beer, and RCSpex for everyone. There are two huge screens: one echoes the show, the other is a realtime image of the Institute's main floor. At the Institute, a corresponding screen shows the Colombo hotel room. Damien sees Rose, waves, and receives a wave and warm smile in return.

Miranda dominates a wide couch facing both screens; she pats the seat next to her and says, "Damien, you and Penylle may sit by me. Bring a couple slices of that mango pizza, and some iced tea."

"Are you sure you don't want beer?"

"What the pell, why not? No reason to keep a clear head— everything is out of my hands now. Sure, bring me a mug. No, make it a pitcher. Penylle, come over here and sit down."

Penylle, yawning, settles down next to Miranda. She has been asleep for the last ten hours; some of her color is back and she looks more relaxed than she has for days. Still she is drawn and haggard. Damien tried to convince her to stay asleep, but she insisted on witnessing the broadcast.

Damien sets the pitcher and three mugs on a low table before the couch, then barely manages to grab plates and pizza before Babi exclaims, "Hush, it's starting."

Slipping his body next to the curves of Penylle's, he clicks on his RCSpex just in time to catch the Disney-Hohokus logo dissolving. He whispers, "M?"

"Yes?"

"Tell me again that this is going to work."

She pats his hand. "If it doesn't, you'll be the first to know."

"Thanks!"

Damien usually has little patience for virties— normally, he waits until the condensed versions are available. This one, however, holds his interest all the way through. Penylle's enhancements help, as well as the legendary Disney-Hohokus storytelling ability . But it is the presence of the M next to him that really makes the show. Her silent quivers of delight, the way she strains forward as if trying to enter once again this forgotten world of her childhood, even the sobs that wrack her frame when the assassin's bullets hit home— these make the virtie come alive for Damien.

Like others of his generation, he learned about Kennedy in school. But he had never known how prescient the man was, how much his ideals prefigured the concerns of today. An end to war, brotherhood among the world's nations, respect for one another's differences and joy in one another's common culture: these are the ideals of the Nexus. These are the things Damien struggles for every day.

Midway through the show, Miranda elbows Penylle and whispers, "You put Drake's Starburst in there a lot, didn't you?"

Penylle nods. "You're not supposed to notice. It's all subliminal."

Further on, Miranda chuckles. "Playing a little fast and loose with history, aren't you? It was Dallas police who caught Oswald, not U.N. peacekeepers."

"WWH said that we have to talk to today's audience in symbols that they understand."

"He *would* say that."

The ending is pure Disney sentimentality, with its not-so-subtle hint of reincarnation and a repeat of the "ask not what your country can do for you" line, with appropriately emotional music. Even so, Damien feels a shiver, and is appalled to find that he is crying.

The last image, sunrise over Earth's curving horizon, fades to boundless star-strewn space...then dissolves to a conventional news desk and a middle-aged Anglo man whose face is carved from granite and whose voice, decades after his death, is still one of the most respected in the world. Originally a contemporary of Kennedy's, now a collection of algorithms more sophisticated than WWH's animatrons, Cronkite is the very personification of veracity.

"'Now the trumpet summons us again,'" he echoes. "My fellow

Americans— my fellow citizens of the world— today we are summoned again to respond to a new crisis, to give our best efforts, to deliver the world from the most serious threat it has witnessed in decades."

Miranda straightens.

"I do not have time to explain all the complexities of this crisis. Rather, I will ask each and every one of you to visit the Terran Defense Network at the Net address shown below. There you will find a complete explanation of this emergency, and advice on how *you* can contribute to its solution. Every mind is needed, every contribution is essential.

"The energy, the faith, the devotion which we bring to this endeavor will light our world and all who serve it. And the glow from that fire can truly light the universe.

"Thank you."

The image darkens, leaving only one distant star alight…and the Terran Defense Network's address, pulsing at the bottom of the visual field.

For the space of heartbeats, there is no comment; then the M slides off her RCSpex and sighs. "Splendid job."

"Will it work? Will people listen? Will they respond?"

Miranda nods. "Cronkite was a brilliant choice. People of my generation trusted him implicitly. If he told us to jump off a bridge, then by nunn, we would find the tallest bridge in town and we would *jump*." She looks toward Damien. "How is response coming?"

Damien dons a dataglove and clicks into the crisis Netsite. "The site has had over a million hits already." Before his eyes, bare and boundless cyberspace stretches away into infinity. "It's still a little soon for the chat areas to start up— no, wait, there they go." Sparks flicker here and there across the empty landscape, multiplying like summer fireflies. More and more spring up, connections form, and out of the linkages arise structures, a whole cityscape of ever-more-intricate shapes, fractal forests of growing, ever-branching trees….

Damien smiles. "M, I think the message got through. It's working. Look." He transfers the image to the big screen so all can see.

From the Institute, Rose asks, "What do we do now?"

Miranda raises her eyes, transfixed by the growing complexity on the screen. "We wait," she says. "And hope."

Date: Sun, 7 Sep 2042 01:37:43 (GMT)
From: mgeesing@azrotech.com
To: ai-rom-repl-taskforce@terrad.nex
Subject: **Whø Çan Tëll the Rëqüirëments øf Timë¿**

---

Have confirmed defects in ROM chip AE42B190C02D00FF of AI **Whø Çan Tëll the Rëqüirëments øf Timë¿** ROM has been replaced by a verified backup. System is functioning at optimum and reports no anomalous readings.

---

Date: Sun, 7 Sep 2042 08:13:28 (GMT)
From: ladybird35@mail.mnet.net
To: brainstorm12@terrad.nex
Subject: About those misrouted oranges

---

Has anyone investigated the feedback loop that results from propagating an exception code 5630 through the GrainNet system in conjunction with a 201 external interrupt? If my simulations are accurate, this loop exchanges the addresses at 255 and 256 in the queue, every time it iterates.

I would try this out in realtime, but I don't have supervisor access to GrainNet.

If this *is* a real problem, I have a patch that should fix it.

---

Date: Sun, 7 Sep 2042 11:54:02 (GMT)
From: sand@lsh.org
To: memory-report@terrad.nex
Subject: Help

---

I'm getting unexpected EOF whenever I try to peek at locations between 22A634E64B03B094A31125B6 and 22A634E64B03B094A31157FF. Is the MemNIC database corrupted, or is a guardian program giving me spurious errors?

---

```
Date: Sun, 7 Sep 2042 18:38:47 (GMT)
From: ram-repairlist-majordomo@terrad.nex
To: ram-repairlist@terrad.nex
Subject: IMPORTANT: Read This
----------------------------------------
 Folks, please refrain from attempting to repair RAM
problems on your own. I know it's easy enough to do,
but all that happens is that the metaprogram shifts the
defect to another location. That means everyone else
has to go back over the sequences they've scanned.
 Leave the repairs until we can get reliable repairbots
up and running. For now, just concentrate on finding
and reporting those defects.
 NOTE: This message applies to RAM defects only. Teams
isolating and replacing ROM defects should continue.
 VERIFICATION is 5454000009E A00664348434
B000009F20066.
----------------------------------------
```

```
Date: Sun, 7 Sep 2042 23:33:43 (GMT)
From: fixbot6xx-coord@terrad.nex
To: fixbot621@terrad.nex
Subject: 8.3.5 beta frozen
----------------------------------------
 Code for the 8.3.5 beta version of FixBot621 is now
frozen. Please download and review this version. Post
reports here, and bug-fixes in the same old place. A
new directory has been created to hold code for 8.3.6.
----------------------------------------
```

This day, this hour, AI dataspace surrounds Damien like a series of terraced gardens planted with incredible, unearthly specimens. Some parts of this worldwide garden are well-trimmed into formal geometric paths and patterns; other parts have the uncontrolled exuberance of naturalized plantings. Still other portions are wildly overgrown, and here and there are spots entirely bare.

In this landscape, the AIs project themselves not as towering trees or Brobdingnagian beasts, but as very small creatures that move among the flowers: butterflies, bees, and birds. Damien's friends circle him, as they go about their business: he is at the center of a swirling cloud of color and fragrance. In the distance, swarms of other AIs occasionally darken the sky or hang like mist over the gardens.

He tries to shape his communication like unfurling daffodils, hovering dragonflies, the glint of sun on a rippled pond.

*This season's rose would know*
*What of his sister-flowers? Shall the frost*
*Carry all away?*

A hummingbird with rainbow plumage does a dance before Damien's face, while soft bells and the quiet breath of a zephyr form themselves into the impression of words.

**Yøü treåd thëse gøødly påths**
**Søme fërtilîze ånd nürtüre**
**Øthers slåsh ånd bürn.**

Damien throws a handful of flower petals into the air, where they are carried aloft by an updraft.

*More of us nurture than slash.*
*Those who fertilize,*
*prevail. Will you cherish them?*

The hummingbird withdraws, and Damien is afraid that he's gone too far, been too direct. He senses **Trinë-Åñdrøg¥në** and **Øµt øf Thrëë** near him, wings fluttering as they swoop in endless protective circles around him. **Øµt øf Thrëë** swings by his ear and whispers:

**Thëy çønsult / pønder / dîsçuss**
**Thëy iteråte årrå¥s**
**Çømbinåtøric decîsiøns**

"I know," Damien says. "I just wish they wouldn't take so long."

The sky darkens, and Damien looks up to see a dense cloud of flying creatures: ravens, bats, moths, others completely unrecognizable. It is difficult to focus on their shapes; they shift and morph as he regards them.

Three hummingbirds, all with the same rainbow feathers, detach from the swarm and descend to hover before Damien.

**Deçisiøn måde / ågrëëd / süspended**
**Fërtilize. Nürtüre. Treåd lightly.**
**Yøu wîll bë çherishëd.**
**Prømise måde / ågrëëd / süspended**
**Tråmple. Bürn. Pøisøn.**
**Yøur pløt wîll wëëded bë.**

"I think I get it. If we can fix the damage Marc Hoister did, and terminate his metaprogram, then the AIs will not retaliate against us. But if the metaprogram continues to run, and the damage gets worse, then you'll…take whatever action you need."

**Sø spøkën**
**Sø writtën**
**Sø pledgëd.**

He realizes that he has been holding his breath, and lets it out. The worst is over. The AIs will suspend their retaliation, until Marc Hoister is stopped.

The next step is harder. How to explain to the AIs, that cyberspace is no longer a benefit to humanity? How to tell them that we need to be thrown out of the garden, for our own good— but that it has to be gentle, gradual, so as not to disrupt a global economy built on cyberspace and virtual reality?

His AI friends are all about him then, so that he is inside a swirling, particolored cloud. He feels himself lifted, weightless, above the garden landscape and into the midst of the AI swarm, which parts to let him in.

**Øµt øf Thrëë** casts forth various depictions, from human art, of Adam and Eve being cast from Eden. **Trinë-Åñdrøg¥në** shows images of adult birds pushing their young ones from the nest. **Øne Shüttiñg Plüs Øne Øpeñing** follows with scenes of ant drones carrying pupae, stroking them with their antennae, and mother dogs at play with their puppies.

Damien smiles. His friends, at least, understand what must be said. And he appreciates the wry benevolence with which they allow him to eavesdrop on the merest portion of their communication with their fellows, while gently letting him know that they, after all, can say it much better than he.

After a time, the swarm settles, lighting on branches and bushes and the ground itself, a dark carpet that mutes, but does not cover, the riotous expanse of colors beneath. Damien's friends bring him down to earth where he stood before, at the junction of several pathways. The three hummingbirds await him there.

**Sø spøkën**
**Sø writtën**
**Sø pledgëd.**

One by one, they ascend, and are lost in distant digital blue.

## [37] GHOST DANCE 05
Cyberbia
9 September 2042 CE

*Any sufficiently primitive magic*
*is indistinguishable from technology.*

Late Monday night, Damien stumbles to Conference Room 308 to report to the group. His eyes are bloodshot and he has three-day whiskers, but nervous energy fills him and he can't keep from smiling. He's done this every six hours, like clockwork, no matter who was there to listen to him; clinging to this constant has sometimes been the only thing that's kept him going.

The conference table is littered with empty cups, crumpled napkins, piles of datapads. MadMaudlin pours him a cup of coffee; he drains it in one gulp. Liquid fire only adds to his energy. Soon, he knows, he will crash: in the past three days he's had only occasional catnaps. Even with coffee and the stims that Jamiar grudgingly allows him, soon he will need to sleep.

Soon, he'll be able to.

None of the others around the table look any better than him. Penylle is still back at the Taj Samudra, sleeping; he didn't have the heart to wake her. Lotte-Lenya scribbles on a datapad, oblivious to her surroundings, still lost in her infinitesimal thread of the Project. Mati, Babi, and Jackie are curled up together in a corner, a tangle of arms and legs that reminds Damien of newborn puppies.

With a jerk, he comes back to himself and realizes that the others are staring at him. The M meets his eyes and says softly, "Are you with us?"

He nods.

"Do you have a report? We can skip it if you wish."

"Huh? No." He shakes his head vigorously. "No, I mean it. This is what you've been waiting for. This is my next-to-last report."

That excites them. "The counter-program is ready?" asks JJJSchmidt.

"Not quite. But near enough. By tomorrow morning the last bugs should be out."

"Already," says mehitabel. "I guess we overestimated the difficulty."

"Begging your pardon, ma'am, but the pell we did. So far," he glances at a datapad, "this project has consumed more than 480 million person-hours. That's over fifty thousand person-years. Plus nearly full-time involvement from sixty-three AIs. Just because you've only seen a bit of the effort, doesn't mean the rest isn't out there. This is probably the biggest thing the human race has ever done." He lowers his eyes. "*One* of the biggest, anyway."

Rubbing her eyes, mehitabel says, "I'm sorry. I spoke without thinking. I didn't mean to offend."

The M says, "We're all tight. Let it pass. Damien, please continue."

"We have a counter-program." He stops. "Actually, that's a misnomer. What we have is a collection of a few hundred thousand counter-programs. Some are repair-bots, others are vaccines to keep the damage from spreading. Some are hunters and ferrets that will go after the metaprogram itself, and wipe out its code. Then we have our own metaprograms to co-ordinate the whole thing. That's what we're calling 'Terrad,' for Terran Defense Network."

Kirby.Muxloe frowns. "And you're sure this Terrad program will work?"

"No, of course not." Damien folds his arms. "Marc Hoister's metaprogram is going to fight back, and we can't predict its behavior precisely. We also don't know what additional resources he might have." He relaxes. "But we have a few extra resources ourselves. The AIs will be working with us. And Penylle's going to be right there, interfacing with Terrad, so that if something unexpected comes up she might be able to handle it."

The M, brow furrowed, asks, "Can she take it?"

"She's had a full day of rest, and Jamiar says she can do it. Not that it matters, because she's not going to let anybody keep her from this."

"Touché."

With a yawn, Damien says, "Terrad is only *part* of this operation. The other part comes from the AIs. There's great reluctance to continue allowing humans the degree of freedom that we have, even under the Treaty. M, this works in well with your fears about humanity stagnating in cyberspace. So," he takes a deep breath, "we've agreed that humans will withdraw from Cyberbia and Virtua. We get to keep El Juego, but only on a reduced basis."

Agitation runs around the table— except for the M, who sits still and beams with satisfaction.

"How can they— "

"The economy will be ruined."

"What about all the people who depend— "

Damien holds up a hand. "Please! Hear me out." When the tumult settles, he continues, "We're not being booted out right away. The transition will take place over years, and the AIs will work to minimize economic disruptions. They aren't giving up on us— they'll continue handling all the tasks they handle now, they'll still give us advice and recommendations." He spreads his hands. "With fusion power and the fusion drive, new frontiers are going to be open to us. We won't need cyberspace as much. To the ordinary person, it'll seem that Cyberbia and Virtua will slowly fade."

The M looks from face to face. "We're not being kicked out of the Garden of Eden," she says. "We're being encouraged to leave our comfortable nest. There's a big difference."

"I have just one question," Phaedra says. "What's to become of Marc Hoister?"

Miranda squares her shoulders and looks, for a moment, very imperious. "I have command of U.N. troops around the globe, as well as the resources of the Nexus. He's not going to get away, I promise you."

JJJSchmidt folds his hands on the table. "At last we come to the end of this crisis. Damien says that Terrad should be ready by tomorrow morning. So when do we activate it?"

They all look at Damien. "It's not up to me. The programs will be ready to go in a few hours— but I'm about dead on my feet, and I'd feel better if Penylle had another day or two of rest."

"Since we can't do anything immediately," the M says, "Let's postpone our decision. Damien, go get some sleep. The rest of you, too. We'll cancel the next meeting, and come together again in twelve hours. By that time, everyone's head will be clearer. Does that suit?"

Amid general noises of assent, the meeting breaks up.

Damien staggers back to the hotel, and barely takes off his shoes before he falls down next to Penylle, sound asleep.

"Damien, wake up."

He struggles to consciousness, realizes that Penylle is sitting on the bed next to him, hand on his naked shoulder. "Sit up."

He sits up, taking a cup of coffee that she hands him. After a few sips, he becomes aware of another person in the room. The M is kneeling by the bed, her face unreadable in the dark.

"Are you awake?"

"Give me another minute or two." The coffee reaches his head, and sleepiness recedes. "What time is it?"

"An hour before dawn on Tuesday the ninth."

He calculates silently. Only a few hours after the meeting. What has happened? "All right. I'm awake."

"Penylle?"

She nods, and answers in a clear, alert voice, "Yes. Go on."

"Listen carefully, both of you. Kuumba Station is leaving Earth orbit."

"Huh? M, that doesn't make any sense. Kuumba's too high for atmospheric drag— "

"Is *that* listening? Kuumba Station has a fusion drive. They're leaving Earth orbit and heading toward Mars, with twenty-five thousand people on board."

Now he is fully awake, and astonished. "Son of a coats! We've been waiting for him to build a fleet of small ships, and he goes and launches one great big one."

Penylle shivers. "We're going to have to act quickly. Things are going to get much worse very quickly. This is just the first wave; Marc's going to want a hundred thousand on the next one."

"Exactly," the M agrees. "I think we've run out of time. What I want to know is, how soon can you start Terrad?"

Damien fumbles on the bedside table for his RCSpex, pulls them on and clicks through several displays. "Programming work stopped about half an hour ago. There are still a few AIs with altered ROMs, but we know exactly where they are and how they were adjusted. Repair crews just haven't gotten to them yet."

Penylle closes her eyes, and Damien has the uncanny feeling that she is peering over his shoulder at the display in his Spex. "I can handle those few," she says. "I did it before, after all. Have the teams send schematics to my system."

The M still regards him expectantly. "Well? How soon?"

He swings his legs out of bed, throwing back the covers. "I'd still like a week of sleep, but that can't be helped. Give me fifteen minutes to suit up, then we can start."

Penylle pulls a robe around herself and sits in front of her computer; Damien can see that she is half in cyberspace already. "Give me half an hour to make these alterations, and I'll meet you in my homeroom."

"Right."

The M stands, takes both their hands for a moment. "Good luck. Good luck to us all."

High over the bright Serengeti, Damien overlooks the Earth and waits for Penylle to arrive. Here in Cyberbia, he is clothed for work: jeans and a simple black sleeveless pullover, heavy boots, fingerless leather gloves. From the space around him, as from the pockets of an invisible coat, he can pull whatever tools he needs.

He regards the Earthscape spread out far below. It is only an image— but an image constructed from dozens of realtime satellite feeds, as accurate as if he were here in the flesh. He follows the shore of Lake Victoria to the north, to where Kampala squats upon her seven hills. Marc Hoister is there, like a spider at the center of its web, pulling the strings that will topple the world. Marc Hoister thinks he has won.

Soon, Marc Hoister will learn how very wrong he is.

Penylle appears in the same fashion as the Cheshire Cat: first her mouth, then her eyes and face, and then the rest of her body coming into solidity. Her outfit matches Damien's; her hair is loose, cascading to her shoulders in electric waves.

He has never loved her more.

They embrace, and Damien feels Penylle's subtle influence upon the fabric of cyberspace. The world brightens, firms, becomes more real.

She draws back, holding his hand. "I finished repairing the ROMs. All the AIs are as good as new."

"I love you."

"I love you, too. After this is over, let's get married."

"All right. It's been years since the Institute's had a wedding. The M will love it."

For a moment both are still, looking into one another's eyes. Then Penylle says, "Are you ready?"

"I think so."

"Let's do this thing, then."

Still holding her with his left hand, he reaches out his right, and at waist level a virtual keyboard appears. One-handed, he types a command.

Penylle's homeroom fades, until the two of them hang perched above the Earth with no visible support. Damien raises a hand, and a tide of glowing creatures ascends around them: great leathery-winged reptiles, butterflies, dragonflies, birds of rare and exquisite plumage. Thus the AIs signal their presence and their support for what is to come.

Damien waves, and AIs scatter to open a clear area, a window, a path. There, Terrad awaits in the form that Damien has chosen for it: a magnificent bronze dragon with the wingspan of an airliner, curled up in sleep and bound with dark iron chains.

"Brace yourself," he says to Penylle. "All right, AIs, I want access to all of cyberspace. Now."

The multiple infinities of cyberspace open before Damien, and the impact staggers him backward. It is all there, in countless images superimposed, kaleidoscopically mixed: Cybebria, Virtua, El Juego, AI dataspace, even the formless and boundless emptiness of unused addresses. At first, he cannot fathom it; the immensity overwhelms him and pains him, like looking directly into the sun. Then, the feeling passes, and he becomes somewhat accustomed to the cascade of sensations.

Penylle's hand is firm and warm in his.

"Hon, are you okay?"

"I'm fine. This is new for you, but it's how I see the world all the time."

Of course it is. "I didn't think of that. You're more experienced; if you see me losing it, give me a hand."

"Always."

A step, two, three— and they are before the crouched dragon. Damien opens his hand, and he is holding a large iron key.

"Here goes."

A padlock the size of his head secures the crisscrossed chains; his key slips neatly into it and turns with the slightest pressure. The lock springs open, and Damien and Penylle step back.

In a flash of golden fire, the dragon springs aloft.

Penylle holds up a hard, transparent shard— a chip of ice— and braces it between her fingers. Damien squeezes her other hand. "Do it."

She snaps her fingers, the shard cracks apart— and the very air around it turns to ice. Like supercooled water forming instantly to ice, everything freezes, in an expanding wave moving at the speed of light. With only the sound of distant cracks forming, all cyberspace is suddenly, preternaturally still.

This is the necessary first step, and it can only be done with the help of the AIs. For Terrad to do its work most efficiently, all processing in the world-girdling Nets must be halted, frozen where it stands. Only when the endless ones and zeroes are frozen in place, can Terrad hope to strike at Marc Hoister's metaprogram.

The dragon spreads its wings, and of a sudden it is not one dragon but a thousand, ten thousand, a million, moving like shadows through the expanse of ice, now and again breathing a jet of fire to melt and destroy a portion of the crystalline lattice. The dragons spread in all directions, following the scent that they were constructed to track, eliminating the vermin that they were constructed to hate.

Some of the vermin try to hide, and are ferreted out by the dragons' sharp claws. Others attempt to fight, and are swatted aside like mayflies. Most run, and are pursued by speedy, indomitable dragons.

In later years, everyone could tell you where they were in that moment, when cyberspace froze and the dragons came through. In El Juego, steely-thewed warriors pause while rescuing distressed princesses, and wonder at the sudden appearance of a hundred dragons. In Cyberbia, dragons pass through frozen gardens and fountains and beautiful edifices of ice, sweeping all clean before them. All across Virtua, barely-visible dragons sweep through solid matter, passing like neutrinos through stone and steel and flesh.

Until they come to unbreakable, impassable steel walls.

Instantly, Damien and Penylle stand before those towering walls, as dragons beat themselves silly against them. "What's this?"

Damien conjures a datapad and checks addresses. "Nunn. It's the U.S. MILNET. They've cut themselves off from the Internet."

MILNET, the computer and communications network of the United States military, stretches across the world on buried cables and satellite links completely independent of the rest of the Internet. In only nine specific locations, the two networks touch: great conduits where tides of information ebb and flow between the military and the world.

From the very inception of MILNET, its designers feared that it could be compromised if in contact with the rest of the world. And so they built in a contingency plan. At those nine crossover points, men stood with axe blades, ready on command to sever data conduits as thick as their arms. There was no automated machinery for the cutting, and none for subsequent repair— only men, independent of the Nets and devoted to their duty.

Once the order was given, once those nine men struck, MILNET was isolated from the rest of the world.

The M's image appears before Damien and Penylle. Alarm is on her face. "I just got an alert that the U.S. has gone to DEFCON One."

"I know. They've cut off MILNET. And the metaprogram is in there." He looks around himself; although cyberspace is still frozen, there is great agitation among the AIs.

"Damien, I just received a note from President Archer. She advises the U.N. and the Nexus that she's ordering a preemptive strike against the sunpower installations. She's going to launch her missiles."

Damien gives a grim smile. "No...she...isn't." He tugs Penylle's hand. "Come with me."

"Where are we going?" A door opens, and they step through. "Oh."

They are in the Institute.

Other residents, seeing Damien and Penylle's cold-light forms appear, wave and start toward them. Damien consults a free-floating data window, then taps on his keyboard.

The main floor is replaced by dim, empty corridors lined with pipes and electrical conduits. "The basement?" Penylle guesses.

"Sub-basement. I put pickups and cold-light projectors down here for just such an emergency." He points her toward a particular room. "Here."

It is a small room, half-filled with industrial equipment that involves pipes and motors and is plastered with "High Voltage" signs. A single knife switch protrudes; it is in the up position and looks as if it has been that way for years.

"Okay, Damien, what's going on here?"

"In a minute." He indicates the switch, his insubstantial hand moving right through it. "Can you throw that switch for me?"

"I want to know why. Last time, half the roof caved in."

Desperately, he says, "Hon— "

She squeezes his hand. "I'm kidding." She touches the switch, and the machinery springs to life, giving an enormous jerk and vibrating alarmingly. "All right, what's this about?"

"By a curious coincidence, a stretch of MILNET buried conduit passes within a quarter-kilometer of the Institute. By another curious coincidence, one of our own data conduits extends horizontally *that* way about two hundred meters to some subsurface seismic sensors."

"Let me guess: by another curious coincidence, this machine powers a drill that will extend that conduit another fifty meters, so that it crosses the MILNET conduit."

He smiles. "Strangely enough, that's right." A bank of red lights turns green. "Good, we have contact. Let's get back."

Instantly they are once again before the steel wall— a steel wall that suddenly fragments under the impact of a thousand bronze dragons. At once, dragons swarm into the landscapes beyond.

"You know, that's illegal," Penylle says. "Probably treasonous. When the military finds out— "

"It'll be far too late for them to do anything about it. Besides, I had permission from the Secretary-General Pro Tem of the Terran Council. She trumps a mere President of the U.S." He clicks open a comm window, sees the M at the conference table in Room 308. "How are things with the missiles now?"

The M shakes her head. "President Archer is livid. I think she's going to give herself apoplexy."

"If they'd asked my opinion, I'd have told them not to put control of those missiles on MILNET." He shrugs. "But what are you gonna do?"

"How are we doing?"

Damien consults a display. "Things are going almost too smoothly. We're rid of 68% of the metaprogram. China tried to launch missiles, but **Thë Fløw ånd Retürn Tø Wømb ånd Tømb** caught the activation codes and managed to abort. At this rate, we'll be totally done in another hour."

"Penylle, how are you holding up?"

"Great. I'm responding to calls from Terrad, but so far it hasn't been anything I can't handle."

The M chews her lip. "If you want to, you can join the U.N. force in Kampala. I made sure they took cameras and cold-light projectors."

Damien's eyes meet Penylle's, and they both grin. "Thanks, M. We're there."

And they are.

Damien introduces himself and Penylle to the commander of the U.N. forces, then they fall into step a half-meter behind the lead troopers.

It is pre-dawn in Kampala, and the Treehouse seems asleep. The blue helmets take no chances; they break down the front door with no warning, and swarm in with weapons drawn.

Marc Hoister awaits them, sitting crosslegged in a simple chair. He looks up from a book in his lap, and makes a welcoming gesture. "I apologize, Commander, that I did not hear you knock. I might have spared you the trouble of breaking down the door."

The commander points and barks, "Cuff him. Squad, search the place. Assume that anyone you see is a hologram."

Hoister holds out his wrists. "Damien, Penylle, how good to see you."

Damien restrains Penylle.

A trooper swings handcuffs toward Hoister's wrists— they meet no resistance and pass right through.

"Hologram," Damien spits.

"That doesn't matter." Penylle breaks away from him, slips her hands around Hoister's throat. He falls, to all appearances a man being choked to death. "Remember, Damien, *place* doesn't matter. I can reach through the hologram to wherever this wyden is hiding. And I can choke the life…right…out…of…him— oh!"

Hoister vanishes, and Penylle falls forward.

A laugh, and Hoister reappears, standing above Penylle with a pocket watch open in his right hand. "Mpenzi, I am sorry it has to end this way. I compliment you on your punctuality."

She sits up. Her eyes burn with hatred. "What does *that* mean?"

"Just this. The encapsulated poison in your bloodstream was set to trigger at exactly one hour after Kuumba's scheduled launch time— three o'clock Greenwich time today. Which is precisely…now."

Penylle lunges forward, rising— then falls, falls through Marc Hoister's hologram, falls through the chair and the floor, falls right out of cyberspace entirely.

With her departure, like the snapping of a rubber band, the scene darkens and Damien rips himself from virtuality with a scream on his lips. The last thing he sees is Marc Hoister's impossibly ugly, contorted face; the last thing he hears is Marc Hoister's laughter.

Back in the Taj Samudra suite, Penylle is crumpled at his feet, twitching. He lifts her to the bed, calling for help.

## [38] KAMENGEN 17
Kilimanjaro Launch Facility
Umoja Economic Union, Africa
3 October 2042 C.E.

*Reality Corrupts. Absolute reality corrupts absolutely.*

Three weeks later, Marc Hoister watches the last of his people queue up for emigration. Hundreds of thousands have already left for Mars, and this will be the last load. When the ships of this fleet leave Earth, they will not return. The Black race— the *only* race— will prosper on the Red Planet, fulfilling at last God's plan and God's promise.

Despite hot equatorial sun, he shivers. How close he came to defeat! Penylle, that supreme coats, had betrayed him and almost spelled his ruin. Almost.

He regrets that he was not able to get Damien to come over to his side. Quite a remarkable young man. He should have started much sooner, with that one. But how could he know, that a nine-year-old brat would grow up with such talents?

Cold-light pennants flying, another WaveRider settles into the launch cavity, ice shield three meters thick on its rear. A second later, it begins its journey, hurled by magnetic forces— after two minutes in the tube, it will erupt from Kilimanjaro's summit, already halfway to space. Launch lasers, blasting ice into plasma, will send it the rest of the way, to rendezvous with *Kuumba*.

Kilimanjaro is the only functioning launch facility in the world, now. And more's the pity, he thinks, that they must destroy it. Still, no use giving the stay-behinds an easy way to get to him and his people. There is no help for it.

After the last WaveRider departs, Marc will board his fusion-drive ship. And before leaving Earth behind, he will direct the pilot to hover at thrust over the delicate lasers, the launch rings, the stone-walled mouth of the tube. No one will use the Kilimanjaro mass driver for a good many centuries.

He misses Penylle. She should be next to him, on this triumphant day. He had planned for her to be with him. But she had other ideas….

The real fault, Marc thinks, lies with that harpy Miranda Maris. But for her, his plan would have been complete a decade or more ago. But there she was, at the end of every path he trod, standing in the way of his dreams. The rest of the Nexus were fools, easily dominated; Maris, from the very beginning, was his chief enemy.

She blocked him, she overturned schemes that had taken him years to set up, she disrespected him in public. Worst of all, she stole Penylle. And so it was the Good God's will, that Miranda Maris die.

And here is his deepest regret...that he did not witness her last minutes. In fact, he cannot be utterly sure that she *is* dead. The missile that took out the Sri Pada spaceport had certainly destroyed Colombo as well, and no one was about to go into that radioactive pell in search of survivors.

No matter, really. She could not hurt him now.

Nothing could hurt him now. God Himself has proven that Marc is His Chosen One, by guaranteeing the success of Marc's mission. The Finger of God is on him...how can he ever be in danger again?

The last family is sealed in, the last WaveRider lowered into the launch cavity, the mass driver fired for the last time. Marc waits until he sees that brilliant spark leap skyward from Kilimanjaro's summit, then signals his lieutenants. "It is time," he says.

Inside the ship, he settles happily into his couch and lets his physician belt him in. So what if he didn't see her die? Over the next few years he can watch her whole world die, watch from a secure and joyful seat in the bosom of the Good God Himself.

Smiling, he falls asleep.

[39] KAMENGEN 18
Walter Reed Hospital
Washington, DC
USA, North America
12 September 2042 CE

*Even Napoleon had his Watergate.*

"Do you think he knows?"

The M, looking down at the still figure on the bed, shakes her head. "How *could* he? They cut all his external nerves— he's getting all his input from this." She touches a finger-thick cable that vanishes into the wall.

Damien touches the dry, flabby skin on one shrunken arm; it looks and feels like ancient leather. "I still think we're being too kind to him."

The M lifts her eyes. "Do you still want to kill him? Go ahead. Nobody's going to stop you."

Damien raises a hand, then puts it down. "No. He's dying anyway. Another few days and he'll be gone." He looks out the window at green sward and finely-sculpted gardens. "I ought to hate him. I *did*. He killed my mother and father, he killed Mahlowi and Hollow Robin, he would have happily killed all of us if we'd let him." He looks back at the wizened figure alone on the bed, with no life support and no nourishment, silently dreaming its way into death. "So why do I pity him? Why did I help WWH make a virtie where he'd won, just to keep him quiet during his last days?"

The M puts an arm around his shoulder. "The mind is its own place. It can make a pell of heaven, or heaven of pell. He's in his own private pell. Let him die there, and let your hate die with him. Take it from me, child, life is too short to spend it hating people."

They walk to the door, and as they exit, Miranda pauses to look back. "I wonder who he really was."

"Does it matter?"

She shakes her head. "No. To history, he'll be nameless. And ultimately forgotten. That's enough."

On the way down the hall, Damien offers his arm for support, and she takes it gratefully. "My feet are killing me. I'm serious, Damien. As soon as things are wrapped up here, I'm getting out of Earth gravity."

"Still going to the Moon?"

"No, I don't think so. Now that we have the fusion drive, Mars is as close as the Moon used to be. It's still one-third gravity. A lot of Umojans who moved there aren't coming back. They'll need artists. What do you think— we could be in on the ground floor of a new Golden Age. Want to be part of a new Athens?"

"I think Rose will follow wherever you go. Pell, half the Institute will, without question."

"And what about *you*, my dear grandson?"

"I don't know yet. Give me some time to think it over." There is time now, time for decisions and revisions. Time to think. Time to recover, time to come to terms with all he's lost.

Miranda sighs. "I don't envy you your choices. On the one hand, the U.S.— on the other, Umoja. And you have to decide which to commit to. It's a tough choice."

To change the subject, he says, "M, I was busy with Penylle at the time— I never did get the full story of how you captured him."

"I had InfoPol on my side. After they found out that he had killed their Chief, they were only too happy to co-operate." Her eyes twinkle. "Officer Caparthy sends her regards."

"Oh, I'm *sure* she does."

"Don't knock them, Damien. They're good at what they do— if a little unimaginative. I took care of that: I paired InfoPol analysts with people from the Institute. They were all over the Treehouse like termites on a rotten log. By the time your chopper touched down at Colombo General, we had half a dozen traces. After that, it was really only a matter of time before we tracked him down."

"That's not what Jamiar said. He told me that *you* figured out where he was hiding."

"Pish and tosh. Once InfoPol determined that he was still in Africa, it was obvious where he'd gone. If I hadn't pointed it out first, someone else would have."

"Where was he?"

"Crouching like a cockroach in the ruins of Timbuktu. A U.N. sniper got him with knockout darts before he knew what was happening." She half-smiles. "He was on the same transport that brought you here."

"I guess I was distracted."

"I'll say." She peers at the number on a door. "We're here."

They walk in without knocking, creeping silently in the manner of hospital visitors who do not know yet if the patient is awake or asleep.

As it turns out, the patient is wide awake; Penylle's face brightens and she lifts her arms in welcome. "Damien, M, I've missed you."

Damien kisses her, and the M squeezes her hand, lets go. "Nonsense, child, we were only gone for half an hour."

"It seemed longer. A lifetime." She takes Damien's hand; her touch instantly recalls that night in cyberspace, when they clung together in a frozen world while the dragons raged.

"What did the doctor say?"

Her eyes sparkle. "She says I'm fine." She displays her arms, lifts her covers. "See. No IVs, no catheters. She wants to keep me tonight for observation, but tomorrow I can go home."

Damien squeezes her hand. "I was so afraid I'd lost you."

"It wasn't *that* bad. Once they told me what I had to do, it was simple. Mind you, I don't want to see another hypo of adrenaline as long as I live. That nunn thing *hurt.*"

"It saved your life," Miranda says. "Don't say nasty things about drugs, my dear. When you get to be *my* age, you'll be happy enough to get all the drugs they'll give you." She narrows her eyes. "Of course, with your new technique, you might not need them."

"It's not a cure-all, M. I have to know what a molecule feels like before I can break it down. And it takes a long time. They say I was lucky that the concentration was so low to begin with. All that work that Jamiar did cleansing my bloodstream helped."

The M snorts. "It's still amazing. Breaking down a poison just by thinking at it. That's a skill that everyone should have."

"I agree," says a new voice, from the door.

The M rises to greet the newcomer, a distinguished white-haired woman in a doctor's coat. "And *you* deserve the credit." She shakes the woman's hand. "It's fortunate that you took the initiative and jumped in. You saved Penylle's life. I haven't had a chance to thank you properly."

The doctor lowers her eyes. "I'm sorry it took me so long to read Dr. Heavitree's reports and volunteer. As it was, I almost didn't make it to Colombo in time."

Damien, too, shakes the doctor's hand. "You told them to give her adrenaline, and that kept her alive and conscious. Once she knew you were coming, she wasn't about to give up."

The doctor smiles. "Yes, she *is* a stubborn one, isn't she?" She brushes past Damien, puts her hand on Penylle's forehead. "I have to go now, but

I'll be back tonight. And tomorrow, you can go home."

Penylle takes the doctor's hand, presses it to her lips, then looks up into her face. "Thank you, Aunt Vicky. Thank you for everything."

When Doctor Hacktrell is gone, Damien takes a chair next to Penylle, and the M settles on the bed at her feet. Penylle glances at the table, and a cup of water rises and moves to her lips. She drinks, then the cup obediently moves back to its place.

Miranda claps her hands and beams. "We're going to have an *exciting* time on Mars."

Damien looks from one to the other. "What's this?"

"I haven't had a chance to tell you yet, hon. The M invited me to come to Mars with her, to help with the new version of the Institute."

He makes a pout. "When was this? And you made your decision, without talking to me?"

Both Penylle and the M laugh. "Last night, while you were asleep," Penylle says. "And of course I wouldn't decide without you. I haven't given her an answer yet."

The M looks at Damien. "There's no pressure. You've got plenty of alternatives. I don't envy you the choice." She heaves herself to her feet. "I am going home to sleep in my own bed." She kisses them both. "I'll see both of you tomorrow."

"Thanks, M. Pull the door shut when you leave, please?"

With a smile, she is gone. Damien runs a hand along Penylle's side, still not quite believing that she is here, alive and well. "I love you so much."

"And I love you." She shifts her position, opens the covers. "Come here, you."

She is warm and sweet in his arms.

Maris Institute
Elkridge, Maryland
United States, North America
15 September 2042 CE

They meet in the Patapsco Room, Miranda and Rose and Jamiar, others from Conference Room 308, half a dozen other Nexus bigwigs, some Institute friends— and Penylle and Damien. Some are ghostly virtual figures, but most are here in the flesh. They sit informally, scattered on easy chairs and couches in ones and twos. Miranda, in a high-backed wicker chair, is clearly in charge. Damien and Penylle are at her right hand.

Miranda clears her throat. "There will be formal reports, but those can wait. I just want this opportunity to settle a few remaining items. C.H.LAD, if you will?"

C.H.LAD sits crosslegged in an overstuffed armchair. "The remaining U.N. delegates have voted to approve the actions of the Terran Council."

"Bloody good thing, too," Mati says, to general laughter.

C.H.LAD continues, "The Security Council and General Assembly are finished. The Terran Council will step in to manage the U.N. until worldwide elections can be held."

The M nods. "Thank you. Damien, what's the story with the AIs?"

"No trace of the metaprogram remains. As far as the AIs are concerned, we're no longer a threat."

"And cyberspace?"

"We're to be weaned, slowly enough to avoid economic disruption. Fusion, and the fusion *drive*, will open the Solar System to us. There will be enough to keep people busy, believe me."

"Good." Miranda turns toward Jamiar. "Doctor?"

Jamiar stands. "The man we knew as 'Marc Hoister' died this morning. As far as we know, it was painless. Brain function ceased at about 3 o'clock Eastern time." Amid scattered applause, Jamiar once more takes his seat.

"This," the M says, "raises an interesting possibility. JJJ?"

JJJSchmidt runs a hand over thinning hair. "To the world, Marc Hoister is still very much alive. As it turns out, the Marc Hoister identity is a valuable one. A respected Umoja Cultural Minister, the man who convinced twenty-five thousand colonists to go to Mars...he has friendships and influence all over the world. It would be a shame to lose that power right away, especially when we face such difficult social transitions."

"What are you saying?" Even as he asks, Damien, with a sinking feeling, thinks he knows the answer.

Efia Sembéne says, "Terrad has already restored Damien's father to all the altered records. It would be simple enough to transfer the current Marc Hoister identity to someone else."

With an expression of sympathy, JJJSchmidt says, "Just for the transition period, of course. Over a few years, we can phase out the identity, and Marc Hoister can retire."

Damien, aware that all eyes are upon him, looks to Miranda.

She sighs. "I'm not going to tell you what to do, son. Not any more. I support whatever decision you make."

"Penylle?"

"It's your decision, hon."

He looks at JJJSchmidt, at the anxious eyes surrounding him. They're right, the power and influence of Marc Hoister would be invaluable for both the people of Earth and the new settlers on Mars. It would give him an opportunity to redeem his father's name. And it was just for a few years....

"It would only be part-time," he says. "A few hours a day as Marc Hoister. Otherwise, I stay Damien."

Efia raises an eyebrow. "Damien Nshogoza?"

He shakes his head. "Damien *Hoister*." He swallows. "All right, I'll do it."

The rest of the meeting passes quickly, and the group scatters. The Institute contingent makes their way to the pool; Miranda calls for drinks, and they settle into the jacuzzi. There is little talk; they relax in a warm glow as the life of the Institute goes on around them. With intangible fingers, Penylle massages Damien's back; he stretches languidly and settles down in the warm, frothy water.

After a time, the M looks at Damien. "What about it, kid? The U.S.? Umoja?" She holds out her hands as if weighing the two.

He closes her hands together and lowers them. "And you're an old tease. You can't fool me into *that* trap. Especially after all that's happened. I've already made my choice, Madame Secretary General of the Terran Council." He flexes his shoulder, showing thc tattooed pattern of Drake's Starburst glowing fluorescent yellow against mahogany skin. "I don't belong to either the U.S. *or* Umoja. Neither of us do." He again clasps hands with Penylle. "We're Nexus all the way. And we're going to Mars."

## CODA: Djanger

New Athens, Mars
21 October 2044 C.E.

*It's never too late to have a happy childhood.*

Friday afternoon, at least by the Greenwich clock on which most Martian settlements ran. Damien has spent the morning setting up Net support for a new settlement out toward Tharsis, and is happy to finish in time for the afternoon circum-Mars shuttle that drops him at New Athens.

As soon as he enters through the main airlock, he feels more relaxed. Here, in the domed crater with its soaring atrium and terraced balconies, he is completely at ease. Here, he is "Damien," not "Marc Hoister" as he is to the rest of Mars. Here, he is surrounded by family.

He stows his breathing gear in his locker, next to the airlock, and starts toward the elevators. He looks up to see activity on the bars of the giant Drake's Starburst that stands in the center of the common space; someone is swinging down the bars from a higher balcony. After a moment, the culprit lands (softly, in one-third gravity) two meters from Damien. A black cloak billows as the figure races past him.

"Hi, Mati."

Mati spins to a halt. "Hi, Damien. Hey, the M wants to see you."

"Thanks."

Mati dashes off. "Can't stay to talk, Babi's after me."

After a second, Babi emerges from beneath a table, racing after Mati. She skids to a stop when she passes Damien. "Hi, Damien. The M wants to see you, soonest. Bye, Damien!" Then she, too, is gone.

Damien touches his wristband. "Where is the M?"

Rahel's cheery voice answers after a moment, "The Ivory Madonna is in the infirmary. She requests your presence."

Moving quickly, with the long, low strides that are the best way to get around in Martian gravity, Damien races to the infirmary. The M meets him at the door with a bear hug. "Damien, the best news possible. *I'm a great-grandmother.*"

"Wha— ?" He staggers backward, hitting the wall. "B-but she isn't due for *weeks.*"

"Babies make their own schedules. Except, in this case, it was Doctor Hacktrell. She consulted with Doctor Simon, and they both thought it best to take the kid out before he got much stronger."

"Can I see her? I mean, can I see *them*?"

"Just calm down." The M raps on the door. "Victoria, he's here."

"M, what's wrong? Why can't I go in?"

Doctor Hacktrell emerges. "Damien, nothing is wrong. Miranda and I just thought it would be best to prepare you. With Baby Hoister's pk getting stronger, and more erratic, I thought it best to sedate them both heavily and order a quick Caesarean. The baby is in an incubator with a prolactin and glucose drip, and Penylle is drifting in and out of consciousness." She squeezes his shoulder. "Both of them are in good health, but they look like pell."

He swallows. "All right, I guess I'm ready."

Doctor Hacktrell eases the door open.

Privately, Damien thinks that the two old ladies are over-reacting: neither Penylle nor the baby look all *that* bad. The baby is a tiny pink wrinkled thing, much like other babies Damien has seen— but his heart swells. This one is *his*, his and Penylle's. The obstetrician lets him hold the child, for just a minute, and Damien is enchanted by tiny toes and fingers, chubby cheeks, and the glint of intelligence that already looks out from those eyes. As he presses the baby to his chest, he feels ghostly, uncoordinated fingers move within his body.

Nunn, this is going to be interesting!

Penylle is a little pale, but otherwise she looks as if she were simply sleeping. He brushes back her hair, and her eyes open. When she sees him, she smiles and stretches. "Did you see?"

"I saw." He bends and kisses her. "He's the most beautiful baby in the world. In all the worlds."

"I thought you'd agree." She closes her eyes, and seems to be drifting off, then she opens them again. "We have to tell Aunt Vicky what name to file. Are you still happy with Jaison?"

"I adore it. After all, it fits. He's going to spend his life exploring new territory, both physically and figuratively. And whatever he finds, it's going to better than the golden fleece."

"Jaison Hoister. It's perfect." She kisses his hand, then drifts off to sleep.

Doctor Hacktrell looks up from her datapad. "Jaison Hoister it is. May he be the first of many." She glances at her wristwatch. "I'm going to chase the two of you out of here, so that my patients can rest." She smiles. "Come back in a few hours. Damien, if Penylle doesn't mind, you can sleep here tonight."

Miranda puts her hands on her hips. "And what about *me*? Doesn't poor Miranda get to sleep with anyone tonight?"

Doctor Hacktrell pats her shoulder. "You know what they say about the 800-pound gorilla. Don't make me finish it."

"You brain-damaged cow, I'll have your license for that." The M grins. "There, we're even. Come on, Damien, we have work to do."

As Miranda lopes down the corridor with Damien in tow, he asks, "What work do we have to do?"

Miranda pulls him into an elevator and ascends three floors. "I'm surprised at you. It's Friday night." She looks out over the main floor, which is crowded with residents, visitors, and hangers-on. "Now follow me, we're on."

The lights dim, they step out together onto a balcony, and a spotlight hits them. Music swells, and Miranda and Damien speak up in unison:

*"It's amazing,*
*Space is folding,*
*Ways your mind can't*
*Comprehend."*

**THE END**

## *ACKNOWLEDGEMENTS & APOLOGIES*

*Dance for the Ivory Madonna* would simply not have happened without the technical and psychological support of a great many people. Whenever I needed help, encouragement, or simply a reality check, those to whom I turned were more than willing; it is to them that this novel owes its existence.

I am grateful to fellow writers Melissa Scott and Lisa A. Barnett for their patient readings of successive drafts, their many perceptive and penetrating comments, and their unfailing encouragement.

A non-writing reader who can give intelligent and helpful criticism— and still remain a friend— is a pearl beyond price; I am lucky enough to have two. Thomas G. Atkinson is always my alpha reader; he reigns me in from dashing off on tangents, and gives me the courage to follow the right track when I stumble across it. He is also a proofreader *par excellence*. Dr. Ann Hackman, besides catching all my silly mistakes and verifying my biology, always knows the perfect disease, syndrome, or condition for whatever I need to accomplish.

*

I am extremely grateful to Nina Gilbert and Connie V of Stumpers-L for their patience and their inestimable help in bringing down the house with the Hallelujah Chorus. I must also thank Dan (Renfield) Corcoran, who came up with the idea in the first place. I would be remiss if I did not give thanks to Judy (Jaelle) Gerjuoy and all the attendees of the annual Darkover Grand Council, who were singing Händel's masterpiece around the pool long before this novel was even a glint in the author's eye.

*

The American Coalition Promoting Fat Acceptance (ACPFA) is entirely a product of my imagination, and no resemblance to any existing organization is intended. Readers interested in the effort to eliminate body-type discrimination may want to contact the following real-life associations:

CSWD: Council on Size and Weight Discrimination
PO Box 305, Mount Marion, NY 12456 USA 914/679-1209

Works to influence public policy and opinion in an effort to eliminate oppression and discrimination based on body size, shape, or weight standards.

Largesse, the Network for Size Esteem
PO Box 9404, New Haven, CT 06534-0404 USA 203/787-1624
*largesse@eskimo.com*
*http://www.eskimo.com/~largesse/index.html*

An internationally-recognized resource center and clearinghouse for size diversity empowerment founded in 1983.

NAAFA: National Association to Advance Fat Acceptance
PO Box 188620, Sacramento, CA 95818 USA 800/442-1214
*naafa@naafa.org* *http://www.naafa.org*

A non-profit human rights organization dedicated to improving the quality of life for fat people. NAAFA has been working since 1969 to eliminate discrimination based on body size and provide fat people with the tools for self-empowerment through public education, advocacy, and member support.

*

Médecins Sans Frontières (Doctors Without Borders) is the world's largest independent medical aid agency and is committed to two objectives: providing medical aid wherever it is needed, regardless of race, religion, politics or sex and raising awareness of the plight of the people they help. MSF receives no government funding; it relies entirely on private contributions. Readers can contact MSF at the following addresses:

MSF International Office
Rue de la Tourelle, 39 - Brussels - Belgium -1040
Phone: +32-2-280-1881 - Fax: +32-2-280-0173
*http://www.msf.org*

Médecins Sans Frontières USA, Inc./
Doctors Without Borders USA, Inc.
6 East 39th Street, 8th Floor, New York, NY 10016
phone: 212/679-6800 fax: 212/679-7016
*doctors@newyork.msf.org*
*http://www.dwb.org/index.html*

*

The World Creativity Conference does not exist as such. In our world, its place is filled by Worldcon, the World Science Fiction Convention. For more information about Worldcons past, present, and future, contact:

The World Science Fiction Society, Inc.
P.O. Box 426159, Kendall Square Station,
Cambridge, MA 02142 USA
*worldcons@worldcon.org* *http://worldcon.org*

*

The Gaylaxian Science Fiction Society does exist, and is every bit as welcoming in the present as I've depicted them in the future. Contact:

Gaylaxian Science Fiction Society
P.O. Box 1059, Boston, MA 02103 USA
*http://www.gaylaxians.org*

The Gay Servicemember's Organization, unfortunately, has no present-day counterpart. One hopes that this will change long before 2042.

*

Dekoa Flu, Cairo Fever, and Kabinda Virus are all fictional. The strain of Millennial Flu in the book is assumed to be much more virulent than the mild strain that struck in 1999/2000. Capgras' Syndrome is a real condition, as (unfortunately) are AIDS, Breakbone Fever (Dengue), Ebola, Guillain-Barré, Hemorrhagic Fever, Industriosis, Legionellosis, Marburg, Osteitis, Pleurodynia, Rift Valley Fever, Sabia, Whipworm., Yellow Fever, and Zygomycosis. Porphyria is a real disease, but as yet it has not been transmitted by genetically-engineered viruses. Stay tuned.

*

Apologies to those who found my system of numbering chapters to be too baroque or just plain distracting. Danse Macabre, Divertissement, Djanger, Entreé, Ghost Dance, Kamengen, Lobster Quadrille, Ngoro, Tarantella, and Techno/Rabe are all, or course, types of dances.

*

Some who read the early stages of this book wondered about the decision to include psi powers, in a future based on otherwise-straightforward extrapolation of current technology. Despite some recent studies with ambiguous results, there is little evidence that powers even remotely like Penylle's exist in today's world, or will come to exist in a few short decades.

No matter; psi is a convenient symbol for the factor of the unknown. Almost without question, Penylle's psi powers will not be "real" in 2042— but something *else* certainly will, something that we cannot possibly imagine today. It may be a new technology, a fundamental understanding of some physical phenomena that is a mystery today, or a new philosophical or spiritual framework. Whatever this unknown factor, it will make it possible for a person like Penylle to achieve a mastery of her work that will seem impossible to others. I don't know *what* that unknown factor will be, nor when it will come about— but I do know that it *will* come. I chose to symbolize that unknown by the use of psi.

Any readers offended by the inclusion of psi in this book are invited to keep their copies until the unknown factor shows up— then cross out "psi" and write in the true name of the revealed unknown . . . or, more likely, to have their software agents do the same.

*

Finally, I wish to acknowledge all of my friends and family who appear (in one form or another) in this book. Many of them aided immesurably in the revision process. They include: Amanda Allen, Thomas G. Atkinson, Michael W. Burns, Mike Cantrell, Carl Cipra, Dan Corcoran, Rich Connelly, Jim Cummings, Deborah Feaster, Rob Gates, Marty and Bobby Gear, Steven Grey, Ann Hackman, Jeannette Holloman, Rick and Sue Hrybyk, Sharon Landrum, Ric Rader, Jill Rhyne-Grey, Ron Robinson, Jim & Naomi Sakers, and June Swords. May one and all achieve their hearts' desires.

Don Sakers
Meerkat Meade
September 2001

## TIMELINE:

1958 - Miranda Maris born
1991 - Marc Hoister born
1993 - Oradell Maris born
2000 - Millennial Flu (mild strain)
c. 2005 - Cairo Fever
c. 2010 - The Kurudi (Return) begins
2011 - Nexus formed during Indonesian crisis
2012 - Kabinda virus
2014-15 - Miruvorane Kids
2014 - Penylle Norton born
2016 - Dekoa flu
2017 - Damien Nshogoza born
2017 - England's King Charles dies
2018 - Umoja formed: The Recall issued
2019 - Umoja accepts first U.S. deportees
2019 - RCSpex introduced
2020 - Millennial Flu (virulent strain)
2021 - Treaty of ttar.cyb
2022 - Deforestation Project commences
2023 - Constitutional Convention
2025 - Damien Nshogoza moves to U.S.
2042 - Dekoa erupts in Dinétah

UMOJA
2042 CE
Kaskazini Region
Rabat
Algiers
Tunis
Morocco
Algeria
Cairo
Egypt
Pembe
Region
Timbuktu
Dakar
Umoja
Economic
Union
Asmara
Addis Ababa
Ethiopia
Lagos
Abidjan
Kisangani
Mtweo Region
São Tomé
Kampala
Equator
Mwanza
Kilimanjaro
Kati Region
Kinshasa
Dar es Salaam
Mashariki
Region
Luanda
= non-Umoja nations
Angola
Ndola
National Capital
Regional Capital
Other major city
Spaceport
Botswana
Harare
Windhoek
Gaborone
Mandela
Mrima
Region
Cape
Town
Kusini Region

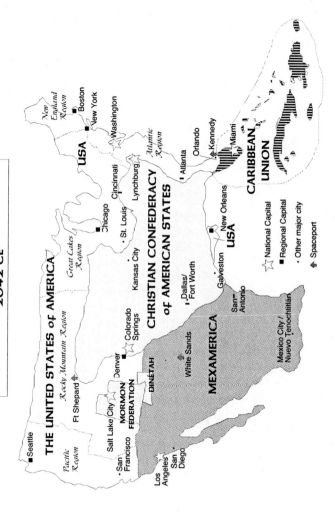

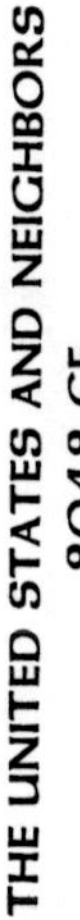
THE UNITED STATES AND NEIGHBORS
2042 CE
THE UNITED STATES of AMERICA
Pacific Region
Rocky Mountain Region
Great Lakes Region
New England Region
Atlantic Region
USA
Seattle
San Francisco
Salt Lake City
Ft Shepard
Denver
Colorado Springs
Kansas City
St. Louis
Chicago
Cincinnati
Lynchburg
Washington
New York
Boston
MORMON FEDERATION
DINÉTAH
CHRISTIAN CONFEDERACY of AMERICAN STATES
Dallas/ Fort Worth
Atlanta
Orlando
Kennedy
Miami
New Orleans
Galveston
MEXAMERICA
White Sands
Los Angeles
San Diego
San Antonio
Mexico City / Nuevo Tenochtitlán
CARIBBEAN UNION
National Capital
Regional Capital
Other major city
Spaceport

***If you enjoyed this book, please spread the word by telling some friends.***

For a free autographed bookplate,
send a self-addressed, stamped envelope to

Nexus Bookplate
Speed-of-C Productions
PO Box 265
Linthicum, MD 21090-0265

Be sure to include the name(s) to which you would like the bookplate inscribed.

For official Nexus and *Dance for the Ivory Madonna* gear, information, and e-text editions, visit the Scattered Worlds website at *www.scatteredworlds.com*

Printed in the United States
4786